SLOW HEAT IN HEAVEN

Schyler raised her chin. "I want you off Belle Terre by the end of the week."

"Who's going to get your timber ready for market?" Cash asked.

"I will."

"Wrong. You can't do doodledee squat without me." He took a step closer. "And you know it. You knew it when you came driving over here, didn't you?" He braced one hand against the post near her head and leaned into her, brushing his body against hers. "Know what? I don't think that's why you came over here at all. I think you came over here for something altogether different."

His lips covered hers in a hard kiss. "Admit it." Cash lifted his mouth off Schyler's only far enough to speak, "This is what you came here for."

"I hate you."

"But you want me."

He kissed her again. The rain beat loudly against the roof, drowning out her whimpers of outrage and then of surrender...

Please turn this page for rave reviews on *Slow Heat in Heaven*

SLOW HEAT IN HEAVEN

"A MASTERY OF STEAMY PROSE!"
—*Affaire de Coeur*

"I LOVED IT! *Slow Heat in Heaven* is an enormously entertaining book. It is fast-paced, with vivid characters, a juicy plot, sizzling love scenes, and the kind of tension that keeps you turning the pages. Sandra Brown has once again proven her talent as a storyteller."

—Lisa Gregory, author of *Before the Dawn*

"FAR EXCEEDS THIS AUTHOR'S PREVIOUS WORKS...REFRESHING, A KEEPER AND A BESTSELLER."

—Mary Grigg,
Romance Consultant, Waldenbooks

SLOW HEAT IN HEAVEN

SANDRA BROWN

POPULAR LIBRARY

An Imprint of Warner Books, Inc.

A Warner Communications Company

Chapter One

At first she wasn't sure he was real.

She had been dozing. Her head rested on her bent arm, which had gone to sleep and had started to tingle. She woke up and opened her eyes, then stretched languorously and turned her head. That's when she saw him. She immediately forgot her discomfort.

She thought he was a trick of her unfocused eyes or a product of late afternoon drowsiness and midsummer ennui. She blinked several times. The image remained.

The outline of his body was as detailed as a silhouette cut out of black construction paper with tiny manicure scissors. It was cast against a showoff sun that was making one hell of an exit. The horizon was as gaudily striped as a sultan's turban. It boasted every vibrant hue ranging from vermilion to gold.

Like the pines, he was motionless. The trees stood as majestic and tall as sentinels. Their spiky branches were still. There wasn't a breath of breeze. Above from where Schyler lay, Spanish moss drooped from the sprawling limbs of the live oak, looking more desolate than usual, mourning the unrelenting humid heat.

The unmoving form was undeniably male. So was the stance. Ah, yes, his stance was definitely, arrogantly masculine. One knee was bent, throwing his hip slightly off center.

It was intimidating to wake up from a nap and discover someone standing not twenty yards away watching you with the silence and patience of a predator. It was doubly disconcerting to find that that someone was a self-assured and cocky male who clearly saw you as the trespasser.

Most disturbing was the garden hoe that lay across his shoulders. It appeared innocuous. His wrists were hooked over the handle, his hands dangling carelessly. On the streets of London, a man carrying a garden hoe across his shoulders would attract attention. In rural Louisiana during the summertime, it was a common sight.

But there wasn't so much as an onion patch on this section of Belle Terre. The fields where sharecroppers cultivated vegetables were miles away. So Schyler had reason to be alarmed. The sun was going down, she was alone and, relatively speaking, a long way from the house.

She should challenge him, demand to know who he was and what he was doing on her property. But she said nothing, perhaps because he looked more a part of Belle Terre than she did. He blended into the landscape, was one with it. By comparison, she seemed out of place and conspicuous.

She didn't know how long they had been staring at each other. At least she thought they were staring at each other. She couldn't distinguish his face, much less tell what he was looking at so intently. But instinct told her he was watching her and that he had been for quite some time. That unnerving thought goaded her to act. She sat up.

He started toward her.

His footsteps hardly rustled the ankle-deep grass. Moving silently and sinuously, he slid the hoe off his shoulders and gripped the long handle with both hands.

All the self-defense instructions Schyler had ever heard burrowed cowardly into the farthest corners of her mind. She couldn't move, couldn't speak. She tried to suck in a deep breath so she could scream, but the air was as dense as quicksand.

Instinctively she shrank against the massive tree trunk and shut her eyes tightly. Her last impression was that of the sharpened blade of the hoe. It glinted in the remnant rays of sunlight as it made its swift, downward arc, making a thunking sound when it landed. She waited for the agonizing pain to assault her before she keeled over dead. But it never came.

"Get your nap out, *pichouette*?"

Schyler blinked her eyes open, amazed that she was still alive. "What?"

"Get your nap out, Miss Schyler?"

She shaded her eyes against the brilliant sunset, but she still couldn't distinguish his face. He knew her name. His first language had been a Cajun dialect. Other than that, she didn't have a clue as to who he was.

Snakes slithered out of the bayous. She'd been taught from infancy to consider all of them poisonous. That reasoning seemed to apply to this situation.

The thunking sound had been made by the sharp blade when it bit into the grass. The man was leaning on the hoe now, both hands innocently folded over the blunt end of the handle. His chin was propped on them. But his benign stance made him no less dangerous.

"How do you know me?" she asked.

A pair of saturnine lips cracked open briefly. The fleeting facial expression wasn't a bona fide smile. It was too sardonic to pass for genuine.

"Why, it's common knowledge around Laurent Parish that Miss Schyler Crandall has come home from Londontown."

"Only temporarily and only because of my father's heart attack."

He shrugged, supremely indifferent to her comings and goings. Turning his head, he glanced at the rapidly sinking sun. His eyes reflected it like the motionless waters of a bayou when sunlight strikes it at the right angle. At that time of day the surface of the water looks as solid and impenetrable as brass. So did his eyes.

"I don't repeat gossip, Miss Schyler. I only listen to it. And I only pay attention when I hear something that could affect me."

"What are you doing here?"

His head came back around. "Watching you sleep."

"Before that," she said sharply.

"Gathering roots." He slapped the small leather pouch attached to his belt.

"Roots?" His answer made absolutely no sense, and his cavalier attitude irritated her. "What kind of roots?"

"Doesn't matter. You've never heard of them."

"You're trespassing on private property. You've got no business on Belle Terre."

Insects hummed noisily in the silence that followed. His eyes never wavered from her face. When he answered, his voice was as soft and elusive as the wished for breeze. "Oh, but I do, *pichouette*. Belle Terre is my home."

Schyler stared up at him. "Who are you?"

"You don't remember?"

Comprehension dawned. "Boudreaux?" she whispered. Then she swallowed hard, not really relieved to know who she was talking to. "Cash Boudreaux?"

"*Bien*! You recognize me now."

"No. No, I didn't. The sun's in my eyes. And it's been years since I've seen you."

"And then you had good reason not to remember." He grunted with amused satisfaction when she had the grace to look away, embarrassed. "If you didn't recognize me, how did you know who I was?"

"You're the only person living on Belle Terre who isn't . . ."

"A Crandall."

She ducked her head slightly, nervous at being alone with Cash Boudreaux. For as long as she could remember, her father had forbidden her sister Tricia and her to even speak to him.

His mother was the mysterious Cajun woman, Monique Boudreaux, who lived in a shanty on Laurent Bayou that wound in and about the forested acreage of Belle Terre. As a boy, Cash had had access to the outlying areas but had never been allowed to come this close to the house. Not wanting to take issue with that just yet, Schyler asked politely, "Your mother, how is she?"

"She died."

His blunt reply startled her. Boudreaux's face was inscrutable in the descending twilight. But had it been high noon, Schyler doubted his features would have given away what he was thinking. He'd never had a reputation for being loquacious. The same aura of mystery that cloaked his mother had cloaked him.

"I didn't know."

"It was several years ago."

Schyler swatted at a mosquito that landed on the side of her neck. "I'm sorry."

"You'd better get yourself home. The mosquitoes will eat you alive."

He extended his hand down to her. She regarded it as something dangerous and was as loath to touch it as she would be to reach out and pet a water moccasin. But it would be unspeakably rude not to let him assist her to her feet. Once before she had trusted him. She hadn't come to any harm then.

She laid her hand in his. His palm felt as tough as leather and she felt raised calluses at the bases of his fingers that closed warmly around her hand. As soon as she was on her feet she withdrew her hand from his.

Busily dusting off the back of her skirt to cover the awkward moment, she said, "Last I heard of you, you were just out of Fort Polk and on your way to Vietnam." He said nothing. She looked up at him. "Did you go?"

"*Oui.*"

"That was a long time ago."

"Not long enough."

"Uh, well, I'm glad you made it back. The parish lost several boys over there."

He shrugged. "Guess I was a better fighter." His lip curled into a facsimile of a smile. "But then I always had to be."

She wasn't about to address that. In fact, she was trying to think of something to say that would graciously terminate this uncomfortable conversation. Before she did, Cash Boudreaux raised his hand to her neck and brushed away a mosquito that was looking for a sumptuous spot to have dinner.

The backs of Cash's fingers were rough, but their touch was delicate as they whisked across her exposed throat and down her chest. He looked for her reaction with frank interest. His gaze was sexual. He knew exactly what he was doing. He had brazenly committed the unpardonable. Cash Boudreaux had touched Schyler Crandall . . . and was daring her to complain about it.

He said, "They know the best places to bite."

Schyler pretended to be unmoved by his insinuating stare. She said, "You're as ornery as ever, aren't you?"

"I wouldn't want to disappoint you by changing."

"I couldn't care less."

"You never did."

Feeling severely put down, Schyler stiffened her posture. "I need to get back to the house. It's suppertime. Good seeing you, Mr. Boudreaux."

"How is he?"

"Who? My daddy?" He nodded curtly. Schyler's shoulders relaxed a degree. "I haven't seen him today. I'm going to the hospital after supper. I spoke with one of his nurses by telephone this morning who said he'd had a comfortable night." Emotion dropped her voice to a husky pitch. "These days even that is something to be grateful for." Then in her most refined, Sunday-company voice she said, "I'll tell him you inquired, Mr. Boudreaux."

Boudreaux's laugh was sudden and harsh. It startled a bird into flight from the top of the live oak. "I don't think that'd be a very good idea. Not unless you want the old man to croak."

If her swift calculations were correct, Cash Boudreaux was approaching forty, so he should have known better than to say something so flippant about a seriously ill man. His manners hadn't improved with maturity. He was as coarse, as rude, as undisciplined as he'd been in his youth. His mother had exercised no control over him whatsoever. She had let him run wild. He was constantly into mischief that had ceased to be cute by the time he reached junior high school, where he fast became the scourge of the public school system. Heaven, Louisiana had never spawned such a hellraiser as Cash Boudreaux.

"I'll say good evening, then, Mr. Boudreaux."

He executed a clipped little bow. "Good evening, Miss Schyler."

She gave him a cool nod, more characteristic of her sister than of her, and turned in the direction of the house. She was aware of him watching her. As soon as she was a safe distance away and beneath the deep shadows of the trees, she glanced back.

He had propped himself against the trunk of the live oak, which half a dozen men standing hand to hand couldn't span. She saw a match spark and flare in the darkness. Boudreaux's lean face was briefly illuminated when he lifted the match to the tip of his cigarette. He fanned out the match. The scent of sulfur rode the currents of Gulf humidity until it reached Schyler's hiding place.

Boudreaux drew deeply on the cigarette. The end of it glowed hot and red, like a single eye blinking out of the depths of hell.

Chapter Two

Schyler slipped through the trees, stumbling over dense undergrowth in her hurry to reach the security of the house. On the creaky footbridge, her head was engulfed by a buzzing cloud of mosquitoes. The bridge spanned the shallow creek that separated the woods from the manicured lawn surrounding the house like a neat apron.

Reaching the emerald carpet of thick St. Augustine grass, Schyler paused to regain her breath. The night air was as heavily perfumed as a Bourbon Street hooker. Honeysuckle lined the banks of the creek. Gardenias were blooming somewhere nearby, as well as wild roses, wax-leaf ligustrum, and magnolia trees.

Schyler cataloged the individual smells. They were resurrected out of her childhood, each attached to its special memory. The scents were achingly familiar, though she was long past childhood and hadn't set foot on Belle Terre in six years.

No English garden smelled like this, like home, like Belle Terre. Nothing did. If she were blindfolded and dropped onto Belle Terre, she would recognize it immediately by sound and scent.

The nightly choir of bullfrogs and crickets was warming up. The bass section reverberated from the swampy creek bottom, the soprano section from overhead branches. Out on the spur, a mile or so away, a freight train's whistle hooted. No sound was as sad.

Schyler, closing her eyes and leaning against the rough bark of a loblolly pine, let the sensations seep into her. She crossed her arms over her chest and hugged herself, almost afraid that when she opened her eyes she would awaken from a dream to find that she wasn't at Belle Terre in the full bloom of summer, but in London, shrouded in a cold, winter mist.

But when she opened her eyes she saw the house. As pure and white as a sugar cube, it stood serenely in the heart of the clearing, dominating it like the center gem in a tiara.

Yellow lamplight, made diffuse by the screens, poured from the windows and spilled out onto the deep veranda. Along the edge of the porch were six columns, three on each side of the front door. They supported a second-story balcony. It wasn't a real balcony, only a facade. Tricia frequently and peevishly pointed that out. But Schyler loved it anyway. In her opinion the phony balcony was necessary to the symmetry of the design.

The veranda wrapped around all four sides of the house. It was enclosed with screens in back, made into what had once been called a sleeping porch. Schyler remembered hearing her mother, Macy, talking about the good times she'd had there as a child when all her Laurent cousins would sleep on pallets during family get-togethers.

Personally Schyler had always preferred the open veranda. Wicker chairs, painted white to match the house, were strategically placed so that whoever sat in one might enjoy a particular view of the lawn. There were no eyesores. Each view was worthy of a picture postcard.

The porch swing that Cotton had suspended for Tricia and Schyler to play on was in one corner of the veranda. Twin Boston ferns, each as plush as a dozen feather dusters tied together, grew out of matching urns on either side of the front door. Veda had been so proud of those ferns and had fussed over them endlessly, scolding anyone who brushed past them too quickly and too close. She took it as a personal injury if a cherished frond was torn off by a careless passerby.

Macy was no longer at Belle Terre. Nor was Veda. And Cotton's life hung in the balance at St. John's Hospital. The only thing that remained unchanged and seemingly eternal was the house itself. Belle Terre.

Schyler whispered the name like a prayer as she pushed herself away from the tree. Indulging a whim, she paused long enough to slip off her sandals before continuing barefoot across the cool, damp grass that the automatic sprinkler had watered that afternoon.

When she stepped off the grass onto the crushed shell drive, she winced at the pain. But it was a pleasant discomfort and evoked other childhood memories. Running down the shell drive barefooted for the first time each season had been an annual rite of spring. Having worn shoes and socks all winter, her feet would be tender. Once it was warm enough and Veda had granted permission, the shoes and socks came off. It always took several days for the soles of her feet to toughen so that she could make it all the way to the public road without having to stop.

The sound and feel of the shell drive was familiar. So was the squeak as she pulled open the screened front door. It slapped closed behind her as she knew it would. Belle Terre never changed. It was home.

And then it wasn't. Not anymore. Not since Ken and Tricia had made it their home.

They were already in the dining room, seated at the long table. Her sister set down her tumbler of bourbon and water. "We've been waiting, Schyler," Tricia said with exasperation.

"I'm sorry. I went for a walk and lost all track of time."

"No problem, Schyler," Ken Howell said. "We haven't been waiting long." Her brother-in-law smiled at her from the sideboard where he was topping off his glass from a crystal decanter of bourbon. "Can I pour you something?"

"Gin and tonic, please. Heavy on the ice. It's hot out."

"It's stifling." Crossly, Tricia fanned her face with her stiff linen napkin. "I told Ken to reset the thermostat on the air conditioner. Daddy's such a fussbudget about the electric bill. He keeps us sweltering all summer. As long as he's not here, we might as well be comfortable. But it takes forever for this old house to cool down. Cheers." She tipped her glass in Schyler's direction when Ken handed her the drink.

"Is it all right?"

Schyler sipped from her drink but didn't quite meet Ken's eyes as she replied, "Perfect. Thanks."

"Ken, before you sit back down, please tell Mrs. Graves that Schyler finally put in an appearance and we're ready to be served."

Tricia waved him toward the door that connected the formal dining room with the kitchen. He shot her a resentful look but did as he was told. When Schyler dropped her sandals beside her chair, Tricia said, "Honestly, Schyler, you haven't been home but a few days and already you're resuming the bad habits that nearly drove Mama crazy up until the day she died. You're not going to sit at the dinner table barefooted, are you?"

Tricia was already aggravated with her for holding up dinner. To maintain peace, Schyler bent down and put her sandals back on. "I can't understand why you don't like to go barefooted."

"I can't understand why you do." Though Michelangelo could have painted Tricia's smile on an angel, she was being nasty. "Obviously there's some aristocratic blood in my heritage that is grossly lacking in yours."

"Obviously," Schyler said without rancor. She sipped from her drink, appreciating the gin's icy bite and the lime's tart sting.

"Doesn't that ever bother you?" Tricia asked.

"What?"

"Not knowing your background. Sometimes you behave with no better manners than white trash. That must mean that your folks were sorry as the day is long."

"Tricia, for God's sake," Ken interrupted with annoyance. Returning from his errand in the kitchen, he slid into the chair across the table from his wife. "Let it drop. What the hell difference does it make?"

"I think it makes a lot of difference."

"The important thing is what you do with your life, not who gave it to you. Agreed, Schyler?"

"I never think about my birth parents," Schyler replied. "Oh, I did now and then when I was growing up, whenever I had my feelings hurt or was scolded or—"

"Scolded?" Tricia repeated with disbelief. "I don't recall a single time. Exactly when was that, Schyler?"

Schyler ignored her and continued. "I'd get to feeling sorry for myself and think that if my real parents hadn't given me up for adoption, I would have had a much better life." She smiled wistfully. "I wouldn't have, of course."

"How do you know?" Tricia's sculptured fingernail lazily twirled an ice cube inside the tumbler, then she sucked her fingertip dry. "I'm convinced that my mother was a wealthy society girl. Her mean old parents made her give me up out of jealousy and spite. My father was probably someone who loved and adored her passionately but couldn't marry her because his shrewish wife wouldn't divorce him."

"You've been watching too many soap operas," Ken said with a droll smile, which he cast in Schyler's direction. She smiled back.

Tricia's eyes narrowed. "Don't make fun of me, Ken."

"If you're convinced that your birth parents were so

wonderful, why haven't you tracked them down?" he asked. "As I recall, Cotton even encouraged you to."

Tricia smoothed the napkin in her lap. "Because I wouldn't want to upset their lives or cause them any embarrassment."

"Or because you might find out they aren't so wonderful. You couldn't stand to eat that much crow." Ken took a final drink from his highball glass and returned it to the table with the smugness of a gambler laying down the winning ace.

"Well if they weren't rich," Tricia snapped, "at least I know they weren't trashy, which I'm sure Schyler's real parents were." Then she smiled sweetly and reached across the table for Schyler's hand. "I hope I didn't hurt your feelings, Schyler."

"No. You didn't. Where I came from never mattered to me. Not like it did to you. I'm just glad that I became a Crandall through adoption."

"You always have been so disgustingly grateful that you became the apple of Cotton Crandall's eye, haven't you?"

Mrs. Graves's appearance gave Schyler an excuse not to acknowledge Tricia's snide remark. The housekeeper's name was appropriate, since Schyler was sure a more dour individual had never been born. Schyler had yet to see the stick-figure woman crack a smile. She was as different from Veda as possible.

As the taciturn housekeeper went around the table ladling vichyssoise out of a tureen, Schyler felt a stab of longing for Veda. Her smiling face, as dark as chicory coffee, was a part of Schyler's memory as far back as it went. Veda's ample bosom was as comfortable as a goose down pillow, as protective as a fortress, and as reassuring as a chapel. She always smelled of starch and lemon extract and vanilla and lavender sachet.

Schyler had looked forward to being enveloped in one of Veda's bear hugs the moment she crossed Belle Terre's threshold. It had come as a crushing disappointment to learn that she'd been replaced by Mrs. Graves, whose meager bosom looked as hard and cold and uninviting as a granite tombstone.

The vichyssoise was as thin and spiritless as the woman who had prepared it, served it, and then slunk back into the kitchen through the swinging door. After one taste of the chilled soup, Schyler reached for the salt shaker.

Tricia immediately leaped to the cook's defense. "I told Mrs. Graves to stop cooking with salt when Daddy's blood pressure started getting so high. We're used to it by now."

Schyler shook more salt into her bowl. "Well I'm not." She tested the soup again, but found it unpalatable. She laid her spoon in the underserver and moved the plate aside. "I remember Veda's vichyssoise too well. It was so thick and rich, you could stand your spoon in it."

With controlled motions, Tricia blotted her lips with her napkin, then carefully folded it into her lap again. "I might have known you'd throw that up to me."

"I didn't mean—"

"She was old, Schyler. You hadn't seen her in years, so you're in no position to question my judgment. Veda had become slovenly and inefficient, hadn't she, Ken?" She asked for his opinion rhetorically and didn't give him time to express it. "I had no choice but to let her go. We couldn't go on paying her salary when she wasn't doing her work. I felt terrible about it," Tricia said, pressing a hand against her shapely breasts. "I loved her, too, you know."

"I know you did," Schyler said. "I didn't mean to sound critical. It's just that I miss her. She was such a part of Belle Terre." Because she'd been living abroad at the time, Schyler couldn't countermand Tricia's decision. But a slovenly and inefficient Veda Frances was something Schyler couldn't fathom.

Tricia paid lip service to loving the housekeeper, but Schyler couldn't help but wonder if she had been acting out of spite when she let Veda go. There had been numerous occasions when her sister had been anything but loving toward Veda. Once she had rebuked Veda so insultingly that Cotton lost his temper with her. There had been a terrific row. Tricia had been banished to her room for a full day and had been grounded from a party she had looked forward to for weeks. Although Tricia was capable of carrying grudges indefinitely, Schyler was sure there had been a more serious reason for Veda's dismissal.

No amount of salt or pepper made the chicken casserole that followed the cold potato soup taste good to Schyler. She even tried seasoning it with Tabasco sauce straight from the bottle, which was a staple on any table belonging to Cotton Crandall. The red pepper sauce didn't help either.

However, she gave Mrs. Graves's culinary skills the benefit of the doubt. She hadn't had much appetite since she had received the overseas call from Ken, informing her that Cotton had suffered a heart attack.

"How is he?" she had asked fearfully.

"Bad, Schyler. On the way to the hospital, his heart stopped beating completely. The paramedics gave him CPR. I won't bullshit you. It's touch and go."

Schyler had been urged to come home with all possible haste. Not that she needed any encouragement. She had pieced together frustrating flight schedules that eventually got her to New Orleans. From there, she had taken a small commuter plane to Lafayette. She had rented a car and driven the remaining distance to Heaven.

When she arrived, her unconscious father was in an ICU at St. John's, where he remained. His condition was stable, but still critical.

The worst of it for Schyler was that she wasn't sure he even knew she had come home to see him. He wafted in and out of consciousness. During one of her brief visits to his room, he had opened his eyes and looked at her. But his face had remained impassive. His eyes had closed without registering recognition. His blank stare, which seemed to look straight through her, broke her heart. She was afraid Cotton would die before she had a chance to talk to him.

"Schyler?"

Startled, she looked up at Ken, who had addressed her. "Oh, I'm sorry. Yes, I'm finished, Mrs. Graves," she said to the woman who was staring down censoriously at her virtually untouched plate. She took it away and replaced it with a blackberry cobbler that looked promising. Hopefully the sugar cannister hadn't been discarded along with the salt box.

"Are you still going to the hospital after supper, Schyler?"

"Yes. Want to come with me?"

"Not tonight," Tricia said. "I'm tired."

"Yeah, playing bridge all day is hard work."

Ken's dig was summarily ignored. "Daddy's Sunday school teacher brought by a get well card from the class and asked us to deliver it. He said it was a shame that Cotton had to recover in a Catholic hospital."

Schyler smiled at the deacon's religious snobbery, though it was typical of the area. Macy had been Catholic and had raised her adopted daughters in the church. Cotton, however, had never converted. "Heaven doesn't have a Baptist hospital. We have no choice."

"Everybody in town is worried about Cotton." Ken's waistline had expanded marginally since Schyler had last seen him but that didn't deter him from pouring heavy cream over his cobbler. "I can't walk down the sidewalk without a dozen people stopping to ask about him."

"Of course everybody's worried," Tricia said. "He's about the most important man in town."

"I had someone ask me about him this afternoon," Schyler added.

"Who was that?" Tricia asked.

Tricia and Ken stopped eating their cobbler and looked at Schyler expectantly.

"Cash Boudreaux."

Chapter Three

"Cash Boudreaux. Well, well." Tricia turned her spoon upside down inside her mouth and, with her tongue, leisurely licked it clean. "Were his pants zipped?"

"Tricia!"

"Come now, Ken, don't you think nice ladies like me know about him?" She flirtatiously batted her eyelashes at her husband. "Everybody in town knows about Cash's escapades with women. When he broke off with that Wallace woman, she told the whole Saturday morning crowd at the beauty shop about their sordid little affair." Tricia lowered her voice secretively. "And I do mean every detail. We were all embarrassed for her because the poor dear was more than just a little drunk. But still we hinged on every scintillating word. If he's half as good as she claimed, well . . ." Tricia ended with a sly wink.

"I take it that Mr. Boudreaux is the town stud," Schyler said.

"He nails anything that wears a skirt."

"That's where you're wrong, honey," Tricia said, correcting her husband. "From what I hear, he's very particular. And why not? He can afford to pick and choose. He has women all over the parish practically throwing themselves at him."

"Heaven, Louisiana's equivalent to Don Juan." Dismissing the topic, Ken returned to his cobbler.

Tricia wasn't yet ready to shelve it. "Don't sound so sour. You're just jealous."

"Jealous? Jealous of a no 'count, bastard, ne'er-do-well, who doesn't have two nickels in his jeans?"

"Honey, when talk comes around to what he has in his jeans, the ladies are not referring to money. And apparently what he's got in his jeans makes him more valuable than pure gold." Tricia gave her husband a feline smile. "But you've got no need to worry. The earthy type has never appealed to me. You must admit, though, that Cash is a fascinating character." She turned to Schyler. "Where'd you run into him?"

"Here."

"Here?" Ken's spoon halted midway between his bowl of cobbler and his mouth. "At Belle Terre?"

"He said he was gathering roots."

"For his potions."

Schyler stared at Tricia, who had supplied what she seemed to think was a logical explanation. "Potions?"

"He took up where Monique left off." Schyler continued to stare confusedly at her sister. "Don't tell me you didn't know that Monique Boudreaux was a witch."

"I'd always heard the rumors, of course. But they were ridiculous."

"They were not! Why do you think Daddy let trash like that live on Belle Terre all those years? He was afraid she'd put a curse on us all if he ran her off."

"You're guilty of melodrama as usual, Tricia," Ken said. "Actually, Schyler, Monique was what is known as a *traiteur*, a treater. It's a Cajun custom. She cured people, or so they claimed. Right up till the day she died she was doling out tonics and tinctures."

"Traditionally, treaters are left-handed and usually women, but folks around here seem to believe that Cash inherited his mama's powers."

"She didn't have any *powers*, Tricia," Ken said impatiently.

"Listen," she said, slapping the edge of the table with her palm for emphasis, "I happen to know for a fact that Monique Boudreaux was a witch."

"Malicious gossip."

Tricia glared at her husband. "I know it firsthand. One

day in town, she looked at me with those big, dark, evil eyes of hers and that afternoon I got my period. It was two weeks early and I've never had cramps that bad before or since."

"If Monique possessed any special powers, she used them to make people feel better, not worse," Ken said. "Her potions and incantations had been passed down since the eighteenth century from the Acadians. They're harmless and so was she."

"Hardly. Those healing traditions were combined with African voodoo when the Acadians came to Louisiana. Black magic."

Ken frowned at Tricia. "Monique Boudreaux wasn't into voodoo. And she wasn't evil. Just different. And very beautiful. Which is why most of the women in this town, including you, want to believe she was a witch."

"Who actually knew her, you or me? You'd only been living here a little while before she died."

"I've heard tell."

"Well, you've heard wrong. Besides, she was getting old and all her former beauty had faded."

"That's a woman's point of view. I tell you she was still a good-looking woman."

"What about Cash?" Schyler cut into what she could see was becoming a full-fledged marital disagreement. It hadn't taken long for her to realize that the Howells' marriage fell short of being sublime. She tried her Christian best not to take pleasure in that.

"What does Cash do for a living?" Schyler could tell the question surprised them. They stared at her for a moment before Ken answered.

"He works for us, for Crandall Logging."

Schyler assimilated that. Or tried to. Cash Boudreaux was on her family's payroll. He had hardly behaved deferentially that afternoon. His manner hadn't befitted an employee in the presence of an employer. "Doing what?"

"He's a logger. Plain and simple." Having demolished the cobbler, Ken wiped his mouth and tossed down his napkin.

"Not quite that plain or that simple, Schyler," Tricia amended. "He's a sawhand, a loader, he drives the skidder. He selects the trees for cutting. He does just about all of it."

"Shame, isn't it," Ken said, "that a man his age, and as smart as he seems to be, has no more ambition than that?"

"Does he still live in that shanty on the bayou?"

"Sure does. He leaves us alone. We leave him alone. Cotton has to deal with him down at the landing, but other than that we all give each other wide berth. Can't imagine him coming close to the house today. He and Cotton had words when Monique died. Cotton wanted to move Cash out. Somehow Cash talked Cotton into letting him stay. Cotton's trust is commendable."

"It's also selfish," Tricia said. "He needs Cash."

"He might need him, but he doesn't like it. I think he's a fool for trusting the man. I wouldn't trust Cash Boudreaux as far as I could throw him." Suddenly Ken leaned across the table and looked at Schyler with concern. "He didn't do or say anything offensive, did he?"

"No, no. We just exchanged a few words." And a touch. And a gaze. Both had conveyed as much contempt as sensuality. Schyler didn't know which disturbed her the most, his interest or his suggested animosity. "I was curious about him, that's all. It's been years since I'd heard anything about him. I didn't expect him to still be around."

"Well, if he ever gets out of line with you, you let me know."

"And what will you do? Beat him up?" Tricia's laughter ricocheted off the crystal teardrops of the chandelier overhead. "Some say Cash stayed in the jungles of Vietnam a tad too long. He kept reenlisting in the marine corps because he loved the fighting and killing so much. Came back meaner than he went, and he was already meaner than sin. I doubt you could pose a threat to him, honey."

Schyler could feel the undercurrents of enmity between husband and wife rising again. "I'm sure that's the last I'll see of Mr. Boudreaux." She scooted back her chair. "Excuse me, please. I'm going to freshen up before I go to the hospital."

The bedroom she was sleeping in now was the same one she had as a child. Through three large rectangular windows she had a view of the back of the property, the greenhouse, what had at one time been a smokehouse and now served as a toolshed, the barn that housed several horses, and the detached garage. Beyond the outbuildings which were all painted white to match the main house, was the woods, and beyond the trees, the bayou.

She closed the bedroom door behind her and stood with her back against it. She paused to appreciate the room she'd missed so much. The hardwood floor was dotted with area rugs that were worn and faded and would bring a premium price should they ever be sold, which they wouldn't be. Schyler would never part with anything that belonged in or to Belle Terre.

All the furniture in the room was made of oak, aged to a golden patina that kept the pieces from looking heavy and masculine. The walls were painted saffron, all the woodwork white. The bedspread, chair cushions, and drapes were white as well. She had insisted on that the last time the room had been redecorated. She hadn't wanted any of the furnishings to detract from the simple beauty of the room itself.

The only modern touch was the bookshelf. It was still cluttered with childhood and teenage memorabilia. She had resolved to clean out and throw away the yearbooks and dried corsages and yellowing party invitations many times. But nostalgia would always override her pragmatism. Nevertheless, she decided that before she returned to London she would give this room a thorough housecleaning and get rid of that junk.

The small adjoining bathroom hadn't been changed. It still had a white porcelain pedestal sink and claw-foot bathtub. She rinsed her face and hands in the sink and, using the framed mirror over it, retouched her makeup and brushed her hair. When she lifted the loose, dark blond curls off her neck, she noticed the pink bump on the side of her throat. A mosquito bite.

They know the best places to bite, she remembered Cash saying.

She tossed down the hairbrush impatiently and, picking up her purse and rental car keys off the bureau in the bedroom, went downstairs. Tricia was speaking animatedly into the telephone receiver in the formal parlor. It was joined to the informal parlor by sliding wooden doors that disappeared into the connecting walls. The doors were always kept open, making one large room out of the two, but each half was still referred to by its traditional name.

The adoptive sisters waved good-bye to each other. Schyler walked through the wide hallway and out onto the veranda. She was on the second step down when Ken spoke to her. He left the rocker he'd been sitting in and came to join her on the step. Encircling her upper arm, he led her toward her car, which was parked in the drive. It made a semicircle in front of the house, then ran along one side of it to the back and the garage.

"Let me drive you to the hospital," he offered.

"No thanks. You and Tricia went this morning. It's my turn."

"I don't mind."

"I know, but there's no need."

He turned her to face him. "I didn't offer because I thought you needed a ride. I offered because we haven't had a second alone since you got here."

Schyler didn't like the direction the conversation was taking, nor Ken's confidential tone. She politely but firmly disengaged her arm. "That's right, Ken. We haven't. And I think that's best, don't you?"

"Best for whom?"

"For all of us."

"Not for me."

"Ken, please." Schyler tried to sidestep him, but he heeded her off. Facing her again and standing close, he ran his fingers down her cheek.

"Schyler, Schyler. I've missed you like hell. Jesus, can you imagine what it was like for me to see you again?"

"No, what was it like?" Her voice was harsh as were her accusing eyes.

He frowned with chagrin and withdrew his hand. "I can imagine how you felt when we found out that Tricia was pregnant."

Schyler's laugh was bitter. "No, you can't. Not unless you've been betrayed like that. Not unless the planet has been jerked out from under you. You can't know what I felt like at all." She wet her lips and shook her head as if to ward off an attack of insurmountable depression. "I've got to go."

Again she tried to walk around him and again he impeded her. "Schyler, wait. We've got to talk about this."

"No."

"You hightailed it to London without ever giving me a chance to explain."

"What was there to explain? We were about to announce our engagement to be married when Tricia upstaged us by announcing that she was pregnant with your baby. Your baby, Ken," she repeated, stressfully enunciating each word.

He gnawed his lower lip, his only concession to a guilty conscience. "We'd had a fight, remember?"

"A quarrel. A stupid, lovers' quarrel. I don't even remember what it was about. But it must have been over a real bone of contention with you because you wasted no time in sleeping with my sister."

"I didn't know she would get pregnant."

Schyler was speechless. She didn't remember obtuseness being one of Ken's character traits. Six years was a long time. She had changed. Apparently so had Ken. Still, it was incredible that he missed the point.

"It was inconsequential that she conceived, Ken. It hurt me just as much to know that she *could* be pregnant with your baby."

He took a step closer and caught her shoulders. "Schyler, you're blaming the wrong party here. Tricia came on to me something fierce. Hell, I'm only a man. I was depressed. I was missing you. At first I thought she just wanted to comfort me, you know, sympathize, but then—"

"I don't want to hear this."

"But I want you to," he said, shaking her slightly. "I've got to make you understand. She, well, you know, started flirting with me, flattering me. One thing led to another. She kissed me. Next thing I know, we're making out. It just happened once." Schyler looked at him with patent disbelief. "Okay, maybe a few times, but it never meant anything. I screwed her, yeah, but I loved you." He tightened his grip on her shoulders. "I still do."

Angrily, Schyler threw off his grasping hands. "Don't you dare say that to me. It insults us both. You are my sister's husband."

"But we're not happy."

"Tough. I am."

"With that Mark character you work for?"

"Yes. Yes, with that Mark character. Mark Houghton has been wonderful to me. I love him. He loves me."

"Not like we loved each other."

She laughed shortly. "Nothing like the way we loved each other. Mark and I share a kind of love you would never understand. But whatever my relationship with Mark, it has no bearing on ours. You're married to Tricia. Whether or not your marriage is happy or dismal is no concern of mine."

"I don't believe you."

He quickly drew her to him and kissed her. Hard. She recoiled and made a small choking sound when his tongue speared into her mouth. But he didn't stop kissing her.

For a moment she allowed it, curious as to what her reaction would be. She discovered, quite surprisingly, that Ken's kiss evoked nothing but revulsion. She dug her fists into his chest and pushed him away. Saying nothing, she quickly got into the rented Cougar and started the motor. She floorboarded the accelerator and put the car into motion with a spray of crushed shells.

Chapter Four

From the cover of a palmetto, Cash watched Schyler drive away, leaving Ken staring wistfully after her. He waited until Howell had dejectedly climbed the steps and entered the house before he slipped into the deeper shadows of the woods and headed toward the bayou.

"So that's how the wind blows," he said to himself.

In Heaven everybody knew everybody's business. The scandal six years ago involving the Crandall sisters had started tongues wagging. The town had buzzed with gossip for months after Schyler's defection to London and speculation on when she would return had varied. Some said weeks. Others said she might sulk for a month or two. No one betted on it being years before she came home, and only then because her daddy's life was in jeopardy.

But Schyler Crandall was back at Belle Terre and, apparently, back in her old lover's arms. If that kiss was any indication, it didn't matter to her that Howell was married to her sister. Maybe she rationalized that she had had him first and that turnabout was fair play.

What mystified Cash was why either woman would want Ken Howell. He must pack more of a punch than it seemed he could. Howell had been known to frequent the upstairs bedrooms of the area honky-tonks, but no more than any other man. He never chased after women who were married, single, or somewhere in between. And he always paid for his extramarital dalliances. Women weren't one of his vices.

Whatever made Ken Howell attractive to the Crandall

sisters escaped Cash. In his opinion, Howell was a sancti-monious son of a bitch. He'd been raised to look down his nose at anybody who wasn't in the social register. Howell had conveniently forgotten that when his folks died in a plane crash, they had left behind more liens than legacy. He still considered all but the upper crust of society inferior to him.

Maybe he also considered himself above morality and felt justified in having a wife in the house and a lover on the veranda.

Deep in thought, Cash continued walking through the forest. He moved through the trees with a stealth that had been developed in childhood and refined with taxpayers' money. The marine corps had honed his natural talent and developed it into a fine art. He didn't have to think twice about finding his way, which was good since he was lost in thought about Schyler Crandall.

It didn't make sense to him that that much woman would want a pompous wimp like Howell. Not that Schyler was a lot of woman physically. He was certain he could almost close his hands around her waist and he would welcome a chance to prove it. Her hips were full enough to make a sensual curve from her slender waist. While her breasts weren't large enough to win a wet T-shirt contest, he was sure she'd find it uncomfortable to sleep on her stomach without making adjustments. He'd been well aware of their shape beneath her blouse.

Thinking of that made Cash smile. Was there a set of tits on any living woman that he didn't take notice of? With that expertise to qualify him, he could say that Schyler Crandall's figure wasn't voluptuous, but remarkable just the same.

She put that figure to full advantage, too. It wasn't so much her body that made her wholly woman, but what she did with it. The graceful way she moved. The feminine gestures she unconsciously made with those slender, ring-less hands. The long legs and narrow feet. The expressive movements of her light brown eyes. And all that sweet, honey blond hair.

She was woman through and through. Cash wondered if

she knew that. It was doubtful she did. But he sure as hell did.

Irritated with himself for dwelling on her, he stepped into the pirogue that he'd left on the bank of the bayou. He picked up the long pole and used it to push off. As silent as his guerrilla progress through the nighttime jungle, the canoe cut as cleanly as a blade through the still, murky waters of Laurent Bayou.

Since he was several years older than Schyler—he wasn't sure just how many because Monique hadn't been a stickler for dates and was never sure exactly what his birthday was—Cash had watched her grow up from a pretty little girl with flaxen braids into the woman she now was.

As a child, being driven around by proud papa Cotton in his newest Cadillac convertible, she had always worn hair ribbons that matched her lace-trimmed dresses. Always so prim. While Cotton looked on proudly, she had entertained his friends with her precociousness.

But she hadn't been like that all the time. Every now and then the little doll had stepped out of her bandbox. From his hiding places in the woods, Cash had often seen her riding Cotton's horses barebacked and barefooted, hair flying, face flushed and sweaty.

He wondered if she still rode horseback. And if she did, did she ride hell-bent for leather like she used to when nobody but him was looking?

That image of her made his sex stretch and grow hard against his zipper. He wiped the sweat that beaded his forehead on his sleeve and cursed the vicious heat. Ordinarily he wouldn't have even noticed it.

But Schyler Crandall had come home. Nothing was ordinary.

Schyler noticed how stifling the heat was as she left the car and made the short walk to the air-conditioned lobby of the two-story hospital. By the time she stepped through the automatic doors, her clothes were sticking to her. Maybe she should have showered and changed before coming to the hospital.

As she waited for the elevator, she surreptitiously checked herself in the mirrored wall and decided that she looked far from outstanding, but okay. There was a grass stain on the hem of her full cotton skirt and her sleeveless blouse was wrinkled, but in this part of the country everybody wore cotton in the summertime. Everybody looked wilted by late afternoon. It was a given that the heat and humidity would inflict their damages, so they were generally ignored.

The very thought of wearing stockings was suffocating. She'd left on her sandals. Her only pieces of jewelry were a plain watch with a leather strap and the gold hoops in her ears. They were eighteen carat but unostentatious. Her shoulder bag was expensive and of the highest quality, but since the designer's signature wasn't obvious, no one would be impressed, even if he recognized the Italian's name.

In the mirror Schyler saw a woman who looked perilously close to her thirtieth birthday. It wasn't the maturity in her face that bothered her, but that she didn't have more to show for those thirty years. No career to speak of. No husband. No children. Not even an address she could call her own.

Her accomplishments added up to nil. She hadn't been able to move forward because of the memories that kept her shackled to the past. By coming home, she had wanted to lay to rest the most disturbing of those memories. She had hoped that the ambiguities surrounding her feelings for Ken Howell would be resolved.

Instead, his kiss had only confused her further. She no longer loved him, not with the intensity she had before. That she knew. What she didn't know was why. She couldn't pinpoint the reason why her heart didn't trip over itself each time he looked at her, why she hadn't dissolved at the touch of his lips on hers.

For six years Ken Howell had been preserved in her mind as she had first seen him, a dashing student leader on the Tulane campus, a stunning basketball star. He was from a good family, in solid with New Orleans society. He was a business administration major; his future had held nothing but bright promise. And he had chosen Schyler Crandall, the reigning belle of Laurent Parish, to pin his fraternity pin on.

They went together for two years. As soon as both had graduated, marriage seemed a natural progression. Then they had had a silly falling out, a misunderstanding over something so trivial as to be insignificant. They didn't date each other for several months.

Schyler never considered the break irrevocable and she had viewed the temporary separation as healthy for the relationship. It gave them time to date others and make certain that they wanted each other for life.

When Ken finally relented and called her, he wanted desperately to see her. Their reconciliation was tender and passionate by turns. He was impatient to get married; she felt the same. They set a tentative date for their wedding and asked both families to gather at Belle Terre for a party.

But Tricia stole the show.

She wore blue that day, a shade exactly the color of her eyes. Schyler had told her earlier how pretty she looked. Schyler had loved the entire world that day. Everybody and everything was beautiful.

In the midst of all the gaiety, Tricia had sidled up to Ken and taken his hand. "Everybody, everybody, can I please have your attention?" When the laughter and conversation died down, she smiled up at Ken and said, "Honey, I suppose I should have told you first and in private, but it seems so appropriate to tell you now, when the people we love most dearly are here with us." Then she had drawn a deep breath and, with a jubilant smile, announced, "I'm going to have your baby."

According to his facial expression, Ken was as stunned as anyone there. He looked flabbergasted, embarrassed, ill. But he didn't deny his responsibility, not even when Schyler turned to him with disbelief and silently begged him to.

Any solution other than marriage was out of the question. Within days and with very little fanfare, Tricia and Ken were married in a civil ceremony. Eight weeks later Tricia miscarried.

But by that time, Schyler had left for Europe. When news of the miscarriage reached her, she felt nothing. Her heart had been as empty as Tricia's womb. Their betrayal had left her numb.

In many ways, she still was. So when the bad memories darkly obscured the good ones, Ken's kiss evoked nothing but revulsion.

Stepping off the elevator on the second floor of the hospital, Schyler thought that if Cotton didn't pull out of this, that if he died as a result of the massive heart attack, at least he would die in the knowledge that his life had amounted to something. So far, the same could not be said of her.

Before she returned to England, she must come to terms with her feelings for Tricia and Ken and their treachery. If she didn't, she might remain stagnant forever. Until her mind and heart had finally closed the door on the past, she would be like a stalled engine, going nowhere, accomplishing nothing.

"Good evening," she said to the nurse she met in the hallway. "How is my father?"

"Hello, Miss Crandall. There's no change. The doctor asked earlier if you had come in. He wants to see you."

"He can find me outside my father's room."

"I'll tell him."

The nurse moved away to find the doctor. Schyler continued down the corridor toward the last ICU. Through a narrow window she saw Cotton lying in a bed, connected to machines that bleeped and blinked his discouraging vital signs.

Schyler's own heart ached to see the man she adored in this condition. Cotton, if he was aware of it, would hate being helpless. He had never been dependent on anyone. Now, the most elemental body functions were being done for him by sophisticated machinery. It didn't seem possible that such a robust man could be lying there motionless, colorless, useless.

Laying her palm against the cool glass, Schyler whispered, "Daddy, what's wrong? Tell me."

Their estrangement had roots in that horrible day when

the gods had decided that Schyler Crandall had had enough good luck and had hurled a life's worth of misfortune at her in the space of one afternoon.

After the bewildered guests had departed, after Ken and Tricia had left to handle the necessary legal aspects of getting married, Schyler had gone to Cotton, expecting him to envelope her in his loving and sympathetic embrace.

Instead he'd metamorphosed into a stranger. He refused to look directly at her. He brusquely set her aside when she collapsed against his wide chest. He treated her coolly. Until that day Schyler had been the apple of his eye. But on that miserable afternoon, when Schyler suggested that she go abroad for a while, Cotton had approved the idea. He hadn't been angry. He hadn't ranted and raved. She wished he had. That would have been familiar. She could have dealt with his short temper.

But he had treated her with indifference. That had pierced Schyler to the core. Cotton was indifferent only to people he had absolutely no use for. Schyler could not understand why her father no longer showed the tender affection she so desperately needed.

So she had left Belle Terre and moved to London. The rift between Cotton and her had grown wider with each year. Other than a letter every several months, and a few civil but chilly telephone conversations on holidays, they had had no formal contact.

He didn't seem to mind. It was as though he'd dismissed her from his life for good. She didn't want him to die harboring the secret grudge. Her greatest fear was that she would never know what had turned him against her, what had changed her from pet to pariah.

"I'm not going to have two patients on my hands, am I?"

The doctor's voice roused her. She raised her bowed head and wiped tears off her cheeks. "Hello, Dr. Collins." She smiled waveringly. "I'm fine. Just very tired." He looked skeptical but didn't pursue it, for which Schyler was grateful. "Any change?"

Jeffrey Collins was a young man who had decided to set up practice in a small community hospital rather than battle the competition in a large city. As he studiously consulted the chart on Cotton Crandall, he reminded Schyler of a boy about to give an oral book report in front of the class, wanting to do well.

"Nothing significant."

"Is that good or bad?"

"Depends on which way you look at it. If it's a change for the worse, we'd rather do without."

"Of course."

"What the patient needs is bypass surgery. Triple, maybe quadruple. The pictures of his chest indicate that." He snapped closed the metal cover of the chart. "But he isn't strong enough yet. We've got to wait, build up his strength, and hope that he doesn't have another attack before we can go in."

"'We'?"

"The resident cardiologist, the general surgeon, and I."

She looked away, trying to think of a graceful way to put what she had to say. "Dr. Collins, at the risk of sounding ungrateful for everything you've already done, and doubtful of your ability—"

"You wonder if I know what the hell I'm doing?"

She smiled helplessly. "Yes. Do you know what the hell you're doing?"

"I don't blame you for wondering. We're a small hospital. But the financial backers who built this facility, your father included, spared no expense. The equipment has the latest technology available. The staff is well paid. We're not doctors and surgeons who couldn't find jobs anywhere else. It's just that we wanted a small-town environment for our families."

"I'm sorry, I didn't mean to imply that you weren't competent or qualified."

He held up his hand, indicating that no offense had been taken. "When the time comes for surgery, if you want to have Mr. Crandall moved to another hospital, I'll be glad to make the arrangements for you and do whatever it takes to move him safely. I wouldn't advise that he be moved now, however."

"Thank you, doctor. I appreciate your candor. I hope you appreciate mine."

"I do."

"And I don't think it'll be necessary to have him transferred."

"That's gratifying to know."

They smiled at each other. "Can I go in and see him now?"

"Two minutes. By the way, I recommend that you catch up on your meals and start getting more rest. You look none too healthy yourself. Good night."

He set off down the hall with a confident stride that belied his wet-behind-the-ears appearance. Schyler took comfort in that as she nodded a greeting to the nurse monitoring the life-saving equipment and stepped into the ICU. Despite the bright fluorescent lighting, the room was sepulchral.

She tiptoed to the bed. Cotton's eyes were closed. A tube had been inserted into his mouth, held in place by tape across his lips. Smaller tubes had been placed in his nostrils. Wires and conduits and catheters attached to the various machines disappeared beneath the sheet covering him. She could only guess at their unpleasant functions.

The only thing that was familiar was his shock of white hair. Tears blurred her eyes as Schyler reached out and ran her fingers through it. "I love you, Daddy." He didn't stir. "Forgive me for whatever I did." She used up the full two minutes before she kissed his forehead and quietly left the room.

Only after the door closed behind her did Cotton Crandall open his eyes.

Chapter Five

Tricia and Ken were in the throes of an argument. From the steps of the veranda, Schyler could see them through the parlor windows. An authentic Aubusson rug was their arena. They were squared off across its muted, pastel pattern. Their voices were muffled, so she couldn't distinguish individual words. She didn't have to. They were gesturing angrily.

Stepping out of the wedge of light coming through the window, she went back down the steps. She didn't want to intrude or have them see her, especially if she were the source of the squabble.

Surely Tricia hadn't seen Ken kissing her before she left for the hospital. Tricia wouldn't have stayed undercover, waiting until Schyler left to confront her husband. She would have charged out of the house immediately and challenged them both.

The visit to the hospital had left Schyler emotionally drained. She didn't want to join the fracas going on in the formal parlor, so she left her purse and keys lying on the hood of her car and struck out across the lawn.

Maybe the exercise would exhaust her enough to make her sleep. She had been tired every night since her arrival but had lain awake, thinking about Cotton, thinking about Tricia and Ken, thinking about them sleeping together in the room down the hall from hers. She hated herself for still caring about that. But she did.

And because she did, it was curious that Ken's kiss hadn't affected her more than it had. For the last six years

33

she had fancied herself still in love with him. The first kiss, after so long and heartbreaking a separation, should have electrified her, regardless that she was kissing her sister's husband. Yet all she had felt was a vague sadness, a sense of loss, which she couldn't explain.

That was just one of the things troubling Schyler as she made her way across the wide lawn and entered the surrounding forest. The evening air was sultry, only marginally cooler than it had been at sunset. Her footsteps disturbed patches of mist that hovered above the ground. Ethereally, it swirled around her ankles and climbed her calves. It could have been a spooky sensation, but Schyler regarded these patches of fog as friendly.

She followed the narrow path that paralleled the road for a few hundred yards before angling off to the left. From there, it meandered through the woods on a gradual decline until it reached the fertile banks of the bayou.

Here, on the higher terrain, there were a few hardwoods, trailing the harmless Spanish moss from their branches. But mostly there were pines, reproducing themselves prolifically until they gave way to the cypress and willow and cottonwood that claimed the muddy shore of the bayou as their domain.

Almost as soon as she could say her ABCs, Schyler could name every tree in the woods. She had never forgotten them. She remembered Cotton's forestry lessons well. She knew the forest by sight, touch, and smell. Her ears could still attach a label to each familiar sound.

Except one.

And it came upon her so swiftly that she didn't even have time to wonder about it until the vicious, snarling dog was blocking her path.

The animal had seemingly emerged from hell and sprung out of the marshy ground to stand only a few feet in front of her. His body was sturdy, with a deep and heavily muscled chest. His face was triangular and had a blunt snout. His sharply pointed tail curved in an upward arc that was aggressive and hostile. He was short-haired, an unattractive, mottled blend of black and brown and tan. Wide-set eyes glittered up at her. His snarling mouth drooled. He stood with his feet planted far apart, like a sailor on the deck of a tall ship. He was ugly, extremely ugly, the most menacing creature Schyler had ever seen. His sinister growl was terrifying in itself.

Instinctively she sucked in and held her breath. Her heart was pounding so hard it hurt. When she raised her hand to it, the animal lurched forward and gave three sharp, rapping barks.

She froze, not wanting to alarm the dog by moving a muscle. "Down, boy, down." The words were ridiculously trite. This wasn't an amiable pet. There wasn't a single friendly aspect to his character. This animal was a killer. His growl modified to a low vibration in his throat, but Schyler wasn't foolish enough to think that he was backing down.

Crying out for help would be futile. She was too far from the house. Besides, the sudden noise might provoke the short-tempered animal to attack her. But this Mexican standoff couldn't last forever. She decided to chance a half step backward. The dog didn't seem to notice, so she took another. Then another.

When she had put several yards between them, she decided to turn and make her way swiftly along the path toward the house. She wouldn't break into a run because he was certain to chase her. But she wouldn't waste any time either.

Dreading the risky result, she turned. The instant she did, the dog barked another sharp threat. The sound was so abrupt, so startling and loud, that she stumbled and fell. The dog lunged at her. Schyler rolled to her back, covered her face with her forearm, and knocked the powerful animal aside with the other.

Actually coming into physical contact with him was like living a hideous nightmare. His moist breath was hot on her arm. She felt the scrape of sharp teeth on her skin. Either his saliva or her own blood felt sticky and wet as it trickled over her wrist. The bone in her arm almost cracked upon impact with the dog's broad skull. The blow numbed the nerves for several seconds.

She had no doubt that the animal would rip out her

throat if she couldn't stop it. Acting on sheer survival instinct, she groped behind her and picked up the first thing she laid her hand on, a fallen pine branch about as big around as her wrist. When the dog launched his next attack, she whacked him in the face as hard as she could. The blow landed solidly but didn't deter him. Indeed, it only infuriated him more.

Swinging the pine branch wildly and, as a consequence, ineffectually, Schyler struggled to her feet and started to run. As she slashed her way through the trees, the dog was literally on her heels. She felt his teeth snapping at her thrashing ankles. Several times she barely escaped his clenching jaws.

Suddenly, from out of nowhere, two brilliant lights cut through the forest as smoothly as a sythe through tall grass. They stopped on her like a searchlight that had found its target, blinding her. Mist and dust danced eerily in the twin beams. Reflexively, Schyler crossed her arms over her eyes.

A piercing whistle rent the still, humid air. She sensed the dog's immediate attention. He ceased his snarling and barking and came to an abrupt standstill. Another shrill whistle galvanized him. He sped past her. His sweaty body brushed against her bare leg, nearly knocking her down. He plunged through the undergrowth in the direction of the bright lights.

Schyler realized then that in her headlong plunge, she had almost reached the road. The lights belonged to a vehicle that had pulled to the shoulder. The steering wheel had been cut sharply to direct the headlights into the woods. She blinked into focus the shape of a pickup truck, made spectral by the cloud of dust that swirled around it.

The noises coming from the truck were surreal. The engine was wheezing and knocking. And from the back of the truck came the raucous sound of barking dogs. They were in a frenzied state, rattling their metal cages as they clambered to get out. Schyler couldn't tell how many there were, but it sounded like every hound in hell.

She reversed her direction and fled in terror, certain that soon the whole bloodthirsty pack would be unleashed on her. She risked looking over her shoulder. The truck was backing up, the gears grinding. Then it turned onto the road and lumbered away. The forest was plunged into darkness again.

But the barking continued, so Schyler kept running from it, blindly clawing her way through the dense trees that had become alien. The moss that brushed against her cheek now was terrifying. Roots and vines were snares that wrapped around her ankles and tried to trap her in this nightmare. In vain, she fought off the mist that rose to embrace her in its ghostly arms.

She actually screamed when she was brought up hard against a solid, impregnable body. She fought it, struggling to scratch and claw her way free. She was lifted up; her feet left the ground. She used them to kick.

"Stop it! What in hell's name is the matter with you?"

Despite her terror, Schyler realized that this phantom in her nightmare had a very human voice. He felt human, too. She flung her head back and looked up at him. It was the devil, all right.

Cash Boudreaux was gazing down at her curiously. Several seconds lapsed, then he swung her up in his arms. Schyler was too relieved to argue. The dog's attack was still too recent for her not to welcome a larger, stronger presence than herself.

Her breath came in short, swift pants that fanned his throat. She clutched the front of his shirt. She shuddered with revulsion at the recollection of the dog's slobbering, snarling mouth. But when the remnant horror began to recede, embarrassment set in.

She drew in a long, unsteady breath. "You can put me down now, Mr. Boudreaux. I'm fine." He didn't set her down. He didn't even stop but kept walking in the direction of the bayou. "Did you hear me?"

"Oui."

"Then please put me down. This is nice of you, but—"

"I'm not being nice. It's just more convenient to carry you than drag you along behind me."

"That's my point. I can manage alone."

"You couldn't stand up. You're shaking too bad."

That was true. From the marrow out, she was quaking like a dead leaf in a gale. Willing, at least for the moment, to concede the point to him, she let him carry her. "You're going the wrong way. The house is back there."

"I know where the house is." There was a trace of sarcasm in his voice. "I thought you might be running scared from something or someone there."

"What would I be afraid of there?"

"You tell me."

"For your information, I was attacked by a . . . a dog." Her voice cracked. It was mortifying to feel tears in her eyes but she couldn't help it.

Boudreaux stopped in his tracks. "A dog? A dog attacked you?" She nodded. "I heard the barking," he said. "Were you bitten?"

"I think so. I'm not sure. I ran."

"Jesus."

He started down the path again, walking more quickly now. The chorus of bullfrogs grew louder. Schyler recognized the willows, whose long, trailing branches bent toward the still, murky waters like a penitent paying homage. This branch of the bayou was distributary, drawing water out of the wider, freer flowing Laurent Bayou. It was a narrow creek. The waters flowed sluggishly if at all, making it appear almost stagnant.

There was a pirogue lying half in, half out of the water. Agilely, Cash put one foot in it and leaned down to deposit Schyler in the narrow, canoe-type boat. Taking a book of matches from the breast pocket of his shirt, he struck one and lit a kerosene lantern. The yellow light made his eyes appear as sinister as the wildcats that prowled the swamps. He blew out the match and turned up the lantern.

"What were you doing here?" she asked with a detached curiosity.

"Hauling in the day's catch." He nodded toward a net trap that was partially submerged in the shallow water. Several dozen red swamp crayfish were squirming inside.

"You seem to have a propensity for trespassing where you don't belong."

He didn't defend himself. "Here, have a drink."

A pint bottle of bourbon was lying in the bottom of the pirogue. He twirled off the cap and passed the bottle to her. She regarded it blankly. "Go on," he said impatiently. "It's not moonshine and it's not bootleg. I bought it this afternoon from a respectable liquor store."

"I'd rather not."

He leaned forward, his face looking satanic in the lantern light. "When you plowed into me you looked like you'd seen a ghost. I don't have any crystal glasses or silver ice buckets like up at Belle Terre. I'm sure it's not as fancy a cocktail as you're used to, but it'll give you a good, swift kick in the gut, which is what you need to stop your shakes. Now take a drink, goddammit."

Not liking anything he had said, liking less the imperious way he'd said it, Schyler yanked the pint of liquor from him and tipped it to her mouth. Cotton had taught her to drink, just like he'd taught her to do everything else. But he'd taught her to drink like a lady, in a manner Macy had approved of. The hefty swig of bourbon she drew out of Cash Boudreaux's pint scalded her throat and every inch of her esophagus along its way to her stomach where it exploded with the impetus of a dying sun.

She gave a hoarse, unladylike cough, wiped her mouth with the back of her hand, and passed the bottle to him. He took it from her and, staring at her with amusement, drank from it himself. "More?"

"No, thank you."

He took another drink before recapping the bottle and tossing it into the bottom of the pirogue. He climbed in and crouched down in front of Schyler. "Did he get you anywhere beside the arm?"

Schyler gasped when he reached out and encircled her wrist, drawing her arm closer to the lantern. His touch elicited a tingle, but what alarmed her was that her arm was oozing blood from several ugly scratches. "I didn't realize. My God."

His fingers were warm, strong, and gentle as he probed the wounds, examining them carefully. "What did it look like?"

"The dog?" Schyler shivered. "Horrible. Ugly. Like a boxer. Sort of like a bulldog."

"Must've been one of Jigger's pit bulls." Cash's gaze rose to meet hers. "You were lucky to get off with no more than this. What'd you do to it?"

"Nothing!" she cried. "I was walking, through my own woods, and suddenly it sprang out of nowhere."

"You didn't provoke it?"

The dubious inflection in his voice made her angry. She jerked her arm free and surged to her feet. "I'm going to the hospital. Thank you—"

Cash shot up and loomed above her. His splayed hand landed solidly in the center of her chest and gave a slight push. "Sit down."

Chapter Six

Her bottom landed hard on the rough seat that spanned the floor of the canoe. Incredulous, she stared up at him. "I'll take care of you," he said.

Schyler wasn't accustomed to being manhandled. Nor was she accustomed to someone dictating to her. In light of the fact that she was on eye level with the fly of his tight jeans, she said as calmly as possible, "Thank you for what you've done, Mr. Boudreaux, but I think I need to let a professional look at this."

"Some consider me a professional." He knelt down in front of her again. "Besides, I refuse to take you to the hospital and you'd never get there under your own power." His eyes lifted to hers again. His were mocking. "Of course you could always get your brother-in-law to take you." He returned his attention to the bleeding wounds. "But you'd have to get to Belle Terre first, and I don't think you'd make it."

"I'll need a rabies shot." Even as she spoke the sudden realization aloud, she felt ill at the prospect of getting the series of painful shots.

Reaching around her for a leather pouch at the rear of the pirogue, Cash shook his head negatively. The light picked up strands of gold in his long, brown, wavy hair.

"None of Jigger's dogs would have rabies. They're too valuable."

She watched with mingled fear and curiosity as he withdrew several opaque brown bottles from the pouch. None were labeled. "Are you referring to Jigger Flynn?"

"Oui."

"Is he still around?"

Cash snorted a laugh. "Every whore in the parish would be out of business if he ever left."

Jigger Flynn's name conjured up childhood fears. Flynn was a reputed pimp and bootlegger, the occupation from which he'd derived his nickname. "My mother used to tell my sister and me that Jigger Flynn kidnapped little girls who didn't behave," Schyler said.

"She wasn't far off."

"At our house, he was one and the same with the Boogey Man. We would stare at his house with awe and fear whenever we drove past."

"It's still there."

"Somebody should have locked that reprobate behind bars years ago."

Cash smiled around a soft chuckle. "Not a chance. The sheriff's office provides some of Jigger's most frequent customers."

Knowing that he was probably right, Schyler nodded vaguely. She'd also been distracted by Cash's low laugh. It had touched an erogenous spot deep inside her. She pulled her arm from his grasp. "What is that?"

He had soaked a wad of cotton with the clear liquid from one of the brown bottles. He lifted it to her nose. The smell was pungently recognizable. "Plain ol' everyday rubbing alcohol. And it's going to burn like hell. Feel free to scream."

Before she could properly brace herself for it, he applied the alcohol to the scratches on her forearm. She felt the wave of pain approaching before it crashed over her full force. She was determined not to scream, but she couldn't hold back the choking sound that escaped before she rolled her lips inward and forcibly held it back.

Her stoicism seemed to amuse him. He was grinning as he laid aside the blood-soaked cotton. "This will help stop the stinging." Quickly he uncorked another of the bottles he'd taken from the bag and, using his fingers, dabbed the contents onto her wounds. Now cleaned of blood, they didn't look so serious. After liberally smearing them with the unguent, he bound her arm from wrist to elbow with gauze. "Keep it clean and dry for several days."

"What was that you put on it?" Amazingly the wounds had stopped stinging.

"One of my mother's homemade salves." At her startled expression, he grinned sardonically. "It's got bat's eyes and ground spleen of warthog in it." His eyes glittered in the lantern light. "Black magic," he whispered.

"I never believed that your mother practiced black magic."

His grin settled into a hard line of bitterness. "Then you were among few. Did the dog bite you anyplace else?"

Schyler nervously wet her lips. "He snapped at my ankles, but—"

She didn't get a chance to finish before he flipped back her skirt and lay the hem well above her knees. Cupping the back of her calf in one hand, he lifted her foot to his thigh and turned it this way and that beneath the light.

"The scratches aren't as deep. I'll clean them, but they won't need a bandage." Checking the other ankle and finding that it only had one faint mark, he doused another ball of cotton with alcohol.

Schyler watched his capable left hand swab the scratches and bites on her ankles. She tried to think of what Ken had called these Cajuns who healed. She tried to think of anything except the intimacy of having her foot propped high on Cash Boudreaux's thigh and his face practically in her lap.

"You said I was lucky to get off this light," she said. "Has that dog attacked people before?"

"There was a kid, a few months back."

"A child? That dog attacked a child?"

"I don't know if it was that particular dog. Jigger's got pit bulls with just enough mongrel in them to make them meaner than junkyard dogs."

"What happened to make the dog attack the child?"

"They say the kid provoked it."

"Who said that?"

He shrugged uncaringly. "Everybody. Look, I don't have the details because it was none of my business."

"Some of that gossip that doesn't apply to you," she said snidely.

"That's right."

"What happened to the child?"

"He got okay, I guess. I didn't hear anything more about it after they took him to the hospital."

"He had to be hospitalized? And no one did anything?"

"About what?"

"About the dogs. Didn't Jigger have to pay a fine, anything like that?"

"It wasn't Jigger's fault. The kid was in the wrong place at the wrong time."

"It's Jigger's fault if the dog was running free."

"I guess you've got a point. Those dogs are mean sons of bitches. He trains them to be. They have to be mean to fight in the pit."

"The pit?"

He looked at her with derision and gave a dry, coughing laugh. "Haven't you ever heard of pit bull terrier fights?"

"Of course I've heard of them. They're illegal."

"So is spitting on the sidewalk in front of the courthouse, but that doesn't stop folks from doing it."

He had finished treating the wounds on her ankles and was restoring his supplies, including Monique's homemade, anesthetizing salve. Schyler shoved her skirt down over her knees. That didn't escape his attention.

Ignoring his lecherous smile, she said, "You mean that pit bull fights are held around here?"

"Have been for years."

"Jigger Flynn breeds dogs to kill and be killed?"

"*Oui.*"

"Well, somebody's got to put a stop to that."

Cash shook his head, obviously amused by the suggestion. "That wouldn't sit too well with Jigger. His pit bulls are one of his most lucrative sidelines. They aren't defeated in the pit too often."

"As soon as I get to Belle Terre, I'm calling the sheriff."

"I'd let it drop if I were you."

"But that animal could have killed me!"

Moving suddenly, Cash closed his fingers around her throat and drew her face closer to his. "You haven't been back very long, Miss Schyler. I'll save you the trouble of finding this out for yourself." He paused and stared deeply into her eyes. "Nothing in Laurent Parish has changed since you left. Maybe you've forgotten the first unwritten rule. If you don't like something, you look the other way. Saves you a lot of grief. Got that?"

Because she was concentrating so hard on his fingers touching her skin, it took her a moment to comprehend his warning. "I hear you, but I won't change my mind about this. I hate to think what would have happened if Flynn hadn't come along when he did and called the dog back to the truck."

"You'd've been chewed to pieces, and that would have been a damn shame, wouldn't it? 'Cause you look pretty damn good just like you are."

His thumb made a slow stroke along the base of her neck. When the pad of it swept over the rounded welt, he went back to investigate more closely. He rubbed it several times. "That mosquito got you, didn't it?"

Schyler felt herself quickly losing control of the situation. The intensity in his eyes was thrilling, but it made her uncomfortable. She liked the structure of his stern face and the sexy inflection of his voice very much. She had covertly admired the breadth of his chest and the tapering shape of his torso. His thighs were lean and hard. The bulge between them testified that his reputation as a stud was well-founded.

But she was Schyler Crandall and knew better than to fall for Cash Boudreaux's disreputable charm.

"Kindly let me go."

He kept stroking her throat. "Not before I put something on that bite."

"That won't be necessary."

However, she didn't move when he removed his hand from around her neck and went foraging through the bag again, coming up with a small vial. He uncorked it. The scent of the oily substance was familiar and evoked memories of summer camp.

"You're a phony witch doctor, Mr. Boudreaux. That's Campho-Phenique."

He grinned unapologetically. "Close."

Schyler never knew why she didn't deflect the hand that moved toward her neck again, why she sat still and let the pad of his index finger, slippery with the camphor-laden substance massage that small, red bump on her neck. She didn't know why, having done that, she let his fingers explore her neck and chest for other welts, and, finding one beneath the neckline of her blouse, let him unbutton the first button. He slipped his hand inside and liberally coated the raised spot with the lotion.

His hand remained in the opening as he asked, "More?"

It was a loaded question. "No."

"Sure?"

"Very sure."

Slitted eyes revealed glints of amusement as he withdrew his hand and replaced the vial in his bag. Standing, he stepped out of the pirogue and offered a hand down to her. This time she declined to take it and came to her feet without assistance. But the moment she stood up, she swayed. Only his quick reaction prevented her from falling. Once again, he lifted her in his arms.

"Put me down. I'm fine."

"You're drunk."

She was. A near impossibility on one swallow of booze. "You lied to me. That drink you gave me wasn't liquor store whiskey." He made a noncommital sound that could have meant anything.

The three-quarter moon had risen above the tree line. As a result, the forest was brighter than it had been earlier. Cash made rapid progress through it, seeming to know even better than Schyler did where each curve in the path was and anticipating each low limb.

The frightening ordeal with the dog, not to mention the potent liquor, had left her listless and dizzy. She gave up trying to hold her head erect. Her cheek dropped to his chest. Her body went limp. Her shape molded pliantly against his. She couldn't keep her eyelids open and they closed. When he came to a stop, she kept them closed for several seconds longer before opening them. They were standing in the shadow of the gazebo.

His face was bending low over hers. "Can you make it the rest of the way on your own?"

Schyler raised her head. Belle Terre looked like an iridescent pearl nestled in green velvet. It seemed very far away. The prospect of covering that distance under her own steam wasn't very appealing, but she said, "I'll be fine," and slid to her feet when he relaxed his arms and released her.

"I'd be glad to carry you the rest of the way, but your daddy would rather have somebody piss in the well than to have Cash Boudreaux's shadow fall on Belle Terre."

"You've been very kind. Thank you for——"

The breath left her body when he planted the heels of his hands in the center of her midriff and backed her against the latticed wall. His fingers closed hard around her narrow rib cage. His breath was hot as it fell on her startled face.

"I'm never kind to a woman. Beware, *pichouette*. My bite is much more dangerous to you than Jigger Flynn's dog."

"You call that making love?"

Cash rolled away from the woman lying beneath him. Her body was shiny and slick with his sweat and bore the reddish markings of rowdy sex. Reaching for the pack of cigarettes on the nightstand, he lit one and drew deeply on it.

"I never have called it making love." He left the bed, peeling off the condom and dropping it into the wastebasket. He was only semi-soft. His body was still taut, still hungry.

Rhoda Gilbreath sat up and pulled the sheet over her breasts. The ludicrously demure gesture was wasted on him. He was standing at the window with his back to her, naked, calmly smoking his cigarette and staring sightlessly at the gaudy, animated, pink neon sign in the parking lot of the Pelican Motel.

"Don't pout." Her purr was conciliatory. "I like it hard and fast sometimes. I wasn't complaining."

His head, with its shaggy, gold-streaked hair, came around. Scornfully he gazed at her over his shoulder. "You've got no reason to complain, Rhoda. You got off three times before I lost count."

In the span of a second her expression went from seductive to furious. "First you sulk, then you get nasty. One would think you'd be grateful."

"What do you want, a tip?"

She glowered at him. "It wasn't easy for me to drop everything and come running tonight. I only accommodated you because when you called it sounded like an emergency."

"It was," he muttered, remembering the state he'd been in when he left Schyler at Belle Terre. Leaving the window and placing the cigarette between his broody lips, he reached for his jeans and stepped into them.

The woman reclining against the headboard sat up at attention. "What are you doing?"

"What does it look like?"

"You're leaving?"

"That's right."

"Now?"

"Right again."

"But you can't. We just got here."

"Don't sound so put out, Rhoda. You rushed over because you were hot to get laid. You always are."

"Aren't you?"

"Yes. But I admit it. You make it sound like meeting me here was an act of charity. We both know better."

She took another tack, reverting to seduction. Raising one knee, wagging it back and forth slowly and enticingly, she said, "I told Dale that I was going to sit with a sick friend and probably wouldn't be home until morning." She let the sheet fall. "We've got all night."

Indifferent to her allure, Cash pulled on a pair of muddy cowboy boots and shoved his arms into a shirt, which he left unbuttoned. "You've got all night. I'm leaving."

"Damn you."

"The room's paid for. There's cable TV. You've got an ice machine right outside. What more could you want? Enjoy." He tossed the room key onto the bed beside her.

"You bastard."

"That's exactly right. Ask anybody." He gave her a cynical smile and a mocking salute before slamming the motel door behind him.

Chapter Seven

They laughed at her.

Breakfast was being served on the screened portion of the veranda at the back of the house. When Schyler made her outlandish statement, Tricia dropped the spoon she was using to dig out a Texas Ruby Red grapefruit. Ken clumsily replaced his coffee cup in the saucer. For a moment they stared at her with amazement, then simultaneously began laughing.

Only minutes earlier Schyler had put in an appearance,

already dressed for the day. By eight-thirty the humidity had topped ninety percent. It had made her hair wave and curl and cling to the back of her neck. Just in the few days since her arrival, the southern sun had streaked the strands nearest her face to a pale and appealing blond. The bandage on her arm had drawn attention immediately.

"What in the world happened to your arm, Schyler?" Tricia had asked.

Pouring herself a cup of coffee from the silver pot on the trolley and declining Mrs. Graves's stilted offer of a hot breakfast, she said, "I was attacked in the woods last night by a pit bull terrier."

Tricia's eyes widened. "You're kidding!"

"I wish I were."

"They're vicious dogs."

"I don't know about the whole breed, but this one was. It scared the living daylights out of me. It could have killed me."

"The dog was in our woods?" Ken asked. "On Belle Terre?"

"Yes. Only a few hundred yards from the house." Schyler recounted the incident for them, omitting any reference to Cash Boudreaux.

"You should have those bites looked at," Ken said worriedly.

"They've been looked at. I had them treated last night." She was deliberately unspecific and hoped that neither of them would ask her for details. To avoid that, she said, "I intend to press charges against that Flynn character."

That's when they reacted first with astonishment, then laughter. "Schyler, you can't sic the law on Jigger Flynn." Ken smiled at her patronizingly.

"Why not?" she demanded. "There must be a local or state law he's violating by keeping those dogs."

"There's not. Folks have been fighting pit bulls around here for a hundred years or more. Jigger doesn't let them roam free."

"One was free last night."

"It probably just got out of its pen by mistake."

"A costly mistake. And that's not the first time. I heard that a child was attacked not long ago."

"The kid was riding his bike past Jigger's place."

"And that justifies him getting mauled?" she cried angrily. "I intend to see that something is done to guard against that happening again."

"Calling the sheriff won't do you any good. Oh, he might make a token visit out to Jigger's place, but they'll likely end up sharing a drink and a dirty joke."

Schyler divided her disgust between her sister and Ken. "You expect me to just let this drop, pretend that it never happened, let bygones be bygones?"

"That would probably be best, yeah." Ken got up, gave Tricia a perfunctory kiss on the cheek and Schyler a pat on the shoulder. "I'm due to tee off at ten. Bye-bye, girls."

Schyler watched him leave with a blend of dismay and resentment. His dismissive attitude toward the dog attack made her furious and all the more determined not to let it pass without taking action against the animal's owner.

She had rolled over and played dead only once in her life, when Tricia announced her pregnancy. Never again. She had learned there was no percentage in being a martyr. As often as not it earned one contempt, not respect.

"I can't believe Ken wants me to let this drop. He's always been ready to crusade for the underdog, no pun intended."

"When he was in college, Schyler. He grew up."

"So you're suggesting that I grow up, too."

"Yes," Tricia declared. "This isn't a campus. We're not trying to end a war or start one or find relief for migrant workers or equal education for black children." Tricia returned the uneaten half of her biscuit to her plate and licked the dripping butter and honey off her fingers. "You haven't been back a week yet. Don't go stirring up trouble, please."

"I didn't start this. I wouldn't have even known that the damn dogs existed if one hadn't attacked me on my own property."

Tricia let out a long sigh. "You just can't leave things alone, can you? You always were poking your nose into business that didn't concern you. Cotton encouraged your activist goings on, but they drove Mama and me to distraction. They were an embarrassment. So . . . so unrefined." She leaned forward for emphasis. "This is my home, Schyler. Don't you dare do anything that's going to embarrass me. I want to be able to hold my head up when I go into town."

Schyler scraped back her chair and tossed her unused napkin into her empty plate. "If I can't get the authorities to do something about that menacing bootlegger and his vicious animals, I'll do something about it myself. And I don't give a damn how much embarrassment it causes you with the Junior League, Tricia."

"He has showed signs of improvement in the last twelve hours," Dr. Collins told her when she arrived at the hospital. "I'm being guardedly optimistic. If his condition continues to improve, even this gradually, we should be able to operate within a week."

"That's wonderful."

"I said guardedly optimistic. He's still a very sick cardiac patient."

"I understand." The doctor smiled at Schyler sympathetically. When someone's loved one had been as close to death as Cotton Crandall had been, relatives grasped at shreds of hope. "Can I see him?"

"Same rules. Two minutes max every hour. But you might want to hang around for a while. He's been semiconscious all morning."

Schyler went to the pay telephone and notified Tricia of the good news, putting aside the argument they'd had earlier that morning. Then she was allowed into her father's ICU for two minutes. She was disappointed that he didn't wake up or otherwise acknowledge that he knew she was at his bedside, but she was encouraged by the doctor's report. Even the nurse's reassuring smile seemed more genuine.

Tricia and Ken arrived early in the afternoon. The three of them whiled away the hours in the hospital waiting room, taking turns going into the ICU once every hour.

Boredom set in. Eventually Ken said, "Schyler, why don't you come on home with us?"

"You two go ahead. I'll be home in time for dinner. I'd like to see him one more time before I leave."

"All right." Ken led his wife to the elevator. They waved at Schyler before the doors slid closed. Sick of looking at the same four walls, Schyler strolled along the gleaming corridors, thinking that she should call Mark.

He had been generous to let her leave without having any idea how long she would be gone. He hadn't even asked. He had helped her pack, had driven her to Heathrow, had kissed her good-bye, and told her to call if she needed anything. He had been as concerned for her as he was for Cotton, whom he'd never met but had certainly heard a lot about.

Schyler decided to wait until Cotton's prognosis was more definite before she called him. There was no sense in phoning until she had something substantial to report, except that she missed him terribly. She would take comfort just in hearing the familiar sound of his nasal Boston accent.

"Miss Crandall?"

She spun around. "Yes?" The nurse was smiling. "Daddy?"

"He's awake. Hurry."

Schyler followed the nurse's rapid footsteps down the corridor and into the ICU. Cotton didn't look much better than he had last night, though Schyler thought his complexion didn't look quite so waxy and that the blue tinge of his lips had faded somewhat. Being careful of the IVs, she lifted his hand and pressed it between both of hers.

"Daddy, hi. It's Schyler. I've been here for several days. How are you feeling? We've all been so worried. But the doctor says you're going to be fine."

The lines in his face were etched deeper. The skin beneath his stubborn, square chin was looser. His hairline had receded. But it was his eyes that arrested her. They had undergone the most remarkable change since she'd last seen him. The change made her own heart sink heavily in her chest. His eyes were the same vivid color of blue, but there was no light in them, no spark of mischief, no life.

His heart condition wasn't responsible for that lifelessness. Schyler knew that she had extinguished that light in his eyes. What she didn't know was what she had done to put it out.

"You've come back." His voice was as whispery and fragile as ancient paper. There wasn't a degree of warmth behind it.

"Yes, Daddy, I'm back. I'm at Belle Terre. For as long as you need me."

He stared up at her for a long moment. Then his veiny eyelids closed over those condemning blue eyes and he turned his head away.

The nurse stepped forward. "He's gone back to sleep, Miss Crandall. We'd better not disturb him anymore."

Schyler reluctantly released her father's hand and moved away from the bed. She watched the nurse make adjustments on the IVs. Feeling empty and alone, she left the room and the hospital.

No daughter had ever loved her father more than Schyler loved Cotton. And vice versa. Only he had stopped loving her. Six years ago. Why? She had been the injured party. Why had he turned against her? *Why?*

The accumulated heat inside her car was unbearable. Even set on high, the air conditioner wasn't sufficient to cool it off, so she rolled down the windows. The wind tore at her hair punishingly. She took the winding road that was as familiar as her own face in a mirror. Her heart began to beat with glad expectation as she crossed the Laurent Bayou bridge. The road came to a dead end in front of Crandall Logging.

It was Saturday afternoon. The landing was deserted. No one was working in the yard or on the loading platforms that lined the railroad tracks. The rigs were parked beneath the enormous shed, their trailers folded up and riding piggyback on the cabs. The air wasn't punctuated by the racket of loggers hauling the timber from the surrounding forests. There was no sound of machinery, no clank of metal wheels on the rails. Except for a few chirping birds, everything was still and silent.

She left her car door open and went toward the small, square, frame building that housed the office. The key that was still on her key ring fit the lock. It hadn't been changed in six years. The door swung open and she stepped inside.

It was stifling. She left the door open behind her. The late afternoon sun cast her shadow across the dull, scarred floor and over the top of Cotton's desk. Unfiled paperwork and unopened correspondence littered it. It always had. He would procrastinate doing the clerical chores for months. Schyler would catch up with them during school holidays and summer vacations.

She crossed to the desk, picked up the telephone and dialed the number that was engraved on her memory forever.

"Belle Terre."

"Hello, Mrs. Graves, this is Schyler. I won't be home for a while. Don't hold dinner for me."

The housekeeper appeared not to have any curiosity and nothing to say; the call was completed within fifteen seconds. Replacing the telephone receiver, Schyler gazed about her. The windows overlooking the railroad tracks needed washing. They were without adornment of any kind, even venetian blinds. Cotton had always insisted on an unobstructed view. He wanted to know what was going on at any given time.

Schyler ran her fingertip along the windowsill and picked up an inch of dust. She should arrange for someone to come in and clean. Returning to the desk, she stood behind the chair and laid her hands on the tall, tufted back.

Cotton's chair.

Years of use had made the brown leather glove-soft and pliable beneath her squeezing fingers. She closed her eyes. Hot, salty tears welled up behind her eyelids as she recalled the times she had sat in Cotton's lap in this chair, listening patiently while he explained the different types of wood and to which lumberyard or paper mill the timber would be shipped.

He had been delighted with his attentive pupil. Tricia hated the landing. She called it a dirty, noisy ol' place and had grown sullen if she ever had to go near it. Macy hadn't cared about the business, even though it had originally belonged to her family. Cotton had audaciously changed its name. No sooner had Mr. Laurent been buried than Cotton set himself up as sole owner and operator.

Macy hadn't cared about much at all, not her family's business, not her husband, not even the two daughters she had adopted out of desperation when she learned that she was barren and could not give Cotton the offspring he desired.

Macy had seen to it that her two daughters were better dressed than any other girls in the parish. They had been educated in an elite private school. Parties held in their honor were more lavish than any the old-timers could remember. She had provided their material needs, but she had neglected their emotional ones. If it hadn't been for Cotton, Schyler would never have known parental love.

But he no longer loved her.

She opened her eyes and wiped the tears from them. Suddenly noticing the long shadow stretched across the untidy desk, her head snapped up. She gave a soft gasp that seemed unnaturally loud in the stillness. Then, recognizing the man indolently leaning against the doorjamb, she frowned.

Chapter Eight

"I wish to heaven you'd stop sneaking up on me. It's giving me the creeps."

"What are you crying about?"

"Cotton."

Cash's body tensed. His brows formed a low shelf over his enigmatic eyes. "He died?"

Schyler shook her head. "No. He regained consciousness. I spoke with him."

"I don't understand."

"You're not supposed to," she said shortly. "Stop meddling in my business."

"All right. The next time you get a dog bite, I'll let your arm rot off."

Schyler pressed the heel of her hand against her temple, where a headache was off to a good start. "I'm sorry. I should have thanked you."

"How is it?" He nodded toward her bandaged arm.

"Okay I guess. It hasn't hurt at all."

"Come here." She only stared at him. He arched one brow and repeated softly, "Come here."

She hesitated a moment longer before stepping around the desk and approaching the open door, where he still had a shoulder propped against the frame. She stuck out her injured arm with about as much enthusiasm as she would thrust it into a furnace.

Her aversion to having him touch her made him smile sardonically as he unwound the gauze bandage he had fashioned the night before. Schyler was amazed to see that the skin had almost completely closed over the wounds and that there was no sign of infection. He touched the scratches lightly with his fingertips. They were painless.

"Leave the bandage on tonight." He rewrapped her arm. "Tomorrow morning, take it off and wash your arm carefully. It should be okay after that." She looked up at him inquiringly. "It's the spleen of warthog that does the trick."

She jerked her arm away. "You're left-handed."

His grin widened. "You believe the legend, do you? That all *traiteurs* are left-handed." Without a smidgen of apology or hesitation, he moved aside the square nautical collar of her dress and brushed his fingers across the top of her breast, where he had located the welt the night before. "How are the mosquito bites?"

Schyler swatted his hand away. "Fine. Was Monique left-handed?"

"*Oui*. She was also a woman. That's where I break with tradition." His voice dropped seductively. "Because I am a man. And if you have any doubts as to that, Miss Schyler, I'd be more than glad to prove it to you."

She looked up at him and said wryly, "That won't be necessary."

"I didn't think so."

His conceit was insufferable, Schyler thought as she watched his lips form a lazy, arrogant smile. What was she expected to do, unravel because big, bad Cash Boudreaux, the man most feared by fathers of nubile daughters, had turned his charm on for her? She was a little old to grow giddy and faint in the face of such blatant masculine strutting.

Still, no one needed to sell her on Cash's masculinity. It was evident in the rugged bone structure of his face, the width of his shoulders, the salty scent that he emanated in the afternoon heat. A bead of sweat rolled from beneath the hair curving over his forehead. It slid down his temple and disappeared into his thick eyebrow.

His walk, all his movements, were masculine. Schyler watched his hands as they went for the pack of cigarettes in his breast pocket and shook one out. He offered it to her, but she wordlessly declined. His lips closed around the filtered tip. He replaced the pack in his pocket and pulled out a matchbox. He struck the match on the doorjamb, then cupped his hands around the flame while he lit the cigarette.

She remembered his hands on her midriff, pressing into the tender center of her stomach, the hard, dominant fingers lying against her ribs. He had imprisoned her against the wall of the gazebo without exercising any force. The only bruises her body bore this morning were a result of her struggles with the pit bull. It made her uneasy to know that Cash Boudreaux could be so overpowering without hurting her.

As he drew on his cigarette, staring at her through the smoke that rose from it, she lowered her eyes. There was a knotted bandanna around his strong, tanned throat. His chest tapered into a narrow waist and lean hips. The soft, washed denim of his Levi's cupped his sex as intimately as a lover's hand.

Schyler knew that his eyes were boring a hole into the crown of her head, just as certainly as she knew that there was something sexual going on. But then, if rumor was correct, everything that Cash Boudreaux had done since he was about thirteen years old had been sexually motivated.

She wasn't flattered. She wasn't afraid. If he'd wanted to assault her, he'd had plenty of opportunities in the past twenty-four hours to do so. Mostly, she was offended. Obviously he had lumped her into the ranks of women who were flattered by his indiscriminate attention.

If she were being entirely honest, however, she had to admit that the prospect of experiencing something sexual with Cash Boudreaux had a certain allure. He was disreputable and dangerous, aggravating and arrogant. He was rude and disrespectful and treated women abominably. Perhaps that was his attraction, what made him desirable.

Geographically they'd grown up in the same place, but the realms of their upbringings were worlds apart. They had nothing in common except these sexual undercurrents, which were invisible but as real as the shimmering heat waves that radiated out of the ground. She was a woman. Cash Boudreaux was indisputably a man.

She raised her head and gave him a direct look, as if by doing that she could nullify the subliminal sparks. "Did you follow me here?"

"No. I just happened by. Thought I'd check on things."

"Check on things? I'm sure Ken is capable of handling things while Daddy is ill."

"Ken isn't capable of finding his ass with both hands."

"Mr. Boudreaux—"

"To keep everybody from discovering that, he shut the place down."

Her protests died on her tongue. *"What*? What do you mean he shut the place down?"

"I mean he told all the employees on the payroll that they were laid off until further notice. He told the independent loggers to find other markets for their timber. He said that Crandall Logging was temporarily out of operation. Then he locked the door and left. Don't you think that amounts to shutting the place down?"

Schyler fell back a step. She gazed about the office with dismay, realizing now why it had an abandoned look. It bore the empty sadness of a house that hadn't been occupied in awhile. "Why would Ken do that?"

"I just told you why."

"I'm serious."

"So am I." Cash flicked his cigarette out the door behind him. It made a red arc before dying in the dust of the deserted yard. "The day after they took Cotton to the hospital, your brother-in-law paid everybody off and hightailed it outta here."

"Does Cotton know about it?"

"I doubt it."

"So do I." She gnawed the inside of her cheek, trying to figure out what could have motivated Ken to shut down. Cotton had had to ride out economic crunches before, but he had never laid off employees. "That must have put scores of men out of work."

"Goddamn right it did."

Schyler pulled her fingers through her hair. "I'm sure Ken had his reasons. They just aren't apparent."

"Well, let me tell you what *is* apparent, Miss Schyler."

He stopped slouching in the doorway and advanced into the room. "About half the families in the parish are running out of groceries. Prospects aren't looking too good that they'll have money to buy more any time soon. While your brother-in-law is languishing around the country club swimming pool, swizzling glass after glass of Lynchburg, Tennessee's finest, kids are doing without breakfast, dinner, and supper."

Ken left the house every morning and returned every afternoon. Schyler had assumed he was at work during those hours. It galled her to think that he was living off the profits Cotton had put a lifetime into earning. But perhaps she was being unfair by jumping to conclusions. Ken had begun working for Crandall Logging when he married Tricia. When his parents were killed, he had sold everything in New Orleans, severed all connections there, and moved to Heaven. He had several years of his life invested in this business. There must be a logical explanation for his shutting down operation.

"Come up with any good excuses for him yet?"

"I won't have you disparaging my brother-in-law, Mr. Boudreaux," she lashed out.

He whistled softly. "Listen to her defend him. That's what I call real family loyalty."

Willfully restraining her temper, Schyler said, "I assure you that I'll look into the matter immediately. I know Cotton wouldn't approve of families going hungry, families who depend on him for their livelihoods."

"I know he wouldn't either."

"I assure you something will be done."

"Good."

She gave Cash a long, steady look. He irritated the hell out of her. He was no better than he had to be. He was a lowlife who seemingly had no scruples. She could use just that kind of man.

"I guess you're off the payroll, too."

"I don't think your brother-in-law likes me. I was the first one to get notice."

"Then I'm sure you're running low on money and could

use some." He shrugged noncommittally. She drew herself up importantly. "I've got a job for you."

"You do?"

"Yes, I do. I'll pay you well."

"How well?"

"You tell me."

"Well, now that all depends on what the job entails." His voice was thick with lewd suggestion. "What do you want me to do for you?"

"I want you to destroy the dog that attacked me last night."

He didn't blink for several moments, only held her in a stare. His eyes, she noticed now, were hazel, but with more yellow and gray than green. They were like cat eyes, predatory cat eyes.

"Kill it?"

"That's what destroy usually means."

"You want me to kill one of Jigger Flynn's pit bulls?"

She raised her chin and answered firmly. "Yes."

He hooked both thumbs into his tooled leather belt and leaned down until his face was almost on a level with hers. "Have you lost your frigging mind?"

"No."

"Well, then you must think I've lost mine."

"I want that animal killed before it kills someone."

"Last night was a freak accident. Jigger doesn't let those dogs run free."

"So Ken told me. But that—"

"Ah!" He held up his hands to forestall her and looked at her through narrowed eyes. "You bounced this idea off your brother-in-law first?"

"Not exactly."

"You asked him to do it. He crapped in his britches at the very thought, so now you're coming to me. Is that it?"

"No!" She drew an exasperated breath. "I told Tricia and Ken about the dog attacking me. They noticed the bandage."

"Did you tell them where you got it?"

"No."

"I didn't think you would," he drawled.

Ignoring him, she rushed on. "I insisted that something be done about those dogs. Ken thought I should let the matter drop."

"Well, for once I agree with the son of a bitch. Let it drop."

"I can't."

"You'd better. Stay away from Jigger Flynn. He's meaner than hell."

"So are you."

An abrupt silence followed her raised voice. Cash treated her to another long, penetrating stare. She moistened her lips and forced herself to speak. "What I mean is, you have a reputation for . . . too much fighting. You went to war and stayed longer than you had to. You must be good with guns."

"Damn good," he whispered.

"I don't know anybody else to ask. I don't know anybody else who has . . . has . . . killed . . ."

"You don't know anybody else low enough to do your dirty work."

"I didn't say that."

"But that's what you meant."

"Look, Mr. Boudreaux, you've spent the better part of your life cultivating a short-tempered, violent image. By all accounts you're as testy as a cobra. Don't blame me for responding to your reputation. I know you must have broken the law before."

"Too many times to count."

"So why do you have a conscience against destroying a public menace, a killer dog?"

"Not a conscience. Common sense. I have the good sense not to provoke Jigger Flynn's wrath."

"Because you're afraid of him," she shouted up at him.

"Because it's not my quarrel," he shot back.

Schyler could see that yelling was a one-way street leading to a dead end. She took another tack. One could always fall back on greed for motivation. "I'll pay you one hundred dollars." His face remained unmoved and unimpressed. "Two hundred."

"Stuff it, Miss Schyler. I don't want your goddamn money."

"Then what?"

His lecherous grin was as good as an invoice. And the sum total of it couldn't be measured in dollars and cents. "Read my mind."

Furious, Schyler shoved past him on her way to the door. "Jerk. I should have known better than to ask you."

He closed his fingers around her upper arm and brought her up against him hard. "You're quite a hothead, aren't you?" His eyes rapaciously scanned her face. "Are you just as eager to make love as you are to make war?"

"Not with you."

"Never say never."

"Let me go," she said through her teeth.

"Come with me."

"Come with you? Where?"

"I'll show you why no sane person would kill one of Jigger's dogs."

"I'm not going anywhere with you."

"How come? What are you afraid of?"

Chapter Nine

"Where are we going?"

Cash was behind the steering wheel of his faded blue pickup truck. Schyler still couldn't guess what had prompted her to accept his invitation. Perhaps because it had been posed in the form of a challenge. Before she took into account the possible consequences, she had locked the office, left her car parked at the landing, and stepped up into the cab of Cash's battered truck.

In answer to her question, he consulted the watch strapped to his right wrist. "It's early yet. Hungry?"

"I thought this had to do with Jigger Flynn."

"It does. Be patient. That's a common trait with you people. You're always in a hurry."

"'You people'?"

He looked at her across the stained, threadbare upholstery. "Rich folks, Miss Schyler."

She refused to acknowledge or address the disparity between their economic levels, so she took issue with the appositive he continued to use with such phony obsequiousness. "Why don't you drop the Miss and call me just plain Schyler?"

He casually took a hairpin curve in the road before turning his sly grin on her. "Because I know it annoys the shit out of you."

"And is that your main goal in life? To be annoying?"

"How come you don't spell it like it sounds?" he asked, ignoring her question. "Why not S-k-y-l-e-r?"

"I didn't have any choice. That's how Mother and Daddy entered my name on my birth certificate."

"When they adopted you?"

She wasn't surprised that he knew. Everybody in the parish knew. She was, however, automatically defensive. "I was only three days old."

"That's still not the same, is it?"

"The same as what?"

"As being their natural born."

Deliberately or not, Cash was rubbing salt into an old wound. "It's the same to me."

He shook his head. "Nope. It's not the same." Before Schyler could argue with him, he whipped the pickup off the road and braked to a hard stop. "There it is."

Schyler hadn't realized where they were going and drew in a sharp, quick breath when she noticed the ramshackle house. It had been in disrepair for as long as she could remember. It was constructed of unpainted cypress. The gray, weathered wood added to the overall dreary appearance of the place.

The window screens were torn; they curled outward toward the snaggle-toothed batten shutters. Forlorn lace curtains hung in the windows. They were tattered and dingy, as pathetic as an aging whore's last fancy dress.

A collection of hubcaps had been nailed on the exterior walls. Once shiny, they were now corroded. A potpourri of junk littered the yard. Tools and utensils lay neglected in the grassless dirt. A disemboweled car was providing a roost for several scraggly hens. An empty Frigidaire on the sagging porch was serving no purpose except to support a dusty wysteria vine, which valiantly struggled for life amid the decay. Behind the house was a dog kennel made of rusty, cyclone fencing. There were no dogs in it presently. In fact, the place appeared to be deserted.

"We picked a good time to come calling. Jigger's not at home."

Schyler rubbed her arms as though chilled. "I used to be afraid to even drive past this place."

"I don't blame you. Jigger's been known to do target practice on motorists from his front porch out of sheer meanness."

"How does he get by with things like that?" Schyler cried angrily. "I didn't know that the saying, 'Justice is blind,' meant that it turned a blind eye? Why hasn't he ever been prosecuted?"

"Simple. People are afraid of him."

"I'm not."

"Well, you damn sure ought to be." Cash slipped the truck into first gear and set off down the rough gravel road in the direction of town. "You didn't answer my question. Are you hungry?"

Schyler was glad to leave Flynn's place behind. Even deserted, it unnerved her. "I hadn't thought about it. I guess I am."

"I'll treat you to supper at a place you've never been to before."

"Oh?"

"Red Broussard's."

"Is the floor still covered with peanut shells?" she asked with a mischievous smile.

He looked at her with astonishment. "Don't tell me."

"Oh, yes. Daddy used to take me to Broussard's often."

Cash's grin faded gradually. "I forgot. Cotton likes Cajun food, doesn't he?"

"Yes, he does. And so do I."

"I never saw you at Broussard's."

"We usually went before sundown."

"Hell, the place doesn't start warming up until after sundown."

She laughed. "That's why he always took me before then."

The accordian music was loud, repetitive, and raucous. It seemed to expand and recess the walls of the clapboard restaurant like the wolf in the tale of the three little pigs, huffing and puffing and trying to blow it down. Cash was humming the French Acadian tune as he came around and opened the passenger door for Schyler.

"Saturday night," he remarked. "They're tuning up for a *fais-dodo*. Drinking, dancing, a party," he said by way of explanation.

She took offense. "I know what it is."

"You're acquainted with Cajun customs?"

"Belle Terre isn't an ivory castle, you know."

"No. I don't know." Having made that oblique statement, he placed his hand in the small of her back and nudged her toward the entrance.

"I hope I'm dressed properly," she remarked uneasily.

"Not quite." When she shot him a swift, worried glance, he added, "They might ask you to take off your shoes."

The square building was set on stilts. Dancing footsteps drummed through the floorboards and echoed in the hollow space underneath. Red Broussard, a barrel-chested, potbellied, bearded man with a Santa Claus countenance and garlic breath, greeted them personally, giving each a boisterous shout of welcome and a rib-crunching hug. He pressed icy bottles of beer into their hands and ushered them toward a table in the corner of the room, affably elbowing aside dancers who blocked their path.

Schyler moved through the crowd self-consciously, but no one stopped to stare as she feared they might. No one seemed to think it noteworthy that she was with Cash Boudreaux. But then, this was his crowd, not hers. If she'd taken him to the country club tonight it would have caused quite a stir. It was much easier to move down a notch in society than it was to move up.

They reached their table and Red held her chair for her. The upper two-thirds of the walls of the building were screened. The hinged, exterior walls had been raised and propped open by two-by-fours. They were only lowered during a severe Gulf storm and the coldest days of winter. Maddened insects, frantic to reach the lights burning inside, kamikazied themselves against the screens.

"Boudin sausage, *mon cher*?" Red asked with a beatific smile that split his furry red beard and revealed nicotine-stained teeth.

Schyler smiled up at him. "No thanks." She hadn't been able to eat the sausage since a Cajun rig driver had bartered some timber for a hog and had insisted that Cotton oversee the slaughtering. Schyler had begged to go along. Over Macy's vehement protests Cotton had taken her. She'd regretted it ever since. "Crawfish, please."

Red threw back his rusty head and bellowed a deep laugh. Then, pointing a meaty finger down at her, he teased, "I seen de day you pack away dem crawfish, don't cha know. More dan your papa, *oui*."

"Bring us a platter, Red."

Red gave Cash's shoulder an affectionate and mighty wallop, then lumbered off toward the bubbling vats where the day's catch of crawfish was boiling in water seasoned with spices that made one's eyes water and nose itch. Over the music, Red shouted at his patrons to eat and drink some more.

Cash reached for the bowl of peanuts in the center of the table, cracked the shell between his fingers, and shook the roasted nuts out of the pod. He tossed them into his mouth, then took a swig of beer to wash them down. He swallowed gustily. His eyes, glowing in the light cast by the red glass candle holder, dared Schyler to do the same.

She accepted the silent dare, dropping the peanut shells onto the floor as Cash and every other customer had done. She didn't request a glass for her beer but drank directly from the bottle.

He said, "I thought you'd be horrified at the thought of coming here."

"Because I'm too snooty and would look down my aristocratic nose at the people here?"

"Something like that." He took a drink of beer, watching her. "So is this an act just to prove me wrong?"

"No. I miss the food."

That's all they had time to say to each other before Red sent a waitress over with a platter of crawfish. She scooted aside the candle and the bowl of peanuts and set the platter between them in the center of the table. Before moving away, she gave Cash a seductive sidelong glance.

Schyler watched her walk away. "Is she one of yours?" She selected a crawfish. Without needing a refresher course on how it was done, she broke off the tail, dug her thumbs into the seam of the shell and split it apart, then used her fingers to pull out the rich, white meat.

Cash followed suit. "She could be if I wanted her." He tossed the remainder of the crustacean body back onto the platter and picked up another.

Schyler blotted her mouth with the paper napkin she took from the metal dispenser. "It's that easy for you? Any woman you want is yours for the taking?"

"Interested?"

"Curious."

"Curious to know what attracts them?"

"No, curious to know what attracts you."

"Curiosity."

With belying composure, Schyler ate another crawfish, took another sip of beer, and blotted her lips before she looked at him.

He took a long drink from his beer bottle first. Then, lowering the bottle back to the table, his eyes captured and held hers. They intimated, "Come and get it."

Up from Schyler's stomach rose a trill of sensation that had nothing to do with the spicy ethnic food and beer. Cash Boudreaux was dangerous in a variety of ways. His allure was undeniable; he was sexually attractive. He was also street smart and cunning, wise in the art of bullshitting. But he was no slouch in serious verbal warfare either.

"You don't like me, do you?"

He answered her intuitive question honestly. "No. I guess I don't. Don't take it personally."

"I'll try to remember that," she said dryly. "Why don't you like me?"

"It's not so much you I dislike. It's what you represent."

"And what is that?"

"An insider."

She hadn't expected so succinct and simple an answer. "That's not so much."

"To an outsider it is."

His prejudice struck her as being unfair. "I had nothing to do with that."

"Didn't you?"

"No. I didn't even know you."

His eyes narrowed accusingly. "You didn't make a point to get to know me either."

"That's not my fault. You weren't ever exactly friendly."

Her flare of temper seemed to amuse him. "You're right, *pichouette*. I guess I wasn't."

She used that to get them off the track the conversation had taken and onto something else. "You've used that word before. What does it mean?"

"*Pichouette*?" He hesitated, watching her face. "It means little girl."

"I'm hardly that."

He twirled the neck of the beer bottle between his fingers as he stared at her across the candlelit table. "I remember you as a little girl. You had long blond hair and long skinny legs."

Schyler responded spontaneously and smiled. "How do you know?"

"I used to watch you playing on the lawn at Belle Terre."

She knew better than to ask why he hadn't joined her to

play. He would have been ordered off the place by her parents if she hadn't run inside out of fear first. Neither Cotton, nor Macy, nor Veda would have allowed her to play with Monique Boudreaux's boy. Not only had he been several years older, he was an unsuitable companion for a young girl under any circumstances. His reputation as a troublemaker was well founded and well known.

"I remember one particular birthday party you had," Cash said. "I think it was the day you turned four. There must have been fifty kids at that party. Cotton was giving them rides on a pony. A clown performed magic tricks."

"How do you remember that?" she exclaimed.

"I remember because I wasn't invited. But I was there. I watched the whole thing from the woods. I wanted like hell to see those magic tricks up close."

His antipathy was understandable, she supposed. He carried a chip on his shoulder, but it was justified. Whether overtly or not, he had been slighted. She hadn't been directly responsible for it, but she intuitively knew how it would affect her now. "You're not going to kill Jigger Flynn's dogs for me, are you?"

"No. I'm not."

She twisted her damp napkin. "I guess it was unfair of me to ask you to do my dirty work, as you put it."

"Yeah, I guess it was."

"I didn't mean to insult you."

He merely shrugged and nodded toward the platter between them.

"Finish eating."

"I'm finished."

Red chastized them for not eating enough and invited them back soon. As they went down the rickety steps of the restaurant, Schyler thanked Cash for bringing her. "I haven't had a good-tasting meal since I got here. The new housekeeper my sister hired took an instant dislike to me. The feeling is mutual. I can't stomach her any more than I can the food she serves."

"Just how weak is your stomach?"

The serious tone of his question brought Schyler's head around. "Why?"

"Because it's about to be tested."

Chapter Ten

"I thought I knew every road in the parish, but I've never been on this one." Schyler braced herself against the dashboard as the pickup jounced over the road. "Where in God's name are you taking me?"

"To a place you've never been." He gave her a sidelong glance. "And this time I'm sure of it."

It was a hot, still night. Away from the town's lights, the stars were visible, a panoply of brilliance. Having lived in a city for the past six years, Schyler had forgotten just how dark it could get in the country once the sun went down. Beyond the beams of the pickup's headlights, there was nothing but inky blackness.

But then the pickup topped a rise, and she spotted the building. She looked at Cash inquisitively, but he said nothing. To reach the building, they crossed a narrow wooden bridge that she prayed would hold up until they were safely on the other side. Despite the difficulty in reaching it, the corrugated tin structure was a popular place.

It was built like a barn and may have served that purpose at one time. Apparently it was some kind of meeting place because there were dozens of cars parked on the flat, marshy ground surrounding it.

Cash drew the pickup alongside a sleek new Mercedes,

which seemed ridiculously out of place in this remote rural area. Schyler looked at him for an explanation. He gave her a smirking grin.

Ill at ease, she alighted when he came around for her, and they started toward the entrance. It was distinguished only by one bare bulb suspended above the uninviting door. There were no signs posted, nothing to indicate what was going on inside the building.

She wanted to turn around and leave. But she wouldn't give Cash the satisfaction of seeing her back down or showing any fear or reservation about stepping through the tin door he held open for her.

It was suffocatingly hot inside, as dank and humid and airless as a sauna. And dark. So dark that Schyler nearly stumbled into the table that was positioned a few steps inside the door. She would have walked right into it if Cash hadn't placed both his hands on her hips and stopped her.

"Hiya, Cash."

The toad of a man sitting in the folding chair behind the table looked Schyler over with a grin so lecherous it made her skin crawl. "Who's the new broad?"

"Two please."

He added Cash's ten-dollar bill to a metal box that was already stuffed with money. "We can always count on you to find fresh meat. Yessiree, that we can do," he said in a singsong voice.

"How'd you like to eat your balls for breakfast tomorrow morning?" Cash's steely tone of voice wiped the grin right off the man's face.

"I was just jokin' with ya, Cash."

"Well don't."

"Okay, sure, Cash. Here're your tickets." The man carefully reached past Schyler to hand Cash two tickets he'd ripped off a roll.

Suddenly a roar issued up from behind the partial wall in back of the table. It rocked Schyler, who wasn't expecting it. Again Cash placed his hand on the curve of her hip just below her waist. The ticket seller glanced over his shoulder at the wall behind him.

"Y'all are just in time for the next fight. If you hurry,

there'll be time for the little lady to place a bet before it starts. Be more fun for her that way, don'tcha know."

"Thanks. We'll keep that in mind." Cash nudged Schyler toward the end of the partition. When she seemed reluctant to move, he pushed a little harder.

She did an angry about-face and hissed, "What is this?"

She had been to the Soho district of London. She had seen the pornographic stage shows there, but it had been her choice to go. She had been in the company of several friends. It had been harmless. She had known what she was getting into when she paid her admission.

This was vastly different. All her life she had lived in southwestern Louisiana, but she had never heard of a place such as this, much less been to one. She was afraid of what she would find beyond the partition and afraid of the man who had brought her here. His hard, sardonic face did nothing to reassure her that his intentions were good.

"It's a dog fight."

Her lips parted in shock. "Pit bulls?"

"*Oui.*"

"Why'd you bring me here?"

"To show you what you're up against if you hold to that fool notion to even the score with Jigger."

That was tantamount to calling her a fool. Schyler resented that, especially coming from someone with as tainted a history as Cash Boudreaux. "I told you I wasn't afraid of him and I meant it." Turning her back to Cash, she led him around the end of the partition.

From the outside the building had looked large. Even so, Schyler was astonished by just how immense it was. It was rimmed by crude bleachers, ten or twelve rows deep. It was difficult to count exactly how many because the whole place was dark except for the pit located in the center of the arena. It was lit by brilliant overhead spotlights. The large rectangular pit had a dirt floor and was enclosed by wooden slats that were bloodstained.

On opposing sides of the pit, the owners and trainers were readying their pit bull terriers for battle. Though it had been years since she had seen him, she recognized the trainer facing her as Jigger Flynn.

Cash moved up close behind her. "Want to place a bet on your favorite dog?"

"Go to hell."

He merely laughed and edged her toward the nearest set of bleachers. There was room enough for them at the end of the fourth row. Those around them were distracted from the activity in the pit when Schyler climbed the bleachers and took her seat. Realizing that she was one of notably few women in the place, she assumed a haughty, parochial school posture that Macy would have been proud of and tugged her skirt down over her knees.

"That won't help," Cash said close to her ear. "You stick out like a sore thumb, baby. If you cover your knees, they'll ogle your tits."

Her hair whipped across his cheek when she brought her head around with a snap. "Shut up."

His eyes glowed threateningly in the darkness. "Be careful how you talk to me, *mon cher*," he said silkily. "When they get all riled up," he nodded toward the crowd, "I might be the only thing standing between you and gang rape."

By an act of will, she kept her face composed, not wanting him to see her anxiety. She returned her attention to the pit. A shudder went through her when she recognized the dog snarling across the dirt floor of the pit at his opponent as the one who had attacked her.

Uglier and meaner looking than the two pit bulls, however, was Jigger Flynn. Schyler watched him in fearful fascination as he closed his hands around his dog's jaws and, straddling the animal's back, lifted it up until only its back feet touched the ground.

Flynn's thinning, gray hair had been slicked back with oil that made his pink scalp glisten beneath the spotlights. His eyes were deep-set, small, and dark. Surrounded by puffy flesh, they looked like raisins set in bread dough. His nose was fleshy, his lips thin and hard. Schyler doubted they could form a smile. His chin melted into the loose, wobbly flesh beneath it. He wasn't tall. Generally, he was a small man, but his neck was thick, and he had a beer gut that hung over his belt. His baggy trousers looked as though they were losing a battle to stay up on hips that were unsupported by a butt. He had thin, bandy legs and comically small feet.

No one knew his worth, but it was estimated that he was one of the richest men in the parish, all of his money earned through illegal enterprises. Whatever his wealth, he certainly didn't flaunt it. His clothes could have been salvaged from a welfare bin. They were old and soiled. He reeked of malevolence.

"What's he doing with that dog?"

Cash, who had been intently studying Schyler, glanced toward the pit. Jigger was holding his dog to face the other. He shook the animal slightly while continuing to squeeze its broad face between his hands. The other trainer was doing likewise. The dogs' back legs were thrashing, kicking up puffs of dirt whenever their sharp claws touched.

"That's called scratching. The trainers are deliberately provoking them, rousing their inbred instincts to fight, infuriating them so they'll charge each other. The fight is over when one dog kills the other or when one refuses to scratch and charge."

"You mean—"

"They try to rip one another's throat out."

The only thing that kept Schyler sitting on the bleacher was her stubborn determination not to lose face in front of Cash. A man whom she assumed was a referee signaled for quiet and enumerated the rules. Obviously this was a routine practice and of no interest to anyone except her. Everyone was shifting restlessly, ready for the action to begin.

She actually jumped when the two animals were released and charged across the pit toward each other. By nature of the sport she had expected violence, but nothing to equal the ferocity with which they attacked each other. The dogs were amazingly strong and tenacious. Time and again they went for each other, but their stamina never seemed to flag.

When first blood was drawn, Schyler turned her head away and pressed her face into Cash's shoulder. She was revolted, but also horrified, realizing how lucky she was to have come away with only superficial wounds from the dog's attack.

Shaken, she raised her head and watched until Jigger's dog clamped down on the other's shoulder. The opposing dog closed his jaws on Jigger's dog's back. They held on.

"That's the way they rest," Cash told her. "They'll be given a minute, but it won't last long. See?"

Both trainers entered the pit. Each had a wedge-shaped stick about six inches long, which he put in his dog's mouth and prized open the jaws. "That's called a break stick. Rest time's over."

The dogs were separated and the scratching process started again. "Do the dogs ever turn on their trainers?" Schyler asked. She was mesmerized by the evil light in Flynn's eyes as he purposefully antagonized his pit bull.

"I've known it to happen."

"Little wonder. They put them in that pit to die."

Cash continued to watch her, even after the dogs had launched another attack on each other. The noise in the tin building began to mount in proportion to the violence going on in the ring. The Saturday night crowd had filled the hall to capacity. Men and dogs were sweating profusely. The dogs waiting to fight sensed the tension. They smelled the blood and anticipated tasting it. They barked with ferocious and crazed intent from their wire cages.

The crowd's sudden gasp drew Cash's attention back to the pit. This time, more than blood had been drawn. Hide and tissue had been ripped from the shoulder of the dog opposing Jigger's. Once the initial shock passed through the crowd, a cheer went up. Jigger's dogs were usually favored to win. Hard-earned wages were riding on this fight and the gamblers holding those vouchers smelled victory.

So did Jigger's dog. It went after its foe with renewed vigor. It sank its teeth into the other dog's neck and tore out a chunk of flesh, severing the jugular. Blood spurted from the wound and splattered the slat walls of the pit.

Schyler covered her mouth and turned her head away again. Cash's left hand came up reflexively, cupped the back of her head, and pressed her face into the crook of his shoulder. His right arm slid around her waist and drew her closer. He glanced over his shoulder and cursed viciously when he saw that the crowd had doubled since their arrival. Between them and the exit was a squirming, shouting sea of men with necks craned to see the finish of the fight.

Schyler couldn't breathe, but that was all right because she didn't want to. The walls of the crowded auditorium pressed in on her. The unventilated air was fogged with the smoke from hundreds of foul cigars. The stifling heat concentrated the unpleasant smells until she tasted them with each breath she drew. Sweat, dog, smoke, blood.

Her fingers curled inward and came up with a handful of Cash's shirt. "Please."

The hoarsely spoken appeal went through him like a rusty nail. It touched a soft spot that he thought had calloused over forever when he was in Nam, where seeing men die was a daily occurrence.

"Hold on. I'll get you out of here."

Caring little now for her pride, Schyler clung to him, listening to his heartbeat in the hopes that it would drown out the yelling of the maniacal, bloodthirsty crowd. It was a futile hope. When the mortally wounded dog fell, the racket reached a crescendo that was deafening.

"Okay, that's it. But take a good look, Schyler, at what you're up against."

Cash hooked a finger beneath her chin and forced it up. In the pit, Jigger was leading his dog around by a leash while receiving accolades from the crowd. The dog's coat was lathered and smeared with blood. Flynn's gloating smile sickened Schyler more than the blood and gore.

When she turned toward Cash, her face was pale. He said to her, "That animal isn't a pet. It's a machine trained to kill. It's a moneymaker. If you harm one of his dogs, Jigger will kill you."

He waited a moment, to make certain she had understood, then he leaped off the end of the bleacher and extended his arms up for her. Placing her hands on his shoulders, she let him lift her down. Holding her close against him and trying to shield her with his own body, he shouldered his way toward the exit. It was bottlenecked with men either coming in or going out, counting their winnings or cursing fate for their defeat, congratulating or commiserating with each other.

From out of that mass of bodies Schyler heard, "Jesus Christ, Schyler, what the fuck are you doing here?"

Chapter Eleven

She stopped, turned in the direction of the familiar voice, and stood still while the crowd eddied around her, Cash, and Ken Howell. Her brother-in-law was looking at her through eyes that were red and glazed by alcohol. Slack-jawed, he gaped at her incredulously, then at Cash, then back at her. "Answer me! What the hell are you doing here?"

"I could ask you the same question," she replied.

"Help me get her out of here, huh, Howell? We're blocking traffic."

Ken gave Cash a withering glance, then clumsily grabbed Schyler's hand and began shoving people aside as they wiggled their way through the exit. Outside, men were milling around, drinking, laughing and joking, and discussing the fights that had already taken place and those yet to come. Ken propelled Schyler toward the corner of the building and away from the crowd before he drew her around and repeated his original question.

"What are you doing here? Especially with him." He hitched his chin toward Cash contemptuously.

"Stop shouting at me, Ken. You're not my keeper. I'm a grown woman, and I don't have to answer to you or to anybody else."

He wasn't hearing too clearly. Either that or he wasn't paying attention. "Did you ask him to bring you here?"

She faltered. "Well no, not exactly, but—"

He whirled toward Cash. Spittle showered from his mouth as he sneered, "You stay away from her, you hear me, boy? You goddamn Cajun bastard, I'll—"

Ken never had the satisfaction of stating his threat. In one fluid motion, Cash came up with a knife that had been concealed in a scabbard at the small of his back and, at the same time, slammed Ken into the wall with enough impetus to knock the breath out of him and to rattle the tin. The gleaming blade of the knife was placed so strategically that reflexive swallowing would give Ken's Adam's apple a close shave.

Schyler fell back a step, astonished and afraid. Cash's nostrils flared with each breath he drew. Ken's glassy, bloodshot eyes were bugging. Sweat ran down his face as copiously as a baby's tears.

"Before I cut you real bad, you son of a bitch, you'd better get out of here." The voice, tinged with the musical rhythm of his first language, sounded as sinister as the razor-sharp knife looked. Cash eased the blade away from Ken's throat and stepped back. Ken clutched his neck as though to reassure himself that it hadn't been dissected. He cowardly slumped against the tin wall.

"Get out of here," Cash repeated. His eyes sliced to Schyler. The cold glint in them made her blood run cold. "And take her with you."

Cash turned his back on them, not the least bit concerned that either would launch a counterattack. Schyler watched him thread his way through the parked cars until he disappeared.

"Where's your car, Ken?"

He raised an unsteady hand to indicate the general direction. She took his arm and pulled him away from the support of the wall. Together they made their way toward his sports car. When they reached it, she asked for the keys.

"I'll drive," he mumbled.

"You're drunk. I'll drive." His prideful resistance snapped her patience in two. "Give me the damn car keys."

He belligerently dropped them into her extended palm. She slid behind the wheel. Once he had closed the passenger door, she peeled out. She didn't even take the insubstantial bridge slowly but roared across it.

She was angry—angry at Ken for behaving like such a fool, angry at Cash Boudreaux for putting her through this ordeal, and angry at herself for letting him lead her to slaughter like a naive lamb.

"What were you doing with him?"

"For godsake, Ken, we just came away from a place where one animal wantonly killed another for the amusement of cheering men. There was illegal gambling going on, and God only knows what else. And you want to talk about what I was doing with Boudreaux?"

Her voice had risen a note on each word until she realized she was virtually screeching. She took a composing breath. "Boudreaux wanted to make a point. I tried to hire him to kill the dog that attacked me. I guess he wanted to show me how important those dogs are to Jigger Flynn."

"Jesus," Ken swore, running a hand through his hair. "I told you to drop that. Kill one of Jigger's pit bulls? You might just as well challenge him to a duel on Main Street."

"Don't worry. Cash declined my offer."

"Thank God. He's right. Leave it alone, Schyler."

She switched topics. "What were *you* doing there, Ken?"

He squirmed in the expensive leather car seat and turned his head away from her. "It's Saturday night. Don't I deserve a chance to unwind every now and then?"

"Were you gambling?"

"Anything wrong with that?"

"No. But there are more wholesome environments for it. The racetrack in Lafayette, a private poker game."

"Don't get on my back." He hunched lower in the seat, looking like a petulant child. "Tricia bitched at me tonight because I wouldn't take her to a goddamn country club dance. I don't need bitching from you, too."

Schyler let it go. It wasn't any of her business what Ken did in his leisure time. She needed to ask him why he had suspended operation of Crandall Logging, but now wasn't the time or place to bring up that delicate subject. He was sullen, no doubt feeling demoralized and emasculated after being so badly shown up by Cash.

"Did he hurt you?" she asked quietly.

He swung his head around. "Hell no! But you stay away from him. See what kind of man he is? He's poison, as low and vicious as those fighting dogs. You can't trust him. I don't know what he's after, or why he's sniffing around you all of a sudden, but he has his reasons. Whatever they are, they're self-serving." He jabbed an index finger at her for emphasis. "I can guarantee you that."

"I'll see who I want to see, Ken," she said icily. "I told you why Cash took me to that fight."

He tilted his head cockily. "Did he also tell you how much money he had riding on the outcome?"

Schyler brought the car to an abrupt halt in the center of the road and turned to her brother-in-law. "What?"

Ken smiled smugly. "I can see that he failed to mention his sizable wager."

"How do you know?"

"Boudreaux always bets on Jigger's dogs, so he won big tonight. I don't know what he told you, but he had a vested interest in that pit bull fight."

"No wonder he turned down my offer," she muttered.

"Right. You think he's gonna kill a dog that earns him winnings like that?" Seeing Schyler's disillusionment, he touched her shoulder sympathetically. "Listen, Schyler, Boudreaux always covers his ass first. Count on that. He has the survival instincts of a jungle animal. You can't trust the conniving Cajun bastard."

She shrugged off Ken's consoling hand and put the car into motion again. Ken reached across the seat and laid his hand on her thigh, giving it an affectionate squeeze that wasn't entirely brotherly.

"You've only been home a short while. There are reasons for the wide gaps in the social structure around here, Schyler. They're not meant to be crossed." He patted her thigh. "Just be sure you remember where you belong, and you'll be back in the swing of things in no time. Stay away from the white trash. And don't provoke the likes of Jigger Flynn. That's only asking for trouble."

Heaped onto what he'd told her about Cash, his condescending, patronizing, chauvinistic tone enraged her. She didn't waste energy on that, however. She let his humoring attitude work to make her more resolute.

Since she hadn't succeeded in enlisting anyone else for her cause, she would take action into her own hands.

Chapter Twelve

She knew that once the dogs started barking, she wouldn't have much time. Flynn would come charging out to see what had caused the ruckus in his yard. It was going to be tricky. She had to get close enough to be effective with the shotgun, but keep enough distance between her and the house so the dogs wouldn't pick up her scent. Once she had accomplished what she had come to do, she would gladly own up to it, but she didn't want to alert Flynn beforehand.

Undertaking this alone probably wasn't very smart. Schyler realized the risks involved and was willing to face them. On the other hand, every time she thought of the evil that Jigger Flynn embodied, she shivered involuntarily.

Last night she had retrieved her car from the landing. Tonight she had left it parked in front of Belle Terre and walked to Flynn's house through the woods. She had dressed for her mission, in old jeans and a dark T-shirt. She had thought about covering her light hair with a cap, but thought that might be a trifle melodramatic.

Earlier in the day, when both Ken and Tricia were away

from the house and Mrs. Graves was outside sweeping the veranda, Schyler had gone into Cotton's den and taken a shotgun from the gun rack. She had given the twelve gauge a cursory inspection, certain that it was cleaned and oiled and in prime condition. Cotton had always kept his hunting guns in working order, ready to load and fire. Schyler hated guns, hated touching their cold, impersonal surfaces of wood and metal. But she had put her aversion aside and concentrated on what she felt compelled to do.

The Howells and she had eaten a large Sunday dinner at midday, so supper consisted of cold fried chicken and fruit salad. Ken and Tricia, who was still peeved because Ken hadn't accompanied her to the dance the night before, had bickered throughout the light meal.

"I got to watch the Saturday night movie on TV all by myself," Tricia complained sarcastically, "while you went out to God knows where."

Schyler's eyes met Ken's across the table. Tacitly they agreed not to mention to Tricia where he had been. "I told you I was with friends," Ken said.

Since they had returned to Belle Terre in separate cars, Tricia didn't know that Ken and her sister had been together. Keeping that a secret smacked of an illicitness that made Schyler uneasy, but she still thought it best for Tricia to remain unenlightened of last night's activities. In this case what she didn't know couldn't hurt her, or anyone else.

The secret that they shared hadn't drawn Ken and her closer. On the contrary, he had been querulous and stand-offish all day. That suited her fine. She thought it best that they give each other breathing room after what had happened last night, when neither had been seen in the most favorable light.

As soon as she had eaten supper, Schyler excused herself and went upstairs. In her room, she changed clothes, then sneaked out of the house by way of the back stairs. She wanted to avoid having to explain where she was going toting a shotgun. Besides, if she thought about it much longer, she might chicken out.

Now, standing hidden behind a clump of blackberry

bushes several hundred yards and across the road from Flynn's house, her hands were slick with perspiration and her heart was racing. She didn't take lightly what she was about to do. The thought of killing anything made her sick to her stomach. Even the idea of maiming an animal turned her stomach.

Only the memory of how viciously the unprovoked dog had attacked her, and the possibility that another defenseless child might suffer such an attack, propelled her closer to Flynn's house. His pit bulls weren't ordinary household pets. They were life-threatening animals, bred to attack and kill. If Flynn demanded it afterward, she would compensate him for his loss, within reason. Apart from that she would offer no apology. She would personally see to it that action was taken to prohibit pit bull fights in the area, even if it meant appealing directly to her congressman.

Flynn's pickup was parked in the yard. A mangy cat was curled on the hood of it. There were no lights on outside the house, but enough light was coming through the windows to illuminate the yard and cast long, eerie shadows. As she crept closer, she could hear a TV or radio playing inside. Every now and then a shadow moved past a window. The tacky lace curtains rose and fell reluctantly whenever the desultory breeze touched them. Schyler could smell pork cooking. She counted on that pervasive smell to keep the dogs from picking up her scent.

From the opposite side of the road, she gave the house wide berth, having planned to approach it from the back side. She hadn't selected the shotgun at random. A pistol was out of the question. She would have to get too close. A rifle would have meant firing with precision accuracy, and since it had been years since she'd fired one, her skill was questionable. Using the double-barreled shotgun to blast the kennel where the dogs were penned would guarantee hits. If the shots didn't kill the dogs, they would at least inflict serious damage.

Crouching low, Schyler watched the house for another five minutes. She could see movement inside. The dogs were prowling their pens restlessly, but not a single bark had been uttered. Drawing a deep breath, she stepped from behind the bushes and onto the gravel road. She was fully exposed for the length of time it took her to run across it. Making it to the back of a dilapidated shed, she flung herself flat against the wall of it, drinking in oxygen through her wide, gasping mouth.

One of the dogs growled. Their movements became more restless. One whined a sound that had a question mark at the end of it. Schyler sensed their mounting skittishness. They couldn't smell her, but they seemed to know she was there. They sensed impending danger, danger she tried not to think about as she checked the shotgun one final time. Two shells were loaded, two riding in her waistband waiting to be. Holding her breath, she pulled back both hammers. The soft metallic clicks elicited another growl from the dog pens.

It had to be now.

She stepped from behind the shed and aimed the shotgun at the fenced enclosure. It was about seventy-five feet away from her. Her finger was so wet with perspiration, it slipped off the trigger the first time she tried to pull it; however, she finally squeezed off the shot.

She had forgotten how deafening a sound it made. The gunshot exploded in the stillness and reverberated like a cannon. She had also forgotten to anticipate the kickback and was painfully reminded of it when the stock rammed into her shoulder with bruising force, nearly knocking the breath out of her.

In the periphery of her mind, she was aware of the racket that erupted around her, the frantic yapping coming from the kennel, the livid cursing and shouting from inside the house. She disregarded both and concentrated only on aiming the shotgun a second time.

As soon as she fired, she flipped the release and the barrels dropped forward. Reaching inside, she pinched out the two empty shells and replaced them with the two she had easily accessible in the waistband of her jeans. She locked the barrel into place again. Her practice that afternoon had paid off. She'd completed reloading in under eight seconds. She fired the third shot and had just gotten off the fourth when Jigger Flynn came tearing out the back door of the house.

He was almost farcically outraged. His face was a florid mask, his sparse hair was standing on end. He was barefooted and was wearing a ratty, ribbed knit tank T-shirt over his drooping trousers. Far from funny, however, was the pistol he was brandishing. Dire threats issued from a mouth that sprayed spittle with each blue word.

Schyler froze in terror. She hadn't counted on him having a gun. She had expected him to be upset, angry, even furious, but she had planned to reason with him once the initial shock had worn off and he had calmed down. One couldn't reason with a madman waving a pistol. The man cursing and damning the whole world to hell looked like he would never be reasonable again.

He hadn't spotted her yet. His first concern was for the dogs. Because none had charged out to attack her through the holes the shotgun had made in the fencing, Schyler assumed that she had inflicted serious damage. Some of the animals were still alive. Their pitiable whimpering would ring in her ears for years to come.

"My dogs . . . What motherfuckin' bastard . . . I'll kill you." Flynn spun around and fired aimlessly into the darkness, intent on killing the culprit who had suspended his lucrative sideline. "I'll kill you, goddamn you to hell. You shithead, you'll wish you were dead when I get through with your miserable, goddamned hide. I'll kill you."

Schyler saw movement beyond Flynn's shoulder. "What's happened?" the woman asked from the window.

Schyler, recognizing her, gasped.

"Shut up, you black bitch! Call the sheriff. Some cocksucker's shot my dogs!" The curtain fell back into place. Flynn, sputtering in his rage, fired the pistol again. This time the bullet slammed into the wall of the shed. Schyler heard the brittle wood splinter near her head. Giving thought to nothing except running for cover, she dashed toward the road, putting the shed between her and Flynn.

Seconds later, she could hear his choppy breathing and knew that he had seen movement. He ran across the yard after her, cursing the obstacles in his path.

All thought of diplomatic negotiating vanished. Schyler ran for her life. Her only chance to escape unharmed was to get across the road and take cover in the dense woods. She slid down the shallow ditch and scrambled up the other side. When she reached the road, the pounding heels of her tennis shoes crunched in the gravel. She prayed she wouldn't twist an ankle, which was a ridiculous prayer. Why worry about a sprain when at any second she could be shot? Jigger Flynn was in hot pursuit and firing the pistol as he hurled vile curses at her.

She had reached the center of the road when a pickup truck careened around the bend, almost running over her. It swerved away just in time and came to a partial stop with a theatrical shower of gravel and a cloud of dust. The passenger door was flung open.

"Get in, you idiot!" Cash shouted at her. Schyler tossed the shotgun into the bed of the truck, grabbed hold of the open door, and hauled herself inside. A bullet struck the door. "Keep your head down!"

"Come back, you goddamned murderer," Flynn yelled. He fired the pistol repeatedly but was too angry to be accurate. By the time he had calmed down enough to take careful aim, the truck had been obscured by a curtain of dust.

Inside the cab of the pickup, Schyler was bent double, her head between her knees, arms crossed over her head. She couldn't stop shaking, even when she knew that they were out of range and Flynn's hysterical cursing could no longer be heard.

Cash was piloting the old truck as though it were a Porsche on a smooth racetrack, taking the twisting turns in the washboard road at a daredevil speed and without the aid of headlights, making it impossible for anyone to follow them. The roads crisscrossed the bayous as intricately as the weaving pattern of the cotton yarn in a Cajun blanket. He knew each one and had no difficulty navigating them.

"You okay?" His eyes left the road for a split second, only long enough for him to glance down at his passenger.

"I'm unwell."

"Unwell? What the hell does that mean?"

Schyler raised her head and glared at him. "It means I'm about to puke."

The truck came to another screeching halt. Cash reached across her and shoved open the door. Schyler leaped from the cab and retched into the dusty bushes that lined the edge of the road.

Hands propped on her knees, she remained bent at a forty-five-degree angle while the spasms gripped her until she was entirely empty. Her ears were on fire. Her skin broke out in a clammy sweat. She was trembling all over. She waited for the terror to subside. It didn't, but eventually it waned. Finally, she opened her eyes. A bottle of whiskey came into focus.

She accepted the bottle and lifted it to her chalky lips. She filled her mouth with the fiery liquor, swished it around, then spat it out. Or tried to. Most of it dribbled down her chin.

"Hell." Cash removed the bandanna that was knotted around his neck and passed it to her. She blotted her chin with it, then dabbed her eyes. They were leaking tears, though she wasn't actually crying. "You can't spit worth a damn. But you can damn sure shoot. There were four holes wider than washtubs in the side of that kennel. Hide and guts were splattered—"

"Please, shut up," she begged weakly. Her stomach heaved again.

"Are you going to vomit again?" She shook her head no. "If you are, tell me so I can pull over. I don't want you doing it in my truck."

She looked at the fresh bullet hole in the door of his pickup, then glanced up at him disparagingly. "Take me back."

"To Belle Terre?"

"To Flynn's place."

He stared at her with patent disbelief. "Have you got shit for brains, lady?"

"Take me back, Cash."

"Like hell. I'm getting tired of rescuing you."

"I didn't ask you to!"

"You'd be dead by now if I hadn't," he shouted back.

"I've got to go back. I've got to offer to pay for—"

"Forget it." His voice sliced the humid air as precisely as his hands did when he made the negative chopping motion. "You don't want Jigger to ever find out who did that to his dogs."

"But I can't just—"

He took her by the shoulders. "Look, why do you think I went in there with the headlights off? I didn't want to spotlight you. I hope to God he didn't recognize my truck."

"I heard him say he was going to call the sheriff. If the sheriff is there, I can explain. Surely—"

Cash shook her hard, and she fell abruptly silent. "Schyler, you don't realize the kind of man you're dealing with. He doesn't settle out of court. He goes for the jugular just like his dogs. I advised you to leave it alone, but now it's done. Stay away from him and don't admit doing this to a soul."

"I've got to go back," she repeated tearfully.

"Shit," he cursed viciously. "Haven't you heard anything I just said?"

"I saw Gayla. Through the window."

"Gayla Frances?"

"Yes, Veda's daughter. You know her? She was inside Flynn's house."

"That's right." Cash released her and stepped back. Clinging to the open door for support, Schyler looked at him incomprehensively. "Gayla's been living with Jigger the last few years."

The earth slipped off its axis. The dark trees spun around her. *"Gayla?* With Jigger Flynn? That's impossible."

"Get in."

Without a shred of compassion, he pushed her into the cab of the truck and slammed the door. He came around and slid beneath the wheel. He had left the motor running, so within seconds they were underway again. He still didn't turn on the headlights. They drove along roads so narrow that sometimes the tree branches slapped against the pickup and interlaced to form a tunnel around them. Schyler didn't suggest that he turn the headlights on; he seemed to know exactly what he was doing. It was a relief to let someone else handle the decisions for a while.

Exhausted, she rested her head against the open window and let the breeze cool her face. "Tell me about Gayla. How did she come to live with that reprobate?"

"When we get home. My home."

"I'd rather not."

"Yeah, well I'd rather not have been staking out Flynn's place tonight, waiting for you to pull some damn fool stunt like you did."

"You were—"

"Parked just around the curve in the road."

"You were that sure I'd do it?"

"I had a strong suspicion you'd try something."

"Even after you had warned me not to?"

He gave her a wry look. "Because I had warned you not to."

After a moment she said, "I guess I owe you another thank you."

"*Oui*. I guess you do."

Chapter Thirteen

He stopped the car. The emergency brake pedal made a grinding noise when he pushed it toward the floorboard. He turned to face her. For a long, tense moment they stared at each other.

"What'll you give me for saving your life again?" he asked softly. "You're running up quite a bill."

Schyler stared him down stonily, though her insides felt

as light and airy as meringue. Her mouth was dry and it wasn't because of her recent nausea.

After several seconds, his lips curved into his character-istically cynical smile. "Relax. I won't collect tonight."

"How kind."

"It's not that. We haven't got that much time." He pushed open his door. "We walk from here, Miss Schyler."

He had deliberately avoided the roads leading back to Belle Terre, so they had approached his house from the far side. Taking her hand, he led her down the overgrown path toward the bayou and the small house that sat on its banks, nestled among the trees.

It had been built of cypress and was probably as old as the plantation house. Like Red Broussard's café, the house was set off the ground on enormous cypress stumps. The metal roof extended over a recessed porch lined with posts, which helped support it. The batten shutters had been left open and revealed screened windows. An exterior stair-case, located at one end of the porch, led to a second story.

Cash guided her up the wooden steps, across the porch, and through a door into the central room. At one end there was a fireplace and small kitchen. The room served as both living room and eating area. It was neater than Schyler had expected it to be, but it definitely bore the stamp of Cash's heritage.

She had toured reconstructed Cajun houses, which were a staple tourist attraction in that part of Louisiana. The architecture of this house was typical, even to the *galerie,* or screened porch, that ran the length of the central room at the back of the house. Through a narrow connecting door, she could see into a bathroom, obviously a modern addi-tion to the original floor plan.

On the *galerie,* there was an iron double bed, a bureau, and a rickety table with a small, portable TV and a deck of cards on it. A bookcase was stocked with best-selling pa-perback novels and recent-issue magazines. In addition to his tidiness, his reading matter, too, surprised her. She gathered that the *galerie* was where Cash spent most of his time when he was at home. It overlooked the bayou.

"What's upstairs?" she asked.

"My mother's bedroom."

Some of the furniture was obviously handmade, but by master craftsmen. There were touches of modernity, like the TV, the microwave oven, and the fan with cane blades that was suspended from a beam in the ceiling of the main room. He reached for the string and gave it a yank. The fan began circulating the still air.

"Drink?" He crossed to the cabinet in the kitchen, parted the calico curtain that was gathered on a rod, and took down a bottle of whiskey.

"Please. Add some water."

"Ice?"

She shook her head no. He came back, bringing the bottle with him, and handed her the drink. "Sit down." He indicated a chair that was upholstered in a regular, all-American fabric, a chair that could have been purchased in any furniture store in the nation. It seemed absurdly out of place in this interesting house beside the bayou, but Schyler sank into it, grateful for the familiarity. Nothing so far this evening had seemed normal. Her teeth clicked against the glass as she took a sip of her drink. "Thank you."

He plopped into the matching chair facing hers and took a swallow of his own drink, having placed the bottle on the low table between them. He propped his booted feet there, too, stacking one ankle on top of the other.

"Where did you learn to shoot?"

"Cotton taught me."

He had been about to raise his glass to his mouth for another drink. He paused momentarily, then drank before he said, "He did a good job of it."

"I'm not proud of what I did tonight."

"Your daddy would be."

"Probably," she admitted grudgingly. Studiously, she ran her finger around the rim of her glass. "We had a disagreement over it, my shooting," she told Cash with a wistful smile. "He wanted me to go hunting with him every fall, but I couldn't bring myself to shoot at anything except inanimate targets. He was disappointed in me." She took another swift swallow, then set her empty glass on the low table beside Cash's feet and stood up.

"Another drink?"

"No thanks." She made a slow, exploratory circle around her chair, trailing her finger over the nubby fabric. "Tonight was different. I had to do it. But I don't want to be complimented on my marksmanship."

Restlessly she prowled the room, making her way toward the window over the kitchen sink. In the sill an herb garden was growing. Apparently it was carefully tended. Inquiringly she glanced at him over her shoulder. He shrugged and poured himself another straight whiskey. "My mother always had things growing in that window."

"You use the herbs to make your potions?"

She asked the question teasingly, but his answer was serious. "Some of them."

Next to the outdated refrigerator, which hummed noisily, there was a corkboard hanging on the wall. Several old pictures had been thumbtacked there. Schyler leaned forward to get a better look at them. There was one of a woman and a child, a young boy with unruly, wavy hair and mature, serious eyes.

"You and your mother?"

"Oui."

The woman's hair was black and curly around her triangular face that tapered from a wide forehead to her impishly pointed chin. Her long, exotic eyes made her look as though she was privy to a thousand secrets. Her mysterious smile said she was sharing none of them. Her lips were heart-shaped, full and voluptuous, enticing and sexy.

Schyler could remember Monique, but never as being this young. And she'd only seen her from a distance. She was captivated by the photograph. "Your mother was very beautiful."

"Thanks."

"How old were you here?"

"Ten maybe. I don't remember."

"What was the occasion?"

"I don't remember that either."

Schyler looked at the other pictures. Several were snapshots of marines in battle fatigues, dogtags hanging from chains around their necks, grinning, acting silly. One had assumed a batter's stance and was holding his rifle like a baseball bat. Another had his middle finger raised to the camera. She recognized Cash in some of the pictures.

"Vietnam?"

"*Oui.*"

"You all seem to be enjoying yourselves."

He made a scoffing sound. "Yeah, we had a helluva good time over there."

"I didn't mean to be facetious."

"The guy with the mustache got it in the gut the day after the picture was taken. The medics didn't even bother to fix him up, just tried to pile all the parts back into the carcass before the chopper got there to cart it out." From across the room, he pointed at one of the other pictures. "I'm not sure what happened to the guy wearing the funny hat. We were out on patrol. When we heard his screams, the rest of us got the hell out of there."

Stunned by his blasé attitude, she asked, "How can you talk about deceased friends like that?"

"I don't have any friends."

She recoiled as though he had socked her. "Why do you do that?"

"What?"

"Retaliate. Repay concern with cruelty."

"Habit, I guess."

"Take me home."

"You don't like it here?" He spread his arms to encompass the modest room.

"I don't like you."

"Most people in your class don't."

"I'm not in a *class*. I'm me. And the reason people don't like you is because you're such a snide, sarcastic son of a bitch. Where's your phone? If you won't drive me to Belle Terre, I'll call someone to pick me up."

"I don't have a phone."

"You don't have a telephone?"

He smirked at the incredulity underlying her question.

"That way I don't have to talk to somebody I don't want to."

"How do you survive without a telephone?"

"When I need one, I go to the office at the landing and use that one."

"That door is always kept locked."

"There are ways around that."

Schyler was aghast. "You pick the lock? You break in and mooch off us?" His unrepentant grin was as good as a signed confession. "Not only are you unlikable, you're a thief."

"So far no one has seemed to mind."

"Does anyone know?"

"Cotton knows."

Schyler was surprised. "Cotton lets you bleed utilities off Belle Terre? In exchange for what?"

"That's between him and me." Abruptly he placed his glass on the table and sat forward, propping his elbows on his knees. "You aren't planning to do anything crazy about Gayla Frances, are you?"

"At the very least I'm going to talk to her."

"Don't. She won't welcome your interference."

"I damn well will interfere. I want to hear from her own lips that she chooses to live with that man. Until then I won't believe it. I can't understand why Veda allows it."

He gave her a strange look. "Veda's dead."

The breath deserted Schyler's body. Her knees unhinged and she dropped into the chair again. She stared at him blankly. "You must be mistaken."

"No."

"Veda's dead?" He nodded. She lowered her gaze and stared into near space, trying to imagine a world without Veda in it. Solid, dependable, loving Veda, who had nursed her through colic and scraped knees and affairs of the heart that had gone awry. "When?"

"Several years ago. Not long after you left. Didn't your sister tell you?"

A cold numbness, like death, stole over her. She shook

her head. "No, she didn't. She told me she had had to let Veda go."

He muttered a foul word. "She let her go, all right. That was the beginning of the end. Veda took sick soon after that. Personally I think it was because that bitch you call a sister booted her off Belle Terre."

He flopped back against the cushions of his chair. "Veda was too old to get another job. Then she got too sick to work. Gayla had to leave college and come home to take care of her. Jobs were scarce. Gayla took what she could find. She got hired to serve drinks in a honky-tonk. That's where she caught Jigger's eye. He liked what he saw and took her under his wing. He coached her in a more profitable occupation."

Schyler stared with disbelief. "You're lying."

"Why would I? Ask anybody. It's the truth. Gayla turned tricks in the cheapest dive in town."

"She would never do that."

"She did, I tell you."

Schyler vehemently denied the possibility. "But she's so pretty, so intelligent and sweet."

"I guess that's why she became such a favorite." Schyler clamped her teeth over her lip and tried to keep the tears out of her eyes. "Among Jigger's girls, Gayla shone like a new penny. That's why he took her for his own. Now he only occasionally loans her out and then at a premium price." Schyler's head dropped into her waiting hand.

Without mercy, Cash went on. "Veda died, mostly of shame and grief. Tricia Howell had spread it around that she was old and incompetent and had almost burned Belle Terre to the ground by negligently leaving an iron on. Then there was Gayla. Veda couldn't stand what her daughter had become."

It wasn't possible. Schyler had known Gayla since she was born to Veda, a late-in-life child. Together they'd cried when Mr. Frances was killed in an explosion at the oil refinery where he worked. That's when Cotton had invited Veda to move into the quarters at Belle Terre. Schyler had watched Gayla blossom into a lovely teenager. She had just seen her off to college when Schyler left for England.

"What about Jimmy Don?" she asked.

Jimmy Don Davison had been Gayla's sweetheart since kindergarten. He'd become the star running back on Heaven's high school football team. He had been known as the Heathen of Heaven on the gridiron. He was such an outstanding athlete that a coach from LSU had drafted him and given him a full, four-year scholarship. He was a handsome, intelligent young man who was popular with black and white students alike. But it had always been understood that he belonged to Gayla Frances and vice versa.

"He's doing time."

"Time? You mean in prison?" Schyler wheezed. "For what?"

"He was still at school while all this was going on. When he heard that Gayla had moved in with Jigger, he got drunk, went berserk, and busted up a bar and just about everybody in it. Nearly killed one guy for boasting that he'd been with Gayla and telling all who would listen what a juicy piece she was. Jimmy Don pleaded guilty to all the charges and is serving his sentence. Three years, I think."

Schyler covered her face with her hands. It was too much to assimilate at one time. Veda. Gayla. Jimmy Don. Their lives had been ruined. And, although indirectly, Tricia was responsible. Schyler felt guilty by association.

She raised her head and looked at the man slouching in the chair opposite her. He seemed to take perverse pleasure in tormenting her. "You relished telling me all that, didn't you?"

He conceded with a nod. "Just so you'll know the caliber of folks you're living with in that big, fancy house. Your sister is a spiteful bitch. Her dick-less husband is a joke. Cotton . . . hell, I don't know what's wrong with him. He stood by and let Tricia do with people's lives what she damn well pleased."

Schyler's chin went up a notch. It was all right for her to acknowledge her family's weaknesses, but it was something else for an outsider to, especially Cash Boudreaux.

"What the people at Belle Terre do is no concern of yours. I won't have you bad-mouthing my family." She stood up and looked down at him, her expression imperious and haughty.

It nudged his temper over the edge. One second his spine was conforming to the cushions of the chair, seemingly indifferent. The next, he was looming over Schyler, gripping her shoulders hard. "I'll say what I goddamn want to about anybody or anything."

"Not about my family."

His fingers slid up through her hair and pressed against her scalp, holding her head in place. He lowered his face to within inches of her. "All right. For the time being, I'll tell you what I think of you."

"I don't care what you think of me."

His lips brushed across hers. "I believe you do."

"Stop that."

Smiling, he briefly touched his lips to hers a second time. "I think you're just about the most interesting woman I've come across in a long time, Miss Schyler."

"Let me go." She tried to dodge his roaming, sipping lips, but they wouldn't be eluded. They gently struck her face with petal softness. She tried to push him away, but her efforts were wasted.

"Any woman who'd go up against Jigger Flynn, hell, she's somebody I've just got to know better." He thrust his hips forward and up, using the fly of his jeans to suggestively nudge the cleft of her thighs.

"You're disgusting."

His laugh was low, deep, dirty. "Ask around, Miss Schyler. Most women don't think so. And I think you're just dying to find out for yourself."

She tried to squirm away, but he pressed his fingers against her head, hard enough to cause some mild discomfort and to effectively stop her from trying to pull it free. Then he tilted her face up and kissed her, covering her lips with his. She made a strangled sound of protest when his tongue slid between her lips and into her mouth. His tongue's lazy, swirling penetration shocked her. She reeled and clutched his shoulders for support.

After a long, thorough kiss, he raised his head. "Just what I thought," he said roughly. "You put on all those ladylike airs, but you're just like a firecracker on the Fourth of July, ready to ignite, ready to explode." His hands slid from her head, down her shoulders and arms to her waist, which he clasped. He jerked her forward and rubbed against her. "Feel that? I've got just the match to light your fuse." She slapped him hard. His eyes narrowed dangerously. "What's the matter, not used to—"

"Filth, Mr. Boudreaux. No, I'm not used to filth."

"Doesn't your brother-in-law talk dirty to you in bed?" Schyler's face went white with indignation. Cash snickered, adding, "How does Howell manage to service both you and your sister?"

"Shut up!"

"Folks in town are wondering, you know. Does he traipse back and forth between bedrooms, or do y'all sleep in one big, happy bed?"

Schyler pushed against his chest so hard that he was forced to release her. She ran out the front door and clambered down the steps. He followed close behind. Encircling her wrist, he brought her up short. "No need to run off. I don't want Howell's leftovers. Now get in the truck. I'll drive you home."

"I wouldn't go anywhere with you."

"Afraid you'll be seen with me?"

"Yes. I'm afraid people would think that your lying, cheating ways might rub off on me."

"Lying, cheating ways?"

"You had bet money on Jigger's dog last night."

"I don't deny that."

"Why didn't you tell me you gambled on those fights when I asked you to kill the dog?"

"It was none of your business."

"You manipulated me!" she cried. "Taking me there, urging me for my own good not to do anything against him. But all the time you were protecting your own interest."

"One had nothing to do with the other."

"Liar. You won a lot of money."

"I damn sure did."

She shuddered with fury over his calm admission. "You're every bit as unscrupulous as people say."

She wrested her arm free. She truly loathed this man. She had tried to communicate with him as an equal, but he wouldn't let her. Ken was right in that respect. The differences between the classes were as deeply ingrained as the rings in an oak tree and seemingly as impenetrable. The system was feudalistic, it was unacceptable, but it was undeniable. Cash Boudreaux had dragged her down to his level and she felt soiled.

"Now that you've told me off, get in the truck," he said.

"Like hell I will."

"Where are you going?"

"Home."

Cash went after her. "Don't be stupid. You can't walk all the way to Belle Terre in the middle of the night."

"Wanna bet?"

He pulled her around again. "You're mad because I said the things you know but don't want to hear. People call me trash. Fine. I don't give a goddamn about anybody's opinion of me but my own. I'll go to hell for some of the things I've done, but I never dumped on an aging black woman who depended on me for her livelihood like your sister did. I wouldn't stand by and let it happen either like that gutless wonder, Howell, did. I wouldn't turn a blind eye like Cotton did."

Schyler glowered at him. Even in the darkness, she could see that he was sneering at her. His kiss had been blatantly erotic, but not sexually prompted. He had used it to insult her, to punish her for being what she was and for what he wasn't and never would be.

"Stay away from Belle Terre and everybody in it. Especially me. If you don't, I'll shoot you for trespassing."

With that, she took the shotgun from the bed of his pickup and struck out for home on foot.

Chapter Fourteen

Gayla sat in the ladder-back chair in the corner. Like a child, Jigger expected her to be seen and not heard, especially when he had company—unless he was using her to entertain his company. Tonight their company was the sheriff. She knew from experience that the sheriff liked his sex straight. He was a swine, but a finicky one. Tonight, though, he was on duty, which relieved Gayla of hers.

"Made any enemies recently, Jigger?"

Sheriff Pat Patout looked longingly at the glass of whiskey Jigger was drinking, but he had declined the offer to join him. He had barely squeaked past his opponent in the last election. He was already sweating the outcome of the next one. Lately he was being as prudent and conscientious as an old-maid school marm.

"I don't have an enemy in the world, Sheriff," Jigger said blandly. "You know that."

They both knew quite the opposite. The sheriff cleared his throat loudly and cast a lustful glance at Gayla. Her face remained impassive, as though she were too stupid to grasp the meaning of their conversation. That passivity was the only way she had survived the last few years. She sat there and let the sheriff ogle her high, pointed breasts. They were as symmetrical and well defined as two sno-cone cups growing out of her chest. Their shape was ill-concealed by the thin, tight dress Jigger made her wear. Gazing back at the sheriff with lifeless eyes, her mind actively conjured up epithets that applied to him.

Patout wiped his mouth with the back of his hand and

fidgeted uncomfortably in his chair. "Maybe I will have just a touch of that." He nodded toward the bottle. "It's a thirsty night. So goddamn hot." Jigger poured him a hefty drink. He downed it in one swallow. Almost immediately beads of sweat popped out on his forehead. "You might not have any enemies, Jigger," his stinging vocal cords wheezed, "but you sure as hell pissed off somebody. I only had to take a gander at those dog pens to ascertain that."

"Bastards," Jigger muttered.

"You think there was more than one?"

"One did the shooting. One did the driving the pickup."

"Did you recognize the vehicle?"

Jigger shook his shiny, oily head. "Too dark. Too fast."

"Did *you* see anything?"

Gayla jumped when she realized that Patout had addressed her. She tucked her bare feet beneath the chair and curled her toes downward, pressing them into the cracked, scummy linoleum floor. Her hands were balled together into twin coffee-colored fists. Straightening her arms, she pressed her fists between her thighs as though to hide evidence. She relaxed her arms and withdrew her hands, however, when she realized that the pose made her breasts more prominent. The goat with the badge pinned to his shirt pocket was staring bug-eyed at her chest.

In answer to his question, she shook her head no. They could torture her, but she would never supply them the name they wanted. That name was Schyler Crandall. Schyler had been in Jigger's yard shooting up his kennel with a shotgun.

It didn't make a lick of sense, but it was true. She would recognize Schyler anywhere. She just prayed to God that Schyler hadn't seen her. Schyler wouldn't spit on her shadow now. Schyler's return had nothing to do with her, but somehow it was heartening to know that her former friend was home.

"I didn't see nothin', Sheriff," Gayla mumbled, deliberately using bad grammar.

Jigger scowled at her over his shoulder. "Where are your manners, gal?" He pronounced it "mannahs." "Fix the sheriff some supper."

"No, thanks, Jigger. I already ate down at the café."

"Fix him some supper." Jigger's eyes were as piercing as pins that impaled Gayla against the tattered wallpaper with the cabbage rose print.

"He don't want none."

"I said fix him some supper," Jigger roared, banging his fist on the table and jiggling the amber contents of the whiskey bottle.

Gayla came to her feet. They whispered across the dirty floor. From the shelf above the old gas stove, she took down a plate. She lifted a graying, greasy pork chop from the pan, dropped it onto the plate, and ladled a spoonful of collard greens beside it. She broke off a piece of cold cornbread from what had been left over and set the chunk on top of the greens, then carried the unappetizing platter to the table and unceremoniously thunked it down in front of the sheriff.

"Thank ya." Patout gave her an uncertain smile.

Jigger wrapped his arm around her waist and jerked her against him. His shoulder gouged her belly. He patted her rump and let his hand linger, caressing her, squeezing the firm flesh through the threadbare dress.

"She's a good girl. Most of the time. And when she ain't . . ." He soundly swatted her fanny with his palm, making it hard enough to sting. Gayla didn't flinch.

A housefly buzzed around the sheriff's plate, which he voraciously attacked once he'd doused the greens with Tabasco. He mopped up the green pot liquor with a hunk of cornbread until it was soggy, then stuffed it into his corpulent mouth. While Jigger continued to maul her, Gayla concentrated on the fly. She watched it light on the dented metal top of the salt shaker. Her mama would have died before she let a fly invade the kitchen at Belle Terre.

But then her mama would have died before she let a lot of things happen, like her girl becoming a whore.

Jigger slipped his calloused hand beneath her dress and ran it up the back of her thigh. She reacted reflexively, though she didn't alter her expression to let her revulsion show.

"How many of your pit bulls were killed?"

"Two. Had to shoot another myself, he was wailing so pitiful like. His brains was hanging out. One more won't fight again. Just as well be dead." He laughed nastily. "But the pregnant bitch wasn't even hit. When she whelps, I'll have the finest litter of fighting pit bulls around."

The sheriff continued to gorge. Occasionally he grunted to let Jigger know he was listening. "I'll do what I can, but there aren't many clues."

"You find the bastards what ruint my dogs, and Gayla and me'll give you a little present, won't we, honey?"

Patout stopped chewing long enough to glance up at her. His lips and chin were shiny with pork grease. She stared down at him, wondering if her eyes revealed just how much she despised all men.

The sheriff swallowed hard and pushed the cleaned plate away. He stood up, tried to hitch his britches over his belly, and reached for his straw cowboy hat. "Then I'd better git on it. I'll keep an eye out for a pickup with a bullet hole in it."

"That accounts for just about every pickup in the parish." Jigger accompanied the sheriff at the screened back door, negligently pushing Gayla aside in the process. "You'll have to do better than that, don'tcha know."

"I don't need you telling me how to do my job, Jigger."

Jigger's mean eyes turned even meaner. "Then I'm tellin' you that whoever done it will be a lot better off if you find them before I do."

The men exchanged a stare of understanding. Patout put on his hat, gave Gayla one last, slavering glance, then went through the door. With a creak and a slap of old wood, it shut behind him. "Bury these dead dogs in the mornin'. They're already stinking in this heat," he said over his shoulder.

"Come out here and bury them your ownself, you blubber gut," Jigger said beneath his breath as he waved the sheriff off.

Jigger wanted the dead animals to stink. He wanted them to stink to high heaven. He wanted everybody in the parish to smell them, to know about what had happened, and the ones who'd done it to be forewarned that he was out for vengeance. He'd get them, but good. He'd show no mercy. He'd set them up as examples. Nobody crossed Jigger Flynn and got away with it. Then he'd see to it that that litter of pups became the meanest sons of bitches in the state of Louisiana and beyond. The thought of the prestige he would gain, not to mention the money, was arousing.

He turned toward Gayla, who was at the sink, scraping off the sheriff's plate. "Time for bed."

Ordinarily she would have dropped what she was doing and followed him into the bedroom. The sooner she capitulated, the sooner it was over with. But she remembered Schyler, who, for unknown reasons, had gone up against him. Schyler's courage had rubbed off on her.

"I c . . . can't tonight, Jigger. I got my period."

He was on her in a flash, backhanding her across the mouth. Her teeth cut her lip and drew blood. "You lying bitch. You got your period last week. What do you think, I'm stupid? You think I don't remember?" He gave her a swift kick in the buttocks that sent her flying face first into the wall.

"Stop it, Jigger. I ain't lyin'." He drove his fingers into her cap of short, curly hair. She kept it short, having learned that when it was long, he could use it as a weapon. He got enough of a grip on it now to bring tears to her eyes.

"I said, time for bed. That means now."

Hand over hand she felt her way along the wall, guided by the twisting, pulling fingers in her hair. She fell through the doorway into the living room. He gave her head a mighty push that almost snapped her neck in two. She stumbled into the bedroom.

Docile now, she stood beside the bed and unbuttoned her dress. She peeled it off her shoulders and let it drop to her feet. Naked she crawled onto the bed and lay down on her back, hoping that's all he wanted her to do tonight.

He undressed. The bed springs rocked noisily when he mounted her. Grunting like a hog, he dryly pushed himself into her. In pain, she arched her back and gripped the coarse sheet beneath her; her heels dug into the thin mattress. But she didn't utter a single sound. He liked her to cry out when he hurt her. She refused to give him the satisfaction. After that initial reaction to his brutal penetration, she lay perfectly still.

This, this gross rutting, bore no resemblance to the loving act she and Jimmy Don had started doing together when she was barely fifteen. They had been so young, so much in love. They couldn't keep their eyes and hands off each other. Their blood had run as hot and sweet as pralines bubbling in a double boiler. Kissing and petting weren't enough. They had followed the urgent dictates of their bodies. And, oh, Jesus, it had felt good.

From that first time, they made love regularly. Afterward she had never felt dirty. With Jigger she always felt as nasty as a spittoon. Mating with Jimmy Don had made her feel pure, loved, cherished. It had not made her feel tainted, or so filthy she would never get clean, or so vile that she wanted to die.

She had thought about it frequently. Killing herself had been a preoccupation ever since she had come to live with Jigger. The only thing that prevented her from ending her own life was the hope, the faint hope, that one day she would see Jimmy Don again and win his forgiveness.

She had also thought about killing Jigger. When he fell into one of his drunken stupors, she had fantasized about driving a butcher knife through his bloated gut and putting an end to her misery. Nothing they could do to her afterward would be as bad as what she lived with daily.

But Veda had made her attend church faithfully, twice on Sundays and Wednesday night prayer meeting. The doctrines were steeped into her. Thundering sermons about hell and damnation had kept her on the straight and narrow for most of her life. She wasn't sure what brimstone was, but she was terrified of having to spend eternity in its midst.

God would forgive her for loving Jimmy Don and "doing it" before they got married. God understood that she was married to Jimmy Don in her heart. And she reasoned that God would forgive her for letting men use her body as a receptacle for their lust. Mama's doctor bills and medicine had been so expensive. Black girls, no matter how smart, rarely got jobs in offices and banks and retail stores. During a recession in the economy they didn't get jobs at all. She was too pretty, her looks too sensual, to get a job cleaning houses. No sane housewife wanted her around a husband or son. So she had done what she had to do. God knew her heart and would understand that.

It might stretch the boundaries of even His understanding and forgiveness if she murdered Jigger Flynn in cold blood. So she hadn't. She had tolerated what he was doing to her now, hoping that she would die a natural death and get out of this life without jeopardizing her chances for spending the next one in heaven with Papa and Mama and maybe even with Jimmy Don.

It was taking longer than usual tonight. Jigger's foul breath soughed against her clammy neck. He sweated like a pig. It dripped from his body and trickled over her breasts.

She couldn't stand it any longer.

Gayla lifted her long, elegant legs and folded them across his back, hugging his pumping hips tightly. She made a moaning, passionate sound that was a tragic parody of the sighs she had once moaned against Jimmy Don's strong, hard, smooth chest.

Her feigned passion worked. Jigger Flynn climaxed, throwing back his ugly, flat head and braying like a jack-ass. He collapsed on top of her before rolling off, precariously rocking the bedsprings. He lay on his back, as white and plump and slimy as a slug.

Gayla turned to her side away from him and gathered her limbs against her body protectively. She held herself still, grateful that it was over and that she had suffered no more tonight than a wallop in the lip and a kick in the rear end.

But she didn't cry until Jigger was snoring beside her. Then she cried silently. While she mouthed her prayers, her tears, remorseful, bitter, and hopeless, slid noiselessly down her satiny cheeks.

Chapter Fifteen

"There was a telephone call for you while you were out," Mrs. Graves informed Schyler. "I put the message on Mr. Crandall's desk in the study."

"Thank you."

Schyler's footsteps echoed off the hardwood floors in the wide central hall as she went toward the back of the house to the small, square room that was tucked behind the sweeping staircase.

The paneled room was dominated by a massive desk. Schyler dropped her handbag and car keys on top of the mounting pile of unopened mail and settled herself in the tufted leather chair. It resembled the one in the office at the landing, but not as many treasured memories were associated with it. Cotton hadn't used this chair as often.

Macy didn't want the girls' heads to be cluttered with talk of timber and its various markets. She had objected to frequently finding Schyler enclosed in this den talking shop with Cotton, so he had done his tutoring at the landing instead. That had helped maintain peace in the household.

Schyler's thoughts focused on her father now. There was still no change in his condition. Less than an hour earlier, the cardiologist had told her that was something to be glad about.

"It's like a tie score, like kissing your sister," he had said. "His condition is nothing to cheer about, but we can be glad he's not getting any worse."

"You still have no idea when you'll be able to do the surgery?"

"No. But the more time we give him to build up his strength, the better. In this case, each day we delay is to our advantage."

After a brief visit to Cotton's ICU, she had returned home. She was dispirited. She missed Mark. The heat was oppressive. She was starved for something good to eat. She was tired of Ken's and Tricia's incessant squabbling. She longed for a good night's sleep.

As she punched out the telephone number Mrs. Graves had jotted down for her, she acknowledged two of the prevalent reasons she hadn't been sleeping well. One was Gayla Frances. The other was Cash Boudreaux.

"Delta National Bank."

Schyler realized her call had gone through. "Uh, pardon?"

"Delta National Bank. May I help you?"

She hadn't expected the call to be of a business nature. On the notepad in front of her was written an individual's name. She referred to it now. "Mr. Dale Gilbreath please," she said with a shade of inquiry in her voice.

"His line is busy. Do you care to hold?"

"Yes, please."

While she waited, Schyler slipped off her shoes and ground her numb toes against the carpet to restore circulation. Tomorrow she would revert to wearing sandals. In this heat, pantyhose and high heels were masochistic.

Who the devil was Dale Gilbreath? The name didn't ring any bells. She searched her memory but couldn't come up with a definite recollection, so she gave up trying and turned her thoughts to matters more pressing.

She had to do something about Gayla. But what? The tale Cash had told her was too outlandish not to be true. He was probably right about Gayla not welcoming her interference. Still, something had to be done. Gayla couldn't continue living with that wretched excuse for a man. The insulting way he had spoken to her was indicative of how horrid her life with him must be. Schyler couldn't stand by and do nothing. The problem was in deciding what to do and how to go about it in a manner that would be acceptable to Gayla. For the moment, she shelved that dilemma, too.

Cash Boudreaux. Lord, what should she do about him? On the surface she could answer that question with, "Nothing." Do nothing. He'd been living on Belle Terre all her life and she'd barely known he was there. Why was it starting to bother her now? So he had kissed her. So what? Forget it.

The problem was that she couldn't forget it. It was like an itch coming from an undetermined source. She didn't know where to scratch to relieve herself of the memory. She shouldn't have liked the kiss. But she had. She couldn't leave the memory of it alone until she had figured out why every time she thought about his kiss, she got a sexual thrill.

"I can ring Mr. Gilbreath now."

Schyler jumped. "Oh. Oh, thank you."

"Gilbreath."

"Mr. Gilbreath? This is Schyler Crandall returning your call."

The tonal quality changed drastically. It went from brusque to ingratiating in a heartbeat. "Well, Miss Crandall, a pleasure to talk to you. A real pleasure. Thank you for calling me back."

"Do I know you?"

He laughed at her straightforwardness. "I've got you at a disadvantage. I've heard so much about you I feel like I know you."

"You're with the bank?"

"President."

"Congratulations."

Either her sarcasm was lost on him or he chose to ignore it. "Cotton and I do a lot of business together. He told me you've been living in London."

"That's right."

"How is he?"

She related the latest doctor's report. "All we can do at this point is wait."

He made a commiserating sound. "Things could be worse."

"Yes, much worse." The conversation lagged. Schyler was anxious to get off the phone and take an aspirin for her nagging headache. "Thank you so much for calling, Mr. Gilbreath. I'm sure Cotton will appreciate your asking about him."

"This isn't strictly a courtesy call, Miss Crandall."

She could have told that by another sudden switch in his inflection. He no longer sounded like he was bending over backward to be cordial. "Oh?"

"I need to see you. Banking business."

"With me? Surely you're aware that my brother-in-law handles—"

"The financial affairs of Crandall Logging, certainly. But since this matter could directly affect Belle Terre, I thought I ought to consult you. As a favor."

More than a headache caused her brows to pull together and form a deep crevice. "What matter is that?"

"An outstanding loan. But look, I think we should discuss this in person."

She didn't like him. Instinctively she knew that. His deference was phony. She wanted nothing more than to tell him to go to hell. Well, not quite. What she wanted most was to undress, take a tepid shower, and lie on the cool sheets of her bed until supper, maybe nap off her headache. But all thoughts of relaxing were tabled. "I'm on my way."

"But I haven't got time this—"

"Make time."

An hour later Schyler entered the fake pink marble foyer of the Delta National Bank. The building was new to her and now took up a whole block right downtown where the five-and-dime had once been. It was a shame that a vault now stood in the spot where the soda fountain had been, that credit applications were dispensed instead of lemon Cokes and triple-decker club sandwiches. She was swamped with homesickness for the old bank lobby that had been paneled in dark wood and filled with subdued furnishings. One could almost smell the currency.

In her opinion this stark, modern lobby was hideous. It was as sterile as an operating room, and as clinical. It had no character or personality. Islands of chrome chairs with stiff mauve cushions floated on a carpet of sea green. Cotton had often said that no chair was worth its salt unless the wood creaked a little when you planted your butt in it. Schyler was of the same mind.

She was led to one of these chairs by a smiling receptionist who was a stranger to her. After situating herself, she glanced around and spotted a few familiar faces. They smiled at her from glass cubicle offices and tellers' windows. She drew encouragement from each familiar face. The words "Belle Terre" and "outstanding loan" kept circling in her head like buzzards waiting for helpless prey to succumb.

"Ms. Crandall, please come this way."

She was led across the lobby and into one of the gold fishbowl offices, this one occupied by Mr. Dale Gilbreath, president of Delta National Bank. He smiled unctuously as they shook hands.

"Miss Crandall, you were lucky I was able to work you in. Sit down, please. Coffee?"

"No thank you."

He bobbed his head to the receptionist and she withdrew. He took a seat behind his desk in the reclining chair and linked his hands over his stomach. "It's a pleasure to finally meet you."

She wasn't about to lie and say, "Likewise." She replied with a cool, "Thank you." Her intuition had proven right. She despised him on sight. He was going to bring bad tidings, cause her trouble.

He assessed her for a moment longer than was flattering. It verged on being insulting. "Well, what do you think of our new bank?"

"Impressive." It had made an impression on her, all right. She didn't feel inclined to expound.

"It is, isn't it? We're proud of it. It's about time downtown Heaven got a facelift, don't you think?"

"I'm sentimental."

"Meaning?"

The man didn't know when to quit. "Meaning that I liked downtown the way it was."

His smile deflated and his reclining chair bounced to an

upright position. "What a surprising attitude for a modern woman like you."

"I confess to having an old-fashioned streak."

"Yes, well, there's something to be said for antiquity, but I always think there's room for improvement."

Schyler was savvy enough to know when she was being baited. Rather than enter into a difference of opinion with a man she didn't know and whose opinion was of absolutely no interest to her, she declined his subtle invitation to spar by picking a nonexistent piece of lint off her hem.

Gilbreath pulled on a pair of eyeglasses and opened a folder lying on the desk. "I regret having to call you, Miss Crandall." Intimidatingly, he glanced up at her over the rim of the glasses. She met him eyeball to eyeball over the glossy surface of the desk and didn't even blink until he looked down to refer to the contents of the folder again. "But it's my responsibility to protect the interest of the bank, no matter how unpleasant that responsibility might sometimes be."

"Why don't you get to the point? No matter how unpleasant."

"Very well," he said briskly. "I wondered if Cotton's unforeseen illness would have any bearing on the payout of the loan I extended him."

Buying time, Schyler recrossed her legs. She tried to maintain her composure, though any time a shadow fell on Belle Terre, she got a sick, sinking sensation in the pit of her stomach. "I don't have any knowledge of the loan. Exactly what were the specified terms?"

He angled his reclining chair back once again. "We call it a balloon note. In this case, Cotton borrowed three hundred thousand dollars a year ago. We set it up for him to make quarterly interest payments. All were made on time."

"Then I fail to see the problem."

Leaning his forearms on the desk, he gazed at her with the earnestness of a funeral director. "The potential problem, and I stress potential, is that the balance of the note, in addition to the final interest payment, comes due on the fifteenth of next month."

"I'm sure my father is aware of that and has the money set aside. I can authorize a transference of funds, if that's what you want."

His sympathetic smile did nothing to calm her jittery stomach. "I wish it were that easy," he said, making a helpless gesture. "Cotton's personal account won't cover the amount of the loan. Not even the interest."

"I see."

"Nor will the Crandall Logging account."

"The bank couldn't be that much at risk. I'm sure a loan of that size was collateralized."

"It was." She held her breath, but she knew what was coming. "He put up Belle Terre as collateral."

She saw stars, as though she'd been struck in the head. "How much of it?"

"The house and a sizable amount of the acreage."

"That's ridiculous! The house alone is worth far more than three hundred thousand. My father would never have agreed to that."

Again Gilbreath made that helpless little gesture, a lifting of his pale hands and a shrug of his shoulders. "At the time he applied for the loan, he had no choice. He was suffering a severe cash flow problem. Those were the best terms I could give him. He did what he had to do. I did what I had to do."

"Usury?"

He made a wry face. "Please, Miss Crandall. I want to make every effort to keep this friendly."

"We're not friends. I seriously doubt we'll ever be friends." She stood up and looked down at him. "Rest assured, I'll see that the loan is paid off in time."

Coming to his feet, he frowned. "I don't blame you for getting upset. You don't need any more bad news. But you can't blame me for being worried in light of Cotton's illness and the shutdown of the business. That could go on indefinitely."

"There is no cause for alarm on either account," she said, wishing such were the case. "The loan will be paid off in time."

Her smile was as fraudulent as the watercolor painting

hanging on the wall behind his desk. Schyler wasn't deceived by either. "It would be a tragedy if we had to foreclose."

"Never." Her smile was no more genuine than his. "And you can engrave that on one of those phony pink pillars in your tacky lobby. Good-bye, Mr. Gilbreath."

Chapter Sixteen

What Dale Gilbreath had told Schyler was the dismal truth. She spent the remainder of the afternoon in Cotton's study at Belle Terre, checking the balances in all his bank accounts. He had virtually no cash at his disposal, not anywhere close to three hundred thousand dollars.

She was staring down at the alarmingly low total at the end of the adding machine tape, when Ken breezed in. "Drinks before dinner now being served on the veranda."

During the first few days following the pit bull fight, Ken had been sullen and crotchety. Recently, he'd had a turnaround and had gone out of his way to be jocular. That jocularity grated on her now like a pumice stone.

"Ken, I need to talk to you." She tossed down the pencil she'd been using and linked her hands together over the desktop. "Why did you cease operation of Crandall Logging when Daddy had his heart attack?"

Ken's wide grin faltered and showed signs of deterioration in the corners, but he managed to hold it intact. "Who told you that?"

"What difference does it make who told me? I would have found out sooner or later. Why, Ken?"

"What brought this on?"

She sighed in resignation. "A phone call from Mr. Gilbreath at Delta National Bank."

"That asshole. He had no right to—"

"He *did* have a right, Ken. We owe his bank a lot of money. And *I* have a right to know what the hell is going on around here, which I'm waiting for you to tell me."

"Well, I have a right to know what you've been up to lately, too." For one heart-stopping moment she thought Ken had found out about her visit to Cash's house on the bayou, possibly even about the kiss. It was almost a relief when he said, "The big news around town is that somebody shot up Jigger Flynn's kennel and killed three of his dogs. He's foaming at the mouth to find out who did it." His eyes narrowed on her. "You wouldn't know anything about that, would you?"

"When did it happen?" she asked, stalling.

"Sunday night."

"I went to bed early, remember?"

He sat on the corner of the desk and carefully gauged her facial expression. "Yeah, I remember." He picked up a brass paperweight and shifted it from hand to hand. "According to Jigger, a pickup truck came barreling down the road like a bat outta hell and picked up the fellow who shot his dogs. He says he fired at the truck with his pistol and hit it on the passenger side." He crossed his arms over his thigh and leaned down low, whispering, "Now guess whose truck is sporting a fresh bullet hole?"

"Whose?"

"Cash Boudreaux's."

"Is Mr. Boudreaux responding to any allegations that he was responsible?"

"Yeah, he's responding. He says he got shot at while fleeing a married man's bedroom, or more specifically, fleeing a married man's wife inside the bedroom."

"Nobody can dispute that."

Ken flashed her a grin. "Not the probability of it anyway. But you know what I think?" Stubbornly and calmly she waited him out. He lowered his voice another decibel. "I think you killed those dogs and that Boudreaux helped you. What I'm wondering is what kind of currency you exchanged, 'cause that Cajun doesn't do anything for nothing."

She came out of her chair like a shot and, feeling trapped, circled the end of the desk. "You're changing the subject."

He grabbed her wrist. All pretense disappeared. His face had turned ugly. "I thought I told you to steer clear of him, Schyler."

She pulled her wrist free. "And I told you that I don't need a keeper. But apparently you do, or my father's business wouldn't be in the shambles it's in."

"It's my business, too."

"Then why did you shut it down?"

"For godsake, what is all the shouting about?" Tricia entered the room, exuding Shalimar and petulance in equal strengths. "Kindly keep your voices down." She closed the door behind her. "Mrs. Graves doesn't talk much around here, but she's probably a blabbermouth when it comes to spreading gossip. Now, what's going on?"

"Nothing you need to concern yourself about," Ken snapped.

"It is something she should concern herself about," Schyler contradicted. "She lives here. She should know that Belle Terre is in jeopardy."

Tricia looked from one to the other. "What in the world are y'all talking about?" She sipped at her highball while Schyler summarized for them her conversation with Gilbreath.

Ken spat the banker's name. "I might have known he'd get you all wound up. He's a persnickety old Scrooge. Only sees the bottom line. Probably a fag, too."

"I don't care if he sleeps with sheep," Schyler declared angrily, "the facts are the same. We have a note coming due and no way that I can see to pay it."

"I'll take care of it," he grumbled.

"How, Ken, how?" Schyler went around the desk again and sat down. Shuffling through the accounts she had just gone over, she raised her hands in surrender and said, "We're broke."

"Broke!" Tricia said on an incredulous laugh. "That's impossible."

"Daddy used Belle Terre to cover a three-hundred-thousand-dollar loan. I can't imagine him doing it, but he did."

"He was desperate," Ken said. "I thought it was foolish myself at the time, but he wouldn't listen to my advice. Not that he ever does."

Schyler jumped to Cotton's defense. "I'm sure he did what he thought was necessary. He couldn't foresee that he would have a heart attack or that you'd close the doors on the business the minute he did."

"You keep waving that at me like a red flag. Well, you finally succeeded in getting me angry, if that's what you're after."

"It isn't. We can't afford the luxury of getting angry at each other. I want an explanation."

Ken gnawed on the inside of his cheek. He shoved his hands into the pockets of his slacks and hunched his shoulders defensively. "It's simple economics. We were losing more money than we were making. No contracts were coming in, but Cotton was paying the regulars the same wages he always had. He was paying the independents a premium price on timber, too."

"He wouldn't cut back on them."

"And that's probably why Crandall Logging is in the shape it's in," Ken said heatedly. "I thought it was better to quit while we were ahead instead of pouring good money after bad."

Ken's explanation didn't quite gel, but Schyler was in no position to dispute it. Cotton had always been a shrewd businessman. It was unlike him to let things get so far beyond his control. Unless he was getting senile, which also seemed an absurd possibility. In any case, the problem was urgent. Solving it had to take precedence over finding its source.

"How are we going to pay this note? We've got until the fifteenth of next month to come up with the cash."

Tricia dropped into a chair and nonchalantly examined her fingernails. Ken moved to a window and nervously jangled the change in his pants pocket. "You could have brought me one of those," he said to his wife, nodding down at her drink.

"When you start being an attentive husband, I'll be an attentive wife."

If they launched into one of their verbal skirmishes, Schyler thought she would scream. She was spared. Ken turned to face her and said, "You and Tricia have money from your mother's legacy."

"Forget it," Tricia said. "I'm not risking my inheritance to get Crandall Logging out of hock or to save Belle Terre. I'd sell it first."

"Don't even say such a thing!" Schyler wanted to slap her. Tricia had never cared for the property the way Schyler did. Her nonchalance now pointed up just how uncaring she was.

But Tricia was right in one respect. Schyler couldn't use her mother's legacy to pay off this note. If Cotton died, she would need that money to maintain Belle Terre in the future.

"What about that guy in London?"

Schyler looked at Ken. "Mark? What about him?"

"He's rich, isn't he?"

"I can't ask Mark for the money."

"How come? You're sleeping with him, aren't you?"

Ignoring the slur, Schyler shook her head adamantly. "Out of the question. I can't and won't ask Mark for the money."

"Then what do you propose to do?"

She resented his condescending tone. "I propose to re-open Crandall Logging and to earn the money to pay off the loan."

"Excuse me?"

"You heard me, Ken."

"You can't do that."

Tricia snickered. "That would be right down her alley, honey, going to that dirty old landing every day. Mama used to have to drag her away from there."

"I forbid it," Ken shouted angrily.

Only minutes ago, Schyler couldn't see a way out of this unexpected dilemma. Now the solution was brimming crystal clear in her mind. The decision was made; it felt right. She wanted to do this for her father. She needed to do it for her own peace of mind.

"You can't forbid me to do anything, Ken," she said tightly. "Tomorrow I want the business records of the last several years brought to the office at the landing. Everything. Contracts, payroll accounts, tax returns, expense receipts, everything."

"Cotton will hear about this," Ken ground out.

Schyler aimed an accusing finger at him. "You're damn right he will. I want to know why Crandall Logging went from a productive business to a nonrevenue-producing company on the brink of ruin in just six short years."

"I guess you think it's my fault. That the company's decline started the day I came aboard."

"Please, Ken, don't be childish," she said wearily. "I'm not blaming anybody."

"Sounds like it to me," Tricia said in unusual defense of her husband.

"It's the economy's fault," Ken said. "You don't understand the economy around here anymore, Schyler. Things have changed."

"Then maybe we should change with them."

"We're up against the big guys. Weyerhauser, Georgia Pacific, huge conglomerates like that."

"There's still a place in the market for small operations like us. Don't try to tell me otherwise."

Ken plowed his fingers through his hair in frustration. "Do you have any idea how complicated running a business like this is?"

"I'm sure I'll find out."

"You're going to make me look like a damn fool. While Cotton's indisposed, Crandall Logging is my responsibility!" he shouted.

"It was," Schyler replied coolly, coming to her feet. "If you wanted to wear the pants in the family, you should have put them on the day Daddy went to the hospital."

She left the room. Ken, fuming, watched her go, then turned on his wife, who was still indolently curled up in the chair sipping her drink. She gave a disdainful shrug toward the entire situation and drained her glass.

Chapter Seventeen

"Schyler?"

"Hmm?"

"What are you doing out here?"

"Thinking."

Hesitantly, Ken sat down beside her in the porch swing. It was after eleven o'clock. Tricia was indoors watching Johnny Carson.

"I guess I owe you an apology," Ken said, staring beyond the veranda at the dark lawn.

Schyler's breasts rose and fell with a deep breath. "I don't want your apology, Ken. I want your help." She turned her head and looked at him. "I need to do this. Don't fight me. Help me."

He reached for her hand and covered it with his. "I will. You know I will. I blew my top, that's all. It's not every day a woman just moves in and takes over, you know."

"Is that what you think I'm doing? I don't intend to usurp your authority."

"That's how it'll look to folks."

"I'll make sure it doesn't."

He traced the delicate bones in the back of her hand with his fingertip. "Why do you feel like you have to do this?"

"I don't really have a choice, do I? That note has to be paid or we'll lose Belle Terre. You were right about Gilbreath. He is an asshole and would show no mercy if it came down to foreclosing."

"I'm sure we could figure out another way to come up with the cash if we put our minds to it."

"Probably. But time is so short, I can't go exploring. I don't want to borrow money to cancel this loan. That would only dig us in deeper and postpone the inevitable. And I don't want to liquidate bits and pieces of Belle Terre. The very thought of parting with one saucer of the china collection, or selling one acre of land makes me shudder. Besides what that would mean to us personally, I have to think about the sharecroppers. I can't sell their homes out from under them."

"You can't burden yourself with everybody's problems."

She smiled at him to relax the mood. "I need something to do. I'm going stir crazy around here between visits to the hospital."

He pressed her hand affectionately. "I know you're accustomed to staying busy, but I'm afraid you're biting off more than you can chew."

"Then if I fall on my face, or make a bigger mess of things, you'll have the supreme satisfaction of saying, 'I told you so.'"

"This is no joking matter, Schyler."

"I know," she said softly, ducking her head.

"I don't think Cotton will find it funny either."

"I'm sure he won't."

Cotton. He was her main motivation. He loved Belle Terre more than he loved anything. He had come to it an outsider and made it his. If Schyler was successful in saving it, maybe his love and affection for her would be restored. He might forgive her for whatever transgression she had unwittingly committed. Their relationship would revert to the loving one it had been before she left for London. As soon as possible, she wanted to present him with the canceled note and watch the love and gratitude well in his eyes. She didn't want that for her sake, but for his.

"You're an exciting woman, Schyler." Her head snapped around at Ken's soft proclamation. It so closely echoed what Cash had said to her only a few nights before. Unlike Cash, however, Ken was smiling gently. "You're a pain in the ass sometimes, but exciting."

"Thank you. I think."

He inched closer, until his thigh was pressing against hers on the bench. The swing rocked slowly. "What I mean is, you're hardheaded. Gutsy. That determination is aggravating as hell. But it's the thing that makes you so damn appealing, too." He reached out and stroked her cheek with a feather-light touch. "Remember all those hours we spent picketing this or that? Lambasting or advocating one cause or another."

"We were a pair of crusaders, weren't we?"

He shook his head in denial. "You were the crusader. I only tagged along so I could be with you."

"That's not true. You were every bit as strong in your convictions as I was. You just don't remember."

"Maybe," he conceded doubtfully.

Honestly, she doubted it, too. But she didn't want to. She wanted to believe that he was uncompromising, that his integrity had been as steadfast as the Rock of Gibraltar. "I've really stuck my neck out this time, Ken. I need your strength and support."

He lightly closed his fingers around her neck. "You make me feel strong." His eyes came to rest on hers. "I made a bad choice. I married the wrong woman, Schyler."

"Don't, Ken."

"Listen to me." Schyler heard the anxiety in his voice, felt it in his touch. He leaned closer. "I regret that indiscretion with Tricia every day of my life. She's not you. She's petty and shallow. Superficial."

"Stop there, Ken."

"No. I want you to hear this. She doesn't even come close to being you. She's nice to look at, she's okay in bed, but she's selfish. She doesn't have your spirit and fire, your zest for living and loving."

Schyler thrilled to the words, but squeezed her eyes shut as though to block them out. "Don't say anything more. Please. I can't stay here if you—"

"Jesus, don't leave. I need you so much."

Closing the short distance between them, he kissed her with passion and desperation. Her initial reaction was to stiffen woodenly, but gradually she relaxed. Her mouth accepted his probing tongue. His hand slid from her neck to her breast. He kneaded it through her clothes. He lifted his lips from hers and, whispering her name endearingly, covered her face with quick, light kisses. She submitted until he tried to reclaim her lips. Then she pushed him away and left the swing.

Encircling the corner column with her arms, she rested her cheek against the cool, fluted wood. "We might regret the way things turned out between us, Ken, but there's no going back. Don't touch me like that ever again."

She heard the chains of the swing squeak as he left it. He moved up behind her and placed his hands on her waist, murmuring her name in her hair. She spun around to face him. "Don't! I mean it."

The light coming through the windows was sufficient for him to see the resolve on her face and in her eyes, which held his without flinching. Disappointment, then anger, caused his lips to shrink into a tight, narrow line. He stormed across the veranda and down the steps. Getting into his car, he gunned it to life and sped off. Schyler watched until the red brake lights disappeared at the bend in the lane.

She didn't realize how exhausted she was until she tried to move away from the column. She had to push herself away from its support. Sluggishly she went inside and climbed the stairs to her bedroom. Once ready for bed, she settled against the pillows and pulled the telephone onto her lap. She would beat Mark's alarm clock by an hour or so, but that couldn't be helped. She needed to talk to him now.

"Hi, it's me," she said when the transatlantic call had gone through to the flat she shared with Mark Houghton.

"Schyler? God, what time is it?"

"Here or there?" She laughed, envisioning his blond hair sticking up all around his head and his clumsy, sleepy groping for the bedside clock.

"Just a sec. Let me light a cigarette."

"You promised you were going to quit while I was away."

"I lied." In under a minute he was back. "You don't have bad news I hope."

"About Daddy, no. He's stable."

"That's wonderful."

"But I won't be coming home anytime soon."

"That's not so wonderful."

"He's got to have bypass surgery." She explained Cotton's prognosis. "I can't leave until he's completely out of danger."

"I understand, but I miss you. At home and in the gallery. Some of our customers won't deal with anybody but you. If I don't produce you soon, I'm afraid they'll lock me in the Tower."

She had first met Mark when he hired her to work as his assistant in his antique gallery. He'd not only been her employer, but also her teacher. She had been an astute pupil with a natural eye and excellent taste. Before long, she knew as much or more about their inventory as he. That's why his flattery was particularly gratifying, if not entirely truthful.

"I know several high-ticket customers who trample over me to get to you." Toying with the coiled telephone cord, she collected her thoughts. "I'll be overseeing the family business until Cotton gets better." She threw out that piece of information like a baited fishing line.

He whistled. "Quite an undertaking. What about Ken?"

Mark knew the entire story, everything. "He resented my interference and objected to the idea at first, but I think he'll come around once he gets used to it."

"You can handle him and the work load."

"Can I?"

"I don't doubt it for a minute."

"Don't be so hasty. There's more. A bank loan is coming due and the coffers are empty."

There was a significant pause. Then, "How much do you need?"

"I wasn't asking."

"But I'm offering."

"No, Mark."

"Schyler, you know that anything I have is yours. Don't

be proud. How much? I'll have my attorney draft a check in the morning."

"No, Mark."

"Please let me help you."

"No. I need to do this on my own."

I need to earn the right to live at Belle Terre is what she meant. She hadn't realized it until that very second.

Belle Terre was hers by chance. If another child had been born hours ahead of her, a child who filled the criteria just as well as she, Macy and Cotton Crandall would have been given that baby instead of her. When Cotton died, she and Tricia would inherit Belle Terre. Tricia would consider it her due.

But not Schyler. No bloodlines linked her to the house and land. She would have to earn it. Pressed, she couldn't have explained to anyone, not even to herself, why she felt working for it was necessary. It was simply a compulsion she had no choice but to act upon.

"Can you do without me for a while longer, Mark?"

He sighed with forebearance. "What choice do you leave me?"

"None, I'm afraid."

"So there's nothing more to discuss."

"I need a hug," Schyler said in a frightened, little girl's voice. "Mark, what the hell do I know about managing a logging company?"

He laughed. "About as much as you knew about antiques before you came to work for me. You're a fast learner."

"In the case of the antiques, I had an excellent teacher."

His voice grew husky with remembrance of good times shared. "I love you, babe."

"I love you, too."

She extended the conversation as long as it was economically feasible, telling him about Jigger Flynn and the pit bulls, which he found difficult to believe. "You mean this young woman, Gayla, is virtually enslaved? I thought the South was decadent only in Tennessee Williams plays and William Faulkner novels."

"Don't judge us all by Jigger Flynn."

He expressed concern for her safety. That's when she mentioned Cash. "I've known him forever. I mean, I've known about him forever. He's somebody who has always been lurking in the background."

"Are you sure you can trust him? He sounds almost as dangerous as this Flynn character."

She plucked at the embroidery on the hem of the sheet. "I guess he's trustworthy, in his own fashion."

Trustworthy? Perhaps. He was certainly dangerous. Dangerous to be alone with if you were a woman emotionally overwrought and temporarily unsure of yourself, when you deliberately compared his kiss to the former lover's and discovered that the former lover's took a distant second place.

Out of sheer curiosity, she had let her lips respond to Ken's kiss to see what would happen. And nothing did. But every time she even recalled Cash's kiss, her heart started beating fast, her nipples tightened, and her insides quivered.

She thought about telling Mark. He was adult about these things. He wasn't judgmental. He would understand. Nevertheless, she changed her mind. She couldn't put into words exactly how she felt about Cash's kiss.

"Schyler?"

"I'm still here, but I've got to hang up. Here I am on the brink of dispossession and I'm running up an astronomical phone bill."

"Call collect next time."

"I apologize for calling so early. Try to go back to sleep."

"Hell, it's time to get up now."

"Sorry."

"I'm not. Call again whenever you need to talk. Whenever you need anything."

"I will."

"Promise?"

"Promise."

Hanging up, she wished all the relationships in her life were as open and uncomplicated as the one she shared with Mark. She switched out the lamp and lay staring at the constantly shifting patterns of moonlight and shadow on the ceiling.

First thing in the morning, she would put out a notice that Crandall Logging was back in operation. The loggers who wanted to work would be immediately reinstated. She would call the independent loggers and tell them that she was actively buying timber. She could get their names from the files. Then the markets would have to be analyzed and contacted. Sales calls would have to be made.

So much to do.

So much to think about . . . namely that Ken's kiss, for all its passion, hadn't disturbed her nearly as much as Cash Boudreaux's.

Chapter Eighteen

"Hey, boy!"

Every muscle in Jimmy Don Davison's athletic body tensed with the sudden realization that he was the only one left in the shower room. That was a dreadful mistake. He lifted his head out of the sputtering stream of lukewarm water and looked toward the man who had addressed him. "You talkin' to me?"

The hulking, muscular man bore a remarkable resemblance to Mr. Clean. He was indolently propped against the damp tile wall. A towel dangled from his extended right hand. "None other, sweetheart."

Jimmy Don ignored the endearment and cranked the rusty handles of the faucet to cut off the shower. He sluiced water off his skin, aware of being watched as his hands skimmed over the muscles he kept supple and strong by daily workouts in the prison yard. He reached for the towel. Razz snatched it out of reach at the last second. After several attempts to take it from the other man, who childishly withheld it, Jimmy Don managed to catch hold. He immediately wrapped it around his waist and tucked the end inside. Without letting his nervousness show, he quickly scanned the shower room. As he had feared, he and Razz were alone.

"Wha'cha looking for, boy? A guard? Don't bother. I brought him a new porno magazine. He's in the crapper happily jacking off." His ribald laughter echoed in the empty, tile chamber.

" 'Xcuse me, Razz. I'm busy."

Jimmy Don brushed past the other inmate, but Razz's meaty fist wrapped around his bicep and stopped him. The former all-star football player was in excellent physical condition. On the running track, he could beat Razz by a mile and not even get winded. Here, however, he was far outsized. The man, whose skin was as pink and smooth as a baby's bottom, outweighed him by nearly a hundred pounds and was as strong as an ox. While Jimmy Don's muscles were kept well honed and sinewy, Razz worked at pumping his up to abnormal proportions. He shaved and oiled his head and body. He was a brute.

Unctuously, he crooned, "What's your hurry, sweetheart?"

"Leave me alone."

For a moment Razz's smile faded and his piggish eyes bore into Jimmy Don's handsome face. Then the nasty smile reappeared. He playfully punched Jimmy Don's arm. "It'd be real stupid of a niggah boy to get Razz mad, now wouldn't it?" He trailed a finger over Jimmy Don's beautifully sculpted chest. " 'Specially since I know what I know."

Jimmy Don shifted away from Razz's touch but said nothing, nor did his face reveal the murderous hate and revulsion he felt. Early enough he had learned the unwritten law of the prison, which was as brutal as the law of the jungle. Only the fittest survived. To survive, one did what was necessary. One found oneself being submitted to unspeakable cruelty by his fellow prisoners, but one stoically withstood the abuse if one wanted to live to get out.

And he did want to get out—just long enough to finish what he had to do. After that, he didn't care what happened to him in this lifetime or in the one hereafter for that matter. Once his scores were settled, the devil could have him.

"Ain't you the least bit curious 'bout this juicy secret I've got concernin' you?" Razz scraped Jimmy Don's nipple with his thumbnail. The muscles surrounding it leaped reflexively, but Jimmy Don's face didn't even flinch. Such molestation was a common occurrence. He had learned to stomach it because to resist was as good as a death sentence according to those in the cell block.

The electric chair was humane compared to what could happen to you at the hands of the inmates, those who governed the prison. Razz was one of them. He was a lifer; the prison was his dukedom. He exercised despotic control over other prisoners and many of the guards. Only the highest administrative officials were ignorant of, or indifferent to, the power Razz and the men like him wielded. Terror was the tactic they used.

"Ask me nice and I'll tell you what I know," Razz taunted.

"What you know ain't worth shit."

Jimmy Don was quick. He could break the hundred in ten seconds. But he hadn't learned to fight in alleys. Razz had. Before Jimmy Don could react, Razz had his hand under the towel and was squeezing Jimmy Don's testicles in a fist as strong as a vise.

"You sure?" He twisted his hand. Jimmy Don came up on his toes. "Ask me nice to tell you," Razz panted close to Jimmy Don's face. Grinning, he applied even more pressure to his fingers. Jimmy Don winced. "Ask me nice or I'll tear 'em off."

"Please. Please tell me." Jimmy Don hated himself for capitulating, but he didn't want to die, and he didn't want to leave there maimed. "Please."

"That's more like it." Razz gradually relaxed his hand, but he didn't remove it. He stepped closer and leaned down to impart his secret. "You're coming up for parole, boy. Soon. Real soon."

Jimmy Don had thought his heart was dead. It wasn't. It sparked involuntarily. His breath rushed in and out. He blinked repeatedly. "You bullshittin' me?"

"Would I do that?" Razz asked, looking wounded.

Hell yes, he would. "How do you know?"

"A little birdie told me." Razz pulled a sad face. "I knew you'd be real glad to hear it, but that piece of news makes me real sad. I kinda like havin' pretty black boys like you around." His hand squeezed Jimmy Don again. This time it was a caress.

Jimmy Don batted Razz's groping hand aside. "Keep your hands off me, you son of a bitchin' fag."

He was lifted bodily and thrown up hard against the shower wall. His cheekbone caught it. The pain was immense. One arm was twisted up behind him. Razz shoved his hand up between his shoulder blades and Jimmy Don cried out in pain in spite of his determination never to show it.

"The only thing that keeps me from cracking your face against this wall like a pecan is that I hate to spoil something so pretty," Razz hissed.

Jimmy Don gouged him in the gut with his elbow. Razz grunted, but his grip on Jimmy Don didn't lessen one degree. He sandwiched the younger man between his massive body and the wall and pressed his lips against Jimmy Don's ear. His voice was sibilant and sinister.

"You'd better be nice to me, sweetheart. You'll do what Razz says when Razz says it, or I'll see that your chances for parole go down the shit hole. You got that? I ain't got much time to enjoy you, but while you're here, you're mine, understand?"

Jimmy Don nodded. Fighting Razz was a waste of energy and time. Fighting only got you hurt and prolonged the inevitable. In this case fighting could mean losing his chance for parole.

Number twenty-one, the Heathen of Heaven, heard Razz's zipper being opened. He felt brutal hands on his flesh. For what was coming, he braced himself, mentally as well as physically.

He could endure it. He *would* endure it. He would endure anything. He had to get out. He lived for the day he would get revenge on Jigger Flynn and his whore, Gayla Frances.

Chapter Nineteen

"Did you do it?"

"Do what?" Cash asked around the sharp fingernail that was seductively rimming his lips. Rhoda Gilbreath smiled at him. It was as bloodthirsty a smile as he'd ever seen. She needed only fangs to make the picture complete.

"Did you kill Jigger Flynn's pit bull terriers?"

"They're not really terriers, you know. That's a misnomer."

"Quit playing word games. Did you?"

"No."

Cash pushed her aside and moved further into the room. She had barely let him in through the back door of her house before molding herself against him. After only one kiss she had posed her question.

"That's what's going around."

"I can't help what's going around. I didn't shoot his dogs."

"Do you expect me to take your word for it?"

"Jigger did."

Rhoda's carefully made-up eyes registered surprise. "You've talked to Jigger?"

"Not more than an hour ago. Get me a beer."

Once she had gotten the can of beer from the kitchen refrigerator, she followed Cash into the formal living room. He plopped down on her finest sofa and propped his boots on the smoked glass coffee table. He sipped at the cold can of beer.

Rhoda sat down beside him. Avid curiosity eked from her like resin out of a pine tree. "Where?"

"Where what?"

"Where did Jigger confront you?"

"He didn't confront me. I was out on the edge of town and saw his pickup parked outside one of his beer joints. I stopped and went in."

"What did he do when he saw you?"

Cash shrugged nonchalantly. "He threw out some fairly strong accusations. I denied them, told him I would have to be nuts to kill off his dogs when they frequently won me money." He slurped at the beer while Rhoda sat hinging on every word. "He said he hadn't thought of it that way. Then he asked me where I got that bullet hole in the side of my truck."

"Where *did* you get it?"

"Some goddamn fool up in Allen Parish got it into his head that I'm humping his wife."

"Are you?"

His grin neither admitted nor denied. He enjoyed tormenting Rhoda. It was rotten of him, granted, but no more rotten than she was for being an unfaithful wife. Cash never seduced a loving wife away from her husband. He took to bed only those he knew were on the make. Rhoda Gilbreath had hit on him one night at the country club. He was hardly a regular with that crowd and had only been there at a divorcée's invitation.

During a break in the penny-ante poker tournament, the divorcée went into the ladies' room. Cash went outside to smoke. Rhoda Gilbreath followed him.

"What do you think of the poker party?" she had asked.

"Boring."

"What do you think of these?" She whipped her sweater over her head and stood before him topless.

While inhaling deeply on his cigarette, he gave her bra-less breasts a casual once-over. "The best money can buy."

She slapped him. He slapped her back. She coolly re-placed her sweater. Holding his hazel gaze, she said, "To-morrow afternoon, three o'clock, the Evangeline Motel."

He put his index and middle fingers together at his tem-ple and gave her a quick and mocking salute. She went back inside. He finished his cigarette before rejoining the party.

The windows of room two eighteen of the Evangeline Motel steamed up the following afternoon. When Rhoda left, she felt bruised, battered, beautiful, and never better.

Since that afternoon, they had met in a variety of motels, but he liked coming to her house. He derived pleasure from violating the domicile she shared with Dale Gilbreath. He enjoyed putting his muddy boots on her expensive furni-ture. He could get by with mistreating her because she had more to lose than he did and both knew it.

She was attractive. When they split, she would find an-other lover, one who would appreciate her frosted blond hair and frosty blue eyes; one who would adore her im-plant-enhanced figure; one whose smile wasn't always tinged with contempt.

Rhoda's face was arresting, but there was a hard aspect to it that kept it from being pretty. There was a calculating glitter in her eyes that never went away, even in the throes of passion. Cash had detected it the night they met. That was part of her attraction. This woman couldn't be wounded too deeply. He never took up with a woman who wasn't tough enough to take the crap he dished out.

Rhoda was. He had her pegged correctly the instant she started sending him it-itches-and-I'd-like-you-to-scratch-it looks across the card table. Women like her castrated their husbands, making them feel inadequate to provide all they wanted in the bank and in the bedroom. They were socially rapacious, fanatical about their looks, money mad, and sexually dissatisfied. They were hungry, restless, selfish harpies. Rhoda Gilbreath led the pack. She deserved no respect.

She deserved no better than Cash Boudreaux.

He drained his beer and set the empty can on the coffee table. "Unless you've started drinking beer, don't forget to throw that away before Dale gets home."

She ran her finger down the placket of his shirt and dug beneath his belt in search of his navel. "Maybe I'll let him discover that I have a lover."

One of Cash's eyebrows rose skeptically. "Don't you imagine he already knows?"

"Probably." She flashed a teasing smile. "Maybe I'll let him worm it out of me who my lover is. That might be exciting. I'd like to see you square off with Dale the way you did with Jigger Flynn."

"Such a thing would never happen."

"Oh? Why not?"

"Because Jigger loved his dogs."

Her coy smile went as flat as a punctured soufflé. She glared at him coldly. "You son of a bitch. You'd better tread lightly with me. I haven't forgiven you for leaving me stranded the last time we met at that seedy motel."

He stacked his hands behind his head and rested it on the back of the sofa. "You can't threaten a man who has absolutely nothing to lose, Rhoda. I don't even have a good reputation at stake."

She angrily pondered his handsome profile for a moment, then laid her head on his chest in conciliation. "That's the hell of it. The more like a bastard you behave, the more attractive you are. I read all about your type in this months's *Cosmo*. They call it 'heel appeal.'" He barked a short laugh.

She plucked at the buttons of his shirt, undoing them one by one. "But you might have something to lose. If the Crandalls lose Belle Terre, you'll be evicted. I doubt if the next—"

He covered her roving hand with his, flattening it against his belly to keep it still. It was a sudden, reflexive move, lightning quick. "What the hell are you talking about? The Crandalls losing Belle Terre?"

She worked her hand free and started on the buttons again. "Dale said Cotton Crandall borrowed money from him last year. He's been making interest payments on it, but the principal is coming due. Dale was worried about it because Ken Howell shut down the business, so he met with that girl, the oldest one, what's her name?"

"Schyler."

"Whatever. Anyway, she didn't even know about the loan. He said she nearly had a caniption when she found out Cotton had used Belle Terre for collateral. Cool as a cucumber and real hoity-toity, you understand, but Dale said she went as pale as death. Right now, it looks like the bank might have to foreclose."

That was one of the reasons Cash had kept meeting Rhoda Gilbreath. Every now and then she supplied him with a tidbit of valuable information. Apparently Dale had no qualms about discussing confidential banking matters with his wife, who in turn had no hesitancy in sharing them with her lover.

Cash stared sightlessly at the ceiling. Rhoda's head moved over his chest, dropping light kisses on the thick carpet of hair. "What would the bank want with an old plantation house like Belle Terre?" he asked.

"Hmm? I don't know." She swirled her tongue around his nipple. "Sell it, I guess."

"Wonder what it would take to buy it?" he mused aloud.

Rhoda lifted her head and looked at him with amusement. "Why? You interested, Cash?"

He knotted his fingers in her hair, drew her mouth up to his, and kissed every single cunning thought out of her head. His tongue swept each malicious idea from her mind and left her thinking of only one thing. Her brain was too fertile a field to sow a single seed of suspicion in. The most farfetched speculation mustn't be given a chance to take root in Rhoda's conniving mind.

"Why don't you finish what you started?" He fished in the pocket of his jeans and tossed her the foil packet he was never without. No bastard kids for Cash Boudreaux. Never.

Holding his hot stare, Rhoda licked her lips. So adroit was she that she didn't even have to look down to unfasten his belt buckle and undo his zipper. She did it all by feel.

Palming his testicles, she lifted him free of his jeans, then lowered her face over his lap.

Cash's head fell back against the sofa again. He stared up through the crystal teardrops of the ostentatious chandelier overhead. He became entranced, not by the rhythmic movements of Rhoda's greedy mouth, but by the name that was chanted in his head like a call to vespers. *Belle Terre. Belle Terre . . .*

"Belle Terre," Cotton Crandall proudly pronounced. "It's a beautiful name for a beautiful house."

Monique Boudreaux smiled up at him, her eyes glowing. Cotton bent his tow head and kissed her lips softly. "You understand why I wanted it, why I married Macy?"

"I understand, Cotton."

Cash, his bare toes curling in the warm earth, angled his head back and watched his mother's smiling face turn sad, though she made sure Cotton couldn't see her smile fade. Cash had hoped that when they moved from New Orleans to this new town where the tall man with the white hair lived that his mother wouldn't be sad anymore. He had hoped that she wouldn't cry and lie listlessly on her bed in the afternoons until it was time to get up and go to work in the barroom where she served bottles of beer to rough, boisterous merchant marines.

She had always told him that one day the man she called Cotton would send for them. Then they would be happy. And she was—happier, anyway. The day she'd gotten that letter from Cotton, she'd squeezed Cash so hard he could barely breathe.

"Look, *mon cher,* do you know what these are? Tickets. Train tickets. See, didn't *maman* tell you? He wants us to come live with him in a wonderful place called Belle Terre." Bubbling and animated with emotion, she had covered Cash's face with eager, exuberant kisses.

Two days later, which was all it had taken to finalize their affairs and pack their meager belongings, they dressed in their best clothes and boarded the train. The ride hadn't lasted long enough for Cash. He had loved it. When they arrived at their destination, he had stood warily against the belly of the steam-belching engine, suspiciously eyeing the man his mother ran to.

She flung herself into his arms. He lifted her up and swung her around. Cash had never seen a man so tall or so strong. Monique threw back her head, laughing more musically than Cash had ever heard. Her dancing, dark curls had glistened iridescently in the sunlight.

She and the man kissed for so long that Cash thought his mother had forgotten him. The man's large hands moved over her, touching her in ways that she wouldn't let the customers of the barroom touch her. Many kisses later, she disengaged herself and eagerly gestured him forward. Taking reluctant baby steps, he moved toward the towering man. He smiled down at Cash and ruffled his hair.

"I don't think he remembers me."

"He was just a baby when you left, *mon cher,*" Monique said softly. Her eyes brimmed with shiny tears, but her mouth was wide and smiling. Cash's young heart lifted. His *maman* was happy. He had never seen her so happy. Their lives had taken a new direction. Things were going to be just as she had said—wonderful. They would no longer live down a dark, dingy hallway in a roach-infested apartment. They were going to live in a house in the country surrounded by grass and trees and fresh air. They were finally at Belle Terre.

But the house Cotton had driven them to wasn't quite as wonderful as Monique had expected. It was a small gray house sitting on the banks of a bayou that he called Laurent. The sunny atmosphere had turned stormy. Monique and Cotton had had a shouting match. Cash had been sent outside to play. He grudgingly obeyed but went no further away than the porch, still distrustful of this man he'd just met.

"It's a shack!" Monique said in a raised voice.

"It's sturdy. A family of moss harvesters used to live here, but it has stood vacant for years."

"It smells like the swamp."

"I can help you fix it up. See, I've already started. I added a bathroom."

Monique's voice had cracked. "You won't live here with us, will you?"

After a short pause, Cotton sighed. "No, I won't. But this is the best I can do."

Cotton had married a lady named Macy and Monique didn't like it. She yelled at him and called him names Cash had overheard in the barroom, but had been forbidden to repeat. She lapsed into her native "Frenglish" and spoke it with such heated emphasis that even her son, who was accustomed to hearing it, could barely translate.

As darkness fell, he gave up trying and concentrated on catching lightning bugs. His mother and Cotton went upstairs to the bedroom and stayed a long time. He fell asleep curled up on the rough board of the porch. When they finally came downstairs, they had their arms around each other's waists. They were smiling. The tall man bent down and touched Cash's cheek, then kissed Monique good-bye and left in his car.

They watched it disappear into the dark tunnel of trees. Monique draped her arm around Cash's narrow shoulders. "This is our home now, Cash." And if she didn't sound very happy about it, at least she sounded content.

Monique worked wonders on the house. In the months that followed, she turned it from an empty, dreary place into a home full of color and light. Flowers bloomed in window boxes. There were rugs on the floor and curtains on the windows. Just as she kept her secret heartache hidden, she disguised the shortcomings of the shanty.

It seemed they had lived there for a long time before Cotton finally gave in to Monique's pestering and walked them through the forest to see the plantation house.

The day would forever stand out in Cash's memory because, up to that point, he'd never seen a house so large. It was even grander than the estates on St. Charles Avenue that Monique had pointed out to him from the streetcar. He was awed by how clean and white Belle Terre was. In his wildest imagination, he couldn't have fathomed a house like Belle Terre.

Standing in the shadows of the trees, with moss serving as a screen, Monique rested her cheek against Cotton's chest as she stared at the large house. "Tell me about it. What does it look like on the inside?"

"Ah, it's beautiful, Monique. The halls have floors that are polished as smooth and shiny as mirrors. In the dining room, the walls are covered with yellow silk."

"Silk?" she had repeated in a reverent whisper. "I wish I could see that."

"That's impossible." Cotton set her away from him and sternly looked down into her face. "Never, Monique, do you understand? The house is Macy's domain. You and Cash can never go beyond this point right here."

Monique's glossy head bowed. "I understand, Cotton. I was just wishing I could see something so fine."

Cotton's face changed. He clasped her to him fiercely. He hugged her tight, lowering his head to cover hers. Cash gazed back at the house, wondering what it would hurt if he and his *maman* went inside to see the yellow silk walls and why they couldn't because of this Macy woman. It was probably because she was married to Cotton.

"Does she dress up for supper?" Monique wanted to know.

"Yes."

"In fancy clothes?"

"Sometimes." Monique inched closer to Cotton, as though to prevent him from seeing her plain cotton dress. He lovingly stroked her riotously curly hair. After a moment, he placed his finger beneath her chin and tilted it up. "Speaking of supper, didn't you tell me you had cooked jambalaya for me?"

She gave him a brilliant smile. *"Oui."*

"Then let's go back. I'm starving." They turned as one and headed back toward the bayou. "Cash, you comin', boy?" Cotton called back when he realized that Cash wasn't following them.

"I'm comin'."

But he remained where he was, transfixed by the beautiful house. Belle Terre . . .

* * *

Rhoda's mouth was avid. She was unaware that Cash's mind wasn't on her, only on the sensations she coaxed from his body. When he swelled to the fullest proportion, when everything went dark around him, when he squeezed his eyes shut and focused only on release, when he bared his teeth in a gripping climax, it wasn't Rhoda's name, but another, that rang in his head.

Chapter Twenty

Schyler's head dropped forward. Closing her eyes, she stretched the back of her neck, then rolled her head around her aching shoulders to work out the kinks of fatigue. Trying to refocus on the fine print of the contracts in front of her proved to be impossible. Her tired eyes refused. She left the desk and moved to the coffee maker across the room.

She poured a cup, more for the distraction and the exercise than because she wanted the coffee. She only took a few sips before setting down the mug and restlessly walking to the window.

She had hired a cleaning team to attack the landing office. They had washed the grime off the windows, but the view was no more encouraging through clean glass. She stared at the inactive platform. Even the railroad tracks were collecting dust. Trains avoided the spur because there was no Crandall timber to pick up and haul to market.

It had been three days since she had asked the newspaper to print a notice that Crandall Logging was open for business. She had anticipated having to turn independent loggers away, thinking she would be unable to buy timber from all of them until she had several contracts in hand. Her optimism had been misplaced.

As yet, not a single one had brought a rig loaded with logs to the landing. She had personally notified the former employees by telephone. None had come to reclaim his job. Without an inventory to sell, it would be senseless to contact the markets.

Dejectedly, she rubbed her bloodshot eyes. Last night she had stayed late at the hospital, hoping to catch Cotton awake. She had only had the opportunity to speak to him that one time. Then he had turned away, not caring that she had returned home to see him. Every time she thought about it, she despaired.

She suspected that he was faking the deep sleeps he lapsed into whenever she was at the hospital. Dr. Collins's prognosis was still guarded but basically favorable. Tricia and Ken had each engaged Cotton in brief conversations. But to Schyler, he still had nothing to say.

Her trips to the hospital were washouts. So was each working day. She spent hours in this office at the landing, waiting for something to happen. Nothing ever did. But she refused to give up. She had to succeed at this even if it meant hiring a forester, someone to coordinate everything, someone who talked the loggers' language, someone who could motivate them to work harder than they'd ever worked in their lives.

It meant rehiring Cash Boudreaux.

His name cropped up everywhere. Like the proverbial bad penny, it kept coming around. She'd heard it so many times in the last few days, she had begun hearing it in her sleep. It was the first thing that came to her mind when she woke up.

The first saw hand she had telephoned said, "You want me back at work? Great! Soon as I hear from Cash, I'll—"

"I'm afraid that Mr. Boudreaux isn't coming back."

"Whadaya mean, Cash ain't coming back? He's the main man."

"Not any longer."

"Oh, well, uh, see, I got this temporary job."

And it had gone downhill from there. By the time she had reached the fifth name on her list, word had apparently gotten around through the grapevine, which had it all over Ma Bell as far as transmitting information expeditiously went.

"Now, Cash, he—"

"I always work with Boudreaux. He—"

"Boudreaux ain't working for you no more? Well, ya see, he—"

She had called every logger Crandall Logging had ever had on its payroll but with no success. She got nowhere. Out of frustration, she had consulted Ken. "I'm beginning to think all Cash Boudreaux had to do was look at a tree and the damn thing would fall down. Exactly what did he do for Crandall Logging?"

"Generally caused trouble."

She curbed her impatience. "Specifically."

"Specifically he . . ." Ken made an encompassing gesture. "He more or less did everything."

"Do you mean at the sites, at the landing, in the office? What?"

"Hell, Schyler, I don't know. My office is downtown. I rarely go to the landing. I wasn't in on the day-to-day operation. Mine is a white-collar job."

"I realize that, Ken. Sorry to have bothered you. Thank you for the information and forgive the interruption." She turned to leave, uncomfortable now every time she was alone with Ken.

"Schyler?"

"Yes?"

Ken seemed to debate with himself before saying, "I overheard Cotton say. . ."

"Well?"

"I once overheard him say that Boudreaux has forgotten more about forestry than other foresters ever knew."

"Coming from Cotton, that's a staggering compliment," Schyler mused out loud.

"But he's a born troublemaker. He continually kept the loggers riled up over something. A day hardly went by that he and Cotton weren't at each other's throats. If you ask me, we're better off without him."

At the time, Schyler had thought they were better off without him, too. He was a disruptive force, especially to her. On principle, she would never approach him about working for her family again.

Staring out the window now, watching the rigs rusting in the garage when they should have been loaded to groaning capacity with timber, she admitted that she couldn't afford to avoid him any longer. The X's on her calendar were multiplying toward the deadline. No amount of principle was going to get Belle Terre out of hock. If getting the money meant humbling herself in front of Cash, then she would be humble. All other alternatives had been exhausted.

Before she lost her nerve, she locked the landing office door behind her. The mare was still tied to the tree across the wide yard, grazing on the short grass in the shade. Schyler mounted. She and Mark had ridden together occasionally, but not so regularly that she wouldn't be saddle sore tomorrow. She didn't care. The muscular discomfort would be well worth the thrill of riding over the acreage of Belle Terre as she had since she was old enough to sit in a saddle and duplicate Cotton's patient instructions.

She set out. The best place to start looking for Cash Boudreaux was at his house. If he wasn't there, she would leave a note. It was damned aggravating not to be able to call him on the phone. Sooner or later she would be forced to look into his gloating face.

Rather than take the roads, she cut across the open fields, wending her way through copses of trees. As the mare daintily picked her way through a particularly dense patch of forest, Schyler heard the whine of a chainsaw. Curious, she led the mare in that direction.

Cash saw her the moment she cleared the trees, but he didn't acknowledge her. He returned his attention to the chain saw he was applying to the branches of a felled tree. Piqued because he had so blatantly ignored her, Schyler drew the mare up but remained in the saddle, watching him.

He wasn't wearing a shirt. The skin of his back and chest was baked a deep brown. His face was beaded with sweat, despite the handkerchief he had tied around his forehead to act as a sweatband. His biceps bunched and strained as he held the saw steady while it ate its way through the pine and sent up a plume of acrid blue-white smoke. Sawdust was sprayed against his shins and over his boots.

When the last major branch had been severed, he cut the power and the saw's whine silenced. He took it in one hand. It weighted down his arm, stretching the skin so thin that Schyler could see each strong vein standing out. He raised his free arm and wiped perspiration off his brow.

"I should have you arrested for stealing timber off my property."

A white grin split his grimy, tanned face. "You should thank me for getting rid of this blowdown for you."

He set the chain saw on the ground beside the trunk of the tree. Over his jeans he was wearing the knee-length suede chaps that served to protect a saw hand's thighs from mishap, at least theoretically. From a wide leather belt around his waist hung a plastic bottle of chain saw propellent. There was a tape measure, used to record the length of felled trees, attached to a back belt loop and riding above his hip pocket. He had on work gloves, which, disconcertingly, only called more attention to his bare torso.

He sauntered to the mare's side and propped an elbow up on the pommel of the saddle. "You want damaging bugs eating away at your forest, Miss Schyler?"

To keep from looking at his chest and its sexy covering of damp, curly hair, she eyed the dismembered pine. "When was it blown down?"

"We had a bad storm about two months back. There's already larvae under the trunk. I checked."

"What are you going to do with it?"

"I'll bring a skidder down here tomorrow and drag it out." He glanced up at her again. "If I can borrow a skidder that is."

She was determined not to be provoked. "I need to talk to you."

"Not from up there, you don't."

"Pardon?"

"I don't look up to anybody. Get down."

She was about to protest when he peeled the yellow leather work gloves off his hands and dropped them to the ground. He extended his hands up to her. "I can manage," she said, swinging her right leg over the saddle and landing on her right foot. She lifted her left foot out of the stirrup and turned around. He was still standing close, allowing her no extra room.

"Funny-looking britches."

She had on black twill jodhpurs and smooth brown leather riding boots. "I left them behind when I moved to England."

"Yeah, from what I hear you left in a big hurry."

Difficult as it was to ignore that, she did. "I'm glad I did. Left the riding clothes, I mean. They came in handy today." A horsefly buzzed past her nose. She fanned it away. Cash didn't move a muscle. "They're a little hot though."

"You used to ride barebacked and bare-legged."

Schyler began to notice another kind of heat. It spilled through her system, making her veins run as hot as rivers of lava. "Mama made me stop doing that. She said it didn't look ladylike."

His eyes lowered to the delta of her thighs, then unhurriedly climbed back up. "Your mama was right. It looked downright dirty."

"How do you know what it looked like?"

"I used to see you."

"Where?"

"Everywhere. All the time. When you didn't know anybody was watching."

Schyler moved away from the horse, away from the man. Both seemed to emanate a musky, animalistic scent. The atmosphere was redolent with sexuality and she couldn't say why, except that the last time she had stood this close to Cash, he'd been kissing her.

Every time he looked at her, his eyes seemed to remind her of that. He remembered that kiss, and knew that she did, too. Restlessly, she rolled back the wide sleeves of her white shirt and pulled away the collar to allow air inside.

"Want a drink?" He bent at the waist to pick up his discarded gloves and tucked them into his low-riding waistband.

"No, thank you. I came here on business."

He walked to the bed of his pickup. It was parked nearby in the shade. The tailgate was down. There was a large, blue thermos sitting on it. He uncapped it and dipped a plastic glass inside. It came up full to overflowing with ice water. He gulped it down thirstily. Some of it ran down his chin and sweaty throat. It formed glistening drops on his chest hair, drawing strands of it into wet clumps.

Intentionally looking elsewhere, Schyler's eyes fell on the hard hat with the screened visor. It was designed to protect a logger's eyes from flying wood particles. "Your hard hat isn't doing you much good in the back of your truck. Why aren't you wearing it?"

"Didn't feel like it."

"But if you had gotten hurt on my land, you would have sued me."

"I don't hold anybody responsible for me, but me, Miss Schyler."

"I've asked you not to call me that."

"That's right. You have." Grinning like a sinner who had no plans to repent, he drained another glass of water. "Sure you don't want a drink?"

The water looked delicious, and so did his cold, wet lips. "Okay, all right. Thanks."

He dipped the glass into the top of the thermos again and passed it to her. She took it from him but didn't drink right away. Instead she gazed dubiously at the dripping glass in her hand. Cash's brows drew together angrily.

"My tongue has been halfway down your throat," he growled. "It's too late for you to worry about drinking after me."

She had never gotten so angry so fast in her life. With one vicious flick of her wrist she threw the entire icy contents of the glass onto the ground. "You are scum."

"That's a British word. Around here people like me are referred to as white trash."

"And worldwide you're called bastards." A muscle in his cheek twitched. A vein in his temple popped out. Schyler immediately regretted her choice of words. "I didn't mean it that way. Not literally." She felt an impulse to reach out and touch him in conciliation, but she didn't. She was afraid to.

He grabbed the glass away from her and tossed it into the pickup's bed. "You came all the way out here, in this heat, to call me names?"

She shook her head. "I came on business."

"Who do you want me to kill this time?"

She deserved that, she supposed, so she disregarded it. "I want you to come back to work for Crandall Logging."

"Why?"

"Because I need you." His eyes snapped to hers. They were disconcertingly incisive. She plunged on. "I've re-opened the business. I can handle the paperwork because I used to do it for Cotton."

She tried to wet her lips, but her tongue, like the inside of her mouth, was arid. "But I don't know how to organize the loggers. I don't know where to tell them to cut, or what to cut, or how much to cut. I won't be a good judge of the quality when they bring timber in and won't know whether I'm over- or underpaying them. From what I understand, you've been in charge of all that."

"That's right."

"Well, then, I need you to pick up where you left off before Cotton had his heart attack."

"In other words, you want me to save your ass."

She drew herself up straight. "Look, I'm sorry for what I said earlier. I didn't mean to call you a bastard. It just slipped out. If you're going to carry that chip on your shoulder, if you're going to hold that against me and be obnoxious—"

"You want me to save Belle Terre from Dale Gilbreath's clutches."

Schyler fell abruptly silent. For long moments they

stared at each other. Cash's expression was belligerent, hers bewildered. "How did you know about that?"

"I know."

"Did Cotton tell you that he had borrowed money from Gilbreath."

He turned his back on her and went to retrieve his chain saw. "Your daddy doesn't confide in me."

"Then where did you hear it?"

Heaven was a small town. Everybody meddled into everybody else's business, but to think that the people of the town were sitting back like Romans at the Coliseum, waiting to see if Belle Terre survived the jaws of the lion, was untenable. She'd been away from it just long enough to resent destructive, small-town gossip.

Angrily, Schyler caught Cash's forearm and spun him around. He glanced down at her hand. Her fingers were biting into his flesh. The hairs on his arms were curled over them. Her nails were making crescent-shaped impressions in his skin. He lifted his eyes back to hers, but she wasn't intimidated by the dangerous glint in them.

"Where did you hear about that loan?"

"In bed."

Schyler snatched her hand back. He smiled a crooked, sardonic smile before continuing on his way back to the pickup. He laid the chain saw in the back. Item by item, he took off his gear and laid it with the saw in the pickup. He pushed the thermos past the hinge and slammed the tailgate shut. He picked up a T-shirt from where he'd left it draped in the truck's open window and pulled it over his head. As he worked it down his torso, he asked, "Want the details? Time, place, with whom?"

"No."

He gave her a lazy smile. She wanted to wipe it off his mouth with the palm of her hand. "Bet you do." She only glared at him. He laughed. "Pity you're not more curious. It's juicy stuff. You might have gotten a kick out of it." He lowered his eyelids to half-mast. "We both might have."

The man was insufferable. He had the manners of a pig and the sexual discretion of a tomcat. If she didn't need him, and need him desperately, she would see to it that he was off Belle Terre by nightfall, and she didn't care what previous arrangements Cotton had made with him.

As it was, she had no choice but to tolerate him and his arrogance, temporarily she hoped. She lifted her heavy, wavy hair off her neck, hoping a breath of air would find it. "Are you coming to work for me or not, Mr. Boudreaux?"

"Depends."

"On what?"

"On who's in charge."

"I believe you were foreman. You will be again."

"Will I have Howell breathing down my neck?"

"Ken's responsibilities will remain what they've always been."

"As the company do-nothing?"

"For your information," she flared, "he spoke very highly of your qualifications as a forester."

"He'd be lying if he said otherwise."

"Don't bother to thank him," she said sarcastically.

"I won't." He gave her another arrogant smile. "But I guess I should be flattered that the two of you took time out from your stolen time together to talk about me."

Schyler clenched her fists to keep from screaming. She forced her voice to remain temperate. "Ken will stay in his downtown office."

"And where will you be?"

"I'll be working out of the office at the landing. I'll handle the contracts and the shipping schedules. You just supply me the loggers and the timber."

"What about the independents?"

"We'll use them as we always have."

"Will the pay scale stay what it was?"

"Yes. And so will the wages of those who work exclusively for us."

"And I'm in charge, right?"

Schyler had the uneasy feeling she was being backed into a corner. He was pressing her for a verbal commitment, but she was unsure why. She hesitated but finally answered. "Right. You're in charge."

"Okay then." While the negotiating was going on, he

had been leaning against the tailgate, arms folded over his chest, ankles crossed. Now he pushed himself away and started toward her. It took all her willpower not to back down. She stood her ground until they were standing toe to toe.

"Stop wearing blouses you can see through."

"Wha—"

"That lacy brassiere you've got on isn't worth a damn. The only thing it's good for is to make a man crazy. If you want full production out of the loggers, we can't have them getting hard and horny. I don't care if they screw their wives and girlfriends through the mattress over the weekend, as long as they report to work bright and early every Monday morning and don't let up till Friday afternoon."

His eyes raked over her hair. "And smooth your hair back. That just-got-laid hairdo will have them sneaking off into the woods by themselves to jerk off."

"You're—"

"No," he interrupted, catching her shoulders, *"you're* going to listen to me." He lowered his face to within inches of hers. "You're up shit's creek without a paddle, Miss Schyler. If you want my help in saving your company from bankruptcy and Belle Terre from foreclosure, you're going to keep your butt to the ground, your mouth shut, and do things my way, understand?" He shook her slightly and raised his voice. "Understand?"

"Yes!"

He released her as suddenly as he had grabbed her. "Good. We start tomorrow."

Chapter Twenty-one

"Gilbreath."

"Hello. It's Schyler Crandall. Thank you for taking my call so late in the day."

The banker angled back his reclining chair and propped his feet on the corner of his desk. "No thanks are necessary, Ms. Crandall. I hope you have good news for me."

"I think so."

"You're prepared to pay off the loan?"

"The news isn't that good, I'm afraid."

Dale's pause was calculated and lengthy. "That's a shame. For both of us."

"Crandall Logging starts full-scale production in the morning, Mr. Gilbreath," she informed him briskly. "I've rehired the previous foreman."

"Mr. Boudreaux, I believe."

"That's correct. My father has a tremendous amount of confidence in him. So do the loggers. I've compiled a promising list of markets. I'll be contacting them as soon as we have enough board feet to make some impressive sales. That shouldn't take but a few days of cutting. Everyone is eager to get back to work."

"This is all very interesting, Ms. Crandall. You've obviously taken some positive steps to reorganize your family's business. But I fail to see how these measures directly affect the bank."

"If I can present you with enough contracts to cover the amount of the loan, would you be willing to let me pay the interest and rollover the principal for a while longer? Six months max."

This was no faint-hearted southern belle with hominy grits for brains. Schyler Crandall was not to be underestimated. She had seized the bull by the horns. It was time to get tough.

"I'm afraid I can't do that, Ms. Crandall, even if you get the contracts, which is doubtful."

"Let me worry about getting them. A signed contract is as good as cash."

"Not quite," he said, oozing chauvinistic condescension. "You might not be able to deliver the orders."

"I would."

"But I would have no guarantee."

"You'd have Belle Terre as collateral."

"I've already got Belle Terre. What would be my incentive?"

"How about decency?"

"That was uncalled for, Ms. Crandall."

She sighed heavily, but didn't apologize. "Deal with me, Mr. Gilbreath," she said imperatively. "It's unrealistic to hope that I can fill enough contracts to come up with that much cash in such a short time."

"That's hardly my problem." He tried to keep a gloating tone out of his voice. He could almost hear her mind working during the ensuing silence.

"What if I paid you the interest and a portion of the principal?"

"Ms. Crandall," he said expansively, "please stop to consider the awkward position you're placing me in. You're making me out to be the heavy. I regret that. This isn't solely my decision to make. I have to answer to the bank's directors. They, as much as I, have been lenient with Crandall Logging and Cotton.

"He's been a customer in good standing for years, but sentiment can only stretch so far. *If* we went out on a limb and extended the loan, we would be placing ourselves in a vulnerable position with the bank examiners. We have to answer to them for every transaction. They don't know Cotton Crandall. They won't be sentimental. They will view this as a nonproducing loan. With the economy being as sluggish as it is—"

"Thank you, Mr. Gilbreath, you've answered my question. Good-bye."

She hung up before giving him a chance to respond. Smiling smugly, Gilbreath replaced the receiver. He enjoyed seeing the mighty humbled and headed for a fall.

When he moved to Heaven from Pennsylvania three years ago, the pillars of the community had treated him with attitudes ranging from mild derision to outright snobbery. Rhoda and he had soon learned that one wasn't considered to have roots in Heaven unless there was a moth-eaten Confederate uniform packed in an attic trunk. Family trees had to have branches sprawling across several generations before the stigma of being an outsider was removed.

Unless one met these criteria, one wasn't embraced by the socially prominent—which is what Dale and Rhoda wanted to be. They wanted to be in the very bosom of Heaven's social circle.

They had been virtually forced to leave their home in Pennsylvania. The couple they had been swapping partners with for several years became born-again Christians during a citywide crusade. In a tearful testimony in front of a large, spiritually emotional congregation, they had confessed everything, naming their partners in sin. The very next day, Dale had been discreetly asked by the staid officers of the bank where he had been a second vice-president to tender his resignation. They agreed to provide a letter of recommendation if he left promptly.

So he had come to the Delta National Bank of Heaven, Louisiana, overqualified and underimpressed. At the time, however, he hadn't had the financial luxury of turning down any job in his chosen field, particularly that of bank president. He had swayed the board of directors with ingratiating charm and gave as his reason for leaving his former place of employment a desire to move to a more temperate climate.

No sooner had the Mayflower van delivered his furniture, than he regretted his decision. He hated the town, hated the heat, hated the narrow-minded people and their closed cliques.

The only person who had treated him in a friendly fashion was Cotton Crandall. Gilbreath had discovered that Cotton was somewhat of a newcomer and outsider himself. Cotton had firmly established himself in the community by marrying the last surviving Laurent in the parish.

Gilbreath had had no such opportunity, but he saw a way to cement his position in this town. It wasn't a perfect town, but since the Pennsylvania episode wasn't the first time he and Rhoda had been asked by moral do-gooders to leave a community, they were determined to stay in Heaven. And if he could help it, they wouldn't remain there as second-class citizens. This was a small pond, but he was going to make sure he was the biggest fish in it.

If he owned Belle Terre, people would have to regard him and Rhoda with deference. It made him giddy just thinking about a couple of Yankees living in Belle Terre. That would set the town on its ear. And there wouldn't be a damn thing that anybody could do about it but kiss his ass and pretend to love him.

Taking Schyler Crandall's phone call was his last piece of business for the day. With a springy gait he left the bank building and walked the two blocks to the parking lot where he left his car each day. Except for his Lincoln, the lot was empty. He opened the door and slid behind the wheel.

"Jesus, it's about time," the person sitting in the passenger side said. "Turn on the air conditioner. It's hotter than hell in here. I thought you said five o'clock. It's almost fifteen after. What took so long?"

Chuckling, Dale turned on the motor and adjusted the air-conditioning controls. "Believe it or not, I was talking to Schyler."

"To Schyler? At the bank?"

"She called me."

"What about?"

"She feels the undertow and is trying to keep her head above the surface. I think she's afraid that everything she holds near and dear is about to be taken away from her."

"Well, she's right, isn't she?"

"For your good, as well as mine, you'd better hope so."

"What did she want with you?"

"To bargain." He recapped their telephone conversation.

"You turned her down, I hope."

Dale's smile was evil. "Of course, but with a great deal of commiseration."

"She won't fall for that. She's smart."

"You're worried about that, are you?"

"You're damn right I am. What are you grinning about? This is serious."

"You're telling me?" Dale snapped. "Schyler's got her foreman back." He glanced at his passenger. "She's confident that she'll line up some good contracts in the next few days."

"They'll have to be more than just good."

Dale nodded in agreement. "Contracts or not, what she hasn't got is time. I don't think we have a problem."

"We do if we don't keep close tabs on Schyler."

"Exactly. That's why I need you to tell me every move she makes. Even things that you don't consider important, I want to know about."

"You want me to spy on her."

"Yes. Not only that, sabotage whatever you can get away with. Just don't get caught at it."

"All right."

"We need something to distract her."

"Like what?"

"I don't know. A love affair? Of course, it would be most fortuitous if Cotton died. That would take her mind off the business for a while." Dale carefully gauged the other's violent reaction. His eyebrows rose inquiringly. "Would that upset you so much?" No answer. Dale frowned. "I can see that it would. Are you sure that your loyalties aren't divided?"

"I'm only loyal to myself. Why shouldn't I be?"

"Then if it gets unpleasant or dangerous before it's over, you won't object?"

"No."

"I hear uncertainty in your voice."

"No!"

"That's better," Dale said, his smile restored.

"Schyler shot Jigger Flynn's dogs."

After a moment of stunned silence, Dale asked, "Are you sure? I'd heard a rumor that—"

"The rumors are false. Schyler did it. She used one of Cotton's shotguns."

"How do you know?"

"I know, okay?"

Dale knew when to back off. He did so, and at the same time, pondered this valuable piece of information and considered its useful applications. "Jigger would love to know that."

"Meaning?"

"Don't play innocent. You're thinking the same thing I am. That's why you told me. I've used Jigger Flynn before to handle sticky situations. He's extremely efficient and relatively inexpensive. If he knew Schyler was responsible for killing his pit bulls, he would do just about anything to retaliate. He would consider Schyler fair game." Dale's thin lips parted in a ferret's smile. "Wouldn't he?"

"I've got to go," the passenger said brusquely, shoving open the door.

"No matter how ambiguous your feelings for Cotton might be, you won't let them stand in your way, will you?"

"No. I won't let anything stand in my way."

"That's what I wanted to hear."

Supremely satisfied with the way the interview had gone, Dale watched his informant disappear into the alley.

Chapter Twenty-two

Ken had a pleasant buzz going when he left the Gator Lounge. He wasn't staggering, but he was drunk enough to fumble and drop his keys as he approached his car. They landed in the gravel. He bent to pick them up, but before he touched them, a shiny black shoe came out of nowhere and stamped on them. His hand was nearly crushed. It froze.

"Hey, Kenny."

Ken straightened slowly. Glancing swiftly over his shoulder, he confirmed what he already suspected. The first man, the one with the expensive shoe, wasn't alone. These types always traveled in pairs, like nuns; except this duo was unholy.

"Hi." Ken gave a nervous little laugh. He shrugged innocently and raised his hands in surrender. "Now before you get pissed, I'll tell you right off that I don't have the cash toni—"

A rock-hard fist landed a solid blow to Ken's guts. He bent over double, clutching his middle. The thug who'd been standing in the background grabbed a handful of Ken's hair and pulled him upright. He yelped with pain. There was no one to hear him. The parking lot, bathed in the ruby light of the neon sign, was deserted. But even if someone had heard his cry for help, he wouldn't have interfered. These guys were deadly.

The first man, obviously the spokesperson, moved forward to stand nose to nose with Howell. "I'm already pissed off. You're three days late paying me what you owe me, Kenny." His voice was silky, but contemptuous. "It does something to me when you lie." The hand he used to cover his heart glittered with diamond rings. "In here, deep inside, it hurts me when you lie to me."

"I can't help it," Ken gasped. "Money's tight. I've had to pay the old man's hospital bills. Doctors."

"Kenny, Kenny, you're breaking my heart." The sullen face turned ugly. "Know what you are? Besides being a liar, you're a loser. You lost bad on that pit bull fight last week. And that nag you bet on in the daily double at Lafayette belongs in the glue factory." He spat in Ken's face. "You're a goddamn loser. I hate losers. They make me want to puke."

Ken was sweating bullets. "Look, man. Give me more time. I—"

He rammed his knee into Ken's groin. Ken screamed in agony. "I don't want any more of your lame excuses. I can't cover my expenses with excuses. I want cash. When do I get my money?"

"S . . . soon," Ken stuttered. "Something big is about to break."

"Something big? Like what? You gonna win at bingo?" The man holding Ken's hair chuckled.

"No," Ken gasped, still in excruciating pain. "Something really big."

"This sounds like more of your bullshit."

"No, swear to God, but I can't give you the details. I haven't worked them all out yet. The logging company—"

"Is reopening. Yeah, yeah, I know. Old news. Boudreaux is back doing his thing." He flashed an oily smile. "Is he bangin' that sexy sister-in-law of yours?"

"No!" Ken angrily put up a struggle against the man who restrained him. The thug only knotted his fingers tighter in Ken's hair and pulled his head back further. "If that's what you've heard, it's a goddamn lie."

His tormentor laughed nastily. "She kicked you outta her bed and outta your position in the family business. Now ain't that a shame?"

"That's not true. None of it. I'm still in control of the books. I'm still vice-president of the company."

"But she's running the show. With Boudreaux coaching her in soft whispers while he's screwing her. Ain't that the way it is?"

Ken tried to shake his head in denial, but the motion only pulled his hair tight enough to bring tears to his eyes. "No. I'm in charge."

"You?" The thug barked a laugh, which he silenced as abruptly as he flicked open the switchblade and slid it between Ken's thighs, directly beneath his manhood.

Ken squealed and rose up on tiptoes. The man behind him, who had been threatening to tear his hair out, now relaxed his grip at a time when Ken wanted to be held up. "I'll get your money," Ken whimpered in panic. "But you gotta give me more time."

"Time's run out on you, Kenny." He pressed the knife's blade against Ken's zipper.

"No, no, please, for the love of God, no. I'll get you your money."

"All of it?"

"Every blessed cent."

"When?"

"A . . . a month." The man behind him opened his fist and let go of his hair. Ken barely kept himself from falling onto the blade. "Two weeks," he amended breathlessly.

Gradually, with a motion that sickeningly resembled a slow, slicing movement, the loan shark withdrew the knife. "Okay, I'm easy. Two weeks." He grinned broadly, then drew his face into a scowl. "Don't bother calling us. We're gonna be on top of you like flies on a pile of dogshit, Kenny." He flashed Ken a hungry crocodile smile. Even his teeth looked like they'd been filed to points. Then he and his comrade stepped out of the pool of neon light and disappeared into the darkness.

With no more spine than a blob of ectoplasm, Ken dropped to his knees. He vomited in the gravel. When the spasms subsided to dry heaves, he crawled around on hands and knees until he located his keys.

* * *

The headlights roused Schyler. Sitting on the porch swing, occasionally giving it a desultory push with her bare toes, she'd almost been lulled to sleep. She hadn't known what fatigue was until she had started working at the landing every day. She rarely left until well after dusk and was always the first one to arrive in the morning.

She smiled at Ken as he trudged up the steps. "Hi. You look as ragged out as I feel."

"I, uh, my stomach's upset."

"Nothing serious, I hope." When he shook his head, she asked, "Is that why you weren't here for supper?"

"No. I just got sidetracked." Crossing the veranda, he reached for the handle of the screen door.

"If you've got a minute, there's something I want to ask you about."

Ken's hand fell to his side and he turned to face her. "There's something I want to ask you about, too," he said heavily.

"Shoot."

"Are you sleeping with Cash Boudreaux?"

Schyler's smile collapsed. She was affronted, not only by his assumption that her bed partners were his business, but also by the insult his question implied. "Certainly not."

His tread was slow and deliberate and angry as he moved toward the swing. "Well you might as well be. That's the gossip going around town."

Darkness concealed the sudden flush of heat in her cheeks. With admirable skill she kept him from seeing how much his comment upset her. She made a dismissive gesture. "You know as well as anybody how people around here love to talk."

"There's usually some basis for gossip."

"Not this time."

"You spend all day with him."

"But not all night!" The instant her temper erupted, she squelched it. She was too tired for an argument tonight, especially since she had nothing to defend. "I work with Cash. I'm required to spend time with him. I've worked with a lot of men, but that doesn't mean I sleep with them."

"Mark Houghton is one exception that springs to mind."

Schyler got out of the swing so fast that it rocked crazily behind her. "I'm not about to discuss my private life with you, Ken. As I've said before, it's none of your damned business. Good night."

He caught her arm as she stalked past him. "Schyler, Schyler," he pleaded, "don't go. Stay and talk to me."

"Talk? Okay. Refute allegations that I'm sleeping with Boudreaux or with anybody, no."

"Hell, what do you expect people to think?"

"I expect people to think exactly what they please. But I expect better from you."

"I can't stand having your name connected to his."

"What would you have me do about that? We're working together."

"Fire him."

"I can't," Schyler cried incredulously. "I don't want to. I need him too much."

"You didn't think so at first."

"I know better now. He's an excellent forester. He does even more than he gets paid for."

"Then *you* quit. Let me take over."

Schyler was surprised by how intensely she loathed that idea. As exhausting as her work at the landing was, she wouldn't think of giving it up. Her efforts to obtain large contracts from former markets had so far met with little success. But the thought of quitting now was untenable. Nor did she trust anyone else, not even Ken, to fight as diligently as she was fighting to keep Belle Terre.

It would be churlish to come right out and say that, so she tried to decline his offer diplomatically. "You can't be two places at one time."

"I'll move my work to the landing office."

"You can't handle both jobs, Ken."

"I can," he argued insistently. "Give me a chance."

"It's unnecessary to wear yourself out. Especially when I'm willing to—"

He squeezed her arm hard. "I'm not willing. I'm not willing to let you turn into a ball-breaking, career broad."

"I'm not like that."

"Fast becoming." He pulled her close. "I remember how sweet and feminine you were when—"

"Ken, please."

"Let me finish, Schyler. I still lo—"

"I thought I heard your voice out here. It's about time you dragged yourself home." Ken jumped away from Schyler and guiltily spun around and faced his wife. "Well, well, well," Tricia laughed lightly, pushing through the screen door. "What are you two up to?"

For a sustained moment, no one said anything. Then Schyler replied smoothly, "I was asking Ken about some files that are missing from the batch he brought to the landing for me."

Only a brief few weeks ago, Schyler woud have welcomed hearing a profession of love from Ken's lips. It would have been icing on the cake for him to profess it within Tricia's hearing.

Now, that kind of reward seemed as cheap and insignificant as a plastic trophy. Having him say he still loved her was no longer worth the tumult it would cause. She no longer wanted to hear it. His love just wasn't valuable to her anymore.

"I'll look for those missing files to be on my desk sometime tomorrow then, all right?" she asked him.

"Uh, sure, okay."

"Good." She bent down and picked up the sandals she'd left beneath the swing. "I'm exhausted. Six o'clock comes early, so I'm off to bed. 'Night." She went inside and padded upstairs.

Tricia, leaning against one of the columns, gave her husband an accusatory and uncharitable look. "It's been a long day for me, too," he said quickly. "I'm going—"

"You, stay where you are, Mr. Howell." Tricia's tone had a ring of authority to which Ken automatically responded. For the second time in only a few minutes, his hand fell away from the handle of the screen door. "You smell like a tavern."

He plopped down heavily in the swing and massaged his eyesockets with his middle finger and thumb. "Makes sense. That's where I've been."

"Drowning your sorrows in an ocean of bourbon?"

"Yeah," he said scornfully, "the chief sorrow being my bitch of a wife."

"Forget me. I'm the least of your problems."

"What do you mean?"

"You're going to let her waltz in here and take over, aren't you?"

"What? Who?"

"Schyler, you idiot. Can't you see what she's doing? Don't you care?"

"I care, but she doesn't listen to me, Tricia."

"Then you're not talking loud enough." She turned her back on him and crossed her arms as though holding in her temper. After a moment she glanced back at him over her shoulder. "Have you even mentioned to her what we discussed?"

He laughed scoffingly, shaking his head in disbelief. "About selling Belle Terre?"

"Belle Terre, Crandall Logging, and everything else."

"Schyler would never hear of it."

"How do you know? You haven't asked her."

"Neither have you." He made it a challenge.

"She has never listened to me. If anybody holds sway over her, it's you." Her eyes narrowed. "Or are you losing ground to Cash Boudreaux? My, my, are the tongues in town flapping about *that*. Imagine what strange bedfellows the two of them make. Schyler Crandall, former belle of Laurent Parish, and Monique Boudreaux's bastard boy. Who'd ever believe it?"

"Nobody who's got any sense."

"You sound so sure."

"I am. I just asked her. There's no truth to the rumor."

"You think she'd tell you?"

"Yes," he said with more surety than he felt. "I think she would."

"Doesn't matter," Tricia said airily. "If folks think they're sleeping together, it's as good as fact." Her smile changed direction and turned downward. "And it would be just like her to lie down with white trash. She never had any discrimination." She gnawed the corner of her lip. "She'll drag our reputation right down into the swill with hers. I wouldn't be surprised if that's why she took up with Cash. To come back here and ruin us for doing . . . for what happened when we got married."

Tricia thumped her fists on the column. "Well, I won't have it. She's provided us even more reason to get away from here. Belle Terre," she sneered. "A pretty name for . . . what?" She waved her hand to encompass the lawn and beyond. "A pile of dirt. Trees. A stinky old bayou that's good for nothing but breeding mosquitoes and crawfish. The house isn't even an original. It's a replica of one the Union army burned down when they were done with it. There's nothing special about it."

"Except that Schyler loves it." Ken gave his wife a calculating look. "Which I believe is the very reason you insisted we live here."

She counterattacked. "Well, I haven't heard you complaining. You haven't had to pay rent, have you? You haven't had to buy groceries. Not one red cent of your money goes into keeping up the place. You've had it pretty damn good for the six years we've been married." She paused before playing her trump card. "Up till now that is."

"Don't threaten me, Tricia."

"Take it as fair warning. If you're not careful, Schyler will replace you, sugar pie. She'll barge right in and make you superfluous. You'll be deadwood around here and Cotton won't hesitate to cut you off."

Because she teased him with his greatest fear, Ken got up and headed for the front door again. As he went past her, Tricia caught his arm and detained him. Changing her tactic, she snuggled against him and laid her cheek on his chest, disregarding the sour smell.

"Don't go huffing off, baby. Don't get mad at me. I'm telling you this for your own good. Our own good. Talk Schyler into getting rid of Belle Terre. What do we need a great big old house like this for? We're sure as hell not going to fill each bedroom with a grandbaby like Cotton expected us to. With our share of the sale money we could buy a modern condo in any city we want. We could travel. We—"

"Tricia," he interrupted wearily, "even if Schyler agreed, which she won't, what about Cotton? He will never agree to selling this place."

"Cotton might die." Ken stared down into his wife's face. It was cold and unfeeling enough to make him shiver. Her expression softened only marginally when she said, "We have to prepare ourselves for that eventuality. It could happen any day. Now, will you approach Schyler with the idea of putting Belle Terre up for sale or not?"

"I've got a lot on my mind," he mumbled evasively. "But I promise to think about it."

He disengaged himself and went inside. Tricia watched him go, despising the dejected manner in which he climbed the stairs, head down, shoulders stooped, hand dragging along the banister like a lifeless appendage.

By comparison, Tricia felt like a kettle about to boil. Flattening herself against the wall of the house, she clenched her fists and clamped her teeth over her lower lip to keep from screaming in frustration. She wanted and wanted and wanted and never got any satisfaction. She thought the people around her, especially her husband, were so unambitious and dull.

No one seemed to care that life was passing them by with the speed of a zephyr, while they had no more forward motion than the waters of the bayou. They were willing to settle for so little when there was so much out there waiting to be had. They seemed content to rot in Heaven.

Her impatience to get away and change her life was so strong that her skin itched from the inside.

Chapter Twenty-three

Heart patients were robbed of all dignity.

Spending weeks in a hospital ICU had made Cotton Crandall expertly familiar with humiliation. His body's weakness, assisted by powerful medications, had kept him drifting in and out of consciousness. But he knew that having his ticker on the blink was as debasing and emasculating as castration.

He pretended to be woozier than he actually was while the nurse exchanged IV bottles because he was only mildly curious about what was being dripped into his veins. His thoughts were more with the nurse. She wasn't one of the bossy nuns who ran the place like military generals. She was young and pretty. From an advantageous angle, Cotton could appreciate the shape of her breasts while she took his blood pressure. He wondered what she would do if he tented the covers with an erection.

He wanted to laugh at the thought but couldn't quite garner the energy, so he satisfied himself with a smile that never quite creased his lips.

There was little hope of an erection, though, since he had a tube running up his cock to drain his bladder for him. "Shit," he thought scornfully. He wasn't even able to piss by himself.

Satisfied with his current condition, the nurse gave his shoulder a kindly pat and left the room. He was left in peace, if not in silence. The computerized machines that monitored all his vital statistics beeped out their information on small, green screens.

How long before he could leave? How soon could he go home to Belle Terre? *God, at least grant me the blessing of dying there,* he prayed.

But he seriously doubted that God, if there even was one, remembered Cotton Crandall's name.

Still, he hoped. His dream death had him sitting on the veranda of Belle Terre, a tall glass of neat bourbon in one hand, his other arm around Monique.

The beeping signals faltered. He heard the glitches before he even felt the palpitation inside his chest. To be safe, he pushed the thought of Monique aside.

Instead, he thought about those living at Belle Terre. As usual his thoughts centered on Schyler. Her name evoked profound love and glaring resentment. These two emotions warred within him, each so strong as to cancel out the other and leave him numb.

When he had regained enough of his faculties to realize that she had come home, his ailing heart had swelled with gladness. But his heart attack hadn't erased his memory. When he recalled why she had gone away, all the bitter anguish returned. He couldn't forgive her.

He thought it was odd that she kept coming to see him. Even though he never acknowledged that she was there, she faithfully visited him each day. He didn't want to admit it, but her visits were the brightest spots of his endless days for in this place there were no sunrises or sunsets. The hours were measured not by the position of the sun in the sky, which couldn't even be seen, but by the switching shifts of nurses and technicians. One could spend months in the hospital and never know the seasons had changed.

Perhaps a season was too much to ask for, but he hoped he lived to see another sunset at Belle Terre. Jesus, he remembered the first sunset he'd viewed from the veranda like it was yesterday.

He had been working for old man Laurent, the stingiest bastard ever to draw breath. The wages he had been earning as a saw hand were paid out in scrip, which could only be used at the company store. The system stunk, but he had been grateful for the job.

Macy Laurent had pulled up at the landing one day in a

sleek red convertible. She epitomized forbidden fruit. With her blond hair and banana-yellow sundress, she looked ripe for the picking. But there might just as well have been a barbed wire fence around her since no one of Cotton's caliber could even get close to her. She didn't notice him any more than she noticed all the other loggers who ogled her while she weaseled her daddy out of a crisp twenty-dollar bill, more than most of them earned in a week.

Cotton credited fate with the flat tire that crippled Macy's red convertible a few days later. He'd been walking to work from the boardinghouse he lived in—it was also company owned—when he spotted her on one of the back roads. She was wearing a swimming suit. Her legs rivaled Betty Grable's, and he'd been a big admirer of Miss Grable for years. He offered to change her tire. Even though he would be docked in pay for being late to work, he considered this good deed an investment.

It paid off. Macy was impressed by his tall, brawny build and intrigued by his pale, almost white, hair. For changing her tire, she offered to pay him a dollar. He declined. So she invited him to her house for fresh peach ice cream that evening instead. He accepted.

"Anytime after supper," she had said, giving him a wave as she sped off.

Supper was at six o'clock at the boardinghouse. He didn't know that rich folks didn't eat until seven-thirty, so he arrived much too early. A massive black woman of indeterminate age—he was later amazed to discover that Veda Frances wasn't nearly as old as he had initially thought; her bearing was more indomitable than some of the sergeants he'd served under in combat in France—sternly told him to wait for Miss Macy on the veranda. He was given a glass of lemonade to quench the thirst he'd worked up on the long, dusty walk from town.

Sipping from that tall, cool glass of lemonade, he had experienced his first sunset at Belle Terre. The colors had dazzled him. He had wanted to share it with Monique, but she was back in New Orleans where he had left her until he could send for her.

Then Macy stepped out onto the veranda and spoke his

name in a drawl that was as thick as honey and soft as a feather and he forgot all about Monique Boudreaux. Monique was as vibrant and vivid as a red rose. Macy was as sweet and subdued as a white orchid.

Her skin was just about that translucent, too. He nearly burst with the protective, possessive instinct that seized him. She was so slightly built, so ethereal, that she barely disturbed the air as she moved to one of the fan-back wicker chairs and gestured him into the one beside it.

The first time he kissed her, which came little more than a week later, he told her she tasted like honeysuckle. Her laughter tinkled like a tiny bell. She called him a foolish poet.

The first time he touched her small, pointed breasts, she whimpered and told him that she felt faint and that if her daddy caught him at that, they'd have to get married.

And Cotton said that was okay with him.

News of their engagement rocked the town, of course. To placate their dainty as china, but stubborn as a mule, daughter, the Laurents allowed her to marry Cotton Crandall. To save face, they created a past for him that included a clan from Virginia. The fictitious family history was rife with calamity. Poor Cotton was the sole descendant of the unlucky bunch.

He didn't care what the Laurents told their snooty friends about him. He was in love, with Macy, with Belle Terre. He didn't care that Macy's mother retired to her room in the evenings to keep from watching him desecrate the hallowed rooms of Belle Terre with his white trash mannerisms and rough language. When she died, he didn't mourn her passing, nor that of his father-in-law only three months later.

Like a well-greased piston, Cotton slipped into the managerial slot of the logging company. The first thing he banished was the scrip system. He sold the company store and had the ratty boardinghouses condemned. When the board of directors unanimously disapproved his innovations, he solved that problem by disbanding the board.

He promised the loggers that he would always put their interests first. They were wary but soon came to learn that

Cotton Crandall was a man of his word. His promise was as long lasting as gold. The name on the company letterhead was changed as a sign of Cotton's sincerity and the dissolution of Laurent's autocracy. Considering the immensity of the changes in company policy, the transition was made smoothly.

The same was not true in the mansion. Cotton discovered that his fair lady was accustomed to and fond of being pampered. To a man who had grown up believing in a strong work ethic, whose next meal depended on whether or not he did an honest day's work, her idleness was incomprehensible.

Equally as puzzling to him was Macy's aversion to sex. In that respect, she was as different from Monique as night to day. Of course Monique hadn't been a virgin. He had met her in a seedy nightclub in the French Quarter during the closing days of the war. The place had been crawling with soldiers and sailors, but she had picked him out.

She flirted vivaciously; he offered to buy her a drink. He boasted his feats in battle; she'd acted suitably impressed. They made love that first night. Godamighty, she'd wrung him out. He had never met a woman with so generous an attitude toward sex. She loved fiercely but faithfully. From that first night Monique's bed was reserved for him.

They had set up housekeeping in a rundown apartment house and hadn't spent a night apart until he had been forced to leave to look for work. By that time they had lived together for three years. The subject of marriage had never been broached. She didn't seem to expect or require it for her happiness.

And in the back of Cotton's mind, he had known that something better was in store for him.

He thought he had found it in Laurent Parish. The irony was that Macy hadn't been exaggerating when she told him his caresses made her faint. She almost fainted on their wedding night when he, after hours of unsuccessful persuasion and coercion, forcibly consummated their marriage.

While she wept, he remorsefully promised that the worst was over. But it never got better. No matter what he did,

she never liked it. Intimate foreplay repulsed her. She refused to touch him "there" because it was so ugly and
nasty. She either accepted him with scathing contempt or
sacrificial stoicism. He distinctly remembered the day
Macy cut him off completely.

"Cotton?"

"Hmm?"

It had been raining, so he wasn't at the landing. His
head had been bent over the ledgers on his desk in the
study behind the stairs at Belle Terre.

"Would you please look at me when I speak to you?"

He raised his head. Macy was standing in the doorway.
Her slender form was limned by the light in the hallway.
"I'm sorry, darling. I was lost in thought." He laid down
his pencil. "What is it?"

"I moved your things today."

"My things?"

Nervously, she clasped her hands at her waist. "Out of
the master suite and into the one across the hall."

He never recalled a time in his life when he was angrier.
"That'll cause you a helluva lot of trouble, my dear. Especially since you'll have to move every single goddamn
thing right back where it friggin' belongs."

"I've asked you not to use profanity—"

When he lunged out of his chair, it went rolling backward and crashed into the paneled wall. "What the hell are
you trying to pull?"

Her narrow chest rapidly rose and fell with indignation.
"Mama and Daddy never shared a bedroom. Civilized people don't. The kind of . . . of . . . nightly rutting you're accustomed to is—"

"*Fun.*" He stamped across the room and loomed over
her. "Most people think it's fun."

"Well I find it revolting."

That cut him to the quick. He admitted that one of
Macy's attractions had been her unattainability. That was
probably most of his attraction, too. He'd been different
from all the smooth-talking college boys who had courted
her. It was the Cinderella story in reverse. He had thought
he had scaled the walls of the castle and won the princess,

but he hadn't. To her, he was still a redneck saw hand, uncouth and unprincipled—in a word, revolting.

His ego wouldn't allow her to see how deeply she had wounded it. "What about children?" he asked coldly. "What about the dynasty we want to establish?"

"I want to have babies, certainly."

He lowered his face to within inches of hers. "Well, to have babies, Macy, you gotta fuck."

He took perverse pleasure in watching her face drain of all color. She swayed as though he'd backhanded her. He had to admire the grit it took for her to stand her ground, though he wasn't surprised. One of her ancestors had been a Confederate hero.

"I'll let you know the days each month when I'm fertile." Without a sound, without a rustle of her clothing, she left him.

A few months later, he discovered the abandoned house on the bayou. He sent for Monique. To this day, he recalled that lusty afternoon when she arrived with her boy. It hadn't all been rosy. She'd pulled a knife on him and threatened to cut off his pecker when he broke the news that he was married. But he'd talked his way clear, and the fight had only heightened their passions.

Naked as jaybirds and sleek as otters, they had loved away that afternoon in the sweltering upstairs bedroom. That was the last time he ever made love to her without using a rubber. All his seed had to be conserved for those periodic visitations he made into Macy's unresponsive, rigid, dry body.

Cotton had never gone into Macy's bedroom without being invited. After they adopted the girls, he never went into it at all. He kept his word to Macy even after she died. Monique had lived according to the conditions he laid down the day of her arrival on Belle Terre.

To the day she died, she had never complained about their arrangement. Each time he made the trip from the mansion to the house on the bayou, whatever time of day or night he arrived unexpectedly, she dropped whatever she was doing and gave him what he needed, whether it be a meal, a fight, sympathy, laughter, conversation, sex.

Her curiosity about Macy never waned, but she wasn't jealous of her. Jealousy wouldn't have improved her situation. It would have been a wasted emotion, and Monique poured all her emotion and energy into loving Cotton.

Jesus, he had loved that woman.

She'd been dead for almost four years, but the pain of her death was as keen as it had been when her smiling lips whispered his name for the last time and her fingers relaxed their grip on his hand.

Now, the guilty memory of her last smile squeezed tightly the fragile walls of his damaged heart.

Chapter Twenty-four

"Cash?" He stopped and turned. Schyler was poised in the doorway of the office. "Are you on your way home?"

He squinted against the setting sun. "It's quitting time, isn't it?"

"Yes, but if you can spare a minute, I'd like to talk to you."

She thought he was going to ignore her because he turned his back and sauntered toward his pickup truck. He left it parked at the landing nearly every day and drove one of the company trailer rigs to wherever they were cutting.

"Have you been cooped up inside that office all day?" he asked over his shoulder.

"Yes."

He leaned over the side of the truck and opened a cooler. He took an iced-down six-pack of beer out of it. "Come on. I'll treat you to a beer."

"Where?"

He looked at her long and hard. "Does it matter?"

Schyler wouldn't back down from a challenge, no matter how subtly it was issued. "Just a sec." She went back inside and turned off all but one light, then locked the office for the night before joining him beside the pickup. He had already downed one can of beer. He crushed the can in his fist and tossed it into the pickup's bed. It landed with a hollow, metallic clatter. He worked a can out of the plastic webbing for her and took another for himself before replacing the six-pack in the cooler.

"Where are we going?"

"Over the river and through the woods."

"To grandmother's house?" Laughing, Schyler fell into step beside him.

"I never had a grandmother."

Both her smile and her footsteps faltered. "Neither did I." He stopped in his tracks and gazed at her. "At least none I knew about," she said in an undertone. He began walking again. After a moment, she asked, "Why do you do that?"

"What?"

"Throw all your deprivations in my face."

"To make you mad."

"You admit it?"

"Why not? It's true. I don't need a priest to confess my sins to."

"You're a Catholic?"

"My mother was."

"And you?"

"I can do without it. My mother's religion didn't do her any good, did it? I prized a rosary out of a dead soldier's hand in Nam. What good did prayers do him?"

"How can you be so callous?"

"Practice."

They walked on, but Schyler wasn't ready to quit. "What about your mother's people?"

"What about them?"

"Where were they from?"

"Terrebonne Parish, but I never met any of them that I remember."

"Why?"

"They kicked her out."

Again Schyler stopped and faced him in the darkening twilight. "They kicked her out?"

"*Oui*. Because of me. When my old man deserted us, her folks didn't want to have anything to do with us either."

Not a trace of sadness was registered on his uncompromisingly masculine features, but she knew that he must hurt. Somewhere deep down inside himself, Cash Boudreaux must feel the pain of rejection.

They continued down the overgrown path that meandered through the woods. "Maybe that's why my real mother gave me up for adoption," she said. "Maybe her family threatened to disown her if she kept her illegitimate baby. Your mother must have loved you very much and wanted to keep you in spite of her family."

"She did. But wanting to keep me sure as hell made life tough on her." He held aside a low dogwood branch for her. "There."

He pointed toward the shallow and narrow tributary at the bottom of a slight decline. Trailing willow branches bent toward the water to tickle the knobby knees of cypress trees that poked out above the surface.

"It's beautiful here," Schyler whispered. "And peaceful. The nearest town could be miles away."

"Have a seat."

She sat down on the boulder he indicated, close to the water's edge. Fragrant, yeasty vapor was belched out of the can of beer when she pulled the tab off. Foam spewed. She sipped it off the back of her hand. She drank from the can, then licked her lips. Cash was leaning against the trunk of a cypress, studying her. She looked up at him and asked, "How do you find these places?"

He gazed around. "I was as wild as an Indian when I was growing up. My favorite place to be was in the woods. I've tramped all over these bayous." He slid down the tree trunk until he was sitting on his haunches. He picked up a stick and dug the tip into the soft mud at the water's edge.

Bubbles popped up. When they burst, tiny holes were left. "Crawfish," he said.

Schyler stared at him. This man intrigued her. He was an enigma, a study of contradictions. He was a diligent worker, but money wasn't his motivation. He didn't seem to mind living with scarcely any amenities. He neither scorned nor coveted material possessions but seemed genuinely indifferent to them.

"Did you ever think of doing something else, Cash?"

He slurped his beer. "About what?"

"With your life. I mean, didn't you ever have any ambition to go somewhere else?"

"Like where?"

"I don't know," she said in exasperation. "Somewhere. Didn't you explore other career opportunities?"

He shook his head. "I always wanted to work in the forest."

"I know. You're excellent at your job. So you could have gotten work anywhere there is timber. Didn't you ever think of leaving Heaven?"

He stared at the still surface of the water for a long time before answering. "I thought about it."

"Then why didn't you go?"

He finished his beer. "It just didn't work out."

Dissatisfied with his answer, Schyler pressed. "What didn't work out? A promised job?"

"No."

"Then what?"

"I couldn't leave." Impatiently, he rose to his feet.

"Of course you could leave. What was holding you here?"

He made several restless movements, then propped his hands on his hips and stared at his booted feet. He drew a deep breath and let it out. "My mother. I couldn't leave because of her."

That was a more thorough answer than Schyler had hoped for, but it still didn't shed much light. She ran her fingertip around the top of the aluminum beer can. "And after she died? Why didn't you leave then?"

He didn't answer her. She looked up expectantly. He

was staring down at her. "I had promised her that I wouldn't." They stared at each other for so long that Schyler began to feel uncomfortable. Intuitively she knew that his reply implied something important, something that involved her, but she doubted she would ever know what it was. Cash Boudreaux was a mystery that would remain unsolved.

That reminded her of why she had detained him. "Cash, didn't you tell me that two of the rigs had flat tires when you got to the landing yesterday morning?"

"*Oui*, but they've been taken care of. I changed the flats myself. The tires are being repaired at Otis's garage."

"I'm not worried about the tires," she murmured absently. "Doesn't that strike you as unusual and unlikely?"

"What?"

"That two rigs would have flat tires on the same morning."

"Coincidence." Her worried frown indicated that she wasn't so sure. "You don't think so?"

The deep breath she drew lifted her breasts and delineated them against her blouse. She wasn't aware of that, nor that the involuntary motion had drawn his eyes. Since the day she had asked him to resume his position with the company, she had been careful to wear modest clothing, not because she felt bound to obey his high-handed directives, but because she didn't want to warrant his criticism.

"I suppose it's just a crazy coincidence. I probably wouldn't have thought any more about it except . . ."

"Go on. What?"

Feeling rather foolish, she looked directly at him. "This morning when I got here, the office door was standing ajar. You didn't arrive before me, did you?"

He shook his head. His brows were pulled into a *V* across his forehead. "Wind?"

"What wind?" she asked with a soft laugh. "I would give my eye teeth to feel a good stiff breeze. Besides, the door was locked. I make certain of that every night before I leave. Did you come in behind me last night to use the telephone?"

He smiled lopsidedly and shook his head no. "What are

you getting at? That the truck tires could have been tampered with?"

"No, I guess not. It sounds ridiculous, doesn't it?" She rubbed the back of her neck. The nagging suspicions she had nursed all day sounded ludicrous when spoken aloud. She wished she had heeded her earlier instinct and kept them to herself.

"Was anything in the office missing?"

"No."

"Disturbed?"

"No."

"No signs of vandalism?"

She denied that, too, with a shake of her head. "It just made me feel creepy."

"I'm sure it's nothing to worry about. But maybe you'd better start going home earlier. Don't stay here so late by yourself."

"Ken said the same thing. He's been driving over to follow me home every night."

"Howell?" Cash's brows drew even closer together. "Was he here the night before last?"

"Yes," she replied, mystified by the question. "Why?"

"Did he go anywhere near the garage?"

She shot him a sour look. "Don't be absurd."

"It's not so absurd. Howell has got two good reasons to be severely pissed off."

"What?"

"You taking over the management of Crandall Logging. And the gossip circulating about us."

"Us?" She knew what was coming. The only reason she had asked was that she was curious to see how much he knew. She braced herself for whatever he might say.

"Us. You and me. Folks say that business isn't all we're doing together. They've put us in the same bed. And they say we're having a damn good time there."

Her preparations fell short. She didn't sustain the blow of his words at all. In fact they caused her breath to catch. She said nothing; she couldn't, no more than she could escape his compelling stare, which, like a chameleon, changed color to match the background. One second it was gray, the next mossy green, the next agate.

"Now if you were Howell, wouldn't you be feeling like shit?"

"Ken's got no reason to hold a grudge. I haven't infringed on his work at the downtown office. As for the other, even though it's silly gossip, it's none of his business. He's married to my sister."

"Right," Cash drawled, taking a long drink from his beer. "But he can't stand the thought of me sampling what he threw away. Finished?"

Schyler had once again been rendered mute. Finally she asked hoarsely, "What?"

"Finished?" He nodded down at the can of beer she was mindlessly strangling with both hands.

"Oh, not quite."

"Well, what have we here?"

Schyler was shakily raising the can of beer to her mouth, when Cash bent from the waist and scooped something up from the muddy ground near her feet. She went rigid with terror when she saw the writhing body of the snake dangling by its tail from his hand. Its dark-banded body was a good two feet long. Its head was black. Inside its open mouth Schyler could see the pinkish-white membrane from which it drew its nickname.

Cash casually swung the snake backward, then let his hand fly as though he were fishing with a casting rod. The cottonmouth tumbled end over end in the air before making a splash in the center of the viscous bayou.

Schyler's eyes backtracked from the dark green splash it made to Cash. "That was a water moccasin," she wheezed.

"Um-huh. Ready to head back?"

"And you just picked it up."

Then he noticed her apparent dismay and said wryly, "I was raised on the banks of the bayou, Schyler. I'm not afraid of snakes. Any snake." He reached down and drew her up. He ran his warm, rough palms over her upper arms. "I guess you are, though. You've got goose bumps." As his hand continued to rub the raised flesh, he whispered, "Not too many snakes make it as far as the mansion, do they?"

Keeping one hand around her elbow, he guided her back toward the landing. Her knees were trembling. The altercation with the cottonmouth had been unsettling. So had his cavalier treatment of it. So was his soft touch and his hot stare and every sexy word that came out of his mouth.

When they reached his pickup, she slumped against the side of it. "Before I forget," she said, "there's something else I wanted to talk to you about."

"I'm listening."

"Today I made an appointment to meet with Joe Endicott, Jr. at his paper mill."

"Over in East Texas?"

"Yes. We've dealt with them before."

"I remember. They gave us several good contracts."

"That's been a few years ago. Do you know why they stopped doing business with us?"

"No."

"Neither do I. He treated me coolly, but I finally wore down his resistance and he granted me an appointment. It's on the twelfth." She paused to draw a breath. "Cash, will you go with me?"

He looked surprised but replied quickly, "Sure."

"I would appreciate it. I'll need your expertise. I got the impression that they need quality timber and have just about depleted their regular suppliers. This could mean a big contract for us. If we can fill their requirements, I might be able to pay off the note at the bank with this order alone."

She was no longer sensitive to discussing family business with him. Since they'd been working together, she had discovered that if anybody had the inside track on Crandall Logging, it was Cash. He knew what dire straits she was in and there was no sense in putting up a falsely optimistic front.

"Glad to oblige," he said. "Aren't you finished with that beer yet?"

She nodded and passed him the can, which was still a

third full. He drank the rest of it himself and tossed the empty into the back of the truck with the two of his.

He curled his fingers over the edge of the truck and straightened his arms, bracing himself against it. His taut, well-shaped rear stuck out. One knee was bent. He turned only his head and looked at her. "You never did come to like beer much, did you?" Schyler looked away. "I guess that beer bust at Thibodaux Pond turned you against it forever."

She stared at the first evening star, showing up silver and shiny against the indigo sky. "I wondered if you remembered that."

"I remember."

She bowed her head so far that her chin nearly touched her chest. "When I thought about it later, I got so scared for what could have happened."

"You were about to get into a heap of trouble and you were only . . . what? Fourteen? Fifteen?"

"Fifteen."

He let the tension in his arms go slack. With an economy of movement, he turned and propped one side of his body against the truck so that he was now facing her. Schyler didn't look at him, but she could feel his eyes on her.

"My mother had died only a few months before that." She couldn't understand why she felt she owed him an explanation for her behavior that night so long ago. But she couldn't hold it back. "She . . . my mother . . . never was a very attentive parent. What I mean is," she rushed to say, "she didn't dote on us the way Cotton did. She was always distracted by other things."

Cash said nothing. "But she was the rule-maker, the disciplinarian. She and Cotton disagreed more often over how Tricia and I should be raised than they did over anything else."

Of course one of their disagreements had resulted in Cotton's banishment from Macy's bedroom. But that had been before she came along. Schyler had never known a time when they'd shared a bedroom. She remembered being shocked to learn at age eight that in most families the mama and daddy slept not only in the same room, but also in the same bed.

"Anyway," she continued, "when Mama died, Tricia and I started testing the perimeters of Cotton's control. I knew that he wouldn't approve of the beer bust. He had bought me a new car, even though my license was restricted. I wanted to go to that party at the pond and show my new car off to all those older kids. I guess I wanted them to think that my mother's death hadn't fazed me." She drew a staggering little breath. "So I went."

"And met up with Darrell Hopkins."

Laughing derisively, she glanced up at him. "How do you remember that?"

"I remember a lot of things about that night." His voice turned husky. "You had on a white dress. I remember how the light from the bonfire picked you out from everybody else. It was made of that material with the little holes in it."

"Eyelet."

"I guess. Your hair was longer than it is now and was sorta pulled up here with a clip." He made a gesture.

"I can't believe you remember that well."

"Oh, I remember. Because I'll never forget that horny kid's hands groping your backside while you danced with him."

Schyler stopped laughing. She lowered her gaze. "Things went too far before I realized what was happening. One minute it all seemed very romantic, dancing under the sky on the shore of the pond with an 'older man.' The next minute, he was grabbing at me. I panicked and started fighting him off."

She lifted her eyes to his. "That's when you interfered. You came out of nowhere. I remember wondering later, when I was lucid, where you had come from and what you were doing there. I hadn't seen you in ages."

"I was home on leave from Fort Polk."

Her memory quickened. "You had a GI haircut."

He ran his hand through his long hair, smiling. *"Oui.* I was cruising the drag downtown and heard about a helluva party with plenty of beer going on out at the pond, thought

I'd go out there and see what kind of action I could scare up."

"You ended up taking me home to Daddy."

"Not before pounding the crap out of Darrell Hopkins. You know, last time I saw him, which wasn't too long ago, he crossed the street to avoid me. He still has a chipped front tooth." Cash closed the fingers of his left hand into a tight fist. "He should have known not to engage in a fight with a soldier on his way to jungle warfare."

Schyler's mellow expression turned serious. "You barely knew me. What made you do it, Cash?"

The air between them seemed to grow thick and electric, as expectant as right before a thunderstorm. His eyes wandered over her face. "Maybe I was jealous. Maybe I wanted to dance with you so I could be the one feeling you up."

He meant to be insulting. Schyler felt like crying and wasn't sure why. "I don't believe that, Cash. I think you did it to be nice."

"I told you before, I'm never nice. Especially with a woman."

"But I was a girl then. I think you interfered because you didn't want an innocent girl to get hurt."

"Could be." He tried to sound nonchalant, but his voice was deep and low. He couldn't keep his eyes away from hers. "But I don't think so."

"Why?"

"Because I liked having your head in my lap too much. Remember that?"

"No."

"Liar."

"I don't remember!"

"Well you should. On the drive home, you laid your head on my thigh. I can still see your hair spread out over my lap. It looked and felt so silky, so sexy. It went . . . everywhere." His eyes turned dark and moved down to her mouth. "I should have taken what I felt I had coming while I had the chance, what I felt I was owed for doing my good deed."

"And what was that?"

Slowly his hand came up out of the darkness. His fingers closed around the back of her neck. His thumb stroked her throat. He drew her forward, until the tips of her breasts grazed his chest. "A taste of you."

"Is that why you kissed me the other day? You felt you had it coming?"

"I kissed you for the same reason I do everything else, because I damn well wanted to."

"Obviously you wanted to the night of the beer bust. Why didn't you then?"

The shield that often screened his eyes dropped into place. "Other things got in the way."

"Like Cotton."

"Yeah, like Cotton."

"Why did he get so angry with you? If it hadn't been for you, I could have lost my virginity to a beer-guzzling, randy kid. I hadn't drunk much. Maybe two beers, but that was enough to make me tipsy and to cloud my judgment."

"So you don't remember everything about that night?"

Schyler was puzzled by the wariness in his expression. "Not really," she answered slowly, probing her memory for evasive facts. "I remember seeing Darrell lying unconscious on the ground, bleeding from his mouth and nose. I wanted to help him, to make sure he was all right, but you practically dragged me to my car. *My* car," she exclaimed. "You drove me home in my car?"

"*Oui.*"

"Then how'd you get back to Thibodaux Pond to pick up your own?"

"I walked from Belle Terre to the highway and hitched a ride."

She had never pieced together all the sketchy details of that night. Now it seemed important that she do so, though she couldn't say why.

Cash had saved her from disgrace, but had characteristically turned the situation to his advantage. It had been in the front seat of the shiny, new Mustang Cotton had given her that she had lain her head in Cash's lap. That made it seem even more forbidden, more erotic, more reason for Cotton to have lost his temper.

She looked at Cash again. "Cotton got angry, didn't he?"

"Not surprising. His pride and joy was brought home drunk."

"Yes, but he was furious with you. Why? It wasn't your fault." Her mind went on a frustrating search for tidbits of memory. "When we got to Belle Terre, you half carried me up the front steps. The veranda lights came on. And . . ." She paused, closing her eyes, conjuring up a mental picture. "And Cotton was standing there."

"Looking as fearsome as Saint Peter at the pearly gates," Cash supplied caustically. "Without even waiting for an explanation, he started thundering at me. Veda came out and hustled you inside and upstairs."

"I remember." Laughing softly, Schyler added, "She undressed me and tucked me into bed. She scolded me for exercising poor judgment and condemned white trash boys who showed no respect for decent young girls like the Crandall sisters."

She recalled Veda brushing the "so silky, so sexy" blond hair that had been spread across Monique Boudreaux's bastard son's lap just minutes earlier.

God rest Veda, Schyler thought, smiling pensively. She would have given Cash a thrashing herself that night if she could have. As it was, he had taken a tongue-lashing from Cotton. While she was upstairs being lulled to sleep by Veda, Cash was being unjustly accused.

"You took the blame, didn't you?" she asked him, puzzled. "You bore the brunt of Cotton's wrath." Gazing into near space, she continued as recollections, like pages of a book, unfolded for her. "I remember hearing the two of you all the way upstairs shouting at each other. Cotton didn't understand that you weren't the one who gave me beer."

"Cotton refused to understand it," Cash said bitterly.

"He should have been thanking you, but he just kept yelling about—" The book was suddenly slammed shut. The pages stopped turning. Her search had led to a dead end, and like all dead ends, it was frustrating. "What was Cotton yelling at you about that night?"

"Bringing you home drunk."

"Something else," she insisted.

"I don't remember," he said curtly. He swiftly ducked his head and brushed a kiss across her lips. "What the hell difference does it make anyway? It's ancient history."

It made a difference. She knew it. There was something significant here being left unsaid, something more important than Cash wanted to let on.

"Why won't you help me remember?"

"I'd rather make some memories," he whispered against her neck. "But if you want to re-create the past, we'll go for a ride in your car now. I'll drive. You can lay your head in my lap again." He cupped her head between his hands and gave her a brief, but thorough, kiss. "While it's there, maybe you can think of something else to do with your mouth besides talk about days gone by."

"Don't!" she cried, angry over his easy dismissal of the subject. "I need to talk to you about this, Cash."

"Talking's a waste of time between a man and a woman." He coiled his arm around her waist and drew her closer. "Tell you what, if it's a walk down memory lane you want, let's take the rest of the six-pack to Thibodaux Pond." He dropped a quick kiss on the tip of her nose. "We could drink some beer. Get naked. Skinny-dip." He kissed her mouth, thrusting his tongue between her lips. "We'll roll in the grass. Engage in some heavy foreplay. I'll kiss you all over. My tongue will stroke you senseless." His lips claimed hers again. The kiss was as rough and wanton as his fingertips on the raised center of her breast. "Who knows? I might get luckier than Hopkins."

Schyler pushed him away and wiped his kiss off her mouth. Her breasts rose and fell with indignation, and to her mortification, arousal. "I should have shot you when I had the chance."

He gave her a slow, lazy smile. "And I should have raped you when I had my chance. 'Night, Miss Schyler." He turned his back on her and sauntered off into the darkness.

Schyler was still fuming over their encounter hours later as she lay in bed, trying to sleep. Cash Boudreaux was the most infuriating man. She wanted to kill him for all his crimes against her, chief of which was making her blood run hot every time she came near him.

He had caused problems for her from their first personal encounter all those years ago. Her memory had kindly obscured that night he had brought her home from the pond. But tonight the memories had flashed like brilliant patches of light in the dark recesses of her brain.

Still, that most significant point, that inexplicable *something* that Cash had said to her father, eluded her. It was vitally important, though Cash obviously didn't want her to remember it. That was curious. What could it be, and why was it important even now?

She was still searching for a plausible explanation when the phone on her nightstand rang hours later. After fumbling for it in the darkness, she said, "Hello?"

"Ms. Crandall?"

"Yes."

"This is Dr. Collins."

She gripped the receiver hard.

Chapter Twenty-five

"Daddy?" she asked fearfully.

"We need you at the hospital as soon as you can get here," Dr. Collins told her. "He's suffered another massive heart attack. We have no choice now but to operate. Even then . . . I just don't know."

"I'm on my way."

She allowed herself five seconds of numbing, immobilizing grief before swinging her feet to the floor. Barefooted, she ran out into the hall. Ken was in his underwear, standing just outside the bedroom he shared with Tricia. "I picked up the extension in our room and heard the end of your conversation," he said. "We're coming, too."

"I'd like that. Downstairs in five minutes."

Even at that hour of the night, the hospital was well lit, though sepulchrally quiet. The trio in the elevator were silent as they rode up to the second floor, where they'd been frequent visitors for several weeks. The women looked pale without their makeup. The fluorescent lighting didn't flatter either. Ken's eyes were puffy and his jaw was shadowed with stubble.

They erupted from the opening doors of the elevator like news hounds on the scent of a big story. Schyler outdistanced the other two and reached the nurses' station first.

"Where's Dr. Collins?"

"He's already scrubbing. He left this consent form for you to sign."

Schyler, barely glancing over the necessary document, scribbled her name on the dotted line. "Has my father been taken to the operating room yet?"

"No, but the orderlies are in his room now."

"Can I see him?"

"He's heavily sedated, Ms. Crandall."

"I don't care. I've got to see him." She didn't add the qualifying words "once more." But that's what she feared it would be.

The stark anxiety on her face appealed to the nurse's compassion. "Okay. Just don't detain them."

"I won't." She turned to her sister and Ken. "Do you want to see him?"

Tricia, vigorously rubbing her hands up and down her chilled arms, shook her head no. Ken looked from his wife to Schyler. "Why don't you go alone? Seeing him in pain like that the first time it happened wasn't pleasant for either of us."

Schyler jogged down the corridor. The door to Cotton's room was open. Two orderlies were transferring him from his hospital bed to a gurney. His body looked as frail as a child's. He was strung with tubes and wires. It was a macabre sight. But that didn't even slow Schyler down. She rushed into the room. The orderlies looked at her curiously.

"I'm his daughter."

"We're taking him to the OR," one of them said.

"I understand, but the nurse gave me permission to speak to him. Is he conscious?"

"I don't think so. They gave him a pre-op shot."

While they were adjusting the IVs and covering Cotton with a stiff white sheet, Schyler moved to the side of the gurney, standing far enough away not to hamper the orderlies, but close enough to take Cotton's hand. The back of it was bruised for having had needles in it for so long. It lay in hers listlessly.

The palm of it, however, was beautifully familiar. She knew each callus personally. A thousand memories were associated with that hand. It had proudly patted her head for getting an A in math. It had soothed her after taking a fall off a frisky colt. It had wiped away her tears while he explained that Macy did love her, she just didn't know how to show it.

She raised his hand to her cheek. "Why'd you stop loving me, Daddy?" Schyler whispered the words so softly that no one could have heard them. But, as though in answer, Cotton's eyes opened and he looked directly at her. She gave a soft, joyful cry and smiled brilliantly through her tears. He wouldn't die without knowing how much she loved him.

"Schyler?" Cotton rasped.

"We've got to go now, miss," the orderly said, trying to edge her aside.

"Yes, I know, but . . . What is it, Daddy? What are you trying to say?" *He still loved her!* He was trying to tell her so in case this was his last chance.

"Why did you . . ."

"Miss?"

"Please!" she shouted in frustration. The orderly stepped back. Schyler bent over Cotton again. "What, Daddy? Why did I what?"

"Why . . . did . . . did you destroy my grandchild?"

* * *

"Boudreaux!"

Cash had been so lost in thought that he hadn't heard the pickup approaching his house, nor the footsteps on his porch. He'd been drinking coffee since three-thirty, waiting until dawn so he could report for work at the landing. Recently, at idle moments such as this, his thoughts turned to the woman he worked for.

That's why he kept himself so busy.

His name had boomed out of nowhere. Now someone was pounding on his door and repeating his name in a voice as finely tuned as a concrete mixer. Cursing his pre-dawn visitor, he left his hot cup of coffee on the table.

Jigger Flynn was standing on the other side of the door Cash angrily pulled open. His eyelids contracted suspiciously, but he was careful to appear nonchalant.

"Bon jour, Jigger. What brings you calling so early in the morning?"

Without any kind of greeting, Jigger snarled, "I need something for my woman."

"Which woman?"

"That black bitch who lives with me, which one you think?"

Cash's eyes turned cold. "Gayla?" Jigger grunted and bobbed his head. "What's the matter with her?"

"She's bleeding."

"Bleeding?" Cash repeated in alarm. "Bleeding where?"

"Everywhere. Wake up, I do, with blood in my bed. She says she slipped a kid."

"Jesus."

Cash ran his hand down his face. This wasn't the first time Jigger had come to him asking for medicine for one of his prostitutes who had either botched a self-induced abortion or taken a beating from a customer who got off on bondage and violence. Jigger avoided doctors because such incidents warranted police reports. Most of the law enforcement officers in the parish were in his back pocket, but Jigger didn't take unnecessary risks.

"If she miscarried a fetus she needs a doctor," Cash told him. "You'd better get her to the hospital fast."

"Your *maman,* she gave me the medicine before, don'tcha know. Fixed them whores right up."

"She knew more about it than I do."

Jigger's eyes gleamed with malevolence. "Be a shame, Gayla should die in a pool of her own blood."

That was his way of telling Cash that he had no intention of taking her to the hospital. He was smart enough not to come right out and say so, but his grin was amoral.

Cash gnashed his teeth. "Wait here."

A few minutes later, he was back with a paper sack. "There are two different bottles in here for her to take. I wrote out the directions." He extended Jigger the sack. Jigger took hold of it, but Cash didn't release it. Jigger looked at him inquisitively. "Leave her alone until she's completely well," Cash said tightly. "Do you understand what I'm saying?"

"No fucking."

"That's right. Otherwise you could kill her."

Jigger leered at him. "You like Gayla? Tell you what, Boudreaux, I'll let you enjoy her for one night. In exchange for the medicine."

Cash's face turned dangerous. He abruptly released the sack. "Give me twenty bucks instead."

Shrugging, Jigger fished a twenty-dollar bill out of his pants pocket and handed it to Cash. "Sure you wouldn't rather have Gayla?" Cash said nothing. Jigger cackled and turned to leave. He had taken only one step, however, when he turned around and asked, "Why do you work for that Schyler Cran-*dall?*"

"The hours are good and she pays well."

Jigger's eyes narrowed to slits. "Did that lady shoot my dogs like Gilbreath said?" Cash said nothing, but he tucked away that piece of information. "She'll pay for it," Jigger hissed threateningly.

"Leave Schyler Crandall to me."

Jigger threw back his head and laughed. He pointed a chipped, yellow index fingernail at Cash. "I forgot. You got an ax to grind with the Cran-*dalls,* too."

"And I'll grind it my own way. You stay away from them."

Jigger winked. "We're on the same side of the fence, Boudreaux, don'tcha know. The same side of the fence."

He ambled down the porch steps to where his truck was parked. He gave another nasal laugh and waved to Cash before driving off.

Cash finished dressing for work, unplugged the coffee-pot, and left his house only minutes after Jigger. He was surprised that Schyler wasn't at the landing when he drove up. He let himself into the office, wondering if he should mention Jigger's visit to her. He decided against it. The news about Gayla would only upset her and more than likely provoke her into doing something reckless. Besides, the less Schyler knew the better.

When the loggers began to report for work and she still wasn't there, Cash dialed the phone number at Belle Terre and was told by the dour housekeeper that Ms. Crandall wasn't at home.

"Where is she?" he asked.

"She's at the hospital. Mr. Crandall had another heart attack and isn't expected to live."

Absently Cash replaced the telephone. He dropped into Cotton's chair behind the desk and stared into near space. Eventually one of the loggers stamped in to get his orders for the day. He took one look at Cash's face and withdrew without saying a word. Something was wrong with the boss, and God help the man who disturbed him when he was in such a mood.

Chapter Twenty-six

Her father's words echoed in her head.

"Why did you destroy my grandchild?"

As many times as she had mentally repeated them, they still made no sense. It was too critical a problem to puzzle through now because her mind could not sustain a thought for more than a few seconds. Her energy had to be used for one purpose, that of holding herself together until the surgery was over.

She covered her face with her hands and drew in a deep breath. He couldn't die before she had another chance to talk to him. He couldn't. God couldn't be that cruel.

"Coffee, Schyler?"

She lowered her hands. Ken was bending over her. "No thanks." He squeezed her shoulder reassuringly, then returned to the other vinyl sofa and sat down beside Tricia. He took his wife's hand and pressed it between his. Schyler watched, feeling a pang of envy. She needed that kind of oneness with someone right now—anyone; anyone who could share her fear and help get her through this.

Tricia happened to catch Schyler's longing stare. She scooted closer to Ken and clung to his arm possessively. Schyler ignored the smug gesture but looked closely at her sister. Without her makeup, Tricia appeared older, harder. There were no cosmetics to alleviate the bitter lines around her mouth or to warm the cold calculation in her eyes.

And then Schyler knew.

In one explosive split second of clarity, she *knew*. Tricia was the culprit.

"Did you . . ." Schyler's voice was as dry and rattly as dead corn stalks blowing in a hot August wind. She tried to work up enough saliva to swallow. "Tricia, did you, at any time, tell Daddy that I had had an abortion?"

Tricia's cheeks, unenhanced by blushing powder, paled even whiter. Her lips went slack and separated slightly, making her look dim-witted. Her blue eyes blinked once, twice. In wordless trepidation, she stared across the waiting room at the woman who was her sister in name only.

"You did. You did."

The knowledge struck Schyler in the middle of her chest. She gasped with pain and sucked in a sharp breath. Her head fell back against her shoulders. She squeezed her eyes shut. Tears rolled down her chalky cheeks.

"Ms. Crandall?"

She raised her head and opened her eyes. Dr. Collins was standing there, looking down at her with concern. He was still wearing his green scrubs. The surgical mask had been untied and was lying flat on his chest like a bib. "The surgeon sent me out. He's closing now."

"Is my father still alive?"

The young doctor smiled. "Yes he is. He survived a quadruple bypass."

Several knots inside her chest unraveled and she took her first comfortable breath in hours. "Will he be all right?"

The doctor scratched his cheek indecisively. "If he recovers, he'll definitely be better than he was. But it'll be touch and go for several days."

"I understand. Thank you for being honest with me."

"Would you like to talk to the surgeon?"

"At his convenience. It's not really necessary, is it?"

"No." He studied her a moment. "It's been a long night for you. I suggest you go home and get some . . ."

His voice dwindled to nothingness. Schyler was stubbornly shaking her head. "No. When Daddy wakes up I have to be here."

"It might be—"

"I have to be here," she repeated adamantly.

The doctor could see that combating such resolve was a waste of time. "I'll keep you posted. He'll be in recovery for thirty-six hours or so. That's an ugly scene, but you can go in periodically if you want to."

"I want to."

"Okay. Then be outside the door every even hour at ten of."

He nodded at the Howells who had remained curiously silent, gave Schyler one last look, and left the waiting room with his characteristic briskness.

Schyler swallowed with difficulty. She didn't want to break down and weep now, though sobs pushed at the back of her throat until it ached. She willed her pounding heart to slow down. She dried her perspiring palms on the handkerchief that was already twisted and soggy with the sweat of anxiety. Her fingertips were white and cold. They felt bloodless.

Making a valiant effort, she stood up. She took only three steps, halving the distance that separated her from her sister and brother-in-law. She looked Tricia straight in the eye. "Get out of my sight." Speaking in a precise, clipped, clear voice, she enunciated each word.

Then she left the waiting room with her dignity and her rage intact.

Schyler became the resident ghost on the recovery floor of the hospital. She refused to leave it. She prowled it endlessly, restlessly, unceasingly, anticipating each report on Cotton's condition, which remained aggravatingly unchanged.

Dr. Collins had tried to prepare her, but nothing he said could have diluted the horror of the recovery room. It was a high-tech torture chamber. She watched from a distance as Cotton struggled against the breathing tube in his throat, which gave him a choking sensation when he regained consciousness. His arms had to be restrained to keep him from jerking free of the necessary needles and catheters and electrodes. She didn't know how any patient survived the recovery room. She didn't know how she did.

The first day, she thought of little else except her father. She was so afraid that the machines monitoring his heartbeat would fall silent and he would die. Every hour he stayed alive was encouraging, the doctors told her. She clung to that hope. On the second day, she started believing it. To help pass the long hours of the second night, she went to the bank of pay telephones and called Mark. Upon hearing his kind and concerned voice, her restraint crumbled and she burst into tears.

"Is he gone, darling?"

"No, no." She brought him up-to-date with wet, noisy, slurpy phrases.

"I hope he recovers. I'm sure he will. The doctors are optimistic, aren't they?"

"Yes. They've said as much anyway."

"But what about you? You sound done in."

"I am," she confessed. She didn't have to pretend with Mark. "I'm exhausted. But I want to be here until I'm sure he's out of danger."

"What good will you be to him if you're on the verge of collapse?"

"I must stay here with him."

He knew better than to argue with her when she assumed that particular tone of voice. Tactfully, he switched subjects. "What about the business? Any progress being made there?"

She filled him in on that, too. "Of course I haven't been to the landing since Daddy's surgery. I assume that Cash has everything under control."

Mark offered her money again. Again she refused it. Finally he said, "I miss you, Schyler."

"I miss you, too. I need to be held."

"Come home and I'll hold you."

She clamped her teeth over her lower lip and tried to keep from crying again. Very expensive tears, these. It was wasteful to cry long distance, but she was dismally homesick for Mark. "I can't, Mark. Not yet. Probably not for quite a while. I need to be here for Daddy. One way or another."

"He doesn't deserve this much loyalty from you."

"Yes he does." He didn't know about Tricia's treachery and she didn't want to go into it over the telephone. "My place right now is at Belle Terre. I have to stay."

They ended the conversation by him telling her a dirty joke. Mark was good at that, at coaxing a smile out of her when she was feeling her lowest. Before she met him, he had experienced his own disillusionment and pain. His suffering had spawned a droll sense of humor and a pragmatic way of looking at life and the rotten pranks it played on people. It was that unique ability of his that had drawn her to him in the first place and that had saved her on more than one occasion from debilitating despair.

But after she hung up, Schyler felt more depressed than ever. Her head was bowed despondently as she made her way down the sterile, over-air-conditioned corridor toward the waiting room, which had become her headquarters.

She didn't see Cash until she walked right into him. He caught her upper arms to steady her. She gazed at him blankly. He stared down at her with dismay, making her realize just how frightful she must look. She had been avoiding the mirrors in the ladies restroom for two days. Defensively she asked, "What are you doing here?"

His hands fell away from her arms and his lip curled sardonically. "This is a public hospital, isn't it? Don't they let Cajun bastards come inside?"

"Oh, that's just great. That's just what I need. Your rank sarcasm." She tried to go around him, but he blocked her path.

"Why didn't you call me when it happened?"

She laughed dryly with disbelief. "Well, I was sort of busy. I had a few other things on my mind."

"Okay, since then. What else have you had to do? Didn't you think I'd want to know?"

"Apparently you found out."

"After calling Belle Terre to check on you."

"So what are you upset about?"

"All that uptight bitch who answered the phone would tell me was that Cotton had suffered another heart attack and that it would probably be fatal."

"Much as I hate to defend Mrs. Graves, that's all she knew at the time."

"Well, word got around to everybody else fast enough. I

found out the details of the surgery at the goddamn filling station when I went to have my truck gassed up."

The nursing nun behind the desk raised her head and peered at them reprovingly over her granny glasses. Cash glared back at her. "You need something, lady?"

"Please keep your voice down, sir."

He resented authority; the look he sent the woman proved it. Taking Schyler's arm, he roughly pulled her down the hallway and through a set of swinging doors that led to an atrium courtyard. It was filled with plastic plants and stone benches. He batted aside a tacky palm frond that happened to get in his way and ignored the benches.

"How is he?"

Each of Schyler's nerve endings felt as raw as an open wound. Everything irritated her.

It was especially aggravating to discover that she was glad to see Cash Boudreaux.

If he wasn't such an ass, if his manners weren't so atrocious, if he knew how to behave like a gentleman instead of a street thug, she would enjoy having him here with her. His wide chest seemed like a perfect resting place for her tired head. If he had placed his arms around her, she would have moved into his embrace because she wanted so much to be held. She would welcome any comfort he offered. But he wasn't doling out comfort; he was being his critical, obnoxious self.

"I said, how is he?"

He barked the question so sharply that she jumped. "He's fine."

"Shit."

"Okay, not so fine," she shouted, flinging out a hand in agitation. "They cut open his chest, prized apart his ribs, and did four bypasses on his heart, which was weak to begin with. How do you think he is? The two of you have never had a kind word for each other. So what do you care anyway?"

His face moved to within inches of hers. "Because I want to know if the business I'm busting my balls for is going to go belly up when the owner of it croaks."

Schyler whirled around. Cash plowed through his hair

with all ten fingers, holding it back off his face for several seconds before letting it fall back into place. He swore beneath his breath, in English, in French, in the mixed language he'd learned from his mother.

"Look," he said, catching up with her at the door, "the loggers are asking about him. I couldn't get anything out of the hospital when I called. Howell has been as tight-lipped as a friggin' clam. I need something to tell the men."

Schyler, her composure restored, turned to face him again. Her expression was stony. "Tell them that he's doing as well as can be expected. The doctor said that by tomorrow we should see a change for the better." Her face softened a degree when she added, "If there's to be one."

"Thank you."

"You're welcome."

"Have they assigned you a bed yet?"

"Pardon?"

"A hospital bed. You look like crap that's been run through the blender."

"How charmingly phrased, Mr. Boudreaux."

"I was putting it mildly. How long since you've had a hot meal? A few hours' sleep? A bath? Why are you punishing yourself for Cotton's illness?"

"I'm not!"

"Aren't you?"

"No. And I don't need you to tell me how bad I look." She drew herself up. "I'll have Ken deliver the payroll checks on Friday. So while you're busting your balls for the company, rest assured that you'll be well paid for your efforts."

She left him cursing amid the artificial forest.

Dr. Collins sought her out the next afternoon at a little past two o'clock. She was in the waiting room, resting her head against the wall. He sat down beside her and took her hand. She braced herself to hear the worst.

"I don't want to be too optimistic," he began, "but he's showing marked signs of improvement."

Her breath escaped in a gust of profound relief. "Thank God."

The doctor squeezed her hand. "I want to keep him in an ICU for another week at least. But I think he's past the critical stage."

"Can I see him?"

"Yes."

"When?"

"In five minutes. During which I suggest you brush your hair and put on some lipstick. We don't want to scare the poor man to death after all he's been through." She laughed shakily.

Five minutes later she entered the ICU where Cotton had previously resided. She noticed his improved color immediately. His skin had lost its grayish pallor. The attending nurse withdrew respectfully, allowing Schyler a modicum of privacy with her father.

She bent over him and touched his hair. His eyes opened and found her. "You're going to be fine," she whispered. Her fingertip smoothed over one of his shaggy white eyebrows, which disobediently sprang back up. "When you get better, I'll explain everything." She licked her lips to moisten them, even though she had just applied lipstick. "But I want you to know something, and it's the truth." She paused to make certain that he was lucid and that she had his full attention. "I've never been pregnant. I've never had an abortion. I would never have killed your grandbaby." She laid her hand along his cheek. "Daddy, do you hear me?"

His eyes clouded with tears. She had her answer.

"I've never lied to you in my life. You know that. What I'm telling you is the truth. I swear it on Belle Terre, which you know I dearly love. I've never been pregnant. It was all a . . . an unfortunate misunderstanding."

The change that came over his face was as dramatic as the first dawn of light breaking out of darkness. His features fell into restful, peaceful repose. His eyes closed. A tear eked from between the wrinkled lids. Schyler wiped it away with her thumb, then bent down and lovingly kissed his forehead.

Exhausted as she was, she left the hospital feeling better than she had in six years.

Chapter Twenty-seven

The first thing Schyler did when she returned to Belle Terre was take a scalding and soapy shower. She ruthlessly massaged her itchy scalp with shampoo, shaved her legs, and got to feeling human again.

Then she went directly to bed and slept for sixteen hours.

When she woke up the following morning, she was ravenous. She dressed in a casual skirt and top, then went downstairs to the kitchen. The three-egg, ham and cheese omelet was almost ready when Mrs. Graves came in.

"Good morning," Schyler said pleasantly as she deftly slid the omelet out of the pan and onto the plate. The housekeeper, incensed that her kitchen had been invaded, made no reply but turned on her heels and stalked out. Amused, Schyler sat down at the kitchen table and consumed every speck of food on her plate, washing it down with orange juice she had squeezed fresh and two cups of coffee.

It was raining, she noted as she cleaned up after her breakfast. The sky was dark with low, scuttling clouds. A good day to sleep late. And apparently that's what Tricia and Ken were doing.

She left the house without seeing them and drove to the hospital. At the door of Cotton's ICU, she came to an abrupt standstill. Using a slender nurse as his crutch, he was standing beside his bed. He raised his head and smiled at his daughter.

"Hurts like bloody hell but feels great."

Dropping her purse on the floor, Schyler rushed forward and hugged him for the first time since Tricia had married Ken.

They were spared a highly emotional scene by the nurse saying, "I hope you have better control over him than I do, Ms. Crandall. He's the most cantankerous, profane patient I've ever had."

"That's a goddam lie."

The women winked at each other behind Cotton's back. Together they eased him back into bed. For all his bravado, the exercise had exhausted him. Almost as soon as his head touched the pillow, he began snoring gently. Schyler watched him sleep for a while, then left his room and went to the lobby gift shop to order flowers for him. They had a lot of sorting out to do. But there would be time for that later. Thank God, there would be time.

She waited around for several hours, but he didn't wake up. Dr. Collins and the cardiac surgeon assured her that the best thing for him now was sleep. She left without speaking to Cotton again, but the fond smile he'd given her when she entered his room had been her reassurance that he remembered what she had told him the day before and that his faith in her had been restored.

She was anxious to attend to business at the landing, but it would keep for another few hours. There was something she must do first. It had been put off long enough. Six years in fact.

It was shortly after noon when she returned to Belle Terre from the hospital. The weather was still inclement. She ran from her car to the veranda through a hard rain. The rooms of the lower story were empty. She heard Mrs.

Graves moving about the kitchen but avoided her. She went upstairs. A radio was playing behind Tricia's bedroom door. Schyler opened the door without knocking and stepped inside.

Tricia, wearing a satin kimono over her slip, was sitting at a vanity table applying makeup. She was humming along with Rod Stewart. When Schyler appeared in her mirror, Tricia dropped the eye crayon and spun around on the tufted velvet cushion of the stool.

"I didn't hear you knock."

"I didn't knock."

Tricia's hand moved to the lapels of her robe and pulled them together, a giveaway of her nervousness, though none of it showed up on her face. "How rude. Has associating with white trash made you forget common courtesy?"

Schyler refused to be provoked or put on the defensive. She went to the radio and switched it off with an angry flick of her wrist. The silence was abrupt and absolute. Schyler confronted her sister.

"You don't deserve my courtesy. Be glad you won't get what you deserve." Schyler was angry, angry enough to cross the room and tear out Tricia's glossy hair strand by strand. But overriding her anger was perplexity. "Why, Tricia? What possible motive could you have had for telling Cotton that I had aborted a baby?"

"What makes you think I did?"

"No more games," Schyler lashed out. "I know. What I don't know is *why*. For godsake, why would you make up such a lie?"

Tricia rose to her feet and gave the belt of her kimono a vicious yank. She went to the window, moved aside the drapes and gazed out at the dreary day. The drape dropped back into place when she let it go. Finally she faced Schyler.

"To get him off my back, that's why. So he would stop condemning me for snatching Ken away from you. Not that I had to do much snatching." She raised her chin haughtily. Her hair swung against her shoulders. "Once he had been to bed with me, there was no question of him ever going back to you."

A statement like that would have destroyed Schyler several years ago, but now her mind concentrated on something else. "Cotton berated you for taking Ken away from me?"

Tricia laughed shortly and without humor. "Berated. Badgered. Bitched. Call it whatever you want. For the way he carried on, you would think I'd driven a stake through your heart. He went on and on about how I had betrayed you, how I had deliberately set out to get Ken only because you wanted him."

Schyler ran her fingers over the carved rosewood back of a chaise longue. She could remember Macy reclining on its linen cushions, distracted and distant, when her daughters came to kiss her good night. Schyler could still feel her mother's cool lips barely grazing her cheek. Tricia had always pushed Schyler aside, clambering to claim those dispassionate kisses that were so miserly dispensed.

"And wasn't he right?" she asked her sister softly. "Didn't you want Ken only because I had him?"

"No!" Tricia answered shrilly. "I fell in love with Ken. You're just like Daddy, always ready to think the worst of me."

"You give people no choice but to think that, Tricia. You've schemed all your life. But this . . . this . . ." Her eyes searched the beautiful room, looking for words suitably descriptive of Tricia's betrayal. She came up empty. "How could you do something so mean?"

"I didn't do it to hurt you, Schyler."

Schyler gaped at her incredulously. "How could it not?"

"Because you're a survivor. You moved to London and started a new life. I thought Daddy would get over it."

"Over his daughter having an abortion?"

"Oh, for heaven's sake! I just said the first thing that popped into my head when he asked me how I could do such a thing to poor little Schyler." Mockingly, she laid a hand against her breast.

"I don't believe you. I think you told him that because you knew it would drive a permanent wedge between us."

"That's bull." Tricia returned to the dressing table and picked up the eye crayon again. Leaning toward the mirror and pulling down her lower lid, she applied color to it. "Don't make such a federal case out of it. An abortion just seemed like a believable reason for you and Ken to have quarreled. I didn't know Daddy was going to mope about it forever."

"When it became apparent that he was, that he was holding it against me, why didn't you tell him the truth?"

"Because I didn't want him to hate me."

"But you let him hate *me*."

Tricia whirled around. "Well it was about time those tables were turned, wasn't it?"

Schyler fell back a step, astonished by Tricia's obvious hatred. Her face was taut with it. "What do you mean?"

"Wasn't it my time to have his approval? To have his attention? To have his love?" Her shapely chest rose and fell beneath the satin. The words had been pent up inside her for years. Now they poured out. "He doted on you. Everything you did was right, perfect. When he happened to see past you and look at me, he didn't like what he saw."

"Tricia, that's not true."

Tricia ignored her. "When he spoke to me, it was always to criticize. But you, you could do no wrong."

She flung off her robe and went to her closet. She jerked a dress off its hanger and stepped into it. Schyler noticed what a beautiful woman Tricia was. Her body was well made. Her figure was slender and compact. Her face would have been beautiful, too, were it not for the bitterness that prevented it from being femininely soft.

Tricia went back to the dressing table and picked up a lipstick. She twirled it out of the gold tube and applied it in smooth rapid strokes to her lower lip. "I don't know why the hell they got me." She rubbed her lips together and dropped the tube of lipstick back onto the dressing table with a clatter.

"They wanted you."

Tricia made a scornful sound. "Your naïveté confounds me, Schyler. Mama was half loony because she couldn't have a baby of her own."

"She wanted to give Daddy children."

Tricia groaned in derision. Wrapping a belt around her

waist, she latched and adjusted it. "She didn't give a damn about giving Daddy anything but a hard time. She wanted to have a baby because that would guarantee a Laurent heir to Belle Terre. At least half a Laurent, which was the best she could do. Being unable to have a child made her less than perfect. She couldn't accept that about herself. So she went a little nuts when she couldn't conceive."

"Don't say that. Mama wasn't a very happy woman, but—"

"Dammit, Schyler, she was miserable. *Yes!*" she stressed when she saw that Schyler was about to contradict her. "She was a miserable, self-centered bitch. Her main occupation in life was to make everybody else miserable, too. She didn't love us. She loved herself. Period. Cotton loved you. You worshiped the ground he walked on. So where do you think that left me? Huh? Out in the cold. Every single day of my life. And when Ken Howell came along with his pedigree in one hand and his broken heart in the other, you're damn right I wanted him. Why shouldn't I? It was my turn," she screamed, flattening a hand against her chest. "You bet I went after him. I would have done anything to keep you from having him."

"*Anything?* There was never a baby, was there, Tricia? You never were pregnant. That was a lie, too. There was no miscarriage after the wedding, was there?"

"What difference—"

"Tell me!

"*No!*"

Their animosity was palpable. Tricia's one-word confirmation of Schyler's long-held suspicion served as a bell ending a round, signaling each to return to her corner. They caught their breath. Schyler was the first to speak.

"Does Ken know you deceived him?"

Tricia shrugged as she lit a cigarette. "I imagine so. He's no Einstein, but he's not that stupid. We've never talked about it." She blew out a cloud of smoke, aimed ceilingward. "I think he prefers to believe that a heavy period was a miscarriage. I say let him, if that makes him feel better about losing you."

She gave Schyler a once-over. "Actually between the

two of us, I'm a much better wife to him than you ever would have been. Your self-sufficiency threatens him. He admires it, but he doesn't like it. It makes his shortcomings too apparent."

"Don't you dare tell me what kind of wife I would have made Ken. I loved him. Deeply."

Tricia's mouth turned up at the corners. "Yes," she said softly, "I know."

"He came back to me. You couldn't stand that." Schyler's words struck home. Tricia angrily flicked an ash into a Waterford ashtray on the vanity. "That's why you made up the lie about being pregnant. You wanted to hurt us both. You saw a way to emotionally destroy me and to trap Ken."

As Schyler sifted through her thoughts, she moved to the windows. The rainfall was heavier than before. Puddles were forming in the grass on the lawn. Even in the rain, Belle Terre was beautiful. Nothing diminished its beauty in her eyes.

"But then you had to justify yourself to Daddy. You knew that what he valued above everything was Belle Terre. He talked constantly about establishing a dynasty. Even though they wouldn't bear his name, he wanted generations of children to grow up in this house. You knew he wanted that more than anything. You knew the thing that would hurt him the most was to find out that one of us had aborted his grandchild."

"Oh, Jesus," Tricia swore as she ground out her cigarette. "You're as sentimental as he is. Our children wouldn't be his grandchildren. Because we're not his! All that dynasty and generational talk was ridiculous. It was embarrassing to hear him carry on about it like a babbling fool. He doesn't belong to Belle Terre any more than we do. Everybody in the parish knows that he only married Macy Laurent to get Belle Terre."

"That's not true. He loved Mama."

"And he screwed Monique Boudreaux!"

Schyler spun around and looked at Tricia with patent disbelief.

Tricia burst out laughing. "Gracious sakes alive. You

didn't know, did you? I can't believe it," she said, flabbergasted. "You honestly didn't know that she was Cotton's mistress? Amazing." Shaking her head, she made a scornful sound. "What do you think he is, a monk? Saint Cotton? Did you think he went without a place to stick it all those years he and mama didn't sleep together?"

"You're vulgar."

"You're right," Tricia purred. "That's why it was so easy to lure Ken out of your bed and into mine."

"That's not altogether true."

Both women reacted to Ken's voice. They turned simultaneously to find him standing in the open doorway. He had addressed Tricia. But he was looking at Schyler. "Let me refresh your memory, Tricia. You came on to me like a bitch in heat."

"Which you seemed to like."

"You also told me the same lie you told Cotton."

"She told you that I had aborted your child?" Schyler asked.

"Out of pique, she said."

"And you believed her?"

Schyler looked at the man standing before her and wondered how she could have ever loved him. He was weak. He was pathetic. That was glaringly obvious now. He had allowed a spiteful woman to dominate his mind and dictate his future. A real man wouldn't have been led around by the nose like that. Cash Boudreaux wouldn't.

Ken made a helpless gesture. "Hell, Schyler, it was easy to believe her. You were always demonstrating for womens' rights, saying a woman had a right to choose."

"Yes, the right to *choose*. That didn't mean that I—" She broke off. There was no sense in rehashing that now. The damage had been done years ago. But thank God it hadn't been permanent.

"I told Daddy the truth yesterday. We've been reconciled." For the time being she ignored Ken and spoke directly to Tricia. "There was never any reason for you to think that Daddy didn't love you. He does and always did.

In addition, you've got Ken. The hatchet is buried as of this second, but I'll never forgive you for adversely manipulating my life."

She turned to leave, but Tricia lunged after her. She stepped between Schyler and the door. "I don't give a good goddamn whether you forgive me or not. I just want my share of this place free and clear. Then I'll be all too happy to get out of your adversely manipulated life forever."

"Your share of this place? What are you talking about?"

"Tricia," Ken said, "this isn't the time."

"We want to sell Belle Terre."

For a moment, the meaning of Tricia's statement didn't register with Schyler. The idea was so inconceivable as to be ludicrous. It was so preposterous that she laughed. "Sell Belle Terre?" She expected them to smile, to let her in on what was surely a private joke.

Rather, it appeared to be a private conspiracy. Tricia hatefully stared her down. She looked toward Ken for an explanation. He looked away guiltily.

"Have you both gone mad?" she asked hoarsely. "Belle Terre will never be sold."

"Why not?"

"Because it's ours. It belongs to Cotton and to us."

"No it doesn't," Tricia sneered. "It belonged to the Laurents. They're all dead."

Schyler drew herself up. "Cotton might not own it through bloodlines, but he has poured his whole life into Belle Terre. He will never sell it."

She tried to go around Tricia, but the other woman, with surprising strength, caught her arm. "Cotton's mind can be changed."

"Never. I wouldn't even try." She shook off Tricia's hand.

"He's an old man, Schyler. He's been critically ill. His business is suffering as a result. He's got himself in debt so deep he'll never get out."

"Your point?"

"We can have him certified incompetent."

Schyler wanted to strike Tricia so badly that she clenched her fists to keep from doing it. "If anything happens to Cotton, then you will truly have an adversary, Tricia. You will have *me* to contend with."

Chapter Twenty-eight

Schyler gripped the steering wheel so tightly her knuckles turned white. She was driving far too fast, but she didn't care. Besides, it seemed only fair that the car keep pace with the windshield wipers. They flapped back and forth furiously, but had little effect in the downpour.

From a sane corner of her mind, she reasoned that she must still be exhausted even after her long sleep. That's why she felt that she had been flayed alive. Her confrontation with Tricia and Ken had left her feeling raw and exposed. Her self-control was tenuous. She feared that it might slip at any moment.

In the meantime, she felt driven to act. If she stalled, she might never get into motion again. If she let herself think about all that had been said in the last hour, she would go stark, staring mad. She had to keep moving to keep her mind from petrifying around one thought: they wanted to sell Belle Terre.

Her objective was clear. She had her sights set on a goal and nothing would keep her from achieving it. She had to preserve Belle Terre, keep it safe, intact, save it for Cotton. She had to work until she dropped. That's what she must do.

Her course of action was so definitely blueprinted in her mind that when she reached the landing side of the Laurent Bayou bridge, she floorboarded the brake pedal. The car skidded several yards before coming to a complete stand-still. The windshield wipers continued to clack out their steady beat. The torrential rain drummed against the roof of the car. Schyler, breathing through her mouth as though she had run the distance from the mansion, stared at the landing.

The inactive scene was so out of keeping with the energy churning inside her, she couldn't believe what she was see-ing. It was incomprehensible. There was absolutely noth-ing being done. The place was deserted.

The office door was dead-bolted, the windows dark. The heavy doors of the hangarlike building that housed the rigs when they weren't in use were chained closed. The loading platforms along the railroad tracks were deserted. The en-tire area looked as forlorn as a ghost town, desolate, empty, and dead.

Schyler swallowed her dismay and tried desperately to remember what day of the week this was. She had lost track of the days, surely. The time she had spent in the hospital had put her off track. Mentally she tallied days against the calendar. No, this was a work day.

Then why wasn't any work being done? Where the hell was Cash? Goddamn him!

She was so upset that she began to shake uncontrollably. She took her foot off the brake and gave the steering wheel a vicious turn. She stepped on the accelerator; the rear wheels spun, trying to gain traction in the soggy ground. They threw up a shower of mud behind the car.

"Dammit!" Schyler thumped her fist on the steering wheel and dug her toe into the accelerator. Finally the wheels found a foothold. The car lurched forward. Its rear end fishtailed and swerved dangerously close to a concrete support of the bridge. Schyler jerked the wheel again and straightened the car out as it shot onto the main road. She met no other cars, and that was a blessing because she positioned her car over the yellow stripe.

Visibility was severely limited by the dark day and the driving rain. She saw the turnoff she wanted too late and slammed on the brakes. The car slid past the side road. Cursing lividly, she shoved it into reverse and backed up.

The side road was a sea of mud, but she aimed the hood ornament down its center and plowed through it. Her fury gained as much momentum as her car. When she brought it to a teeth-jarring stop, she wrenched the door open and cannoned out. Heedless of the rain, she marched toward the house. It was the same color as the gray sky and blended into its setting so well as to be almost invisible.

He was sitting on the covered porch but far enough back to keep dry. Rainwater was rolling off the tin roof and dripping over the eaves, splashing in puddles that bordered the porch. The chair he was sitting in had a cane seat and a ladder back. It was reared back to a precarious angle. He had balanced himself by propping his bare feet on a cypress post that supported the overhang.

He was without a shirt. His jeans were zipped, but unsnapped. A bottle of whiskey and a glass with two finger's worth in the bottom of it were sitting beside his chair. A cigarette was occupying one corner of his sullen lips. His eyes were squinted against the smoke that curled from its tip. They widened a trifle when Schyler bounded up onto the porch and yelled her first question.

"Just what the hell do you think you're doing?"

In no apparent hurry, Cash took the cigarette from between his lips and looked at it curiously. "Smoking?"

Schyler quivered with outrage. Her arms were stiff at her sides, and she kept opening and closing her fists. She seemed impervious to her chilled, wet skin and her hair, which dripped rain onto her rigid shoulders.

With an angry, grunting sound, she reached out and knocked his feet away from the post. The front legs of his chair landed hard on the porch. As though catapulted from the seat, Cash was instantly on his feet and towering over her. He flicked his cigarette over the porch railing.

"You live dangerously, Miss Schyler." His voice had the sinister lisp of a sword being withdrawn from its scabbard.

"I ought to fire you on the spot."

"For what?"

"For goofing off when you thought I'd be away. Why isn't any work being done? Where are the loggers? The rigs haven't even been out today. I went to the landing.

The office is closed. The garage is locked. Nothing is going on. Why the hell not?"

Cash's temper had never had a very long fuse. He didn't take reprimands well and had never walked away from a fight. On any application, he filled in the blank space after RELIGIOUS PREFERENCE with the word Christian, but the concept of turning the other cheek was alien to his nature. The army had trained and sharpened reflexes that were already lightning quick.

He might have appeared to be totally relaxed, a man enjoying a smoke, a whiskey, and a good, hard rain, but in fact, Cash's nerves were as frazzled as Schyler's. For the last few days, he hadn't slept any more than she. His short supply of patience had been used up days ago; he was fresh out. He had consumed more whiskey than was prudent for a man to drink in the middle of the day. He had been spoiling for a fight even before Schyler had charged onto his territory slinging unfounded accusations.

Had she been a man, she would already be picking herself up out of the mud and spitting out teeth. But Cash, for all his meanness, had never physically abused a woman. He resorted to contempt. He was oozing it when he said, "The weather, lady. Do you expect me to let loggers work in this?" He made a broad, sweeping gesture with his hand; water running off the leaves splattered it.

"I hired you to work in any kind of weather."

"This isn't a brief April shower."

"I don't care if it's a hurricane, I want the loggers out there cutting timber."

"Are you *crazy?* The forests become death traps when it rains this much this quick. We can't even get rigs in. The mud—"

"Are you going to put them to work or not?"

"I'm not."

Her breasts heaved with the extent of her anger and frustration. "I should have listened to everybody. They told me you were worthless."

"Maybe so. But saw hands can't cut, haul, or load in this kind of rain. If you've ever been around loggers you damn well know that. Cotton wouldn't send men out in this and neither am I."

Suddenly remembering Tricia's words, Schyler drew a staggering breath. "Your mother. And my father. Is it true? Were they . . .?"

"Yes." He pushed the *s* through his teeth. "They were."

Schyler sucked back a sob. "He was *married*. He had a family," she cried with anguish. "She was a slut."

"And he's a son of a bitch," Cash snarled. "I hated him being with her." He moved forward threateningly, backing Schyler into the cypress post. "But I had to live with it day in and day out practically all my life. You didn't. You were protected up there at Belle Terre, while I had to watch him use and hurt my mother for years. There wasn't a damn thing I could do about it."

"Your mother was a grown woman. She made her choice."

"A rotten one in my estimation. She chose to love a stinking son of a bitch like Cotton Crandall."

Schyler raised her chin. "You wouldn't have the guts to call him that to his face."

"I have. Ask him."

"I want you off Belle Terre by the end of the week."

"Who's going to get your timber ready for market?"

"I will."

"Wrong. You can't do doodledee squat without me." He took a step closer. "And you know it. You knew it when you came driving over here, didn't you?" He braced one hand against the post near her head and leaned into her, brushing his body against hers. "Know what? I don't think that's why you came over here at all. I think you came over here for something altogether different."

"You're drunk."

"Not yet."

"I meant what I said. I want you gone—"

She had moved away from the post. He caught her arm and slammed her back up against it, hard enough to halt her condescending speech. His palm supported her chin while his fingers bracketed her jaw.

"The trouble with you, Miss Schyler, is that you just

don't know when to quit. You keep pushing and pushing, until you drive a man over the edge."

His mouth covered hers in a hard kiss. Schyler reacted violently. She struggled against his hand to release her jaw, while her body bucked against his. Her arms flailed at him.

"Admit it." He lifted his mouth off hers only far enough to speak, "This is what you came here for."

"Let me go."

"Not a chance, lady."

"I hate you."

"But you want me."

"Like hell I do."

"You want me. That's what's got you as mad as a hornet."

He kissed her again. This time he succeeded in getting his tongue inside her mouth. The rain beat loudly against the roof, drowning out her whimpers of outrage and then of surrender.

It wasn't a conscious decision. She didn't voluntarily capitulate. Her emotions superseded her will and responded on their own. For days they'd been seeking an outlet. It had just presented itself, and they eagerly funneled toward it.

Still, her stubborn nature balked at total compliance. She succeeded in tearing her mouth free. Her lips felt swollen and bruised. When she dragged her tongue over them, she tasted whiskey. She tasted him. Cash Boudreaux.

The thought was untenable. She laid her hands on his bare shoulders, intending to push him away. But he lowered his head again. His lips ate at hers. Her fingers curled inward, forming deep furrows in the tense muscles of his upper arms.

When the kiss ended, she rolled her head to one side. "Stop," she moaned.

He did. At least he stopped kissing her lips. But he laid his open mouth against her neck. "You want this as much as I do."

"No."

"Yes." He flicked her earlobe with his tongue. "How long has it been since you got fucked real good?"

A low groan escaped her. It dissolved against his lips. They kissed ravenously, engaging in an orgy of kissing, cruel and carnal. He swept her mouth with his tongue, as though to rid it of pride and resistance.

His hands moved down her chest until each covered a breast. He massaged them roughly. He wasn't easy on the buttons of her damp blouse, nor on the clasp of her bra. He wasn't too much kinder to the soft flesh that filled his hands. "Jesus," he sighed as he kneaded her. He supported her breasts with his palms while he whisked the erect nipples with his thumbs.

"Very nice, Miss Schyler."

"Go to hell."

"Not yet. Not until we've finished what we've started here."

Schyler's head ground against the post. Her eyes were squeezed shut, but she blindly knotted her fingers in his dense chest hair. He grunted, with pain, with pleasure. He bit her lower lip. She went in search of a full-fledged, open-mouth, tongue-thrusting kiss, and got it.

Abruptly they broke apart and gazed into each other's eyes. Their rapid breaths soughed together. It was the only sound they could hear over the incessant rain.

He bent at the knees and lifted her into his arms. The front door crashed open when he landed his bare foot against it. The rooms of the house were dim and shadowed and stuffy. He carried her straight through it to the screened back porch.

The iron bed had been left unmade. The sheets were white and clean, but had a rainy-day rumpledness that was as sexy as the heat their two bodies generated. His knee made a deep dent in the mattress. Springs creaked like settling wood in a beloved old house. The instant her wet hair made contact with the pillows, his body covered hers with mating possessiveness. Their mouths came together hungrily as Cash gathered her beneath him.

Kissing her deeply, he slid his hand beneath her skirt and up her smooth thigh. He palmed her. She was warm, damp. He gently squeezed her mound. Her responding gasp was soft and yearning. Quickly he sat up and plunged his other hand beneath her skirt. Hooking the fingers of both hands in the elastic of her panties, he peeled them down her legs.

Then he straddled her, planting his knees solidly on either side of hers. Schyler's heart was fluttering wildly as she gazed up at him. His thighs looked hard and lean inside the faded jeans. From her perspective his shoulders looked broader, his arms more powerful, like he could break her in two if he wanted to.

His belly was flat and corrugated with muscles. Copper nipples nestled in a forest of light brown hair. He was wearing no expression, but intensity had made the bone structure of his face more pronounced. His eyes seemed to be the only spot of color in the gray room. They burned.

She focused on them as he pulled her blouse open. Impatiently he tugged it out of the waistband of her skirt and pushed aside the flimsy lace cups of her brassiere. Her breasts lay softly upon her chest, but the areolas were wrinkled and puckered with arousal. Her nipples were very pink and very hard.

Cash bent over her and stroked one with his tongue. Schyler's back arched off the bed. He touched her again and again with the pointed tip of his tongue, then he drew one of the shiny, wet nipples into his mouth.

The pleasure was so exquisite, the heat so fierce, Schyler clutched at him. Her seeking hands came to rest on his upper thighs. Her thumbs settled in the grooves of his groin. He bridged her body with his stiff arms and dipped his head low over her breasts. His hair fell forward, tickling her skin.

"Unzip me," he directed huskily between the soft, damp caresses he was giving her breasts. After a few moments, when it became apparent that she wasn't going to, he stood on his knees again and reached for his fly. He winced as he worked the zipper down. Schyler stared, fascinated, as the wedge widened. It filled up with body hair that was darker and denser than that on his chest.

When the zipper was undone, he hooked his thumbs into the cloth and pulled the jeans down over his hips. Schyler caught her breath and held it, shocked by his flagrant immodesty and the fullness of his erection. The tip was as round and smooth and voluptuous as a ripe plum.

He reversed the position of their knees until hers were on the outside. He raised the hem of her skirt to her waist. Schyler closed her eyes.

At that instant, she wanted desperately to call it off.

But then he touched her there. His fingers lightly tweaked clumps of dark blond curls, then slid between the soft folds of her body and up inside, stretching into the wetness.

He made a groaning sound before he said, "You'd better hold on. This is going to be a rough ride." He moved her hands to the iron rails of the headboard behind her head and folded her fingers around them. She gripped the cool metal.

His hands spread wide on the insides of her thighs and separated them. She made a small, helpless sound. "Open your eyes. I want you to know who this is."

Her eyes sprang open in direct challenge to his insulting words. But there was no doubt as to who drove into her. She was wet, but she was tight. She winced with momentary pain. He tensed with momentary surprise. Then he gave another swift thrust and embedded himself inside her with absolute possession.

He withdrew, almost leaving her, before sinking into her again. "My name is Cash Boudreaux."

"I know who you are."

"Say it." He ground his pelvis against hers. "Say it." She caught her lower lip between her teeth. Sweat dotted her upper lip. She tried to keep her hips on the bed, but involuntarily she raised them to meet the next plunging stroke of his strong, smooth penis. "You're going to say my name, damn you."

He flattened his hand low on her belly, fingers pointed toward her breasts, and worked it downward until the heel of his hand was at the very lowest point of her body. He rubbed it back and forth slowly. A low, choppy moan rose out of Schyler's chest. Warm sensations began to spiral up through her middle and radiate outward until her fingertips and toes began to throb with an infusion of blood. She gripped the headboard tighter.

"Say my name." His forehead was bathed with sweat, his teeth clenched in restraint. He lowered his head to her breasts and nuzzled them with his nose. His stubbled chin rasped the delicate skin. His buttocks rose and fell with each rhythmic stroke. The heel of his hand caressed her until he felt moisture against it. He swept his thumb downward, over the tuft of hair, and into the source of that moisture. The pad of his thumb was soft and sensitive against that softer, more sensitive spot.

Pleasure speared through Schyler. She gave a sharp cry.

"Say my name," he panted.

"Ca . . . Cash."

Her eyes closed. Her neck arched. Her head thrashed on the pillow. Her thighs hugged his buttocks tight. Cash stared down at her. Yielding to an urge he had never had before, he lowered himself over her and buried his face in the hollow of her shoulder. His hands joined hers on the headboard. Their fingers interlaced over and around the iron rods. His chest crushed her breasts. Their breathing escalated and turned harsher. He hammered into her. The walls of her body milked him.

When the climax came, neither said anything coherent, but their moans of gratification were simultaneous and long.

Chapter Twenty-nine

On the one hand, he stayed inside her far too long.

On the other hand, it was much too brief.

Cash eased himself away from her. He glanced down into her face. Her eyes were closed. Her face was smooth and still. Resisting an impulse to kiss her mouth, he slowly disengaged their arms and legs and rolled to one side of the bed. Automatically he reached for the pack of cigarettes and lighter on the bedside table.

As he lit one, Schyler sat up and threw her legs over the opposite side of the bed, keeping her back to him and her head averted. She shoved down her skirt and groped among the twisted sheets for her panties. Finding them, she bent at the waist and stepped into them. She pulled them on in the same motion she used to stand up. She replaced the cups of her bra, clasped it, then rebuttoned her blouse. She didn't tuck it in.

She turned around and looked down at him as though there was something she wanted to say. She swallowed visibly. Her lips opened but closed without uttering a single sound. He stuck the cigarette in his mouth and stacked his hands behind his head in a pose that looked insolent and uncaring, especially since his jeans were still bunched around his thighs.

He would have bet a month's salary on what she would do next, and he was right. She turned her back on him and left the house. He listened to her footsteps fade as she went through the front door and across the porch. Shortly, he heard her car's motor starting.

He lay motionless for a long time, until the cigarette between his lips became a fire hazard. He ground it out. He took off his jeans, balled them up, and angrily threw them as far as he could. They hit the opposite wall and dropped to the floor.

Naked, he rolled to his side and stared sightlessly through the screen. It was raining harder than ever. He could barely see the opposite bank of the bayou through the silver curtain. The limbs of the trees drooped with the weight of the rainwater.

His eyes moved to the pillow beside his. He laid his hand in the imprint her head had made. It was still warm.

"Schyler."

Schyler. Cash remembered the day he first heard that name. He had thought it was a funny name for a baby girl. So had Monique. They had talked about it later, after Cotton left.

It had been a cold November day. The bayou was shrouded in fog. Cash had made white clouds of vapor by blowing into the cold air. He had pretended he was smoking Camels like the older boys at the pool hall did.

Cotton had caught him at it. "Why aren't you in school, Cash?" he had asked the minute he alighted from his long, shiny car.

"*Maman* didn't make me go today. Are those doughnuts?" He pointed to the white bakery sack Cotton was carrying. Cotton rarely came empty-handed. He usually brought something for both of them, like flowers, a trinket, a bottle of perfume for Monique; comic books, a sack of candy, a small toy for Cash.

But he never gave them money. He had tried, but Monique would never take it. They'd had fights over it, but Monique always won.

They didn't fight that day. Monique stepped out onto the porch, drying her hands on a dish towel. "You must have smelled my roux," she teased Cotton. "How can you always tell whem I'm making gumbo?"

Cotton smiled back at her. "Good day for gumbo." Then his light eyebrows furrowed. "Why isn't Cash in school?"

Monique shrugged one shapely shoulder. "We slept late."

"He should be in school, Monique. You'll have the truant officer back out here."

She laughed her deep contralto laugh and bent down to hug Cash's disheveled head against her warm breasts. "I need him to deliver medicines today. Everybody's sick with the croup."

"Medicines my ass," Cotton muttered, stamping the mud off his boots as he came upon the porch. "What you're selling folks is mumbo jumbo, voodoo bullshit."

Laughing and sandwiching the eight-year-old boy between them, she caught the lobe of Cotton's ear between her strong, white teeth. "It works on you, *mon cher.*"

Cotton sighed. "It sure as hell does." He kissed her long and deeply, rubbing her back with his large, work-worn hands. "When will the gumbo be ready?"

"Hours. Can you stay that long?"

He looked down at Cash. The lad read the gravity of Cotton's expression. "I need to talk to you about something."

At the table in front of the fireplace, while they demolished the doughnuts and a fresh pot of coffee, Cotton broke the disturbing news.

"We're getting a baby."

Cash, who had been licking powdered sugar off his fingers, quickly looked at his mother. Instinctively he knew that she would be distressed. She was. He watched her delicate hands come together. She interlaced her slender fingers and held them so tightly that her knuckles turned the color of bones.

"A *bébé?*"

"Yes. We're adopting a child. Macy... Macy..." Cotton sighed and stared into his coffee cup for a long moment before going ahead. "It appears she's barren. It eats on her." His blue eyes spoke eloquently to Monique. "Especially since she knows about you. She wants children. Belle Terre needs children."

Monique glanced down at Cash. "*Oui,* it does," she said

quietly. "You should fill it with as many children as possible."

Cotton forced a laugh. "Well, we're only starting with one. It's a baby girl. Macy wanted a boy, but . . ." He shrugged. "This girl was born and she jumped at the chance to get her. Father Martin is handling the adoption for us. I had to agree to raise her a Catholic."

"Better than a Baptist."

Her teasing was as forced as his laugh had been. He cleared his throat noisily. "She's only three days old."

"What does she look like?"

"She was born in Baton Rouge, so we haven't seen her yet. But Macy has already named her Schyler."

"A strange name for a baby girl. But pretty," Monique said with hollow enthusiasm.

"It's a Laurent family name."

Their mouths were saying one thing, but their eyes were communicating quite another. Finally both fell silent. The logs in the fireplace popped and crackled. Cash's eyes warily shifted between his mother and her lover.

After a time, Cotton reached across the table and covered Monique's clasped hands. "This doesn't change anything."

"It must."

"It doesn't. You know it doesn't. You *know*." She continued to stare into his eyes, hurt and unsure. He continued to send her unspoken assurances. "When did you say the gumbo would be ready?"

Her face brightened. Her jet-black eyes sparkled through unshed tears. "Can you stay?"

"I can stay."

"Until it's ready?"

"Until I've had at least two bowls."

She flew from her chair and threw her arms around his neck. They kissed with a passion made stronger because it was illicit. Then she hurried to get the fish, shrimp, vegetables, and spices into the pot, where they would simmer together in the roux until they were tender and the gumbo was rich and thick and properly murky.

Meanwhile Cotton helped Cash load the red wagon he

was often seen pulling through the streets of town. In the back of it bottles of unguents and potions, salves and tinctures clinked together musically. His mother was a *traiteur*. He was her delivery boy.

"You're not smoking for real, are you?" Cotton asked him, referring to the clouds of make-believe smoke he'd been blowing earlier.

"No, sir." Monique had coached him on how to address Cotton respectfully.

"Good. It's a nasty habit and very bad for you."

"How come?"

"It damages your lungs."

"You smoke sometimes."

"I'm a grown-up."

Cash gazed up at Cotton, hoping that someday he would be that tall, that strong. "Will the new baby live in the big white house?"

"Of course."

Cash thought about that, envying the baby a little. "Will you still come to see us after you get her?"

Cotton stopped what he was doing. He gazed down into Cash's earnest, anxious face. With a half smile, he reached out and touched the boy's cheek. "Yes, I'll still come to see you. Nothing could keep me from coming to see you."

Cash gauged the honesty behind Cotton's answer and decided it was genuine. "What'd you say the baby's name was?"

"Schyler."

Cash laid his hand in the bowl her head had made in the pillow. Her wet hair had left the pillowcase damp. He closed his fist. It came up empty. There was nothing there.

For Monique Boudreaux's bastard boy, there never had been.

Chapter Thirty

"You're restless tonight. If you don't stop pacing you'll wear a path in the carpet." Dale Gilbreath missed the dirty look his wife sent him. He had chastised her from behind his newspaper. He tipped the corner of it down and smiled at her in the patronizing manner she loathed. "Is something wrong, dear? Don't you feel well?"

"I feel fine." Rhoda's strained tone of voice wasn't very convincing.

"You've been on edge and out of sorts all evening." With only bland interest he scanned the page of newsprint he'd been reading.

"It's the rain." Rhoda moved to the window and jerked on the tasseled cord. The drapes swished open. "God, the weather in this place is wretched. The humidity is so goddamn high, it's like trying to breathe lentil soup. It threatens to rain. It doesn't. Then when it does, it's a goddamn flood."

"We traded severe winters for a little stickiness."

Dale was on the receiving end of another whithering glance. She could do without his half-baked philosophy tonight, especially when she knew he hated the Louisiana climate as much as she.

"Shoveling a few feet of snow wouldn't hurt you," she said snidely. "You're beginning to get a real gut. Which is no wonder since you sit on your ass behind a desk all day. Don't you ever feel the need to exercise?"

Rhoda attended a workout class every weekday morning. The strain and sweat and self-abuse was like a religious rite to her. To point up to him just how superior her physical condition was to his, she sucked in her tummy, tightened her derriere, and thrust out her breasts.

Dale exchanged his newspaper for a pipe and calmly began filling it with his special blend of tobaccos, scooping it from a leather pouch. "When you're right, you're right. I could use some exercise." He put a match to the bowl of his pipe and drew on the stem. Fanning out the match as he watched her through the rising cloud of smoke, he asked, "But do you really want to swap insults with me tonight, Rhoda?"

Dale could get nasty. He didn't take pot shots but hit below the belt every time with well-aimed punches. Rhoda wasn't in a frame of mind to suffer one of his soft-spoken, but malicious attacks. Her ego was bruised. She didn't think it could withstand further injury.

Cash had told her he would call this afternoon and arrange a time and place for them to rendezvous. He hadn't. She couldn't call him; he didn't have a damn telephone. She had often wondered if the sole reason he didn't have one installed was so he could avoid a woman when he wanted to. That was probably it. The Cajun was a class A son of a bitch.

She would have driven to his out-of-the-way house, but she wasn't sure where it was. He'd been aggravatingly unspecific about that when she had asked him for directions. As the dreary afternoon had worn on, she had given serious thought to gambling her reputation and sacrificing her pride for one roll in the sack with him, but damned if she was going to risk getting her BMW stuck to the hubs on one of the backwoods quagmires. They were called roads. Some even had designated state highway numbers, but she considered them pig trails that were to be avoided at all costs.

Now, just thinking about her thwarted plans for the afternoon heated her temper back up to a slow simmer. And apparently Dale wanted to swap insults whether she wanted to or not.

Casually he said, "For instance, I could start with this juvenile fixation you've developed for your latest lover."

Rhoda's posture stiffened marginally, but she was adroit at controlling knee-jerk reactions. Dale wanted her to fly into a tirade of denial. He loved pricking her with innuendo and half-truths. He enjoyed provoking her until she blew.

Slowly she turned to face him, affecting bewilderment with admirable skill. "Latest lover?"

He puffed on his pipe and smiled around the stem clenched between his teeth. "You really should have pursued an acting career, Rhoda. You're very good. But I know you better than you know yourself. I can smell when you're in heat. You exude a musky odor like an animal."

"Well I'm glad you didn't pursue a career as a poet. Your phraseology is revolting."

"You're also very good at changing the subject."

"I find your subject tiresome."

Dale chuckled. "Rhoda, you and your lovers are never tiresome."

"How do you know there is a current lover?" she challenged. Hands on hips, she faced him where he sat in an easy chair.

"There's always one." Drolly, he added, "At least one."

"Jealous?"

"You know better."

"Ah, that's right," Rhoda said with a catty smile. "You were always a much better spectator than participant."

"Because you always put on such an entertaining and engrossing show."

It wasn't a compliment and Rhoda was smart enough not to mistake it for one. "Let's talk about something else. Or better yet, let's don't talk at all. You're in a foul mood tonight."

Dale puffed the pipe with deceptive contentment. "You'd be well advised not to anger me, my dear." Just as Dale had intended, that got her attention.

Figuratively she laid down her weapons. "Oh? Why not?"

"I'm about to pull off a big deal."

"At the bank?"

"Hmm. Something you'll be extremely pleased about."

"Is it legal?"

He frowned at her, but neither one of them took his reproachful expression seriously. "Shame on you. Of course it's legal. In fact it will be the culmination of a year's work."

"What does it mean to me?"

"Nothing short of the realization of a dream. For both of us. Instead of us being on the outside of Heaven's social circle looking in, these rednecks will be kissing our asses. There won't be anything we can't do and get away with."

Rhoda tingled with an excitement that was almost sexual. She sat down on the arm of his chair and wiggled close to him. "Tell me about it."

"Not yet. I'm saving it for a surprise." He emptied the bowl of his pipe into an ashtray and turned out the lamp on the end table.

Rhoda fell into step behind him as he left the chair and headed toward the bedroom. "Damn you, Dale. I hate it when you dangle carrots in front of me like this."

"On the contrary, darling, you love it. You thrive on intrigue."

"I can't if I don't know about it. Let me in on what you're up to."

"I'll give you a hint." He switched the light on in their bedroom. "What's the hottest topic of conversation around town these days?"

She thought for a moment, watching with detachment as Dale took a 35mm camera from a glass shelf in the étagère. He loaded a roll of film and reset the ASA. Suddenly Rhoda's throat vibrated with a low, nefarious laugh. "Not Cotton Crandall!" she exclaimed. "Your scheme doesn't involve Crandall and Belle Terre, does it?"

"Why shouldn't it?" Dale adjusted the lamp shades on the bedside tables to his satisfaction. He looked at his wife pointedly. She began removing her clothes.

"Belle Terre? You mean there's a chance—"

Dale reached out and cupped his hand over her mouth. "It's not to be discussed outside this room, understand?" She nodded her head. He removed his hand and began undoing the buttons of her blouse.

"That daughter," Rhoda whispered. "I understand she's a firecracker, that Cotton coached her well."

"Schyler? Not to worry," Dale replied with dismissive smugness. "She's being taken care of."

"What do you mean?"

"That's one of the details you needn't be concerned about. The stakes are high on this one, Rhoda. That's why we must be extremely careful." He slipped her blouse off and tossed it onto a chair. He ran his hands over her breasts. "It would be regrettable if a senseless indiscretion screwed this up, wouldn't it?" He tweaked her nipple, a pinch too strong to be classified as foreplay. She winced. "And screw is the operative word."

"Be specific."

"All right. Find a lover who isn't so personally involved with the Crandalls and preferably one who didn't crawl out of a trash can."

She met him eye to eye without flinching. She wasn't alarmed that he knew about her affair with Cash. In fact she was pleased. Dale knew that Cash's reputation with women was legendary. That Cash had chosen her from so many elevated her desirability.

"You've never cared who my lovers were before," she said in a voice as sultry as the weather.

"They've always come from a suitable strata of society before. You're scraping scum off the bayou this time."

By tacit agreement the name Cash Boudreaux would never be uttered. They had learned from experience that mentioning names was unwise. Names could result in more complicated resolutions once affairs were over. Admit nothing was the credo that each adhered to.

"He could be useful to us."

"He is," Dale said. "Extremely useful. But I'm using him my way. He's of more value to us someplace other than your bed. He can't be screwed by both of us at the same time."

Again she laughed deep in her throat. "We've used that tactic before."

"But not with this kind of man. I don't think he'd like that, do you?"

"No," she said without a second's hesitation. "He definitely would not."

"I don't blame you for selecting him. He's attractive, if you like the vulgar, brutal type. But until all the details are finalized, amuse yourself with someone who's closer to being your social equal."

"And yours." Rhoda knew that that was at the crux of this entire discussion. Dale didn't mind being a cuckold. He did mind who made him one. It was a matter of ego.

"And mine," he admitted. He helped her step out of her skirt and paused to admire the dark hosiery, the lacy garter belt, and the patch of hair in between. He slid his hand between her thighs. "You're wet."

"You knew I would be."

Stroking her, he laughed. "Money hungry, bitch. You can come just talking about money."

"We share the same ambition, darling."

"I remember the time you told me that if my cock were as monstrous as my ambition, you wouldn't have to seek outside diversions."

"And in reply you said that my sexuality was one of your greatest assets."

"It's served its purpose profitably many times."

Later, as she languished against the pillows on the bed, the lips of her sex as rosy and glistening as those of her mouth, Dale moved in for a closeup with the camera. He snickered as he clicked the shutter.

"Let me in on the joke."

"I was just thinking what some of the bank board members would say if they saw you this way."

Rhoda reached out and stroked his cheek in a parody of affection. "Most of them have, my dear, most of them have."

Chapter Thirty-one

It was the dead cats that did it.

Schyler had returned to Belle Terre after being with Cash and went straight to her room. She filled her bathtub to the rim and soaked until the hot water turned cold. She asked Mrs. Graves to bring her dinner up to her on a tray. She ignored both the housekeeper's long-suffering sigh and the dinner. She wasn't hungry. She doubted she ever would be again.

How could she have done something so stupid?

Not that she was new at making severe errors in judgment. She had underestimated her sister's jealous hatred and ability to manipulate. She had given Ken up too easily, but had clung to a dead love for too long. She had almost let Tricia destroy her relationship with their father. But of all the serious mistakes she had made in her life, going to bed with Cash Boudreaux championed them all.

To save herself from having to think about it that night, she took a sleeping pill and went to bed early. Before the effects of the mild narcotic overpowered her, though, she suffered through several replays of the afternoon.

In her imagination, she felt again his hands, his lips, his body. Beside hers. Inside hers. She kept remembering him naked and strong and hard and beautiful. He made love as he did everything else, with intensity and passion and a total absence of discipline. His reputation as a stud was well earned. Even the memory of the act was more potent than any other sexual encounter Schyler had ever had. She had never felt so bloody marvelous in her life.

That is, until it was over. Then she'd never felt so wretched. She hadn't cried, but she had wanted to. Thank God she had held back her tears. They would have spelled her final and absolute humiliation and Cash's unqualified victory because what had happened on that bed had been a battle. He had set out to prove that there was a way he could best her, and he had.

He had fought to win. If there had been one kind and tender word spoken, she might not have taken defeat so hard. Nothing had softened the blow to her pride, not even that she had been forced or coerced. No, when he had carried her to his bed, she had wanted to go.

She had left his house and driven home under her own power. She had spoken intelligently with Dr. Collins over the telephone, and had even had a brief and animated conversation with Cotton. Under the circumstances, she had done well. She was confused and angry, but she was made of stern stuff. The matrix of her spirit had held her together. She hadn't crumbled; she hadn't broken apart.

But when she saw the dead cats she began to shake.

Mrs. Graves's scream rattled the crystal in every chandelier in the house. It was a clear morning, promising a better day than the one preceding it. Birds were splashing in the rain puddles on the lawn. A new sun was disintegrating sheer pink clouds. God was in his heaven . . . but all was not right with the world.

The scream woke Schyler up. She bolted out of bed. She was naked, so she grabbed a robe and charged out her door, almost colliding with Ken and Tricia. By the looks of them, they had been roused by the housekeeper's scream, too.

"What the hell is going on?" Ken mumbled.

"I don't know."

Schyler beat them downstairs. Mrs. Graves was standing in the open front door, her face in her hands. She was making retching sounds. Schyler pushed her aside and stepped across the threshold.

Her empty stomach contracted. She tasted bile in her throat. No more than three feet beyond the front door lay the two cats. The female was on her back, spread-eagled beneath the male. The symbolism was blatant and crude. The female's throat had been slit. Blood and gore still oozed from the wide wound. Black fur was clotted with it. Her dead eyes were crawling with ants. The male was dead, too, but whatever had killed him wasn't apparent.

"Jesus!" Ken hissed. "Stay back, Tricia. And for chrissake, shut her up." Impatiently he gestured toward Mrs. Graves who was still gagging behind her hands.

The two women gladly withdrew. Ken stepped around Schyler, who seemed rooted to the threshold. He bent down on one knee and investigated the macabre sight. He looked up at Schyler. "Do you know anything about this?"

"Of course not." But she was afraid she did. Two dead cats found on the front porch could be attributed to teenage pranksters, playful vandalism. Two dead cats, brutally murdered and arranged to depict human beings making love, was the product of a sick mind. The question was, whose?

"Guess we ought to call the sheriff."

Schyler shook her head. "No. He wouldn't do anything. Just get rid of them. Clean up the mess."

"Like hell!" Ken exclaimed. "I'm not a yard nigger."

Schyler began to tremble. Her hands balled into fists. She could feel herself losing control. "Clean it up," she angrily enunciated. "Unless you'd rather go to the landing and deal with the loggers."

Ken's face worked with indignation, but in the end, he stamped off the porch and toward the toolshed. He crossed the wet grass in his bare feet, having to dodge mud puddles in his path. Schyler looked down at the floorboards of the veranda. They were clean. There were no muddy footprints on the steps either. Whoever had placed the cats there could have come from inside the house. Either way, the perpetrator was clever—very, very clever.

She went back inside and upstairs to her room. She returned to the bed, but she didn't give in to the second impulse to hide beneath the covers. Instead, she sat on the edge of it and folded her arms over her middle. Rocking back and forth, she indulged in a good crying jag.

Someone knew about Cash and her. Someone knew that

they'd been to bed together. But who except the two of them?

Cash? She had fired him. He hadn't liked her in the first place. But could he be so violent as to wantonly kill two cats? Of course he could. That's why she had asked him to do away with Jigger's pit bull terriers. She had witnessed him pulling the knife on Ken. He had a reputation for violence.

Jigger Flynn could be violent, too. But he wouldn't know about Cash and her going to bed together. Would he? How?

Tricia and Ken were no doubt furious with her after the confrontation yesterday. They stood on opposing sides regarding the sale of Belle Terre. But they wouldn't resort to something like this even if they knew about Cash and her.

Suddenly Schyler realized that there were several people in Heaven, and on Belle Terre in particular, who would have been much happier if she had never come home from England.

But it was going to take more than a couple of grisly dead cats to scare her off. She had to pay back the loan before the deadline. Yesterday's production had been sacrificed to the weather so they would have to work twice as hard today to make up for it. Now that Cash was out of the picture, she would have to handle everything alone. That shouldn't slow her down. She had been relying solely on herself for a long time.

Wiping the salty tear tracks from her cheeks, she removed her robe and headed for her closet.

When she arrived at the landing three loggers were there. They were hoisting chains and pulleys onto a flat trailer. It was obvious they were wasting no time. Their expressions were grim. They didn't even take time to stop and speak to her. Something was wrong.

"What's going on?" she called out as she left her car.

"Accident," one informed her around a wad of tobacco. "'Xcuse me, ma'am." Moving her aside, he slung a coil of heavy rope over his head and threw it onto the truck.

"An accident? Where? What kind of accident?"

"Rig overturned."

"Did anyone get hurt?"

"Yes, ma'am. One man's down."

She didn't need more details than that. This was an emergency. Loggers loved to swap horror stories of work-related accidents. She had hung around the landing enough to know that. The tales rarely needed embellishment to make them gory. Logging accidents were usually disastrous, if not fatal.

"Is he badly hurt? Why wasn't I notified?"

"We called the house. You'd already left."

"Did you call an ambulance?"

"Sure did. Told 'em where we're cuttin'. It's back deep in the woods. Be tough to get anything that's not four-wheel drive in there, but they said they could. Hey, Miz Schyler ma'am, whadaya doin'?"

"Since I can't take my car, I'll ride there with you." She was met with three argumentative stares.

"No sense in you goin' at all, ma'am."

"A cuttin' site ain't no place for a woman."

"We're wasting time." She stepped into the cab of the truck and decisively slammed the door behind her.

Shrugging and muttering that it was no skin off his ass what the boss lady did, the driver slid in beside her. The other two climbed onto the trailer.

The truck labored its way along a twisting, narrow highway. Once they made it to the turnoff, it had the muddy, bumpy skid rows to navigate. They drove for what seemed like miles through a forest so dense that daylight barely penetrated. The driver colorfully cursed the truck's reluctance as it chugged over the rough terrain toward the site where they had been cutting towering pines.

"Up yonder," the driver told Schyler with a nod of his head.

Logs were scattered about the clearing like a giant's set of pick-up sticks. The floor of the forest was littered with severed branches and pine needles. The air was damp. The skidder, a piece of machinery that dragged the logs through the woods to be loaded onto the rig, had left the earth freshly plowed. The scent of pine was as pungent as a

Christmas candle. Later in the day, the site turned hot and dusty, but at this early hour it was verdant.

Schyler had always enjoyed being in the woods early, but today she didn't pause to enjoy its green freshness. In the middle of the clearing the overturned rig looked like a fallen dinosaur lying on its side. She didn't wait until the truck came to a full stop before putting her shoulder to the cranky door and shoving it open. She jumped to the ground. Her shoes were immediately swallowed by the mud. She worked them free and, lifting her skirt above her knees, tramped toward the silent group of men.

"Excuse me, excuse me." She elbowed her way through the somber huddle of loggers. The sound of her voice acted like Moses' rod. The men parted as cleanly as the waters of the Red Sea to let her through.

She drew up short when the last crewman stepped aside and she saw what was in the center of the ring of men. A massive pine log had pinned down a logger's leg. He was lying on his back, obviously in excruciating pain. Taking a deep breath, she moved to his side and dropped to her knees.

His lips were rimmed with a thin, white line of agony. His face was as waxy and pale as a peeled onion. Each hair follicle of his dark beard stood out in contrast. He was drenched with sweat. His teeth were clamped shut, but bared, and his hand was gripping another as though his life depended on maintaining that grip.

He was holding on to Cash Boudreaux for dear life.

Cash was speaking softly. ". . . the fanciest whorehouse I've ever seen. Right there in downtown Saigon. Did you get to any of those whorehouses while you were over there, Glee? Those Asian girls have got tricks—"

The logger screamed.

"Where's the goddamn whiskey I asked for?" Cash roared. Through the crowd of men a bottle of Jack Daniels was passed from hand to hand until it reached Schyler. She handed it to Cash. His eyes locked with hers. Something odd happened to her insides. They experienced a flurry.

Cash said nothing to her but took the bottle and uncapped it. He held it to the man's lips and used his other hand to support his head.

"Where's the fucking ambulance?" Cash asked her out of the side of his mouth.

"The men said they called. It should be here soon."

"Cash?" the injured man asked, refusing any more liquor. "Will they take it off. My leg? Will it have to come off?"

"Shit, this little scratch? It ain't nuthin'." Cash passed the whiskey bottle back to Schyler and wiped the man's drooling lips with his bare fingers.

"Don't bullshit me. Will they take it off?"

Cash dropped the false joviality. "I don't know, Glee."

The man's lips quivered. "It hurts like hell, Cash. No foolin'." He gasped with pain.

"I know it does. Hang in there."

"How am I gonna feed my kids, with my leg all fucked up, Cash? Huh?"

"Don't worry about it." He smiled and winked. "Worry about something important, like how you're going to keep the rest of these buzzards from flocking around Marybeth at the next dance. You might have to sit that one out."

"Marybeth's pregnant again. Seven months gone. She can't work. How am I gonna feed my kids?"

The man began to cry. Schyler stared down at him. His despair was tangible, real, basic. Disappointing love affairs, sad movies, disillusionments. Dead cats. Those were the things one cried over. She had never seen anyone cry because he might not be able to feed his children.

My God, where had she been? This was life. People suffered. People actually went hungry. She had marched and picketed on behalf of the downtrodden and unfortunate, but this was the first time she'd ever experienced human misery firsthand. His tears touched something deep inside her.

"Feeding your family will be the least of your problems," Cash said softly. "I'll see to it that they don't go hungry. I swear that on my mother's grave." He raised his head suddenly. "Well, thank Jesus, Mary, and Joseph. I hear an ambulance. Hear that, Glee? You're on your way to a nice, long vacation."

"Cash?" The man gripped the front of Cash's shirt. "You won't forget your promise?"

"I won't forget," he said, squeezing tighter the hand he held.

Glee's anguished face relaxed a second before he passed out.

Cash eased the man's head to the ground, then surged to his feet. "Get out of the way," he shouted, waving the loggers aside. He didn't mince words with the tardy paramedics. "You took your goddamn time."

"We were eating breakfast."

"What were you having? Pussy? Give this man something for his pain, something to keep him knocked out."

"We know what to do," one of them said defensively.

"Then do it," Cash said through his teeth. "Tank, Chip . . . where are you?" Two men sprang forward with the discipline of young Nazi troopers. "Did you get the loader into place?"

"Set to go, Cash."

"All right, everybody knows what to do."

Everybody but Schyler. She stood there, looking around her stupidly and helplessly, while the men scrambled in 360 different directions. Cash spun around, nearly knocking her down. "Move. You're in the way," he said harshly.

She opened her mouth to speak, but knew that now wasn't the time to take issue with his high-handedness. With as much dignity as she could muster, she waded through the mud back toward the truck that had transported her there from the landing. This scene clearly belonged to men. No amount of legislated equality between the sexes would change the fact that she was as glaringly out of place as one of the loggers would be at a quilting bee.

She watched as Cash, sitting in the knuckle boom of the loader, maneuvered the crane himself and carefully lifted the log off Glee's leg with the enormous pinchers. Glee's shin was shattered. It was a mass of crushed bone and torn flesh, barely held together by his shredded trousers. He remained blessedly unconscious as the paramedics lifted him out of the mud and onto a stretcher.

The others watched somberly as the stretcher was loaded into the ambulance. The cheerful chatter of birds seemed grossly inappropriate in the respectful silence. It lasted until the ambulance disappeared into the forest on its way back to town.

Then Cash bellowed, "What's going on here? A frigging holiday? Get to work." Then, to soften the order, he added, "Cold beer on me if we make up half of what we missed yesterday." A roar of approval went up. "Haul ass. Get that rig back on its feet. We'll need a new bolster on the rear. And keep the loads light. Everybody look alive."

He watched to see that his orders were being carried out to his satisfaction, then consulted his wristwatch. He seemed impervious to everything except the tremendous task at hand.

"I fired you yesterday. Apparently you've forgotten."

His head snapped around. "What are you still doing here?"

"I'm the boss. Did you hear what I said?"

The once-over he subjected her to was purely sexual. "*Oui*, I heard you. And in answer to your question, I haven't forgotten anything that happened yesterday."

She tried to peel away the layers of deception in his eyes and get to the truth, but there were no layers of deception masking them. They were clear, cool, incisive. Either he didn't know anything about two dead cats being obscenely placed on the veranda of Belle Terre, or he felt no guilt over doing it.

Neither was a comforting thought. If Cash hadn't done it, then the culprit was still a mystery. And if Cash wasn't ashamed of doing such a hideous thing, then he was psychotic. But it just didn't seem his style to sneak around like that, leaving symbolic messages. He usually issued his threats in a straightforward manner.

"I fired you," she repeated. "Why did you report to work this morning?"

"Because it's not that easy to get rid of me, Miss Schyler. You hired me to do a job and I'm going to do it.

Not for you, and not for Cotton, but for me," he said, tapping his chest. "I've got more years of my life than I like to count invested in this company. It's not going to go bankrupt without a helluva fight from me."

"And it doesn't matter what I say about it?"

He smiled arrogantly. "Say whatever makes you happy. The bottom line is that you need me. We've both known that from the beginning."

She glanced at the well-oiled team of loggers, who were attaching pulleys to the overturned trailer. "I guess I can't fire you after the way you handled this emergency. Thank you for what you did for that man."

"His name is Glee."

"I know that," she said in angry reaction to his subtle rebuke. "Glee Williams. I'll see that his family is compensated fully while he's in the hospital."

"He'll probably lose his leg." It was a gauntlet Cash threw down to see how far she would go.

"For as long as it's necessary, he'll draw full wages."

Cash stared down at her. For some inexplicable reason she felt like she was on the witness stand pleading her innocence to an unforgiving judge. "What else can I do?" she shouted up at him.

"We shouldn't have been cutting today." He hitched his head backward in the direction of the overturned rig. "I knew it was dangerous. The ground is too soft. If the logs shift a fraction of an inch while they're being loaded, the rig can go over because it's got no ground support. That's exactly what happened. My bad judgment cost me a good man. It cost Glee his leg.

"But I didn't want you bitching at me about goofing off and letting valuable work days go by. I didn't want you to call me worthless." He pulled on his yellow leather gloves with quick, angry motions. "Think about that every time you sign a paycheck made out to Glee Williams."

He flipped down the screened visor on his hard hat and turned his back on her.

Chapter Thirty-two

Jigger came home in a bad mood. He was also drunk. Sober, he was mean. There was no one meaner in the world compared to Jigger Flynn when he was drunk. At those times Gayla thought he must be the devil incarnate, the Antichrist she'd read about in the Book of Revelations.

Sometimes she felt feisty enough to stand up to him and give him some sass, but never when he was drunk. Then, she did nothing that might provoke him.

Tonight was one of those nights. The screen door slammed closed behind him. He stumbled to the kitchen table and yanked out a chair. It barely cleared the table before he dropped into it.

Silently Gayla filled a plate with food and set it in front of him. With an oath of disgust, he shoved the plate aside and demanded whiskey. She poured him a glass.

"That bastard Boudreaux," he grumbled between deep swallows of straight whiskey. "Mighty smart, that Cajun."

Gayla pieced together the almost unintelligible words and phrases until some sense emerged from them. Earlier that evening, Cash Boudreaux had bought beer for all the loggers who worked for Crandall Logging. It was their reward for doing two days' work in one.

"Big shot, he thinks he is." Jigger's bleary eyes found Gayla and squinted her into focus. "I tell you, he's headed for a fall, he is. He brags now, but wait. All his work goes up like that." He clapped his hands together loudly. His face turned darker and his eyes glittered as he unsteadily tipped the whiskey bottle toward his glass again. "And that Schyler Cran-*dall*. Bitch."

Gayla ran her moist palms down her thighs, drying them on her cheap cotton dress. "What's Schyler ever done to you?"

"Killed my dogs that bitch did." He swigged more whiskey. "I get her. Good, I get her."

"What are you going to do to Schyler?"

He looked up at her and cackled the evil laugh that sent chills down her spine. "You think 'cause your mammy work at Belle Terre the Cran-*dalls* have anything to do with you? Ha! That highfalutin bitch, she spits on black whores like you."

Gayla's head dropped forward in shame. He was probably right. It had been her daily prayer since she had seen Schyler toting the shotgun that her old friend hadn't recognized her before she ducked out of sight. Schyler was fine and good. She would never understand or forgive what Gayla had become.

"What are you going to do to Schyler?" she repeated, keeping her head bowed. If she knew what Jigger's plans were ahead of time, she might be able to thwart them. She could warn Schyler anonymously, prevent her from being hurt. Gayla had lived with Jigger long enough to know that he kept his vows of vengeance. He wouldn't be afraid to take on Belle Terre and everybody in it, especially with Cotton laid up and that worthless Ken Howell in charge.

"That's my business, don'tcha know," he growled. He stood, swaying so that he had to brace himself against the edge of the table to remain upright. "Your business is to get ready for that fancy gentleman that's coming to pick you up."

Fearfully, Gayla backed against the wall. "I can't go with nobody, Jigger. You know that. I'm not healed up yet."

He made a snarling sound. "That sorry Cajun gave me sorry medicine. I git him for that, too." He aimed a finger at Gayla. "You're goin' tonight. Earn your keep."

"I can't!"

He weaved forward and backhanded her across the

breasts. He was gifted at inflicting wounds that wouldn't spoil the perfection of her face. "He's paid one hunerd dollars for you. You're going."

Tears rolled down Gayla's cheeks. "I can't, Jigger. I'm still bleeding. Please don't make me go. Please."

"I do bizness with this man. You're part of our deal."

Her pitiful pleas had no effect on him. At the sound of tires crunching on the gravel road outside, he grabbed her hand and dragged her across the kitchen floor and through the screen door. She tried to wrest her hand free. Her heels dug into the rain-softened earth. She stumbled along behind his staggering tread toward the long car with the opaque tinted windows.

The headlights almost blinded her. It was God, she knew, spotlighting her sin. She averted her head. Jigger pulled open the passenger door and shoved her inside. The air-conditioning had made the upholstery cool. It surrounded her in a clammy caress.

"Is there a problem, Jigger?" asked the man behind the steering wheel. Gayla recognized the voice. She'd been loaned out to him before.

"No problem," Jigger told him. "She likes you."

"Good," the man said softly. "Because I like her, too."

Gayla kept her head down. She didn't see the threatening look Jigger gave her before he closed the door. The man put the car in motion, but they'd barely driven out of sight of the house before he braked and turned toward her. He ran the backs of his fingers down her cheek and felt the wetness of her tears.

"I won't hurt you, Gayla."

She knew he wouldn't. He wasn't one of the violent ones. He just liked to take dirty pictures. He would barely touch her.

He wouldn't affect her emotionally at all. She had collapsed into herself, like a dying star, leaving a black void of such density that no light could escape or enter. She couldn't be touched. That's the only way she had survived. She didn't allow herself to feel.

* * *

"Joe Jr., he's a cagey son of a bitch," Cotton said from the pillows of his hospital bed. "Inherited old man Endicott's shrewdness. Arrogant as hell, too. A real smart-assed buck. He'll haggle you down to bottom dollar if you let him."

Schyler smiled, glad to see that her father had reverted to his normal speech patterns. He was regaining strength each day. The stronger he got, the more profane his language became.

That afternoon he'd been moved from the ICU to a regular room. His prognosis was favorable, if guarded. He was now holding court like a king who had defied death and lived to rule again. Schyler liked to think that one cause for his vast improvement was that she had begun talking shop with him. Dr. Collins had agreed to the idea when she broached the subject. Cotton shouldn't be made to feel like an invalid, he had said.

"Heart patients go through a period of depression that is almost as debilitating as their physical illness. By all means, discuss business with him. Nothing catastrophic, you understand, but let him feel like a useful human being. Don't mollycoddle him."

She had brought Cotton up-to-date on the progress Crandall Logging was making in his absence.

"I'm sorry I saddled you with that balloon note, Schyler," he had said. "Jesus, I didn't realize how soon it was coming due."

"You could hardly schedule a heart attack around a bank loan," she had said with a smile. "Don't worry. We'll make it."

"How?"

"I've got several irons in the fire."

He didn't press her for details, so she was spared having to tell him that none of the irons she boasted having were large enough to cover the debt. Timber was leaving the landing daily on the train, but the accounts she had negotiated were peanuts compared to the sizable contract she desperately needed from Endicott.

Cotton didn't seem to resent her management. On the contrary, he seemed pleased that she had seized control. She'd been careful not to mention Cash's name, unsure how Cotton would feel about him playing such a vital role in their business.

That's just what his role was—vital. As difficult as it was for her to admit, Schyler didn't know how she would have managed without him. He worked circles around every other logger. She saw him several times each day at the landing, but they hadn't engaged in any lengthy conversations since Glee's accident. Things seemed to go more smoothly when they stayed out of each other's way.

Something Ken said drew her back into the present. "Maybe I should go to East Texas with Schyler tomorrow," he offered.

Tricia and he had joined Schyler in Cotton's room, in a sort of celebration over his rapid progress. It was the first time the three of them had been in the same room since their argument. For Cotton's benefit, they pretended to be as staunchly devoted to each other as the three musketeers. "I've dealt with Joe Jr. before."

"Which might be the reason we're in dutch with Endicott's," Cotton said crossly. "Let Schyler handle it herself."

"She doesn't have any experience," Ken argued.

Cotton looked at his daughter with affection and admiration. "Then she'll get some, won't she? Dealing with Joe Jr. will be a baptism of fire."

"Well, if she blows this deal, don't blame me."

"No one would think of it," Cotton said sharply.

Schyler intervened to keep her father from getting upset. "I visited with Glee Williams before coming up here."

"How is he?"

She had told Cotton about the accident, but not until after she'd been told by the doctors that Glee's leg had been spared amputation. During a painstaking and lengthy operation, his fibula had been knit back together with the help of synthetic materials. He would always walk with a pronounced limp, and it was still undetermined what jobs he would be physically capable of handling, but at least he wouldn't be an amputee.

It was gratifying to learn that Cotton had taken an interest in the logger's welfare. He had known Glee personally. He'd even referred to the man's wife by name.

"He looked much better than he did yesterday," Schyler told him. "He said he wasn't in pain, but they're keeping him heavily sedated. The flowers you ordered have been delivered. He and Marybeth sent their thanks. She doesn't look old enough to vote, much less to have three children and one on the way."

"I don't think she is," Cotton said, laughing. "Glee knocked her up when they were in the eighth grade."

Tricia rolled her eyes heavenward. Schyler smiled. Despite Macy's admonitions, Cotton had never ameliorated the saltiness of his language in front of his daughters.

"The insurance company will probably raise our premiums after what they had to shell out for that operation." Ken made a face. "Schyler brought in an orthopedic specialist from New Orleans."

"And he worked a miracle to save that leg," she said, annoyed that Ken had placed her in a position to defend her decision.

He ignored her and spoke directly to Cotton. "Then she offered to pay Williams full wages. Indefinitely. That's going to cost us a fortune and we won't be getting anything in return."

"I approve of her decisions," Cotton said in the ironclad voice that indicated the subject was closed to further discussion.

Sensing the mounting tension, Schyler again acted as a deflector. "Tricia is organizing the Junior League to gather used clothes for the Williams children and to give the family a pounding. I'm sure they could use the extra groceries, especially with another baby due in a few weeks."

Cotton looked at his younger daughter appraisingly. "That's right decent of you, Tricia. They'll appreciate that."

Flustered, Tricia replied, "I'm glad I could help in some small way."

"Well, we'd better go and let you rest." Schyler gathered

her handbag and leaned over to kiss Cotton's cheek. "Good night, Daddy. Sleep well."

"Can't help but sleep like a frigging corpse after absorbing that goddamn suppository they shove up my ass every night." His querulousness didn't camouflage his fatigue. They left a few moments later.

As soon as the heavy door closed behind them, Tricia's hand clamped like a talon around her sister's arm. "Why in the hell did you tell him that? I'm organizing nothing, do you understand me? Pounding, indeed. Do you think any of my friends would be caught dead toting bags of groceries into that rundown neighborhood?"

Schyler slung off Tricia's hand. "Then don't. I thought it would make Daddy happy to know that you were taking part in company business. And I was right. It did make him happy."

"I don't need you to make me look good in front of Daddy, thank you very much." Tricia spoke through thin, tight lips. She looked ready to kill. "I'm taking part in company business, all right, but in ways you might not like, big sister."

She headed toward the elevator, where she endangered her sculptured fingernail on the button she punched. Ken touched Schyler's elbow. "Sure you don't want me to go with you tomorrow? That's a big deal you're negotiating all by yourself."

Schyler had kept it to herself that Cash was going to Endicott's with her. That had been one of the smartest decisions she had made lately. She wasn't certain he still planned to go. If he didn't, she wouldn't have to explain the reason to anybody. If he did, Ken could find you after the fact. She didn't want to justify her reasons to him now.

"No, thank you, Ken. I'd rather you stay here and oversee things while I'm away."

Sighing, he ran a hand through his hair. "You're still mad at me, aren't you?"

"No. This isn't personal."

He gazed at her longingly. "Let's bury this hatchet, Schyler. I can't stand all this tippy-toeing around each other."

"You and Tricia took one stand. I took another."

"Forget Tricia. I'm talking about us. I don't want to quarrel with you anymore."

"I have only one quarrel with you, Ken, and that's over Belle Terre. If you and Tricia persist in wanting to sell it, I'll fight you. Otherwise, we remain friends."

"Just friends?" he asked, lowering his voice.

"Just friends." She gave him a cool stare. "The elevator's here." She walked away from him and joined Tricia, who was impatiently waiting for them in the open elevator.

Fuck you, bitch.

Schyler stared up at the words. They'd been ineptly scrawled in spray paint on the door of the landing office. She glanced around. No one was in sight. It was well past nine o'clock. She hesitated to go inside, but reasoned that the vandal had done his dirty work for the day. It was unlikely he would still be lurking around. She unlocked the door and stepped inside.

The red glowing tip of a cigarette winked at her out of the darkness. With her heart in her throat, she reached for the light switch and turned it on. Cash was sitting behind the desk, his boots propped on the corner of it.

"I guess you got the message." He nodded toward the door she was holding open.

"Did you leave it there for me?"

He snorted a laugh and swung his feet to the floor. "Hardly. I wouldn't waste good paint on what I could easily say to your face."

She closed the door. "I don't guess you would sacrifice two perfectly healthy cats either, would you?"

His brows drew together as he eased himself out of the chair. "What are you talking about? Two cats?"

She told him. "Ken disposed of the carcasses. He told me later that the male had been gutted. Do you use cat guts in any of your potions?"

Cash's face remained impassive, his reply noncommittal. "None that I recall. I've strung a few fiddles with them though."

She tossed her purse and keys onto the desk and stepped around him. "I could use a drink. How about you?"

"I've had one already. But I'll take another."

Schyler shook her head ruefully when she spied the glass on the desk. There was a fraction of an inch of amber liquid in the bottom of it. She took a secreted bottle of bourbon out of the lowest desk drawer and poured them each a drink. "Besides stealing my liquor, what were you doing here?"

"Homework." He flipped open the manila file folder lying on the desk.

Schyler sat down in the chair he had recently vacated. The leather still retained his body heat. It felt wonderful against the backs of her thighs and buttocks. She forced herself not to squirm.

"Endicott," she said, reading the letterhead on the top sheet of correspondence.

Cash sat down on the corner of the desk, facing her. "According to those letters, Cotton's initial dealings with the senior Endicott went well. Both parties came away happy."

Schyler dragged her eyes away from the crotch of Cash's jeans, which rested against the corner of the desk. She reached for her glass of whiskey and took a quick drink. "Cotton said Joe Jr. was a cagey son of a bitch, but he seemed to respect him, too."

"How is he? Cotton," he elaborated when she looked up at him quizzically.

"Much better. He's been moved out of the ICU."

Cash nodded. He pointed down at the file with his high-ball glass. "I've read through all the correspondence. I can't figure out what soured the Endicotts on us."

"Well, I guess we'll find out tomorrow."

"We?"

"Aren't you going with me?"

"You still want me to?"

It cost her some pride to admit it, but she did want him along. For Crandall Logging and Cotton. For Belle Terre. And—who was she kidding?—for herself. "Yes, Cash. I do."

Staring at her over the rim of his glass, he tossed back the rest of his whiskey. "What time in the morning?"

"I'll meet you here at nine."

"Okay." He stood up. "Let's go for now."

"I'm not finished here." She waved her hand over the cluttered desktop. "I need to catch up on some paperwork."

"I don't think you should stay here by yourself. Let's go." He hooked his thumbs into his belt and assumed a stance that said arguing would be futile.

"I am tired," she confessed.

"And tomorrow is going to be a long day. Besides, the bully might still be around."

Or the bully might be standing right in front of her, shoulders pulled back, pelvis thrust forward, looking like a wolf in sheep's clothing. Before capitulating, she drained her glass just as he had. When she stood up, he was smiling as though he knew that last draught was a gesture of defiance.

She went ahead of him out the door. "I'll have someone take care of this first thing in the morning," he told her.

"Thank you, Cash."

"You're welcome."

His phony obsequiousness was irritating, but she let it pass. When they reached her car, he drew her around and pulled her close. "Whoever the son of a bitch is," he said, hitching his thumb over his shoulder toward the door, "he's got a damn good idea."

Schyler's temper went off like a rocket. "You want to talk about it, I suppose?"

"About what? Fucking you?"

"Yes."

His grin formed slowly. "Sure. Why not? Let's talk about it."

"All right." She drew a deep breath to show him how bored she was with the subject. "It was a mistake to go to bed with you. I regret it. It happened. I wish it hadn't, but it did. I take full responsibility for my actions, but I intend to forget the whole thing. I expect you to as well."

"You do?"

"Yes I do."

His whiskey-flavored breath was as balmy as the night air when he laughed into her stormy face. He leaned forward, aligning his body against hers. "Not bloody likely. Do you know what it means to a poor white trash, bastard kid like me to make Miss Schyler Crandall come?"

She shoved him away from her and yanked open the car door. "Don't flatter yourself. It had been a long time for me, that's all."

She peppered his boots with gravel as her car peeled out of the lot. He watched her red taillights disappear in the darkness.

Cash drank straight from the brown paper sack. The liquor sloshed in the bottle, indicating that the pint was almost empty. He belched sourly.

Where was that bitch?

After Schyler left he had gone back into the office, snickering at the crude message written on the door, and made a phone call. That had been an hour ago. He was at the filling station and liquor store on the Lafayette highway. Across the street was the motel. He was waiting for Rhoda.

She had been pathetically happy to hear from him. Oh, she'd acted aloof at first. She'd obviously been pissed off. He explained how busy he'd been. She hadn't been impressed or sympathetic and kept making snotty comments that had made him want to strangle her.

He had said something to the effect of, "Fine. In the dark, one honey pot is as sweet as another. You don't want to play tonight? Fine." That had knocked her on her elegant ass. He named the time and place and she had agreed quicker than a sailor's zipper on shore leave.

But now he wished he had just drowned his anger in the bottle of cheap whiskey and left Rhoda out of it. The newness was wearing off their affair. He was bored with her, especially since she had become possessive and clinging. She had served her purpose. He didn't need her anymore.

Except tonight.

Tonight he needed something or someone to work out his frustration on. Damn Schyler Crandall. She had loved cutting him down like a loblolly sapling, reminding him that she had only used him as a substitute for the boyfriend in London who kept her sexually satisfied and in uptown style.

"Shit." He drained the bottle and tossed it into the overflowing oil drum that served as a trash can outside the men's toilet.

So, Schyler wanted to forget their afternoon together? She didn't want anybody to know about it. Well, that suited him fine. He would never let himself become an object of ridicule like Cotton Crandall had. People kowtowed to Cotton because he was rich and powerful, the biggest timber contractor around. Behind his back, however, they still remembered him as the redneck logger who'd romanced his way into Belle Terre. In these parts "money marries money" was the eleventh commandment. Cotton had had the gall to break that unwritten law and hadn't been forgiven for it yet.

That wouldn't satisfy Cash Boudreaux. He wanted to be able to look himself in the mirror without knowing that his wife's last name had earned the respect he was shown. Schyler's slender, silky thighs opened to the sweetest, tightest piece of woman he'd ever had, but he wouldn't use it as a portal by which to enter Belle Terre.

He'd get what he had rightfully coming to him in his own way and under his own terms.

Amid his brooding he noticed Rhoda's black BMW pulling into the motel parking lot. He watched her alight. She kept the engine running. She went inside to check in and did so, using her gold card. Clasping the room key like a wino with a handout, she returned to her car, her phony tits ajiggle beneath her sleeveless sweater.

Cash felt a yearning to fondle, to kiss, to suck—but not Rhoda's breasts. Cursing his susceptibility, he went to his pickup and got inside. He stared down at the ignition key lying in his palm and gave serious consideration to standing up Rhoda and driving home to nurse his misery in private.

Cutting his eyes across the highway, he watched her

enter a room. She'd be hot, eager, grasping, willing to please, *determined* to please.

What the hell was he waiting for?

Resolve thinning his lips, he crammed the key into the ignition and revved the motor. A hazard to other motorists, he sped across the highway and brought the pickup to a bucking stop outside the door Rhoda had gone into.

Wanting Schyler Crandall, he went inside to join the banker's unfaithful wife.

Chapter Thirty-three

"What's the matter? Have I got egg on my tie?"

"Your tie is fine."

"Then why do you keep staring at it?"

"Because it's there."

Cash, failing to see Schyler's humor, scowled."I might have grown up with bayou mud between my toes, I was poorer than Job's turkey, but I'm not ignorant. On good days I can even read and write. I know when the occasion calls for a necktie."

"Do you want me to drive?"

"No."

"You don't mind driving?"

"I told you I didn't."

"I thought maybe that's why you're being such a pain in the butt today."

"Why should today be any different?"

"Right."

She flopped back in the passenger seat and turned her head to stare out the window at the scenery. It whizzed past her car, a blur of colors. Cash drove too fast. She remembered that from the night he'd picked her up at Jigger Flynn's house. They'd been escaping a derelict's wrath then. She couldn't account for his excessive speed now, except that he had been in a grumpy mood since she'd met him at the landing earlier that morning.

He had mumbled his replies when she asked him about the assignments he'd given the loggers for that day. He accepted her offer to drive with a grunt. Beyond that, he hadn't spoken three words to her.

His expression was surly, his attitude defensive. His shoulders were hunched as though he were ready to take offense at the slightest affront. His eyes were glued to the road. At least Schyler assumed they were on the road. She couldn't see them behind his aviator sunglasses.

"Maybe I should have taken Ken up on his offer," she mused out loud. Cash didn't bite. She elaborated anyway. "He offered to come with me."

"Maybe you should have."

"He would have been better company."

"He's quite a charmer, all right. Can charm the pants off anybody." He gave her a sidelong glance. "The Crandall girls seem to be particularly vulnerable to his charm."

"You just love being vulgar, don't you?"

"Too bad your hero can't fight worth a damn."

"You pulled a knife on him!"

"You're always jumping to his defense, aren't you?"

Schyler ground her teeth, angry at herself for letting him draw her into an argument. It was obvious he was ready to do battle. She watched all ten of his fingers extend and stretch, then curl back around the padded steering wheel, gripping it tightly, as if he wanted to uproot it from the dashboard.

"You're a sore loser, Mr. Boudreaux."

His head came around abruptly. "What's that supposed to mean?"

"I turned you down last night. Apparently most women don't say no to you."

By slow degrees his whole demeanor changed. His posture relaxed until it became a veritable slouch. He laid his arm along the back of the seat. He no longer looked like he might, at any minute, ram his head through the windshield in the throes of a tantrum.

"You're right about that, Miss Schyler. In fact, the second one I asked last night said yes."

This time it was Schyler's head that snapped around. The teasing smirk had been wiped right off her face. She felt like she'd been clubbed in the middle with a two-by-four. She recovered quickly and hoped Cash hadn't seen her stunned expression. "Congratulations."

He flashed her a killer smile. "Thanks. Coffee?" He nodded toward the rest stop complex they were approaching at an unsafe speed.

"Yes, please."

As soon as he braked, Schyler alighted and headed for the ladies' room. She used the toilet even though she really didn't need to. As she washed her hands in the lavatory, she addressed herself in the mirror. "If you didn't want to know, you shouldn't have provoked him."

It was unrealistic of her, having become one of Cash Boudreaux's conquests, to demand his respect. Fidelity, of course, was never even a possibility. His women were as disposable as the coarse paper towel she was drying her hands on. One was as easy to come by as another.

In order to salvage her ego, before she left the restroom she smoothed the wrinkles out of her linen business suit and applied fresh lipstick. She even ran a hairbrush through her hair. When he looked at her today, she wanted him to see his boss, not a has-been lover.

"Can you drink that in the car?" Cash asked, passing Schyler a Styrofoam cup of coffee when she rejoined him in the refreshment area of the convenience store.

"Sure."

"Good. I can't take the smell of those hot dogs."

There was a rotisserie on the counter, slow-cooking fat, red frankfurters for the lunch trade. Cash replaced the sunglasses, which he'd pushed to the top of his head when he went inside. Schyler noticed his tired eyes, the green cast to his skin.

"Now I know what's wrong with you," she said as they walked back toward the car. "You've got a hangover."

"A real bitch." He grimaced.

"It must have been some night."

"A real bitch." This time he smiled.

Sliding into her seat while he held the car door open for her, Schyler wondered at what point Cash's other affairs had become such a bone of contention with her.

"I guess we have a deal, Mr. Endicott," Schyler said, "if that's the very best price you can give us."

"That's top dollar. Compare us with other markets. I'm not bullshitting you."

She resented his taking the liberty to use that kind of language in front of her in a strictly business situation. One slightly raised eyebrow indicated her displeasure. If he saw the censure, he ignored it. What could one expect from a man was was thoroughly obnoxious and continually cracked his knuckles?

Joe Endicott, Jr. was a pompous ass, leaning back in his chair, a smug expression on his face. He seemed to think that he held all the aces. Unfortunately he did.

One thing he didn't know, however, was that the deal they had negotiated would put Crandall Logging in the black with some left over. Schyler was elated, but she carefully concealed her excitement from Joe Endicott, Jr.

"We've always thought Crandall's timber was top grade."

"I'm delighted to hear that," Schyler replied to the complement. "Now to the terms of our contract, would you prefer paying us upon receipt of each delivery, or would you rather send us a check at the end of each week for the cumulative amount?"

"Neither one."

"Neither one?"

Joe Jr. popped a knuckle loudly. "I didn't stutter."

"I don't understand."

"I'm not paying you at all until I receive every board foot of the order."

"Then you must think we're stupid." Cash was slumped

in the second chair across the desk from Endicott. Up until now he hadn't said much, only muttered in direct response to a question or comment Schyler made to him.

"I know you're not stupid, Mr. Boudreaux."

"Then how can you expect us to ship you timber for nothing?"

"You'll get your money, Ms. Crandall. I get my timber. *All* my timber."

"We can't operate that way."

Endicott spread his hands wide and smiled pleasantly. "Then we've got no deal."

Schyler glanced at Cash. He was staring at Endicott over his tented fingers as though he wanted to pulverize him beneath his boot like any other cockroach. His solution to this dilemma was likely to be violent. With as much composure as she could garner, Schyler turned back to Endicott. "May I ask why you're placing this restriction on us?"

"Certainly. You don't always deliver the goods."

"I beg your pardon."

"I didn't—"

"He didn't stutter," Cash supplied in a tight voice.

Endicott smiled at him, but his smile wavered beneath Cash's steady stare. "Crandall Logging took us for several thousand dollars. My old man advanced you money on an order, but we never received the last shipment. That's why we haven't done business with you folks the last coupla years."

Schyler drew herself up straight. "I assure you, Mr. Endicott, that there must have been an oversight or a bookkeeping mistake. My father's reputation as an ethical and honest businessman has stood for decades. If Crandall was advanced a check—"

"It was. And it came back endorsed and cashed.

"By my father?"

"Yep."

"I don't understand." She was at a loss. Cotton was competitive. He believed in free enterprise and capitalizing on every business opportunity. But he played by the rules. He wasn't dishonest. He didn't have to be. "Why didn't you inquire as to why—"

"Don't you think I did?" Knuckle pop, knuckle pop. "All our letters and threatening notices went unanswered."

"Why didn't you file suit?"

"Because my daddy has a sentimental streak." Joe Jr. shrugged. "He always said ol' Cotton Crandall was one of the best contractors in southwest Loosiana. He'd been doing business with him for a long time. He said to let it drop, so I let it drop. Against my better judgment."

"Well I don't intend to let it drop," Schyler informed him firmly. "I'm going to dig until I get to the bottom of it and am able to offer you a full explanation. In the meantime, your refusal to pay us on each shipment is unrealistic. How are we supposed to pay our operating expenses?"

Resting his linked hands on top of his head, he said, "That's not my problem, is it?"

"So we won't receive any money until the last shipment is delivered?"

"Right down to the pulp wood."

"Nobody does business like that." Cash almost came out of his chair, like a testy animal whose leash had just snapped.

"I don't . . . usually." Endicott made a half turn in his swivel chair to look through the wall of glass behind him. It overlooked the railroad yard where logs were unloaded before being run through the paper mill. "But I've got to cover my own ass. I want the shipments to be delivered on a specified schedule, but I won't give Crandall one red cent until the whole order has been filled." He spun his chair around. *"Comprende*, y'all?"

Schyler looked helplessly toward Cash. He looked at her, then back at Endicott. "I need a smoke." He came to his feet abruptly. "Schyler?" He extended a hand down to her. She took it. He helped her out of her chair and they headed for the door.

"Hey, do we have a deal or not? You're taking up my valuable time here. What am I supposed to do while you're out smoking?" Endicott demanded.

"Relax, Junior," Cash said. "Take a nap. Take a leak. We'll be right back."

He slammed the door behind them. The secretary looked

up reprovingly. She was ignored as they went through the reception area. The long hallway opened into various offices. At the end of it there was a large window and a seating area. It was there that Cash escorted Schyler. He shook a cigarette out of the pack in his breast shirt pocket. Schyler watched him light it. He angrily exhaled toward the skylight overhead.

"Well?" she asked. "What do you think?"

"I think I'd like to put my heel to his nuts and send him and that rolling chair straight through that glass wall."

"What should I tell him?"

"To eat shit and die."

"Cash! I'm serious."

"So am I." When he saw her retiring expression, he said, "Okay, okay, I'll get serious."

"Do you know anything about us welshing on a deal?"

"I guess you think I'm the company crook."

"I wasn't making an accusation. I just asked you a straight question."

He took a long drag on the cigarette, then unmercifully ground it out in the nearest ashtray. "No, I don't know anything about why that shipment wasn't delivered, or letters going unanswered, etcetera, etcetera. Want to strip search me?"

Sighing, she rubbed her temples. After slowly counting to ten, she appealed to him for advice. "Should I accept his terms? And don't tell me what you think I want to hear. What do you think I should do?"

"What are your alternatives?"

"To go back home and start making calls. That's backtracking, of course. It took me days to set up this appointment. I really haven't got time to start over from scratch."

"There are plenty other markets, Schyler."

"I know, but none on this scale. I could fill a small order here, another one there like I've been doing. We'd work ourselves to death and it would still be piecemeal, just barely enough to meet payroll and stay open. This one order could pay off the bank note and give us comfortable operating capital for months."

"Then I guess you have your answer."

"What if we deliver all the timber, but he doesn't pay us the full amount?"

"He wouldn't dare. We'd have it in writing. Besides," Cash added, cracking his own knuckles in imitation of Joe Jr., "he values his life."

"*Can* we fill the order?"

"Let me do some quick figuring." He sat down on the edge of a small sofa and reached for a magazine lying on the spindly coffee table. Using its back cover as his scratch sheet, he did some quick calculations. "We've got six rigs hauling every day. That's not including any independents we pull in. At five thousand board feet per load, that's—"

"Thirty thousand board feet."

"Times three loads per day." He glanced up at her. "We can ship ninety thousand board feet each day, in addition to what we buy from independents."

"He's ordering over two million. We've got under a month before the loan comes due."

"Say thirty days."

"It's less than that, Cash."

"So we'll work some overtime."

"What about the weather?"

"We'll be really screwed if it rains."

"Oh, Lord."

He rechecked his figures. "We can do it, Schyler," he said.

"Are you sure?"

"I'm sure."

"By the deadline?"

"Yes."

"I'm placing a lot of trust in you."

He stared at her for a long moment. "I know."

His expression and his soft, almost sad, tone of voice disconcerted her. For a moment she was distracted by them. Then she asked him, "If I weren't here, if you had to do this alone, if you were responsible for this decision, what would you do?"

He stood up, moved to the window, and stared out. He slid his hands into his pockets, a gesture that parted his unbuttoned sport coat. His dress slacks fit his seat as well as the jeans he always wore. His shoes looked new, as though he might have bought them especially for this business appointment. That was endearing. Schyler was touched.

He turned around slowly. "I hate kissing anybody's ass, particularly a guy like that." He jutted his chin toward the executive office at the other end of the hall. "I'd be tempted to tell him to shove it. I guess it would come down to how badly I wanted or needed the deal. How important is it to you?"

Suddenly she remembered the expression on Cotton's face when he'd looked up at her from the gurney and asked, "Why did you destroy my grandchild?" She would never forget that as long as she lived. Cotton's faith in her, his love, had been shattered. She needed to restore it completely.

"It's very important, Cash," she said huskily. "Not just to me. But to Cotton. To Belle Terre. Its future is at stake. I'll do anything, sacrifice anything, even my pride, for Belle Terre. Can you understand that?"

A muscle in his cheek twitched. *"Oui*, I can understand that."

"Then shall we go back in and sign Joe Jr.'s contract?"

"I'm right behind you."

Ken Howell collapsed on top of his wife the second after his climax. When he regained his breath, he raised his head and dusted kisses along her hairline. "That was great. Was it good for you?"

She pushed him off her and rolled to the side of the bed. She thrust her arms into a peignoir. "Did you ask Schyler that every time you made love to her?"

His face, already flushed from intercourse, turned a deeper red. "With Schyler, I didn't have to ask."

Tricia cast him a glance over her shoulder. "Touché." Her mules slapped against her bare heels as she walked into the bathroom. Over the sound of running water, she called out to him, "Are you still in love with her?"

Ken padded naked to the bathroom. He stood in the

doorway and waited until Tricia finished brushing her teeth. "Do you care?"

She straightened and blotted her mouth on a towel, watching him in the mirror over the sink. "Yes, I think I do."

"Only because you don't want her to have something that you can't."

She shrugged and dropped the sheer robe. "Probably."

"At lease you're honest."

Tricia turned on the shower. Reaching in to test the water temperature, she swiveled her head around and looked at him over her smooth shoulder. He was morosely staring at the tile floor. "I haven't always been."

He raised his head. "What, honest? Yes, I know."

For a moment husband and wife stared at each other across the bathroom that was rapidly filling up with steam. Their expressions were tinged with regret, maybe remorse, but neither kidded himself for long. Neither was righteous and never would be.

"When did you know?"

"That there never was a baby?" he asked. Tricia nodded. He pushed back his tousled hair. "I don't know, maybe from the beginning."

"But you still married me."

"I didn't see an easier way out of the mess. It was more expedient and less trouble to go along with your lie."

"You would rather be stuck with me than to beg Schyler's forgiveness for screwing me."

"I never claimed any medals for heroism."

"What about those cats?"

He looked at her quizzically. The question was seemingly out of context. "Disposing of them made me sick to my stomach."

"Don't play dense, Ken. Did you do it?"

"Of course not. Did you?"

"Of course not."

Neither was convinced of the other's innocence. Tricia stepped into the shower but didn't close the door. "You've got to stop her, you know."

"I'm trying," Ken said defensively.

"Try harder. She's in East Texas today negotiating a deal that will get Crandall Logging out of hock. We'll have a harder time convincing Cotton to sell if everything is solvent."

Ken gazed at his reflexion in the mirror, running a hand over his stubbled jaw, not liking what he saw. He was beginning to look jowly, old, soft, dissipated. He looked useless.

"Cash Boudreaux bears watching, too," Tricia said from the shower. "I understand that he and Schyler are thick as thieves."

"He works for her, that's all. She depends on him to manage the loggers."

Tricia's laugh echoed loudly in the shower when she shut off the water. "How naive you are, Ken. Or are you burying your head in the sand? You don't want to believe that they're lovers."

"Who says?"

"Everybody." She wrapped herself in a bath sheet and began applying baby oil to her wet limbs. "Any woman Cash's shadow falls on eventually goes to bed with him. If he wants her, that is. Those who have been with him say that he's the best lover they've ever had. They say his cock's a good ten inches."

Ken frowned at her as he stepped into the shower and twisted the taps wide open. "Female bullshit. Is that all you and your cronies talk about? Men and the size of their cocks?"

"No more than men talk about tits and ass."

"That's a male prerogative."

"Not anymore, baby," she chortled.

Ken shook his head in disgust, then thrust it beneath the needle spray. Tricia finished drying and sailed the towel in the general direction of the hamper in the corner.

She left the bathroom, confident in the knowledge that what she wanted, she went after, and usually got. If Ken couldn't or wouldn't keep up with her, he would be left behind. That would be all right, too.

Chapter Thirty-four

"Having chateaubriand and asparagus tips for lunch was decadent."

Cash indulgently propelled Schyler toward her parked car. She was comically tipsy. They'd stopped at the steakhouse to have a celebratory, late lunch. When they discovered that it didn't open until four, they had decided to wait, passing the time by milling around the parklike setting on the edges of a national forest. Even though the contract they had obtained from Endicott had a definite drawback, it had boosted their spirits.

The meal had been delicious, the portions generous to a fault. They had demanded and gotten the royal treatment, being the only customers in the place at that early hour. Schyler had ordered champagne to toast their success. Cash figured the two bottles she had bought probably depleted the restaurant's wine cellar of its stock. There wasn't much call for champagne in a restaurant that catered mostly to upper-crust tourists and local regulars.

One bottle had washed down their steak dinners. Schyler was affectionately clutching the other to her breasts now as she sashayed toward the car.

"Let's roll down the windows and drive real fast," she said excitedly.

Her eyes were more animated than Cash had ever seen them. They sparkled with amber lights. Champagne was good for Schyler Crandall's soul. She had shed her snooty air along with her inhibitions. She wasn't the boss lady. She wasn't the reigning princess of Belle Terre. She was one hundred percent pure woman. And one hundred percent of his body knew it. Her effect on him was being felt from the top of his head to the soles of his new shoes, which were almost as tight as she was.

"Okay, but I'll do the driving." Smiling to himself, he opened the car door for her and stood aside as she got in. "Why don't you take off your jacket?"

"Good idea." She set the bottle of champagne beside her on the seat and shrugged out of the linen jacket. Leaning forward, she shimmied her shoulders to get the sleeves off. Her breasts swayed beneath her blouse.

His penis took notice.

He laid her discarded jacket in the back seat along with his. As he went around the car, he whipped off the necktie and unbuttoned the first few buttons of his shirt. By the time he steered the car out onto the highway, Schyler's alligator heels were lying on their sides on the carpeted floorboard and her head was lolling against the seat. One foot was tucked up under her opposite thigh. Her knees were widely spread. It wasn't indecent. Her skirt was bunched between them.

What Cash was thinking was decidedly indecent.

"Such an odious man," she said around a wide yawn that would have mortified Macy Laurent. Schyler didn't even attempt to cover it.

Two of her jaw teeth had fillings, he noticed. He had never been in a dentist's chair until he went into the army. It hadn't mattered because he'd been blessed with good teeth. Neglecting semiannual checkups would have been unheard of in the mansion at Belle Terre.

"Who's odious? Me?" he asked.

Her head remained on the seat, but she turned it to look at him. A placid little smile was curving her lips upward. She had eaten off her lipstick. He liked her lips better without it. She had a real bedroom mouth, suitable for kissing, suitable for lots of things.

"No, not you. Joe Endicott, Jr."

"He's a prick."

She giggled. "Crude but true." For a moment she studied

him. "How come when you say bad words they don't sound bad?"

"Don't they?"

"No," she replied, puzzled. "Just like Cotton. He cusses something terrible. Always has. Some of the first words I learned to say were swear words I'd overheard him using. Mama nagged him to clean up his language all the time." She yawned again. "I never thought bad language sounded bad coming from Cotton."

"Is the wind too strong?"

Her breasts rose on a deep, supremely lazy breath. They strained against her linen blouse, which by now had lost its starch. It looked touchable. Cash ached to feel her. He couldn't understand why he didn't, why he didn't just reach across the short distance and cover one of those soft mounds with his hand, pinch up one of her nipples with his fingertips. He had never exercised caution with a woman before. What he saw and wanted, he took. He usually got away with it, too.

"No, the wind feels wonderful," Schyler sighed. Her eyes slid closed. "Wake me up when we get to Heaven." She giggled again and began to sing, "When I get to Heaven, gonna put on my shoes, gonna walk all over God's Heaven." Her smile was winsome. "Veda used to rock me in the chairs on the veranda and sing that spiritual."

Cash thought she'd fallen asleep, but after a moment she said, "Silly name for a town, isn't it? Heaven. I love it and I hate it, know what I mean?"

He took her question seriously. *"Oui."*

"It's like this mole I have on my hip. It's ugly. I don't like it, but . . . but it's a part of me. It wouldn't do any good to have it removed because every time I looked at that spot, I'd be reminded of that mole anyway. That's how I feel about Heaven and Belle Terre. I can leave, go to the other side of the world, but they're always there. With me." Her eyes popped open. "Am I drunk?"

He couldn't keep from laughing at her alarmed expression. "If you're sober enough to wonder, then you're not too far gone."

"Oh, good, good." Her eyes closed again. "It was delicious champagne, wasn't it?" She dragged her tongue over her lower lip.

Cash shifted the swollen flesh in his trousers to a more comfortable position. "*Oui, delicieux*."

"Are we home?" Schyler sat up, groggy and disoriented.

"Not quite. I want to show you something."

"There's nothing to see," she said querulously.

Beyond the car in any direction was dense woods. Judging by the long slanting shadows the tree trunks cast on the ground, it was getting close to sunset.

Cash pushed open his door and got out, taking the unopened bottle of champagne with him. "Come on. Don't be a spoilsport. And don't forget your shoes." Schyler put her heels back on and got out but leaned against the side of the car unsteadily, holding her head. "You okay?" Cash asked as he came around the rear of the car.

"A bowling tournament is being played inside my head. My eyeballs are the pins."

He laughed, disturbing the birds in the nearest tree. They set up a chattering protest. "What you need is the hair of the dog." He wagged the bottle of champagne in front of her face and she groaned. Taking her arm, he led her forward, into the temple of trees that surrounded them.

"These aren't hiking shoes, Cash," she complained. Her high heels sank into the soft ground. Milkweed stalks broke against her legs, spilling their white sap on her stockings.

He strengthened his grip on her arm and helped her along. "It's not far."

"To what?"

"To where we're going."

"I don't even know where we are."

"On Belle Terre."

"Belle Terre? I've never been here."

They were working their way up a gentle hill. The ground was garnished with purple verbena. Wild rosebushes were tangled around lesser shrubs, their pink blooms fragrant in the dusty, shimmering heat of late afternoon.

They crested the hill. Cash said, "Careful. It's steeper going down on this side."

At the bottom of the hill, Laurent Bayou made a gradual bend. Between there and the higher ground on which they stood grew hardwoods and pines, then, along the muddy banks of the bayou, cypresses. Late sunlight dappled the floor of the forest with golden light. It was lovely, wild, and primeval—a place for pagan worship.

"Cash!" Schyler exclaimed in fright when a winged animal went sailing from one tree to another not far from them. "Was that a bat?"

"A flying squirrel. They usually don't come out until dark. He's getting a head start."

She watched the squirrel's acrobatics until it disappeared among the leafy branches. Stillness descended. One could almost hear the beetles crunching paths through blowdowns. Iridescent insects skimmed along the brassy surface of the water. Bees buzzed among the flowering plants. A cardinal flitted through the trees like a red dart.

Schyler stood in awe of this spot unsullied by man. It was Nature in balance. Left alone it had beautifully perpetuated itself century after century, eon upon eon. She must still be drunk, she thought ruefully. She was waxing poetic. She commented on her observations to Cash. He didn't seem particularly surprised or amused.

"It does that to me, too. We're seeing a transformation take place." She looked around her but didn't see any drastic changes in progress. He laughed. "We'd have to stay here several centuries to see it completed."

She consulted her wristwatch. "I probably should get back before then." He actually laughed at her joke. She liked that. It was the first time he had laughed without it being tinged with sarcasm. "What transformation?"

He propped his foot up on a boulder as his eyes swept the forest surrounding them. "I speculate that the original forest was destroyed by fire. It happened, oh, maybe a hundred years ago. See back there behind us," he said, pointing. "What kind of trees do you see? Mostly."

"Oak. Other hardwoods."

"Right. But after the fire, the first ones to grow back were pines, loblolly mainly. They were probably as thick as a nursery in just a few years after the fire. The saplings brought in birds, who carried seeds from the hardwoods of neighboring forests."

"And they took over."

He looked pleased that she knew. "Do you know why?"

She searched her memory, but shook her head. "I remember Cotton telling me that the deciduous usually outlive pines."

"The pine seeds germinate quickly in sunny soil. But deprived of sunlight, the saplings die out."

"So the taller the hardwoods get, the shadier the forest floor gets and—"

"You end up with what we've got here. The pines eventually giving way to the hardwoods."

"Then why don't all forests eventually become deciduous?"

"Because man tames most of them. This," he said with a sweep of his hand, "happens when a tame forest reverts to wilderness."

"It is untamed." She was impressed with his knowledge. Gazing up at him she said, "You like it best this way, don't you?"

"Yes. But it's damned hard to earn a living by admiring a view." He extended her his hand. "Come on."

He led her down the steep incline. They waded through pine needles that were ankle deep. He guided her to a blowdown near the water's edge. She could now see that the bayou wasn't really stagnant at this point, as she had thought when looking down on it from above. But the current was so lacking in energy, the water appeared motionless.

"I thought you didn't allow blowdowns to remain in the forest."

He tore the foil off the bottle of champagne, carefully putting it in his pocket. He disposed of the wire the same way after twisting it off. "Ordinarily I don't. Not here." He looked around him with reverence and awe, as one does in a cathedral. "Everything here is left alone. Nature works out its own problems. Nobody messes with the natural order of things here."

"But this is part of Belle Terre."

The cork popped out. The champagne spewed over his hand and showered Schyler. They laughed.

In that same jocular vein, she asked, "Aren't you taking a rather proprietary attitude over my land?"

He looked down at her for a long moment. "I'd kill anybody who tried to bother this place."

Schyler believed him. "You shouldn't say that. You might have to."

He shook his head. "Cotton feels the same way I do about it."

"Cotton?" Schyler asked, surprised.

"My mother is buried up there."

Schyler followed the direction of his gaze to the top of the hill they'd descended minutes earlier. "I had no idea."

"The priest wouldn't let her be buried in consecrated ground because she . . ." Cash took a drink of the champagne straight out of the bottle. "He just wouldn't."

"Because she was my father's mistress."

"I guess."

"She must have loved him very much."

He blew out a soft puff of air that sufficed as a bitter laugh. "She did that. She loved him." He took another drink. "More than she loved anything. More than she loved me."

"Oh, I doubt that, Cash," Schyler protested quickly. "No mother would put a man who wasn't even her husband above her child."

"She did." He set his foot on the log, almost but not quite touching her hip, and leaned down, propping himself on his knee. "You asked me why I've stuck around all this time."

"Yes."

"You want to know why I still live around here where everybody knows me as a bastard."

"I've wondered, yes."

His eyes penetrated hers. "Before she died, my mother made me promise never to leave Belle Terre as long as

Cotton Crandall was alive. She made me swear that I wouldn't."

Schyler swallowed emotionally. "But why . . . why would she ask you to do that?"

He shrugged. "Who knows? I guess I'm supposed to act as his guardian angel."

"Guarding him against what?"

"Himself maybe." He switched subjects suddenly. "Want some champagne?"

"I shouldn't."

"What the hell?"

He nudged her shoulder with the bottle. She took it from him and drank. The wine foamed in her mouth, in her throat. "It's too warm."

Schyler passed the bottle back to him, but was arrested by the intensity with which he was watching her. The forest, which had been full of activity only moments ago, fell absolutely still. Nothing moved. She could feel the heat waves emanating up from the ground, through the dead log, through her clothing and entering her body through her thighs. Her ears began to ring with the profound silence. Despite the drink of champagne she'd just swallowed, her mouth was as dry as cotton.

"We'd better go." She stood up. Cash lowered his foot to the ground, but he didn't make a move to retrace their path. He continued to stare at her. Nervous, and eager to fill the silence, she started babbling, "Thank you for helping me out with Endicott and for showing me this place. I would have never known it was here. It's beautiful. It's—"

He still had the bottle of champagne in his fist when he threw his arm around Schyler's neck and trapped her head in the crook of his elbow. He sealed her lips closed with a hot, wet kiss.

Schyler's arms closed around his lean torso. Her fingers dug into the supple muscles of his back. They turned toward each other until one's body was imprinted onto the front of the other.

They shared an eating kiss, where lips and tongues tried to taste as much as they could as quickly as possible. They came up for air and gazed deeply into each other's eyes. Their breathing was harsh and uneven.

"I broke all my rules with you." Cash watched his own hand slide down to her breast. He cupped it, lifted it, used his thumb to bring the nipple to a hard peak against her clothing. "I didn't use a rubber. I never do that," he confessed, mystified by his own neglect. "My motto is fuck 'em and forget 'em." Swiftly his eyes came back to hers. "I can't forget it. I've tried." His hand slid over her belly; he pressed the *v* at the top of her thighs. "Damn you, I want it again," he said gruffly.

"Me too."

"*Oui?*"

"Yes. Where?"

"Here."

"Here?"

"*Oui.*"

"I—"

"*Oui.*"

They started kissing again. His tongue probed the silky recess of her mouth with carnal implication. The muscles of her cheeks contracted, squeezing his tongue. He groaned and rubbed his erection against her belly. She reached down to touch him and made of her hand a gentle, caressing, sliding fist. He uttered a hoarse cry. As one, with mouths clinging, they dropped to their knees on the forest floor.

He pressed her shoulders between his hands and angled her backward. She landed on a bed of fallen leaves and pine needles that rustled more enticingly than satin sheets. Responding to a primitive masculine need to possess and dominate, Cash stretched out on top of her.

Schyler reacted with the same degree of passion, though her response was purely feminine. She opened her thighs. He burrowed, hard and urgent, against the warm, vulnerable softness of woman. The elements that made them different made this wonderful. Each released a long, soughing sound that was usually reserved for climaxing.

Raising her hips, Schyler struggled to work her skirt up her legs and out of his way. Cash was roughly rubbing his face against her breasts, his mouth open, moist and hot. He grappled with his belt buckle, but his desperation to be inside her made him clumsy and ineffective.

Between choppy gasps for breath, he cursed with frustration. Schyler knocked his hands aside and attacked the stubborn buckle herself. But she wasn't very dexterous either. Their hands batted at each other in their rush to undo his belt.

And then, simultaneously, they realized that their agonized sighs weren't all that they heard. Abruptly, Cash rolled off her and sat up.

"Cash? Did you hear—"

"Shh!" He held up one hand for quiet.

They listened. It came again—a low, unrecognizable sound.

Cash stood up. As fleet-footed as a deer and as silent as a shadow, he slipped away from Schyler and through the trees in the direction of the noise. His training as a jungle fighter served him well. He didn't even disturb the leaves of the plants he skimmed past. He drew his knife from the scabbard at the small of his back. He crept along the muddy banks of the bayou and circled the ropy trunk of a cypress.

"Jesus."

Schyler, leaving the love nest their bodies had ground into the undergrowth, scurried after him, sliding in the mud. "What is it?" she asked, stepping around him. "*Gayla!*"

Chapter Thirty-five

The young black woman looked up at them fearfully. Her eyes were red. Swelling and bleeding scratches had distorted one whole side of her face. Her clothes were in tatters. The exposed skin was covered with abrasions and cuts. She was missing one shoe.

Cash scanned both banks of the bayou and the hill above them. His eyes were as sharp as a machete. Schyler dropped to her knees in the mud. "Gayla, my God, Gayla." She repeated the name softly and reached out to touch her childhood friend. Gayla flinched.

"Don't be afraid, Gayla. It's me, Schyler." Distraught, Schyler glanced up at Cash. "She doesn't know me."

"Yes I do, Schyler." Gayla ran her tongue over the deep and nasty cut on her lower lip. It had dribbled blood onto her chest. "Don't look at me. Just go away. Please."

Tears welled in her chocolate-colored eyes. She gathered her limbs against her body and curled inward in an effort to make her shame invisible. Schyler lifted Gayla's head onto her thigh and laid her hand along the smooth uninjured cheek. It was the only feature that made her recognizable. Schyler hoped the disfigurement done to her face would be temporary.

"Oh, I'm going to look at you plenty," Schyler whispered, "because I've missed you so much. We're going to talk. We're going to reminisce about old times and, when you're feeling better, we're going to giggle like girls."

A tear slid into one of the scratches on Gayla's cheek. "I'm not a girl anymore, Schyler. I'm a—"

"You're my friend," Schyler stressed.

Gayla closed her eyes and began to cry in earnest. "I don't deserve to be."

"Thank God none of us gets what she deserves." While she continued to hold Gayla, gently stroking her head, Schyler looked up at Cash. He'd been scouting around the immediate area. "Do you see anybody?"

"No." He knelt down and assessed a madman's handiwork. He touched Gayla's shoulder. "Did Jigger do this to you?" Gayla nodded. "That filthy son of a bitch," Cash mouthed. "He must have beat her up, then dumped her. Looks like she slid down the hill."

There was forest debris ensnared in her tight cap of hair. Twigs and leaves clung to her clothes. Her bare arms and legs were streaked with dirt.

"No, Mr. Boudreaux." Gayla pronounced his name correctly, in a musical, contralto, West Indian voice that was made even huskier because of her tears. "I slid down the hill, but Jigger didn't dump me here. I ran away from him."

"You came all this way on foot?"

"Yes."

"Is he looking for you?"

"No. I don't know. Just leave me alone. Forget you saw me. Let me die lying right here and I'll be happy. I can't go back. He'll kill me. I don't want to live, but I don't want to give him the pleasure of killing me."

"He's not going to kill you. He's not going to do anything to you because I'm going to protect you. And I'm damn sure not going to leave you here to die," Schyler said sternly. "Can you carry her up the hill?" she asked Cash. "If we can get her that far, I'll stay with her while you go call an ambulance."

"No!" Gayla nearly came up off the ground. "No, Jesus, no, please. He'll find me and kill me."

"You'll be safe in the hospital, Gayla."

Gayla, bordering on hysteria, shook her head emphatically, despite the pain it must have caused. "Jigger beat me, then locked me in the toolshed. But I got out. When he discovers I'm gone, he'll go crazy."

"He's already crazy."

"He'll find me no matter where I am. He'll kill me for running away, Schyler. Swear to God he will. He's told me he would and he will." She clutched double handfuls of Schyler's blouse. "If you help me, he'll hurt you, too. Go away, please. Don't touch me. I'm dirty. You don't want to mess with a whore like me."

"That's enough!" Schyler cried. "I'm not afraid of Jigger Flynn. Let him come anywhere near us and I'll shoot him myself." Gayla began to weep again; Schyler softened her tone of voice. "If you won't feel safe in the hospital, we'll take you to Belle Terre. I promise to keep you safe there."

Cash nudged Schyler aside. "Come on, Gayla. Can you put your arms around my neck? Yes you can," he urged gently, when she shook her head no. "Try. That's it. Clasp your hands now. That's good." He slid his arms beneath her back and knees and lifted her up.

"Cash, she's bleeding," Schyler gasped. The back of Gayla's dress was soaked with bright red blood. "Gayla, what did he do to you?"

"She fainted," Cash told her. Gayla's head was lolling against his shoulder. "It's just as well. This is going to be a rough trip."

He started up the hill. Schyler picked up the bottle of champagne that he'd dropped and scrambled after him. Her high heels were caked with mud. Branches snagged the cloth of her expensive skirt. She paid them no heed. She was wondering how Gayla had survived tumbling down the steep hillside.

After what seemed like a trek up Mount Everest, they reached the car. Schyler hobbled ahead and wrenched open the back door. She jumped inside. "Lay her head in my lap. Get to the hospital as fast as you can. I don't care what she said, she's got to get to the emergency room."

Cash laid Gayla on the back seat as Schyler had instructed, but he didn't withdraw his head and shoulders from the door. He stayed bent over, looking at her. "Well, what is it? Get going," she ordered curtly.

"They'll take care of her injuries at the hospital, but they'll have to call the sheriff about this." He nodded down at the unconscious woman. "He'll conduct a routine investigation, but he won't do a frigging thing to Jigger. In a few days the hospital will release her. Jigger will be waiting for her. Next time it'll be worse."

Schyler stared down into Gayla's brutalized face and knew that he was right. "All right, let's take her to Belle Terre. I don't know if I can get a doctor to come out there—"

"I can."

Cash slammed the door and ran around to the driver's side of the car. Within seconds they were under way, speeding down the highway through the closing twilight.

"Another drink, Tricia?"

"No thank you, darlin'. Mrs. Graves should be calling us in to supper any minute now."

Tricia was fanning herself with the insubstantial afternoon edition of *The Heaven Trumpet*. There had been a full accounting of the generous pounding the Junior League had sponsored for the Glee Williams family. Tricia was feeling smug and piqued—smug because she was given credit for the astounding outpouring of generosity, piqued because Schyler had been the one who had actually organized the benevolent gesture and had done most of the legwork involved in collecting the food, staples, and used clothing.

"It's really getting tiresome," she said petulantly, "having to hold supper for Schyler every night. She's always late."

"She didn't know for sure when she'd be getting back from Endicott's." Ken sucked on a bourbon-flavored ice cube he'd shaken from the bottom of his glass. "It's a long drive."

"You'd think she'd at least call."

"Relax. Here she comes now." Ken set his empty glass on a wicker table and stepped off the veranda onto the steps. "Driving like a bat outta hell, too. That's not like her."

"Maybe she finally got the message about being perpetually late." Languidly Tricia laid down the newspaper and left her chair to go inside.

"What the hell?" Ken asked rhetorically.

Cash pulled the car to a jarring halt just a few feet from the steps. He opened his door, rolled out, and wrenched open the rear door. Bending at the waist, he reached inside and lifted Gayla out.

"What the hell is going on here?" Ken blocked Cash's path as he set his foot on the first step leading up to the veranda. "Schyler, I'm waiting for you to tell me—"

"Move out of the way, Ken. Tricia, are any of the guest rooms made up?" Both Howells were staring at Cash and Gayla as though they were aliens who had hatched in the bayou. "Well, answer me," Schyler demanded. "Are any of the guest rooms made up?"

Tricia's eyes found her sister's. "What's the matter with that girl?"

"She's been beaten to within an inch of her life. Which bedroom should I put her in?"

"You don't mean to bring her inside the house, do you?"

Schyler emitted a breath of disbelief and disgust. She looked toward Ken for support. He was glaring at Cash where they stood eye to eye on the steps, Ken one up from Cash and directly in his way.

"What is the matter with you two?" Schyler exclaimed. "Don't you recognize Gayla?"

"I know who she is," Tricia snapped.

"She's seriously hurt."

"Then I suggest a hospital."

"She's coming inside."

Schyler went around Ken and indicated to Cash that he should do the same. She was glad that he was holding Gayla in his arms; otherwise he would have used physical force to move Ken out of his path. From the murderous look in his eyes, he would have enjoyed that immensely.

Schyler crossed the veranda and reached for the handle on the screen door. Tricia stepped in front of her and flattened herself against the door to hold it shut. "Mama would turn over in her grave if she knew you were bringing them inside Belle Terre."

"Gayla's been inside. Many times. We used to play with her, remember? Her mother ironed your clothes, washed your dishes, cooked the food you ate. And Veda was blacker than Gayla."

"This has got nothing to do with race."

"Then what?"

"You force me to be unkind, Schyler. She's Jigger Flynn's whore," Tricia shouted.

Schyler went hot with fury. "And whose fault is that?"

Tricia faltered but recovered quickly. "I suppose you're going to suggest it's mine."

"Well isn't it?"

"You blame me for everything that goes wrong around here!"

"I can't argue with you about anything now, Tricia," Schyler said, having lost patience with Tricia's childish tantrum. "This is a house. It isn't the holy of holies. Neither Gayla nor Cash can or will defile it. Mama will never know who comes inside. Even is she's watching with disapproval from on high, there's not a damn thing she can do about it. Now get out of my way."

Schyler pushed her sister aside and jerked open the door.

"You know what Cotton thinks of *him*," Ken shouted behind her.

She turned and thought about that for a moment. Then she said, "There's nothing Cotton can do about it now either." Schyler looked at Cash and inclined her head toward the spacious foyer beyond the door. For the first time in his life, Cash Boudreaux stepped over the threshold of Belle Terre.

Mrs. Graves was standing in the foyer, looking like the last formidable guard at the gates of heaven. "Are any of the guest rooms made up?" Schyler asked her.

"Not for the likes of her." She crossed her arms over her shriveled breasts as though visibly withdrawing any responsibility for what was about to take place.

"Then she can use my room." Schyler said calmly. "Make up a guest room for me." She headed for the stairs.

"By the way, Mrs. Graves, that will be your last official duty at Belle Terre. Kindly rid the quarters of all your personal belongings. I'll have a severance check waiting for you on the hall table within an hour."

Schyler ran ahead of Cash up the sweeping staircase. He took the stairs two at a time. Mrs. Graves was left standing slack-jawed in the hall. Tricia and Ken were stone-faced. Schyler ignored their glares from below as she reached the second-story landing and pointed out her room to Cash. He went ahead of her. By the time she reached the doorway, he was already depositing Gayla on her bed.

"It's going to make a helluva mess." When he withdrew his arms from beneath Gayla's limp body, the front of his shirt was bloodstained.

"It doesn't matter. I just made a bigger mess downstairs," Schyler muttered as she bent over Gayla. "While I undress her, you call the doctor."

"No doctor."

"What?" Schyler sprang erect and stared at him incomprehensively.

"Have her undressed by the time I get back." He headed for the door.

"Wait!" Schyler charged after him. Her fingers slipped on his bloody sleeve, but she managed to stop him. "I thought you said you could get a doctor here. Where are you going?"

"I'm the doctor, but I've got to go get my stuff."

Her face turned pale. "Are you crazy? She needs professional help. She could die. This isn't a mosquito bite, Cash. She's bleeding and I don't even know—"

"It's vaginal bleeding. She's had a miscarriage." Schyler sucked in a sharp breath and held it. She gaped at him speechlessly. "I recognize it. My mother lost a baby. There was nobody else to take care of her. I had to. She told me what to do. I know how to deal with it."

Schyler spun around and lurched for the phone. She picked up the receiver, but before it ever made it to her ear, Cash yanked it out of her hand and slammed it back down. "You promised Gayla."

"I can't take responsibility for this."

"You promised."

"But I didn't know it was anything this bad. What if she dies?"

They'd been shouting at each other. Cash pressed her shoulders between his hands and lowered his voice drastically. "I can help her. Trust me." He gave her shoulders a hard squeeze. "Trust me."

For ponderous moments, Schyler stared into his eyes. She glanced down at Gayla. When her eyes moved back to his, her posture went as limp as her linen blouse. Lips barely moving, she said, "If anyone downstairs tries to stop you—"

"I'll take care of it. Nothing would give me greater pleasure."

Schyler watched him go, praying that she had made the right decision. Then she turned back to the bed and the grim chore ahead of her.

Chapter Thirty-six

Schyler had time to sponge Gayla off before Cash returned. Dirt and dried blood had concealed evidence of previous beatings. With each swipe of the wet cloth, Schyler's pity for her friend increased in proportion to her hatred for Jigger Flynn. By the time Cash came rushing through the door, there were tears of pity standing in Schyler's eyes.

"She's got marks and scars all over her," she told him.

"I doubt Jigger is a tender lover."

"He's an animal that should be locked up."

"Don't hold your breath." He sat down on the edge of the bed and studied Gayla's face. "How is she otherwise?"

"No more bleeding."

"Good. Shown any signs of coming around?"

"She's conscious. She moaned while I was washing her."

Cash laid his hand on Gayla's forehead and called her name softly. "Gayla, wake up and talk to me. I need to ask you some questions." Her eyelids flickered open. She looked at him, then over his shoulder at Schyler. "You're at Belle Terre. Safe."

"Safe." They watched her cut and swollen lips form the disbelieving word. Her eyes closed peacefully.

"Don't go back to sleep yet," Cash said, shaking her awake. "I'm going to treat you, but I have to ask you some questions first."

She struggled to keep her eyes open. "Okay."

He opened his leather pouch and took out a jar of salve. He folded back the sheet and began applying the waxy, yellow substance to the scratches on her chest and arms. "How far along was your pregnancy?"

Tears sprang into her eyes as the old fears swamped her again. Her face twisted in anguish. "I couldn't have his baby. Devil man that he is, I just couldn't."

"There is no baby. Not anymore." Cash clasped her hand reassuringly. "How far along were you before you started bleeding? How late was your period?"

"Six, eight weeks maybe."

"*Bien.*"

"I took the medicine you sent me."

"Medicine?" Schyler exclaimed. She turned on Cash. "You knew about this before today?"

He shushed her. Gayla was still speaking in a faint, far-away voice. "Jigger said you told him it would fix me right up."

Schyler demanded Cash's attention again. "You gave that man medicine for her?"

"*Oui*, now shut up."

"You dealt with him?" Schyler asked, flabbergasted.

Cash whipped his head around. "I did. He came to my

house, told me Gayla was bleeding. That she'd had a miscarriage. What was I supposed to do, ignore him?"

"You could have told me."

"So you could do what? Go butting into business that didn't concern you? So you could shoot up his place one more time and get him really pissed off at you?" She fell silent, but she was still fuming. "Besides, that was when Cotton was at his worst. It didn't look like he was going to pull through. You had your hands full and didn't need anything more to worry about."

He went back to his unpleasant task. He laid his finger against a circular scar on the side of Gayla's breast. "Cigarette burn," he said softly. Gayla whimpered with a terrible memory. Cash's face turned compassionate. "What brought on the miscarriage?"

Gayla rolled to her side and buried her face in the snowy pillowcase. Schyler and Cash looked at each other, puzzled. She had said she didn't want Jigger's baby, but now she seemed upset at the mention of her miscarriage. Cash touched her bare shoulder and turned her over. "Gayla, tell me. What happened? Did Jigger get too rough with you?"

She shook her head slowly from side to side. Tears rolled down her ravaged cheek, liquifying dried blood. "I did it myself. I started the bleeding."

"Jesus," Cash breathed.

Schyler raised both hands to her lips and pressed them until they were white.

"I couldn't have his baby," Gayla averred in a hoarse voice. "I'll go to hell, won't I, for killing it? God'll send me to hell for murdering my own baby."

She was on the brink of hysteria. Cash leaned over her, pressing her back onto the pillows. "You're not going to hell, Gayla. You're not the sinner. You're the one sinned against. Did the medicine I sent help you?"

"Yes. Thank you, Mr. Boudreaux. I was real sick till Jigger brought me the medicine. I followed the directions and took it all. It stopped the bleeding. I was feeling better, but then . . ."

She looked around the room warily, as though she were

in the witness box and the defendant on trial was likely to kill her on the spot if she told the truth.

"Then what, Gayla?" Cash prompted softly, dabbing at a cut on her shoulder with peroxide-soaked cotton.

Gayla looked up at Schyler. Her dark eyes were shimmering with tears of remorse. "He made me go with one of the gentlemen." The words were almost inaudible. "I didn't want to. I told him I couldn't because I wasn't completely healed up yet, but—" She turned her face into the pillow again. "The man paid a hundred dollars for me. Jigger made me go."

Cash glanced at Schyler. She shook her head in wordless incredulity. Gayla's tale was medieval. That kind of subservience couldn't occur in the twentieth century. But it had.

"Did this gentleman," Cash said with a sneer, "make you have sex with him?" Gayla nodded her head. Cash swore viciously. "Why did Jigger beat you today?"

"I refused to go again today. I told Jigger I wasn't feeling good, that I'd started bleeding again. But he didn't want to make the man mad."

"Was it the same man as before?"

"I think so. I saw his car."

"Who? Who is he?"

"I don't know his name. But he . . ."

"What?"

"He . . . he takes pictures of me."

Schyler shivered. Cash mentally filed the information. "Exactly what happened this afternoon?"

"I said I wouldn't go. The man got tired of waiting and went away. After he left, Jigger whipped me with his razor strop. He did this," she gestured at her swollen jaw, "with his fist. It had a chain wrapped around it."

Cash called Jigger a gutter name, which Schyler thought was well deserved.

"He told me to reconsider my decision while I was locked in the shed." Gayla's lips began to quiver. "That's the worst beating he's ever given me. The next time, he'll kill me. I know it. I had to run away while I had the chance." Her face contorted with anxiety. "He'll kill me when he finds me."

"He can't touch you as long as you're here." Schyler laid a reassuring hand on Gayla's arm. "You don't have to ever be afraid of him again."

Gayla didn't look so certain. "You don't hate me, Schyler, for what I've done?"

"Of course not. You were victimized."

"Mama couldn't work. She was sick. I had to feed her, buy her medicine. I couldn't find a job, so I took one serving drinks in the beer joint. Mama would have killed me if she'd known what I was doing. I told her I was working at the Dairy Mart."

She wet her lips and twisted the hem of the sheet Cash had pulled up over her. "Mama got sicker. I asked Jigger for a raise. He said there was only one way I could make more money."

"Shh, Gayla, don't," Schyler said.

"I went with that first man 'cause I was gonna get fifty dollars out of it. I cried and cried afterwards because of Jimmy Don. I knew he would hate me if he ever found out. I thought it would just be that once. That's all, I swear. I didn't set out to become a whore."

"I know. You don't have to tell me anymore."

"But that fifty dollars went fast. And I needed some more." Her shoulders shook. "I went with another man. Then another. Jigger kept bringing them to me."

"Gayla, nobody needs to hear a confession," Cash said. He cradled the sobbing woman in his arms and said to Schyler, "I need to examine her. Can you bring her something to drink? Hot tea? Something?"

Schyler pressed Gayla's arm once more before withdrawing. Outside the door she pulled closed behind her, she let go a long, deep breath and for a moment leaned back against the wall. She was fatigued, physically and emotionally, but she couldn't rest yet. She went downstairs.

Ken was nowhere in sight. Tricia was in the front parlor. She stopped pacing when she saw Schyler and stormily followed her into the kitchen. Schyler put the kettle on the stove and turned on the burner beneath it.

"You weren't serious when you fired Mrs. Graves, were you?"

"Thank you for reminding me, Tricia. I need to write her a check."

"I won't let you fire her."

"I already have. I despise the woman. I have ever since I came home."

"But you can't fire her just like that," Tricia said, snapping her fingers inches in front of Schyler's nose, "just because she expressed out loud what Ken and I were thinking. Something's happened to you, Schyler. You've gone off the deep end. Lately, you've become unreasonable."

"I fired Mrs. Graves because she insulted a friend of mine. And even though the friend was unconscious at the time and didn't hear the insult, I did. As to being unreasonable," she said reflectively, "perhaps you're right." She calmly set the pot of hot tea she'd prepared on a tray. Picking up the tray, she faced her sister. "Mrs. Graves can wait until morning to leave. I really don't have time to write out a check now."

Tricia's face fell. She was right on Schyler's heels as she headed toward the stairs. "You won't get away with this, Miss High-and-Mighty. Where do you get off, coming home after six years and throwing your weight around, undoing everything that I've done?"

Schyler turned and confronted her. "Everything you've done needs undoing, Tricia."

Tricia went as straight and rigid as an arrow. Through clenched teeth she warned, "First thing in the morning, Cotton will hear about this."

Schyler set the tray on the hall table and backed Tricia into the wall. "Cotton will hear about nothing," she said through clenched teeth. "Do you understand me?"

"Watch and see."

"If you go barging into the hospital and upset him, what might happen? He could have another heart attack, right? He could die. Suddenly. And then where would all your

plans for selling Belle Terre be? Out the window. Because
I'm sure Daddy's will divides it equally between us, and
I'll see you in hell before I'll ever let my half of it be sold.
Your chances of talking Cotton into it are so slim as to be
negligible. But your chances with me are positively zero."
She picked up the tray again. "Think about that, baby sis-
ter, before you go to Cotton and start tattling."

Inside the bedroom, Cash was gently tucking the covers
around Gayla. Schyler looked at him for information.

"I don't think she did much damage, though God knows
how she kept from it." He ran his hand through his hair,
which was already untidy. "Believe me, you don't want to
hear the details. It's a miracle she didn't bleed to death."

"Does she need a transfusion?" Schyler asked, looking
down at Gayla and keeping her voice low.

"I was afraid she might, but I don't think so. If I did, I'd
drive her to the hospital myself. She wasn't bleeding from
her uterus. She'd been . . . well . . . scratched up inside."
Schyler winced. "Those scratches had opened up, thanks to
the shutterbug. I found some Kotex in the bathroom.
Change the pad often. If the bleeding increases, let me
know. If she stays in bed a few days, she'll be all right."

"What about her face?"

"No structural damage. Once the swelling goes down,
she'll be as pretty as ever. The scratches and cuts will
heal."

"After the trauma she's lived through the last few years,
I don't know if she'll ever be completely healed." Schyler
extended him the tray. "Here's the tea."

Cash reached into his bag again and took out a small
vial. He uncorked it and poured several drops of the contents into the tea. "What is that?" Schyler asked.

"The narcs don't know about this one. It's an ancient
recipe handed down through generations of *traiteurs*. It'll
keep Gayla asleep for several hours." He cupped Gayla's
head in his hand and lifted it off the pillow. "Gayla, drink
this." He placed the rim of the china cup between her bat-

tered lips. "It'll make you feel like you're on a flying carpet headed for Nirvana."

Gayla sipped the strong, potion-laced tea. She gazed up at Schyler. "How come you're doing this for me?"

"Stupid question, Gayla. I loved your mother. And I love you."

"I don't deserve anybody's love," she said solemnly. "Not even God's."

"He loves you, too."

Gayla shook her head with conviction. "Not after I killed my baby. That's a mortal sin." She lapsed into a moment of self-examination. "It doesn't matter though. Jimmy Don couldn't ever love me again after all the men who've had me. And I loved Jimmy Don more than I loved God." She gazed up at them, her eyes now made lambent by Cash's potion. "Do you think that's why God let Jigger get me? Was God jealous of Jimmy Don?"

Cash set the empty cup on the nightstand. "I'm a long way from being a prophet, Gayla. But I don't think God shits on people the way other people do."

Gayla seemed to take comfort in that unorthodox piece of theology. Her eyelids closed. Seconds later, her entire body went limp. "She's out," Cash said, standing up.

Schyler looked at him, noticing for the first time how tired he seemed. He had changed shirts while he was gone, but otherwise, he looked worse for wear. She cleared her throat and began awkwardly, "Cash, I don't know how to thank you."

"Forget it. I didn't do it for you."

"Yes, but—"

The sudden pounding on the door halted whatever she was about to say. She was too stunned to respond. Cash grunted a dangerous, "Who is it?"

"Deputy Sheriff Walker."

Cash uttered an expletive beneath his breath. Then he called out, "Hold on a sec."

His hand caught Schyler around the back of the neck and yanked her forward. He kissed her mouth soundly, rolling his tongue over her lips until they were red and wet and shiny. He roughly rubbed his stubbled chin against her throat. He tore open two buttons of her blouse, reached inside and pushed down her bra strap.

"Try to look like you've been screwing."

Chapter Thirty-seven

"What the hell do you want, Walker? It better be damned important."

Deputy Sheriff Walker flinched when Cash Boudreaux querulously yanked open the door. He cursed his rotten luck. Sheriff Patout would have his ass if he didn't follow through on this call, but, hell, he didn't want a hassel with Boudreaux. From the looks of it, the Cajun was in a tetchy state of mind, too. He was a far cry from a good ol' boy any day of the week. Anybody who went up against the ornery cuss was likely to get a knife between his ribs. Still, it was his duty to check out this complaint.

Cash had one arm braced on the doorjamb. His body was blocking the narrow opening. The deputy peered around him, trying to look stern and official. That wasn't easy for a man who had to shave only every other day.

"Hiya, Cash. Miss Schyler." He tipped his hat at her. She was standing in the background wearing whisker burns around her mouth and a dazed expression in her eyes. Damn Boudreaux's luck. His legendary dick got him invited between even the classiest thighs.

Walker drew his thoughts back to professional matters.

domestic quarrel in here. Is that right?"

"A domestic . . ." Cash rolled his eyes and cursed. "That dumbass. Is he talking about Gayla? Gayla just had a little accident. She got banged up a little. A few scratches. I'm hurting a whole helluva lot worse than she is."

"Whadaya mean, Cash? What's goin' on?"

"Well," Cash drew out the word and glanced over his shoulder at Schyler, "I don't have to tell you *everything*, do I?"

The deputy cleared his throat importantly and said, "Yeah, you do. Everything."

Cash stared him down, then cursed in apparent exaspera-tion. "All right. You see me and Schyler were having a little picnic out in the woods." He tilted his head. Walker followed the direction he indicated and spotted the half-full bottle of champagne standing on the nightstand. "I wasn't exactly nibbling on fried chicken. Understand what I'm saying?" Walker swallowed hard and bobbed his head. "In fact," Cash said, "I was really getting with it, when here comes one of Jigger's whores tumbling down the hill."

Walker guffawed. "You and me both've seen whores with their heels in the air."

Cash's face changed. His eyes turned cold. Walker began sweating and cursed his stupidity. He'd gone too far.

But Cash went on easily. "Right. I didn't think anything about it. I was anxious to continue what we'd been doing." He frowned. "I'd forgotten that Schyler knows Gayla from way back. She got upset because Gayla was hurt and asked me to fix her up. So, we called off our . . . uh, *picnic* and brought Gayla here. She's sleeping, but if you want to come on in and look for yourself . . ." He stepped aside and swept his arm wide.

The deputy glanced at the bed, where Jigger's whore was indeed sleeping peacefully. He looked at Schyler and blushed to the tips of his ears. Sure enough, she looked like she could have been the main course at a picnic with Cash Boudreaux. Her clothes and hair were in a mess. She seemed embarrassed and guilty as hell to be caught seen with Boudreaux. Shifting from one foot to another, she raised one hand to her blouse and nervously fidgeted with an unfastened button. A spectacular amount of cleavage was showing. He'd like to get a closer look, but the Cajun probably wouldn't want him ogling his current woman. Cash was touchy about things like that.

"No, that's okay, Cash. I don't need to come in." Walker started to move away, but paused. "Only . . . Well, Mr. Howell said that maybe Jigger Flynn was involved."

"Jigger? Did you see Jigger anywhere around, Schyler?" Boudreaux consulted with her over his shoulder.

"Uh, no." She self-consciously smoothed her hand over her tousled hair. "I didn't see him."

Cash shrugged. "All we saw was Gayla barreling down that hill end over end."

"What was she doing out in the woods all by herself?"

"How the hell should I—No, wait. On the way here, she mumbled something about communing with God."

"God?"

"Look, I don't know what the hell she was muttering about, okay?"

"Uh, yeah, okay."

"So is that it?"

"Well—"

"If so, beat it. We've got better things to do." He leaned forward and whispered, "Give me a break, Walker. I've got a hard-on that's stiff as a pike and I'm beginning to fear this just ain't my day to get laid."

Walker laughed and jabbed Cash in the ribs. "I know what that's like, man."

"Then have a little pity and get the hell out of here."

Louder than was necessary, Walker said, "Well, I'd better let y'all get about your business. Sorry to have bothered y'all." He gave Cash a broad wink. "Miss Schyler, ma'am." He tipped his hat and turned away. He had almost reached the top of the stairs when she surprised him by catching up.

"I'll show you out, Mr. Walker."

She fell into step with him. Walker thought that showed real moxey. Catch a lady with her pants down and she's still a lady. As they went downstairs side by side, he gazed about him. He hadn't done too badly. He had parted company with Boudreaux on a friendly basis and he'd got to take a gander at the inside of Belle Terre.

He would have something exciting to tell the wife after his shift. She would pester him with questions, wanting to know what this and that looked like. Damn! He hadn't noticed the color of Miss Schyler Crandall's bedroom. What the hell, he'd make something up. The wife would never know the difference.

There was a tense moment when they went past the parlor. Ken and Tricia watched from the arched opening. "Well?" Ken demanded, stepping into the foyer.

"Cash and I explained everything to Deputy Walker. He's agreed that Gayla should stay here," Schyler said smoothly. She guided the deputy to the door. "Thank you so much for stopping by."

The door was closed behind Walker before he fully realized what had happened. Schyler turned to face the Howells. They both looked ready to bludgeon her. Before she could give it much thought, something at the top of the stairs attracted her attention. Cash was coming down them, casually trailing his hand along the banister.

Tricia and Ken turned to stare with open animosity. His appearance only fueled their hostility. "I won't have that black whore sleeping under my roof," Tricia ground out.

"You have no choice," Schyler said evenly. "Gayla is here to stay for as long as she wants to. When I've had a chance to explain the situation to Cotton, I'm sure he'll be in full agreement with my decision." Tired as she was, Schyler dared either of them to take issue with her.

Ken accepted the challenge. "What about him? Have you asked him to spend the night, too?"

"Thanks, but I've already made other plans," Cash replied politely, a sardonic smirk on his lips.

Tricia looked at Cash with condescending speculation as she passed him on her way upstairs. "Excuse me," she said with hauteur.

Ken was less subtle when he went past. "You'll be sorry, Boudreaux."

"I doubt it."

Seconds later, the slamming of their bedroom door reverberated through the house. Schyler blew out her breath. "I won't be winning any popularity contests around here any time soon."

"Does it matter?"

"Not if I'd have to do anything differently, no." She stood facing him awkwardly, clasping and unclasping her hands at her waist. She was able to stand up to her sister's and Ken's angst, but she faltered beneath Cash's steady stare, especially in light of the lie he'd told the deputy. She could feel the whisker burns around her lips. She hadn't looked in a mirror lately but knew they must be obvious. At the very least she looked well kissed. That couldn't have won her any points with either Ken or Tricia.

"I don't like being indebted to you," she told Cash candidly.

"What'll you give me?"

"What do you want?"

"You know damn well what I want," he growled. "But for now, one drink would cancel all debts."

"This way."

She turned and led him toward the formal parlor; however, he paused in the doorway of the dining room with the yellow silk walls. Schyler, turning, watched him curiously for several seconds. "Cash? Coming?"

"*Oui,*" he replied absently. Beneath his breath he whispered, "For you, *Maman.*"

Schyler went to the sideboard that served as a liquor cabinet and withdrew a decanter of bourbon. She poured a generous portion into a tumbler. "Ice? Water?"

When he didn't answer, she turned and caught him pivoting slowly, taking in every aspect of the room. "Cash?" she repeated. He came to attention with a start. "How do you want your drink?"

"Neat." He came to her, took the glass from her hand and tossed back the contents. He extended the glass, she poured more of the liquor. He drank it the same way.

"That's two drinks," she remarked.

"Then I guess I'll be indebted to you."

"That would be a switch." Since he had set his glass down, she capped the Waterford decanter.

"You're not having one?"

"Ice water." The two ice cubes she took from the silver bucket rattled noisily in the glass. She splashed water over them and took a drink. "Champagne always makes me thirsty."

"And drunk."

"I should have warned you."

"I didn't mind."

He was the first to look away from their long stare. He took in the luxurious surroundings, which bespoke wealth and refinement that was generations old. "You've never been inside Belle Terre before, have you?"

"No," he answered tersely. "Pretty fancy."

"Most of the furniture and accessories in this room are replacements of the originals. The Union army didn't have much of an appreciation for the house. When they left it, they burned what little could have been salvaged. Only the rug and that clock on the mantel are originals. An enterprising Laurent was able to sneak them out."

"How'd they get so rich to start with?"

"There was always timber, of course. But they invested the money they brought from France in several plantations. Sugarcane. Rice. Most of the family never even saw those. They were miles away. They only grew their household crops around here."

"Who's that?"

She glanced toward the oil portrait hanging above the marble mantel. "Macy's great-grandmother."

Cash gazed at the thin, pale woman in the portrait. "Not bad. Not a knockout, but not bad."

"How sexist!"

He looked down at Schyler, letting his eyes rove over her hair and face and figure. Unlike Walker, he didn't avoid looking at her exposed cleavage. He even touched the smooth skin with his fingertip and watched it glide over the soft curves as he asked, "Will your portrait hang up there some day? Will a couple of descendants stand in this spot and discuss your attributes?"

"I doubt if I'll ever have a portrait painted. And if I did, it wouldn't be right to hang it up there."

"How come?"

"I'm not a Laurent. Not even half of one. I came to live at Belle Terre purely by chance."

He studied her for a long moment, then abruptly withdrew his caressing hand. "I gotta go. Gayla should be fine in a few days. I left some ointment on the table by the bed. Apply it twice a day to those scratches on her arms and legs."

"Do you think Jigger will come looking for her?"

"I wouldn't be surprised. Be careful."

He had made it to the front door before Schyler caught up with him. She was puzzled over his rush to leave. She was also irrationally disappointed. "Will you be at the landing in the morning?"

He shook his head no. "I'll go straight to where we're cutting and start marking trees. We've got that order to fill, remember?"

"Actually I didn't. So much has happened since our meeting with Joe Jr." She trailed Cash out onto the veranda, inexplicably reluctant to have him go. "Cash?" He turned. "That lie you told the deputy. . . ."

"It wasn't exactly a lie, was it?"

"Yes, yes it was. And I didn't approve."

"Tough. I didn't have time to consult you first."

"It'll be all over town tomorrow that we were making out in the woods."

"That's the price you'll pay for taking in Gayla. Sorry?"

"No, of course not. Only. . . ."

"Only . . . ?"

"I just wish you had told Walker something else."

"I had to get his mind on us and off her."

"Well your lie certainly worked to do that."

"*Oui*, it did."

She wet her lips. They still tasted like him. The whisker burns stung. "Do lies always come to you that easily."

He backed into the darkness and was swallowed up by it. "Always."

Chapter Thirty-eight

"I suppose you expect me to wait on her hand and foot."

"On the contrary, Tricia. I expect you to pretend that Gayla isn't here."

"Good. That's what I plan to do."

The two sisters were in the downstairs hall. Schyler was dressed and ready to go to work. She had just spoken to Cotton over the telephone, promising to visit him that afternoon with a full account of her interview with Endicott.

"Gayla only drank tea for breakfast and then went back to sleep," Schyler told Tricia. "I imagine she'll sleep most of the day. I've left fruit juice on the nightstand beside her bed, along with the muffins Mrs. Graves baked yesterday. If Gayla gets hungry before I come home, she can eat those without having to disturb you. I've left her a note to call the office if she needs me."

"Mrs. Graves left this morning."

"Good. That's one less thing I have to worry about."

"Don't expect me to do any housekeeping. This place can rot and fall down for all I care."

"I'll start looking for a housekeeper as soon as I get to the office."

"And what am I supposed to do in the meantime?"

Impatiently Schyler said, "In the meantime, you can fend for yourself or go hungry."

Tricia's eyes narrowed. "You can't order me around like you do everybody else, including my husband. It's going to stop, Schyler, do you hear me?"

"I'm sure everyone in the neighboring parish heard you, Tricia. Kindly stop yelling at me."

"I have every right to yell. You've got Cajun white trash and a nigger whore traipsing through my house."

Schyler came close to slapping her. Perhaps she would have had the telephone not rung just then. Instead of raising a hand to Tricia, she yanked up the receiver. "It's for Ken." Laying the receiver on the table, she picked up her handbag and left before she submitted to an impulse to throttle her adopted sister.

Ken took the call upstairs. "Hello?"

"Hiya, Kenny."

Sweat popped out on his forehead. "I've got it, Tricia." He waited to make sure that she had hung up the extention downstairs before he said anything more. "What the hell do you think you're doing by calling here? I told you never to call me here."

"What you told me ain't worth shit. If it was, Kenny, I'd have my money by now, wouldn't I? It really pisses me off when people don't keep their word to me."

"I asked you for more time." Ken slumped down on the unmade bed and massaged his forehead.

"And like a sap I granted you more time. Have I got my money yet? No."

"I'll get it to you."

"Tomorrow."

"But—"

"Tomorrow."

The telephone went dead. Ken stared vacantly at it for a long time before hanging it up. He didn't have the energy to move, so he sat dejectedly on the edge of the bed. When he finally raised his head, he saw that Tricia was standing in the doorway looking at him curiously.

"Who was that?"

"Nobody." He stood up and went to his closet, randomly selecting a tie. As he tied it, he was uncomfortably reminded of a noose.

"It was somebody," she said petulantly. "I didn't like the sound of his voice."

"I don't like the sound of yours," Ken said, shooting her a hateful look. "Not when it's got that edge to it and not this early in the morning."

"We need to talk."

"We talked until the wee hours last night."

"And nothing was resolved. What are you going to do about her?" She aimed a finger in the direction of Schyler's bedroom where Gayla Frances lay recovering.

"There's not much I can do. We called the sheriff. You saw how that turned out. Personally I don't want to get involved with Jigger Flynn. If you're smart you won't either."

Lighting a cigarette, Tricia snorted. "Hardly. All we need around here is another lowlife. They seem to be taking over Belle Terre. If Schyler had her way we'd become a branch of the Salvation Army."

Ken laughed. For once Tricia wasn't flattered that her joke had gone over.

"I'm glad you think all this is funny," she snapped. She was on his heels as he went downstairs. "I don't think it's at all amusing that we've got a former servant's daughter residing here like she was the Queen of Sheba. Or that my sister," she sneered the word, "has her trashy lover strutting around here like he owned the place."

"Boudreaux isn't her lover."

Tricia laughed out loud. "Will you grow up? Of course he's her lover. Didn't you see the way she looked at him when he came down those stairs? Are you blind? Or is it that you just close your eyes to what you don't want to see?"

On top of his recent telephone call, Ken didn't need Tricia's harping. "Look, I don't like the way Schyler has come in and taken over everything either, but I don't know how to stop her."

Tricia flung back her hair and faced him challengingly. "Well you'd better find a way, darling."

"Or what?"

"Or I'll take matters into my own hands." She gave him a feline smile. "And you're a lot nicer than I am."

"Knock, knock?"

Schyler, holding the phone in the crook of her shoulder, signaled for Ken to come in. He closed the door of the landing office behind him. If he noticed the fresh coat of paint on it, he made no remark.

"That will be wonderful, Mrs. Dunne," Schyler said into the receiver as she smiled at Ken. "Yes, it does seem like providence, doesn't it? . . . And we'll look so forward to having you at Belle Terre . . . This afternoon then? . . . Very good. Good-bye."

She hung up and whooped loudly. "I can't believe it. Mrs. Dunne was a cook in the public school cafeteria and comes highly recommended. She quit several years ago so she could stay at home with her ailing husband. When he died, she contacted an agency in New Orleans that specializes in domestics. When I called them, they referred her. Isn't that a coincidence? She won't have to relocate, except to move into the quarters. And I won't have to exhaust myself with interviews. She won't mind looking after Daddy either." She paused for breath and smiled broadly. "Well, what do you think?"

"Will all our meals taste like school cafeteria food?"

"It can't be any worse than what Mrs. Graves served." She shuddered. "Where did Tricia find that stick woman?"

"Search me. That's Tricia's department."

She let him get seated comfortably before asking, "Why didn't you interfere when she fired Veda, Ken?"

"It wasn't my place to," he said defensively. "I didn't grow up sitting on Veda's knee the way you did. To me she was just a housekeeper."

"To me she was a member of the family," Schyler said sadly. "I'm surprised Tricia didn't feel that way about her, too." Then, forcing herself out of her unsettling reflections, she asked, "What brings you to the landing? While you're here, you can take this. It's your copy of the Endicott contract."

"You didn't even mention it last night."

"I hardly had a chance, Ken."

"Boudreaux went with you, didn't he?"

"Yes, he did," she confessed with chagrin. "His assistance was invaluable."

"Hmm. You were with him all day then."

"It's a long drive."

He had more questions to ask but lost his nerve. "How'd it go?"

"I know you'll be pleased."

She handed him a copy of the contract and braced herself for criticism when he got to the clause about receiving no payment before the entire shipment was received. Ken barely glanced at it before folding it and stuffing it into the breast pocket of his summer blazer.

"Aren't you even going to read it?"

"I'll go over it later," he said. "I'm sure everything is in order." He wouldn't look her in the eyes and he was fidgeting as nervously as a kid at a piano recital. "Actually, I came here this morning to talk about something personal."

Schyler sighed and rose from her chair. "If it's about Gayla, I've said all I have to say."

"It's not about that."

Schyler sat down on the corner of the desk, her legs at a slant in front of her. "Then what?"

"Money." He finally looked up at her. "I need some money."

"Don't we all?" she asked lightly.

His grin was half formed and fleeting. "No, I mean now. Immediately."

He was serious. This was no laughing matter. Schyler matched her mood to his. "How much, Ken?"

He shifted in his chair and cleared his throat. "Ten grand."

"Ten thousand dollars?" She didn't even attempt to disguise her dismay.

"It rounds off to that." Again, his smile vanished as soon as it was formed. "It's for a good cause."

"Your health?"

He seemed to find that funny and laughed out loud. "In a manner of speaking."

"Ken?" She stood up and placed a hand on his shoulder. "You're not ill, are you? Is something—"

"No, no, nothing like that." He came to his feet. "But it's important, Schyler, or I wouldn't come crawling to you like a goddamn beggar. Trust me, you're better off not knowing what it's for. And I'll repay you. I promise."

"I don't want guarantees or explanations from you. If you need the money, you need the money. If your reasons for needing it are personal, I honor your privacy."

"Then you'll loan it to me?"

"I wish I could, but I can't."

"Can't?"

"I don't have it."

"Don't have it?"

His echo was bothersome, but she tried not to show her irritation. "I'll barely have enough to live on until I get my next check."

Ken ran his hand through his hair in befuddlement. "What next check?"

"I put my legacy from Mama in a trust. My attorney in London doles out allotments on the first of every month. Those allotments come out of the interest. I've never touched the principal and don't intend to unless it's absolutely necessary."

"You mean you can't have use of your own money when you want it?"

"I could, but I'd have to pay costly penalties to take out lump sums and later replace them. Besides, if Crandall Logging doesn't pull out of this slump and pay off that loan, I'll have to use part of my inheritance as collateral on another loan. I can't start depleting the account."

"Doesn't that Mark character you work for pay you anything?"

"Yes, but I insisted on working strictly on commission. As you know I haven't been there for almost a month."

He began to pace. He looked like a man who had run out of options. Schyler took sympathy on him. "I'm sure you could make arrangements for a personal loan at the bank."

"My old man didn't trust me with my own inheritance. I

can't touch it until I turn forty. I don't have shit to use for collateral."

"Tricia?"

He softened. "She spent the last of the money her mother left her years ago. Since then she's been sponging off Cotton and the paltry salary he pays me."

"When the business is in the black again, I'll see that you get a well-deserved raise."

"That's not going to help me now, Schyler," he shouted. At her stunned expression, he moved toward her and clasped her shoulders. "I'm sorry. I didn't mean to yell at you."

"Ken, you're frightening me. Just how desperate are you for cash?"

Her concern set off warning bells. He couldn't afford to reveal too much. His face relaxed and he forced himself to smile. "Not so desperate that you need to worry about it." He ironed the wrinkle of worry out of her forehead with his index finger. "It'll take care of itself. Something will turn up."

His finger didn't stop with the furrow on her forehead, but slid down her cheek and then along the rim of her lower lip. "So pretty. And so strong." He drew a deep breath of longing. "My God, Schyler, do you know how sexy you are? The air fairly crackles when you walk into a room."

Schyler tried to move away. "Ken, stop it. I've asked you more than once not to touch me."

"You know I still want you. I know you still want me."

She denied that with a hard shake of her head. "Your come-ons are not only wrong, but tiresome. We've said everything that need be said . . . repeatedly. Now for the last time, cut it out!"

Again, he refused to take no for an answer. If anything, he seemed more determined than ever. He moved forward and embraced her tightly. She pushed him away. He only clasped her tighter.

"Schyler, don't snub me. Let me love you." His breathing accelerated. "Damn! Wouldn't it be exciting to make love right here? Right now." He backed her against the edge of the desk.

"Have you lost your mind?" she gasped.

"Yes. I'm crazy about you."

"Don't you see how wrong this is?"

"It's not wrong. It can't be. Not when I love you so much. What we had is still there. You'll see."

Schyler had too much dignity to engage in a sopho-moric, physical struggle. Sternly she said, "No, Ken."

"Why not? We're alone here."

"Not quite."

They sprang apart at the sound of the intrusive third voice.

Chapter Thirty-nine

Cash Boudreaux was lounging against the doorjamb.

"I hate to break up such a tender scene, but I need to see you about something, Miss Schyler."

She tried to appear composed, but doubted that she pulled off the act. "That's all right, Cash. Ken was just leaving."

Ken's jaw dropped. "You're sending me packing so you can talk to *him*?"

She would have to make amends for the slight later, but she couldn't have Cash believing that she was carrying on an affair with her brother-in-law. "Cash and I need to talk business. What you and I were discussing can wait till later."

He glared at her furiously. "Okay, sure," he said curtly. He nudged Cash aside on his way out the door.

Cash waited until Ken's car had cleared the other side of the bridge and the dust had settled before he turned back to Schyler. "Is that how he earns his salary these days, by keeping the boss lady's hormones well tuned?"

"What Ken was doing here is between him and me."

"That much was obvious."

"And none of your business, Mr. Boudreaux."

The atmosphere in the room was explosive. If one had struck a match, the whole place could have gone up in flames. Cash's eyes flayed her with censure. She stared him down. She would be damned before stammering any self-defensive explanations. Let him think what he would.

"I just don't get you, lady," he said.

"Not that I'm all that interested, but what don't you get?"

"You've got a house like Belle Terre, but you run off and live on the other side of the world."

"I had my reasons."

"For leaving, *oui*. But why'd you stay so long?" He slid his hands, palms out, into the rear pockets of his jeans and tilted his head arrogantly. "But I guess that guy you live with over there has something to do with that."

"Mark has a great deal to do with that, yes."

His lip curled cynically. "What's your game, huh? What are you doing, playing Howell and this English dude against each other, and taking on anybody else who gives you a crotch throb in the process?"

"I'm not playing anybody against anybody," Schyler said, seething. "Ken is my sister's husband. As for Mark, he's not English. In the second place, a man like you couldn't begin to understand our relationship. There's much more to it than lust and sweat."

"Lust and sweat should be enough."

"Maybe for you, but not for me. And not for Mark."

He nodded slowly, still treating her to a judgmental stare. "Something else confounds me. You take in a woman with Gayla's past when most respectable ladies wouldn't spit on her if she was on fire, but you have no conscience against screwing your sister's husband."

Schyler wanted to launch herself at him, scratching and

clawing, but she knew that's what he wanted her to do. He wanted to drag her down to his level. She wasn't about to let him do that. If she didn't need him to keep Crandall Logging running smoothly, she would fire him on the spot. Sadly, she did need him. If she had to suffer his insults for the sake of Belle Terre, she would.

"You overstep your position, Mr. Boudreaux," she said loftily. "If you've come to me with a business concern, kindly state what it is. If not, then we both have better things to do."

His eyelids were still half-closed and his expression sardonic, but he removed his hands from his jeans pockets. "How's Gayla?"

"She slept through the night. Drank some tea this morning. Went to the bathroom. Slept again."

"Anymore bleeding?"

"No."

"Good. Let me know if there's any change."

"I will."

By now he was standing close. He smelled like the forest at daybreak. She could feel the edge of the desk against her buttocks. She wanted him to back her against it, and that made her angry with herself. "Is that all?"

"No."

"Well?" Her heart was beating rapidly, thinking that he might kiss her yet.

"This was tacked to the office door this morning when I got here. You were late. I've been holding on to it. Thought you ought to see it."

He reached into the breast pocket of his shirt and came up with a snapshot. He passed it to her. Disappointed, she took the photograph from him and studied it, but after a moment quizzically looked up at him. "The significance escapes me."

"It's a pit bull bitch and her litter. Four puppies, if I'm counting teats right."

The significance of it struck her full force then. "Jigger," she said softly.

"*Oui*. Guess he wanted you to know he's not quitting the gambling trade, even though he's suffered a setback."

"I called the state representative's office several times, but never got through to him personally. His secretary didn't seem impressed by my problem and suggested that I take it up with local authorities."

"And?"

"I got nowhere. Jigger's probably laughing up his sleeve at me."

"I warned you."

She thumped the snapshot with her finger and dropped it onto her desk. "He's still holding a grudge."

"I told you he would."

"Would you kindly stop rubbing my nose in your superior knowledge of the subject," she snapped. "If you want to say something, tell me what I should do."

"All right." He bent over her, until she had to reach back and support herself on the desk. "You want my advice? Get the hell out of here and go back to England."

"What?!"

"Things have been shot to hell ever since you got here."

"That's not my fault."

"Isn't it?"

"No."

"Name one mess you haven't made messier."

"What would all those loggers be doing for work if it weren't for me?"

Because what she said was true, Cash straightened suddenly. He spun around and rammed his fist into the nearest wall. He shook his head to clear it of angry frustration, then looked back at her. "Why didn't you just leave well enough alone?"

"Because everything wasn't 'well enough.'"

"It was a freak accident that Jigger's dog attacked you."

"I doubt you would have thought so if it had been you. Or your child."

"I don't have a child."

"That's not my fault either."

They fell back strategically to plan their next attack. Cash came out fighting first.

"Cotton would have figured out a way to pay off that loan."

"How? He was out of cash."

"That's bull. He's got friends, friends with money, drinking buddies, who would have covered that note for him in a minute. But no, you had to go butting in. You had to undertake all this," he shouted, waving his hand to encompass the entire landing. "To feed your own goddamn ego."

"It has nothing to do with ego."

"Then why are you doing it?"

"That's my business."

"Why? Why didn't you just leave us the hell alone?"

"It was something I had to do!"

"And fuck up everybody else's life in the process!"

He headed for the door. Schyler stepped between him and it. "Cash, don't fight me. Help me. Just how ruthless could Jigger be?"

"You saw Gayla."

"Ruthless enough to jeopardize that Endicott shipment if he got wind of it?"

"Probably."

Laying her hand on his arm, she looked up at him in appeal. Anger and pride were diminished by worry. "What am I going to do?"

His eyes reflected no emotion. They seemed uncaring and indifferent to her problems, as if they had no direct bearing on him. "You're a smart lady." Cruelly he shook off her restraining hand. "You'll land on your feet."

Rhoda's long fingernail twirled a clump of body hair on Cash's lower belly. Her tongue lapped at his nipple like it was the curly tip on the top of a frozen custard cone. She made snuffling noises that gave the impression she thought it was just as sweet.

"We haven't had a nooner in so long," she sighed, taking a love bite of his tough, heavily veined bicep. "I'm glad you called."

Cash had one arm crooked behind him, his head resting in the palm of his hand. His eyes were focused on the water rings on the ceiling as the smoke from his cigarette snaked upward toward them. He was wondering if Rhoda knew, that for all her talent and trouble, he was still soft. His jeans were unsnapped, but so far she hadn't investigated inside them. She would be mad as hell when she discovered he wasn't loaded and ready to fire.

His cock was lusting for somebody else. Rhoda wasn't going to appease it. He had known that before he had called her, but on the outside chance that she would temporarily distract him, he called her anyway.

So far nothing she had done had worked. That left him feeling mad as a hornet and mean as hell. He pushed Rhoda off him and left the bed.

"Where are you going?"

"It's hotter than hell in here."

"It is not. If anything it's too cold. The air conditioner is blowing full blast."

"All right then, it's too cold." He located an ashtray on the dresser and ground out his cigarette, wishing he could put out the fire in his belly as easily.

"You're in another stinky mood."

"It's been a stinky twenty-four hours."

Not really. This time yesterday he'd been watching Schyler get delightfully tipsy on champagne, becoming softer, sexier with each sip. He'd watched her reclining in the car with her knees spread wide, her hair tangled and blowing in the wind, her lips slightly parted while she gently snored through them. All her defenses had been down.

"Cash?"

"What? Goddamn it. Can't you see I'm thinking?"

"I thought you came here to think about me," Rhoda said shortly.

He was ready to hammer home a scathing comment, but he checked himself. What the hell was the matter with him? He had a hot and willing broad in bed waiting for him. She was naked and she was nasty, and he was moping around like a dumb-assed kid with a big red zit on prom night.

"That's right, Rhoda. I did. Give me something to think about."

He dove on top of her and covered her mouth with his.

He held her head between his hands. His kiss was rapacious. Cruelly he ground his pelvis against hers.

"Cash, my God," she gasped several moments later when she came up for air. "Calm down, baby. We don't have to rush it, do we?"

"Yes," he muttered against her neck. "We do." He fumbled to draw out a semi-erection that was showing promise. He had to get it inside Rhoda before he remembered she wasn't his first choice.

"Wait, I want to show you something." She ignored his cursing impatience and smiled seductively. "Look at these." She reached for her handbag on the nightstand, letting her nipple drag across the starched sheet. When she lay back down, both nipples stood out.

Cash sat up, snarling with disgust for himself, for her, for everything. Apprehensively he stared down at what she had handed him. "Pictures?"

His attitude changed after glancing at the first snapshot. He thumbed through the stack of photographs, carefully studying each one before going on to the next. Without moving his head, he glanced up at Rhoda from beneath his brows. Her smile defined licentiousness. He went back to the photographs and looked at all of them a second time.

"That's a really wide . . . smile you've got there, Rhoda." His pause was deliberately timed so that his observation had an insulting double entendre.

Rhoda, however, was too in love with the pictures to notice his intentional slur. "Guess who took them?"

"I don't like guessing games."

"Dale," she said on a high giggle.

"He likes to take pictures of naked women?" Cash's passions hadn't just cooled. They'd gone cold. He thoughtfully tapped the pornographic prints against his thumbnail, remembering Gayla's tearful account of a john who got his highs with a camera. A rage inside him was being stoked, but Rhoda didn't know that.

She lay back against the pillows in one of the indolent poses captured on film. "Which one do you like best?"

"I couldn't begin to choose."

"What's the matter? Jealous?"

"Pea green with it."

She frowned. "You don't seem very excited over the pictures."

"Oh, I am, I am." He bent over her and took both her hands. "Put one hand here," he said, placing it on her breast. "And the other one here, just like in the picture." He laid her hand between her splayed thighs. "And before you know it, you won't even miss me."

He had his jeans buttoned and was pulling on his shirt before Rhoda realized what was happening. "You can't do this to me again, you bastard."

Cash slammed out the motel room door. Rhoda lunged off the bed and flung open the door, uncaring that she was stark naked and in full view of anyone on the highway. In a voice that disturbed truckers napping in the neighboring rooms, she screamed, "Screw you, Boudreaux! I'll get even with you for this."

"Schyler got a contract from Endicott Paper Mill."

Dale Gilbreath hissed a curse beneath his breath. "How large?"

"First I have to know if our deal still stands."

"It does," the banker said. "I get the house. The rest of Belle Terre you can do with as you wish."

"The *bank* will get Belle Terre."

Dale dismissed the clarification. "It'll be as good as mine."

"How so?"

"There'll be a foreclosure auction. Private bids."

"And you'll act as the auctioneer."

"Precisely," he said with an evil grin.

"You'll see to it that your bid is the highest." Dale nodded. "What if the bids are checked?"

"I'll fudge them."

"Even then, you'll have to come up with a tidy sum of cash. Will you have it?"

"The acquisition of Belle Terre is just one of my, uh, hobbies. I've always got more than one deal going."

"You're very clever, aren't you, Mr. Gilbreath?"

"Very."

Dale gauged the individual across from him. His own motivations for participating in this scheme were clear. He wanted Belle Terre because of the power and respect that went with the address. But what about the other's motivations? Were they as clearly defined as his, or were they murky, linked to the past, and related to the emotions? It didn't matter to him really. He was simply curious. Did one have to have concrete reasons for one's actions? Probably not. His coconspirator held a grudge. He couldn't care less where it had its roots, as long as it resulted in the downfall of the Crandalls and Belle Terre.

"How large is the Endicott contract?" Dale asked.

"It's sufficient to pay off the loan and then some."

"Damn!"

"But there is a catch. Crandall Logging has to deliver the entire order before Endicott lets go of one red cent."

"How do you know all this?"

"I know."

Dale examined the other's face and decided that the information wasn't speculation, but fact. He expulsed a deep breath. "So the key is to make sure that the last shipment doesn't go through."

"Right. A shipment will go out every day or so on the train. But, as you said, stopping the last one is the key."

"How soon will that be?" Dale asked.

"The order is so large, she'll be working right up to the deadline. And that means everybody working overtime and the weather holding out. She'll barely be able to get the timber there before the note comes due."

"You'll help me see that she doesn't succeed?"

"She's dumped on me for the last time. I'll do whatever needs to be done."

Gilbreath smiled, tasting victory that was only a few weeks away. "I'll speak to Jigger again. He was agreeable when I first mentioned our little project to him."

"Something else the two of you should know. Gayla Frances is at Belle Terre, lying in Schyler's own bed."

"Jesus. Flynn would love to know that."

"Wouldn't he though?"

"What happened to the girl?"

"Why?"

"Just curious."

"Are you sure? You look pale. You're not a regular customer, are you?"

"What happened to the girl?" Dale repeated with an implied threat.

"Jigger beat her up. She ran away from him. Schyler took her in. That's two strikes against Schyler as far as he's concerned. He'll be more than willing to help us out."

"And if anything should go wrong and he's caught—"

"He'll be the one to take the rap."

"Not quietly, he won't. He'll implicate us."

"And we'll say he's lying. It'll be our word against his. Who's going to take Jigger's word for anything?"

Gilbreath smiled at his conspirator. "Keep me posted."

"Don't doubt that for a minute. Schyler Crandall's comeuppance is long overdue."

Jimmy Don Davison stared at the envelope for a long time before opening it. It had been unsealed and the contents read by prison officials before being delivered to him. The flap on the stiff, cream-colored envelope was embossed with the return address: *Belle Terre, Heaven, Louisiana*. Now who in hell at Belle Terre would be writing to him in prison? Who at Belle Terre knew or cared that he was there?

Finally, slumped on his bunk with his back against the wall and his heels at the edge of the thin, lumpy mattress, he took out the single sheet of stationery. Before reading the lines of neat, cursive script, he glanced down at the signature.

"Schyler Crandall?"

"D'you say somethin', Jimmy Don?" his cell mate asked from the bunk above his.

"Nothin' to you, Old Stu."

"Dear Mr. Davison," the salutation read. In between that and the unexpected signature, he was apologetically reacquainted with the sender, as though anybody from Laurent Parish needed to be reminded who Schyler Crandall was. She inquired after his well-being. Then she got down to the purpose of the letter. It had been sent to inform him that Gayla Francis was living at Belle Terre for an indefinite period of time and that, should he want to contact her, all correspondence should be addressed to her there.

He read the puzzling letter several times to make certain he understood its meaning. On the surface it amounted to a change of address notification, but what Miss Schyler was telling him in a roundabout way was that he should get in touch with his old girlfriend. Some girlfriend; Gayla was a whore. Apparently she'd sunk so low that even Jigger Flynn wouldn't have her under his roof any longer.

Jimmy Don coined epithets for Gayla and the rich, white bitch who went meddling into other folks' business. The embossed cream paper became a wadded ball in his fist. He hurled it against the wall opposite him.

"Hey, man, what's in the letter?"

"Shut up," Jimmy Don growled to Old Stu.

Schyler Crandall seemed to think he was interested in Gayla's whereabouts. He was, but only to the extent of knowing where he could find her in a hurry when he got out. He'd have to move fast. She must have no warning. His revenge must be as swift and sure as the sword of God.

His black eyes snapped with anger. His fists clenched and opened subconsciously. He probed at Gayla's betrayal like a tongue poking at a sore tooth. No matter how much it hurt, he kept returning to it and asking how, how she could have ever resorted to that kind of life.

They'd talked about graduating college, getting married, having kids. Hell, they'd even named the first three or four. She'd been a virgin the first time they went all the way. He hadn't been far from one. They'd coached each other on how to make love, frankly expressing what felt nice, when to rush, when to tarry.

The idea of her applying those sexual skills for hire made him sick to his stomach. That she could be loving Jigger Flynn with the same sweetness and consideration that she had once loved him made him livid enough to kill them both and laugh while he was doing it.

He was so steeped in thoughts about their slow and tor-turous executions that he didn't notice the group of prisoners that collected outside his cell. It was free time and all the cell doors were opened. Prisoners were at liberty to walk about in unrestricted areas. Jimmy Don didn't see the nefarious group until they came strolling into his cell, crowding together to fit into the small space. Razz propped his elbow on the upper bunk and smiled down at him.

"What's happenin', boy?"

"Nobody invited you in, Razz."

Jimmy Don didn't like the odds. Razz and three of his lieutenants against Old Stu and him. If the prison were a microcosm, Old Stu was the village simpleton. He had been given life for killing a cop, almost assuredly a frame-up. Old Stu didn't seem to mind the injustice. He had no family. The prison was his home. He was useless; he was harmless. His credo was to hear no evil, see no evil, speak no evil, and by doing so, survive.

Razz smiled down at Jimmy Don. "That don't sound very friendly. We came by to give you a going away party, right?" The other three brutes nodded their heads in agreement.

"I'm not going anywhere."

"You're outta here, boy. Soon. Paroled. Ain't you heard about it yet?"

Jimmy Don had an appointment with the parole board, but he wasn't going to divulge the date to Razz. "I haven't heard anything official."

"No?" Razz asked, feigning surprise. "Well now, it would be a damn shame if you caused a fuss right before meeting with the parole board, wouldn't it?" He touched Jimmy Don's cheek affectionately. Jimmy Don jerked his head aside. When he did, he happened to catch one of the other inmates leafing through his Bible.

"Get your filthy hands off that," he said testily.

"Hey man, don't go messin' with Jimmy Don's Bible," Razz said to the other prisoner. "His mama must have give it to him, right, Jimmy Don?"

Jimmy Don moved to the edge of his cot. "I said to leave the Bible alone."

The other prisoner, ignoring his warning, read the inscription on the inside cover. "Say what? Now ain't that sweet? You into religion, Jimmy Don?" He ripped out the illuminated page and crumpled it in his fist, just as Jimmy Don had done the letter from Belle Terre.

"Goddamn you!" Jimmy Don lunged off the cot, hands aimed at the other prisoner's throat.

Razz caught him by the neck of his T-shirt and held him back. Mockingly he scolded Jimmy Don's tormentor. "Leave the boy's Bible alone. Didn't you know he's into all that? It's always revival time at Jimmy Don's church. They get baptized, speak in tongues, handle serpents, all that weird shit."

Several more gilt-edged pages of the Bible were maliciously ripped out and divided between the prisoners. Laughing at their own cleverness, they tore them to shreds before letting them flutter to the floor.

"You sons of bitches," Jimmy Don snarled.

"Now is that any way to talk to your friends? Hmm?" Razz cooed. "We come to give you a little going away present."

"Make that a *big* going away present." The prisoner stroked the fly of his pants. The joke earned him loud, approving laughter.

Jimmy Don put up a fierce struggle, but it was a token struggle and he knew it. He was as strong as a young bull, but he couldn't overpower the four of them. It would be useless and even more dangerous to call for a guard because the guard, out of fear of retribution, would side with Razz. If Jimmy Don called attention to himself or caused any trouble in the cell block, he wouldn't make parole. If he didn't make parole, he wouldn't have the chance to do what God had sanctioned him to do to Jigger and Gayla.

So he gritted his straight, white teeth and endured the gang rape while Old Stu lay in the bunk above him, picking his toenails, and thanking the Lord he was too old and ugly for any of Razz's gang to want him.

Chapter Forty

"Damn!"

Schyler's terse expletive was directed toward the bank statement she had been trying to balance for the last hour. Either she had no head for figures or her calculator was broken or several thousand dollars in the Crandall Logging account was indeed missing.

She needed Ken's help with this. He was the accountant. He was being paid to track down misplaced money. She reached for the telephone on her desk but before she touched it, it rang.

"Hello?"

"Schyler? Jeff Collins."

She and the doctor had been on a first-name basis since Cotton's surgery. "There's nothing wrong I hope."

"Why do people always think the worst when a doctor calls?"

She laughed. "Sorry. Are you the bearer of good news?"

"I hope you'll think so. Your father can leave tomorrow."

"That's wonderful," she exclaimed.

"You might want to check with the nurses before you say that," the doctor remarked around a chuckle. "Within a week you might want to send him back. Not that we'd take him back. He's gotten to be a real pain in the ass."

"Feisty old codger, isn't he?"

"The feistiest."

"I can't wait to have him home."

"If you want to come by this afternoon, I'll have all the

release forms ready for you to sign. That way you won't bottleneck with the other dismissed patients in the morning."

"Thanks for the consideration, Jeff. I'll be right over."

Before she could hang up, he said, "We haven't told him yet. I thought you might want to break the good news yourself."

"Thanks, I appreciate that. See you shortly."

Grimacing with distaste, she folded all the canceled checks back into the folder, along with the bank's computerized printout of her account. The damn thing would have to remain unreconciled for the time being.

In fact, everything could be put on hold. Cotton Crandall was coming home.

"Seen Ms. Crandall?" Cash asked a logger who was weighing in the load on his rig. The scale at the landing was so delicate, the amount of board feet the load contained could be measured precisely.

"She left 'bout five minutes ago," he answered around a chaw of tobacco. "What are you doing here?"

"I brought Kermit back," Cash replied absently. It was unusual for Schyler to leave this early in the afternoon. "Did Ms. Crandall happen to say where she was going?"

"The hospital."

Cash, who'd been wiping his perspiring face with his bandanna, froze. The logger had his back turned and was shouting directions to the driver of another rig. Cash caught his shoulder and turned him around. "The hospital?"

"That's what she said, Cash."

"Did she say why? Did it have something to do with Cotton?"

"The lady don't inform me of her comin's and goin's. All I know is that she was in a big hurry. Shouted out to me that she'd be at the hospital if anybody asked, then herded that car of hers outta here lickety split."

Cash's face settled into a deep frown. His brows were pulled down low over his eyes. He stared toward the bridge in the direction Schyler had taken.

"Anything wrong, Cash?" the logger asked worriedly.

"No. Probably nothing." He roused himself from his private thoughts and tried to appear casual. "Keep an eye on things here, okay? Get all this timber ready to load on the train before quitting time. If I don't come back, see that the office is locked for the night before you leave. And tell Kermit to sit in there for the rest of the afternoon and man the phone. He got red in the face because of the heat, but he doesn't want to miss out on the overtime."

"Okay, Cash, but where're you goin'?"

Cash didn't hear him. He was already running toward his pickup.

"I'm going to turn the downstairs study into a bedroom for you. It might not be finished by tomorrow, but when I get through with it, you'll be able to lie in bed and look outside at the back lawn of Belle Terre."

"I liked my old bedroom."

Cotton sounded grumpy, but Schyler knew how pleased he was to be going home. She tried to hide her indulgent smile. "Dr. Collins said you shouldn't be climbing the stairs."

He aimed an adamant index finger at her. "I won't be babied. Not by you. Not by anybody. I've had enough of that in here. I'm not an invalid."

That's exactly what he was. He knew that's what he was, but Schyler knew better than to let on that he was. "You're damn right you're not. Don't expect to be pampered. I'm going to put you to work as soon as you're rested up."

"From what I hear you've got more help around the place than you can use." He shrewdly gauged her reaction from beneath his bushy white eyebrows.

"Tricia told you about Mrs. Dunne?"

"She did. Said she's bossy as all get out."

"Maybe that's why I like her so much. She reminds me of Veda."

"'Xcept she's white."

"Well, yes, there is that difference," Schyler said, laughing.

"Can she cook as good as Veda?"

"Yes." She waved a sheet of paper in front of him. "She can cook everything on this diet Jeff gave me for you."

"Shit."

"Come now, it's not that bad," she teased. "But there'll be no grits and sausage gravy for you. And I won't have you bribing Mrs. Dunne either. Her first loyalty is to me. She won't be swayed, no matter how persuasive or ornery you get."

Cotton's expression remained disagreeable. "I wasn't just referring to the housekeeper when I mentioned the new help."

Schyler kept her smile intact. Was he referring to Cash? Had Tricia, in spite of Schyler's warning, come tattling?

"Veda's girl," Cotton grunted. "I hear she's taken up residence at Belle Terre."

The tension in Schyler's chest receded. "Yes, Gayla's there at my invitation. I felt like we Crandalls were responsible for her misfortunes."

"I heard she's trashy as the day is long."

"I'm sure you have," she said, thinking of Tricia's vicious tongue. "But there were extenuating circumstances. Jigger Flynn's been abusing her for years. This time he nearly killed her. Luckily she was able to get away from him. While she's recuperating, I want her to stay with us."

"That's mighty generous of you."

She pretended not to notice his sarcasm. "Thank you."

Schyler's motives were not purely unselfish. She treasured Gayla's friendship. Lately, her list of friends had dwindled drastically. Because of their most recent altercation, every time Tricia looked at Schyler, resentment wafted from her like cheap perfume.

As for Ken, Schyler apparently had bruised his pride when she asked him to leave her alone with Cash. On the heels of turning down his request of a loan, she had added insult to injury. He, too, was avoiding her these days. He spoke only when it was absolutely necessary and then with rigid politeness.

Cash had dispensed with their coffee-drinking sessions in the mornings. She knew he had been in the landing office ahead of her each day when she arrived, but since their latest quarrel, he had made it a point to leave before she got there. If he returned to the landing before she left in the evenings, he spent the time in the yard among the men, making daily inventory of the timber that had been cut, weighing the loads, recording the figures, and supervising the loading of it onto the freight cars.

If it was necessary for him to consult with her on something pertaining to business, he did so as briefly as possible. His face looked like it would crack if he smiled. His hazel eyes seemed to look straight through her. He was as remote and quick to take offense as when they had first met. His hostility was sexually charged. She knew it, felt it, and recognized it because she felt the same way.

She was restless. During the hot days, she used exhausting work to keep that internal turmoil on simmer. But at night she tossed and turned in bed, unable to sleep, her mind occupied with disturbing thoughts and even more disturbing fantasies. She hated acknowledging how much she missed Cash. Even having him around when he was surly and insulting was preferable to not having him around at all. Also, recollections of that rainy afternoon kept her in a constant state of dissatisfaction.

So she had taken solace in the quiet talks she shared with Gayla. She talked frequently about Mark and their life in London. Gayla, tearfully and over a period of days, revealed what her nightmarish life with Jigger Flynn had been like. Schyler urged her to press charges against him, but Gayla wouldn't hear of it.

"He'd kill me, Schyler, before he ever came to trial. Even if he was in jail, he'd find a way. Besides, who would believe me?" she had asked.

Who indeed? Gayla's tales were unbelievable.

"There was a girl who worked in the Pelican Lounge," Gayla had told her one afternoon. "Jigger strangled her for not giving him his fair cut of what she earned. One morning she was found dead in a dumpster out behind the building. Her murder went down as an unsolved crime. I even tipped the sheriff with an anonymous phone call, but nothing was ever done about it."

"How could a law officer just blow off a murder like that?"

"Either he was scared of Jigger, or, most probably, he thought the girl had it coming for holding out on him."

Gayla had also told her, "Another of the girls got pregnant by one of her johns. Only he wasn't just a customer to her. She loved him and wanted to have the baby. Jigger found out about it and knew that if she carried the baby, he'd lose a valuable employee. He beat her with his fists until she aborted.

"He gets crazy if somebody welshes on a bet. One man owed him a lot of money over a pit bull fight. Jigger sent thugs out to get it, but they couldn't collect. The man went out in his fishing boat one day and never was seen again. They ruled it an accidental drowning and dragged the lake for his body. I guarantee you, it's anchored to the bottom and never will be found."

Day by day, with the help of Cash's ointment and Mrs. Dunne's plentiful meals, Gayla recovered physically. The scratches on her face diminished and eventually disappeared. The swelling went down until her beautiful bone structure was evident again. The bleeding stopped, but she was jittery; she jumped at every loud noise. Schyler realized that it would take months, maybe years, for Gayla to get over her recurring fears and to recover emotionally from the hellish existence she'd been subjected to.

Still, she was fiercely proud. "I can't stay here indefinitely, Schyler," she had insisted on more than one occasion.

Schyler had been just as insistent. "I want you here, Gayla. I need a friend."

"But I can't ever repay you."

"I don't want you to."

"I can't take your charity."

Schyler had considered it for a moment. "I can't afford to pay you a salary just now. Would you be willing to work for room and board?"

"Work? You just hired Mrs. Dunne."

"But there's plenty for you to do."

"Like what?" Gayla had asked skeptically. "You've got a

crew that takes care of the yard. Somebody else tends to the horses. What is there for me to do?"

"I'd like the books in the small parlor to be cataloged. Those shelves haven't been inventoried in years. No telling what's up there. You can start on that. And don't rush it. Don't wear yourself out now that you're regaining your strength. Work only when you feel like it."

Gayla had seen through Schyler's ploy. She knew the job had been invented and was unnecessary. "All right. I'll inventory the books. Some of the houseplants need attention, too," she had said, holding her chin at a proud tilt. "Mama would have a fit if she could see how they've been neglected. And there's mending that needs to be done. I've noticed tears in some of the bed linens."

Gayla had moved out of Schyler's bedroom and into a small room off the kitchen. She refused to eat with the family in the dining room as Schyler had wanted her to. Instead she stubbornly ate her meals with Mrs. Dunne in the kitchen. They had established a fast friendship because Mrs. Dunne's kindness was extensive.

"Gayla has fit in beautifully," Schyler told her father now. "In fact, I don't know how I managed without her. I think you'll find everything at Belle Terre to your liking."

He frowned doubtfully. "You'll hear about it if I don't."

"I'm sure I will." She eased herself off the edge of his bed. "See you in the morning. Not too early. You'll have breakfast here. Take your time getting showered and shaved. I'll be here around ten, okay?" She bent down and kissed him good-bye.

He caught her hand. "I'm proud of that Endicott deal. You did a good job, Schyler."

She hadn't told him why Endicott had stopped using them as a supplier. Until she could satisfy herself with an explanation, she didn't want to get Cotton worked up over it. "Thanks, Daddy. I'm glad you approve."

For the first time in days, Schyler's step was springy as she crossed the hospital lobby on her way out. She had almost reached the sliding glass doors when they opened for a man coming in.

Upon seeing him, she stopped dead in her tracks. "Mark!"

Cash lit a cigarette with the smoldering butt of his last one. He inhaled the acrid smoke while staring at the facade of St. John's Hospital. At any moment, he expected someone to appear with a black wreath to hang over the sliding glass doors.

For the last half hour, he'd been sitting in a widening puddle of his own sweat in the cab of his pickup, smoking, and trying to work up enough courage to cross the street and inquire at the front desk whether or not Cotton Crandall had died.

He didn't want to know.

But he had a strong suspicion that's why Schyler had left the landing in the middle of the day. She wouldn't have done that unless there was a crisis of some kind. Her periodic reports to him on Cotton's condition had been fairly optimistic.

His heart was stronger, but still weak.

He was improving, but not altogether out of the woods.

The operation had been a success, but there was a limited amount of repair that could be done.

Cash knew that Cotton's life was still in danger. Any little thing could go wrong; obviously something had.

The endless cigarettes had made his throat dry and irritated. Impatiently he tossed the one he'd just lit out the open window of his truck. When he did, he noticed a man walking toward the entrance to the hospital.

He was arresting in that he was so different. He fit into the southwestern Louisiana backdrop about as well as an Eskimo would in Tahiti. He looked out of place in his white slacks and navy blazer. He had on white shoes. White shoes, for chrissake! A jaunty red handkerchief was sticking out of his breast pocket. His hair was blond and so straight it could have just come off an ironing board. It was neatly parted on one side and glistened in the sunlight. He was wearing dark sunglasses, but the eyes they shaded would have to be as blue as the sky.

He jogged up the steps of the entrance with the self-confidence of a man who knew that everyone he passed turned to get a better look. He looked polished and cosmopolitan enough to be at home in cities that the people who gawked at him had never even heard of. He was so handsome he could have stepped off the cover of a flashy magazine.

Cash got a real sick feeling deep in his gut.

His worst suspicion was confirmed when the man came face-to-face with Schyler in the doorway. Cash heard her squeal his name in surprise. A smile of pure delight broke across her face a split second before she launched herself against the man's chest. Well-tailored sleeves enfolded her. They hugged each other tightly, rocking together joyfully. Then the man kissed her full on the mouth.

Even from across the street, Cash could see that her face was radiant as she gazed up at the blond god, babbling questions while quick, excited little laughs bubbled out of her smiling lips.

One thing was for damn certain—the broad wasn't in mourning.

Cash nearly broke off the key in the ignition when he cranked it on. He nearly stripped the transmission of his pickup, making it to third gear before he reached the stop sign at the nearest corner. He wanted to get Schyler's attention. He wanted her to see just how unimpressed he was with her affluent, well-dressed, sophisticated roommate.

When Cash glanced in his rearview mirror, however, he saw that she hadn't even noticed him. She was engrossed with her lover.

Chapter Forty-one

"My God, it's Tara."

Schyler beamed beneath Mark's praise. "It's lovelier than Tara."

Mark Houghton glanced at her from the passenger side of her car. "And you're lovelier than Scarlett."

"You're an angel for saying so, but that's crap. I'm exhausted and it shows."

He shook his head. "You're gorgeous. I'd forgotten how much."

Schyler had forgotten how nice it was to hear a compliment. Her face glowed around her smile. "If I look pretty it's because I'm so happy to see you."

He clasped her right hand. "Hurry. I can't wait to take the grand tour."

She began honking the horn when she was only halfway down the lane. By the time she braked the car, Mrs. Dunne and Gayla were waiting expectantly on the veranda to see what all the commotion was about.

"Good news," Schyler called out to them as she alighted and ran around the hood of the car. "Mark is here. And Daddy's coming home tomorrow."

Mark placed his arm around her waist, not only in affection, but as a means of holding Schyler earthbound as she ran up the steps. She was as exuberant as a child at her first circus.

"You must be Mrs. Dunne," Mark said, addressing the housekeeper. "I'm the one you spoke with on the phone a while ago. As you said, I found Schyler at the hospital. Thank you."

"Throw another chicken in the pot, Mrs. Dunne. There will be a guest for supper."

"What a coincidence. I'm baking Cornish hens with wild rice stuffing and I just happen to have an extra one," she said, smiling at the attractive blond couple.

"Good. Is the guest room still made up?"

"I changed the linens today."

"Then you go see to the extra hen. We'll get Mark's bag upstairs. He travels light." Mrs. Dunne went back inside. "Mark," Schyler said, "this is my dear friend Gayla Frances. Gayla, Mark Houghton."

"I'm delighted to meet you, Miss Frances." Mark lifted her hand and kissed the back of it.

"Pleased to meet you, too, Mr. Houghton," Gayla said, flustered. "Schyler has told me a lot about you."

"All good I hope." He smiled disarmingly.

Gayla looked nervously toward Schyler for help. She still found it difficult to make small talk, especially with men. She was spared having to when Tricia stepped out onto the veranda.

"What in tarnation is—" She broke off and gaped at Mark, her eyes going wide with stupefaction and then narrowing with feminine approval. "Hi, y'all." Her slow, honeyed accent matched her smile.

"Hello," Mark said blandly. He was accustomed to having people stare at him. He wasn't obnoxiously vain, but he wasn't oblivious to his good looks. He knew that the way he looked had been either an asset or a hindrance, depending on the situation.

Schyler conducted the introductions. Tricia laid a self-conscious hand at her neckline. "You should have told me, Schyler."

"I didn't know. Mark's visit is a complete and delightful surprise."

"I hope it's not an inconvenience," he said to Tricia politely.

"Oh, no, no. It's just that if I'd known we were going to have company, I would have dressed."

"You look very attractive to me, Mrs. Howell."

"Please call me Tricia." She glanced down at her designer dress with chagrin. "I just put this on to attend a meeting in town. I'll go call right now and tell them I'm not coming."

"Not on my account, please."

"Oh, I wouldn't hear of missing supper with you. Schyler's just raved about you so much," Tricia gushed breathlessly. "Excuse me while I change. Honey, would you bring up that dress I asked Mrs. Dunne to press for me?" She directed that to Gayla before disappearing through the screen door.

"Tricia," Schyler called out in vexation.

Gayla laid a hand on Schyler's arm and said, "It's all right. I was going upstairs anyway to check the guest room. You visit with Mr. Houghton."

"But you are not Tricia's handmaiden. The next time she orders you to do something, tell her to go to hell."

"I'll sell tickets to that," Gayla said, laughing good-naturedly as she went inside.

"Lovely woman," Mark observed when Gayla was out of earshot. "Is she the one who—"

"Yes." During one of their lengthy overseas calls, Schyler had told him about Gayla.

"Hard to believe," he said, shaking his head. "You've worked wonders for her."

"I've been her friend. She would have done the same for me."

Mark faced her and ran his hand over her hair. His eyes were full of love and adoration. "Is that a habit of yours?"

"What?"

"Collecting people who desperately need befriending? I recall a certain aimless wanderer in London, an expatriated American who was terribly lonely. You nurtured him, too."

"Your memory is bad. That's what *he* did for *me*." She went up on tiptoes and kissed his lips softly. "I'll never be able to repay you for all you've meant to me, Mark. Thank you for coming. I didn't realize how much I needed you until I saw you."

As always, when he didn't have an audience, his beautiful smile was tinged with sadness and self-derision. "Before this gets too pithy, show me Belle Terre."

"Where should we start?"

"Did you mention horses?"

Ken was the last one to meet Mark.

By that time they were having predinner drinks in the formal parlor. Mark had been given the grand tour of the house, including all the outbuildings. When they returned, Schyler had excused herself to freshen up before dinner. Mark, already impeccable, had nonetheless gone to his room, ostensibly to do the same.

When Schyler came downstairs wearing a cool, frothy voile print dress, Mark was being entertained by Tricia in the parlor. Schyler was amused by her sister's transformation. Tricia's dress was fancier than the occasion warranted, but Schyler wasn't surprised that Tricia had chosen to wear it. It showed off her voluptuous figure and an immodest amount of suntanned cleavage.

When Schyler entered the parlor, Tricia was saying, "I don't actually remember when Mr. Kennedy was president, but I've watched old films of him. You sound just like him. Of course you probably think *I* have an accent."

Mark's eyes lit up when Schyler entered. He went to greet her, taking both her hands and kissing her cheek. "You look wonderful. This stifling climate suits you like a hothouse does an orchid. Drink?"

"Please." Blushing with pleasure over his compliment, she sat down on one of the love seats while Mark, making himself at home at the sideboard, prepared her a tall gin and tonic. His thoughtfulness didn't escape Tricia, whose effervescence had fizzled since Schyler had come in. Schyler said to her, "Mark actually knows the Kennedys. Did he tell you that?"

Tricia's eyes went round with amazement. "No! *Those* Kennedys? Why I think that's simply fascinating." Mark carried Schyler her drink. He started to sit down beside her, but Tricia was patting the cushion next to her. Politely he sat down beside her again. "Tell me how you met them. Did you know Jackie, too?"

"Actually the Kennedys were neighbors of ours. My parents have a home at Hyannis Port."

"Really? Oh, I've always wanted to go there." She laid a hand on his thigh. "Is it truly beautiful?"

"Well—"

Just then Ken walked in. He took in the parlor scene with one sour glance. Schyler said, "Hello, Ken."

"I called the landing. The ignoramus who answered the phone said there was an emergency at the hospital. I called there. Nobody knew anything about it."

"No emergency. Daddy's coming home tomorrow." That piece of news did nothing to lighten Ken's dark frown. "Mark paid me a surprise visit," Schyler said hastily. "Everything happened so fast, I didn't have a chance to call you."

She introduced him to Mark. Mark stood up, causing Tricia's hand to slide off his thigh. He met Ken halfway and the two men shook hands. Ken's face was sulky. Schyler had known that Ken was prepared to hate Mark on sight, and it was obvious that he did. He took one look at Mark's bandbox appearance and excused himself to go upstairs.

When he came back down, he was dressed in a summer suit and pastel tie. He had also showered; his hair was still damp, and he smelled like the men's cologne counter at Maison-Blanche in downtown New Orleans.

"Can I refill anyone's drink?" he asked, crossing to the sideboard.

He glared at his wife who was monopolizing Mark and prattling on about her reign as Laurent Parish's Mardi Gras Queen. "I was eighteen that summer. Lordy, has it been that long?" she said with a sigh. "I can remember how anxious I was to get all my dresses made in time. You can't imagine how many parties there are. My parade float has never been equaled. Everybody says so. I loved it." She pursed her lips sadly. "Schyler missed out on all that. They passed her up for . . . Who was queen that year, Schyler?"

"Dora Jane Wilcox, I believe."

Schyler was furious. For almost an hour she had watched Tricia's hand slide up and down Mark's thigh. She had watched her simper and flirt until she wanted to throw up. Her sister's saccharine performance for Mark was nauseating.

Whether Tricia was doing it to make her jealous, or Ken jealous, or for the sheer fun of it, it was aggravating the hell out of Schyler. Tricia was dominating Mark and he was too polite to excuse himself from her.

"That's right," Tricia exclaimed. "Dora Jane Wilcox. Well I told you, Schyler, that you spent too much time with Daddy at the landing and not enough time at the country club getting to know the people on the selection committee."

"And I told you, Tricia, that I didn't give a damn about that society stuff. Then or now."

"I was involved for Mama's sake. Before she died, all she talked about was our coming-out parties and such. I felt like we owed it to her to participate in the things she loved."

Tricia made a tsking sound and shook her head at Mark as if to say that Schyler was a hopeless case. "She still spends all her time at the landing. I invited her to join my clubs, but she won't hear of it.

"All she does is work, work, work. She's taken it upon herself to run Belle Terre even though it just wears her out. About the best thing you could do for her is whisk her right back to London." Flirtatiously she gazed at him through her eyelashes. "Not that I'm anxious for you to leave, of course."

"Dinner's ready, Ms. Crandall," Mrs. Dunne announced from the archway.

"Thank you." Schyler was so angry she could barely speak. "We're coming."

Tricia shot the housekeeper a dirty look for announcing dinner to Schyler instead of to her. Possessively she latched onto Mark's arm as they stood up. She nestled it against her breasts. "Mark can escort me to the dining room. Ken, you bring in Schyler."

Ken, who had been slamming back straight double bourbons at a reckless rate, carried the decanter with him. He gripped Schyler's elbow with his other hand. Together they crossed the wide entry hall and went into the dining room. Mark was holding out Tricia's chair. She was smiling up at him over her shoulder.

"Sit here beside me, Mark. Ken and Schyler can take the other side. Daddy always sits at the head of the table. It would be just about perfect if he was here, wouldn't it?"

Things were far from perfect. In fact they started off badly with the fruit compotes when Tricia, with no small amount of asperity, told her husband he was drinking too much. After that, she ignored him and directed her animated conversation to Mark, who responded with noble charm.

With each wonderfully prepared course, tension around the table mounted. Schyler got angrier, Ken was mad at the world, it seemed, and Mark was anxious because the light had gone out of Schyler's eyes. Tricia was the only one having a good time.

That came to an abrupt finish during dessert.

She had said something she thought incredibly witty. As she giggled, she leaned toward him, mashing her breasts against his arm. Mark laughed with her, but it was strained laughter. Then he blotted his mouth with the stiff linen napkin and said, "I'll spare you anymore efforts, Tricia."

Her laughter ceased abruptly and she gazed at him blankly. "Efforts? What do you mean?"

"You can stop pressing my thigh beneath the table. Give your fluttering eyelids a rest. And stop giving me glimpses of your breasts. I'm not interested."

Tricia's fork clattered to her plate. She looked at him whey-faced.

He smiled pleasantly. "You see, I'm gay."

Chapter Forty-two

"That wasn't very kind."

Schyler was leaning against the corner pillar of the veranda. Her hands were folded behind her lower back. The balmly breeze blew against her, molding the soft dress to her body. Fair strands of hair stirred against her cheeks.

The night was almost as beautiful as the woman. The sky was studded with brilliant stars. The moon limned the branches of the live oaks with silver light. The orchestra of insects had tuned up and was in full swing. Floral scents hung heavily in the sultry air.

"What she was doing to you wasn't very kind either." Mark was lounging in one of the fan-back wicker chairs. He'd been appreciating a snifter of brandy for the last half hour. He now drained it and set it on the small round table at his elbow. "You know that it's not like me to be unkind. I couldn't help myself. I stood it for as long as I could. Tricia deserved to be taken down a peg for what she was doing to you."

"Which was?"

"Trying to steal me."

He was right. It was just painful for Schyler to admit it. She stared off into the distance. "You took her down more than a peg. You knocked the slats out from under her."

Mark raised his hands above his head and stretched, shoving his feet out in front of him at the same time. "That's probably why she flounced upstairs. The look she gave me was so venomous I should be dead by now. Your sister is a viper."

"You shouldn't say things like that about her to me."

"I refuse to apologize."

"As her husband, Ken should have jumped to her defense. Instead he laughed."

"Yes," Mark said wryly, drawing his long, elegant limbs back in. "Your brother-in-law was delighted by my announcement. Now he knows that I don't pose a threat."

"A threat?" Schyler's head came around. "To whom?"

"To him. Don't you realize that the man was eaten up with jealousy?"

"Over Tricia."

Mark's blond head reflected moonlight as he shook it. "Over you. He still loves you, Schyler."

"I don't think so." Pulling her hands from behind her, she made a dismissive gesture. "Maybe he thinks he still loves me, but I think what he feels is something else. I'm an anchor, something he needs to hold on to."

"Why? Is he slipping?"

Mark had intended that as a joke, but Schyler answered him seriously. "Yes, I think he is. At least he feels that he is. There's something wrong . . . no, that's too strong a word. There's something *not right* with Ken. I'm not sure what."

"I do." She glanced at him inquiringly. "He knows he made a grave error. He married the wrong woman. He has let Tricia and your father make all his decisions for him. His life isn't worth shit. That's hard for a man to take."

One of the things she had always admired about Mark was that he didn't mince words. Even when it hurt to be blunt, he was. "I think you're probably right," she said softly. "He's made several advances."

"Of a romantic nature?"

"Yes."

"How pathetic. What was your reaction?"

"I've warded them off, of course."

"On moral grounds?"

"Not entirely."

"Then you don't love him any longer?"

"No," she said sadly. "I don't. There wasn't so much as a spark when he touched me. I think I had to come back to realize it though."

"Want to know a secret?" He didn't wait for her reply. "I think you stopped loving him a long time ago, if you ever loved him at all."

"Why didn't you tell me?"

"I was tempted, but you wouldn't have believed me. You had to find it out for yourself."

"I wasted so much time," she said with regret.

"I don't believe time is wasted when one is healing. You had a lot of healing to do. Does the brandy come with the room?" He nodded at the silver tray Mrs. Dunne had brought out bearing two snifters and a decanter.

"Please help yourself."

"You?"

"No thanks." Schyler watched him pour himself another drink. He took a sip, leaned his head back against the wicker and closed his eyes to fully appreciate the bouquet of the potent liquor. "Mark?" His eyes came open. "I believe what you said about Ken is right. But I hope you weren't obliquely referring to anyone else I know when you said his life isn't worth shit."

He smiled at her ruefully. "Live with a woman for six years and she thinks she knows you."

"I do know you."

He held up the snifter and studied the moon through its amber contents. "Perhaps you do."

"I recognize the melancholia."

"Don't be too alarmed. You know I go through these phases periodically. They're almost as regular as your menstrual cycle. I'll get over this funk in a day or two. In the meantime I'll wallow in self-pity. I'll wonder why I didn't let my parents go on deluding themselves that I was straight and marry the woman they had chosen for me. Everyone would have been much happier."

"No one would have been happier, Mark. Especially not the woman. You couldn't have fooled her for long. And certainly not you. As honest as you are with everyone, including yourself, you would have been miserable living a lie."

"But my mother and father would have been happy. They wouldn't have looked at their only son and heir with horror and disgust."

Schyler's heart ached for him. He'd been banished by his parents, who maintained a high profile among Boston's elite. That their son was gay had been an abomination, something untenable. Like a malignancy, they had cut him out of their lives.

"Have you heard from them recently?"

"No, of course not," he said, draining the snifter for the second time. "But that's not why I'm melancholy."

"Oh?"

"No. I'm depressed over losing my roommate."

Schyler smiled wanly and ducked her head. "How did you know?"

Mark left his chair and came to stand in front of her. He laid his hands against her cheeks. "My analogy comparing you to a hothouse orchid was outrageously poetic, but accurate, I believe. You've flourished here, Schyler." He gazed around him, taking in the density of the night. "This is where you belong."

She sighed deeply. "I know. For all its drawbacks, I love it." Tears formed in her eyes. "The ratty little town, the narrow-minded people, the forests, the bayous, the smell of the earth, the humidity and heat. Belle Terre. I love it."

He hugged her hard, pressing her head into the crook of his shoulder. "God, don't apologize for it. Stay here, Schyler, and be happy."

"But I'll miss you."

"Not for long."

"Always."

He tilted her head away from him and wiped the tears off her cheeks with his thumbs. "When we met we were emotional cripples. Whether you had come home or not, I'm not sure it was healthy for us to go on depending on each other for support and safekeeping. We had a mutually beneficial arrangement. You didn't have to fight off unwelcomed attention from men. I hid my homosexuality behind your skirts. Most married couples aren't as good friends as we are." His smile was wistful. "But we can't go on living together indefinitely. You need more than that. You need more than I can give you." He leaned forward and whispered, "You need Belle Terre."

"It needs me, too."

She had kept him abreast of her tribulations because she knew he was genuinely interested. During their tour of the house, he had listened patiently while she brought him up to date.

"Tomorrow Daddy will be home. I'm delighted. But that means I'll be dividing my time between him and my work at the landing. I can't sacrifice one to the other. I want to include him on decisions so he doesn't feel useless, but I can't let him become too emotionally involved or he could suffer another attack. It'll be a real juggling act."

"You can handle it."

"Do you really think so?"

"I really think so." He combed his fingers through her hair. "When were you going to tell me that you were here to stay, Schyler?"

"I don't know. I'm not even sure I knew for certain myself until you said that about losing your roommate. I guess my final decision was lying there in my subconscious, waiting for someone to pull it out."

"Hmm." He nodded thoughtfully. "Does your subconscious decision to stay have anything to do with the cigarette?"

"The cigarette?"

He hitched his chin in the direction of the woods beyond the yard. "There's been one glowing out there for as long as we've been on the veranda."

Schyler whipped her head in that direction. "Cash," she whispered.

"Mr. Boudreaux," Mark said dryly. "His name pops up frequently in your conversation. I wonder if you realize how often it's, 'Cash says this,' or 'Cash does that.'"

She couldn't quite meet the amusement in his eyes, so she stared at the carefully knotted necktie at his throat. "It's not what you think. It's very complicated."

"It usually is, love."

"No, Mark, it's more than just boy-girl games. He's . . ."

"Wrong for you."

"That's an understatement."

"His reputation with women is dubious."

"Not dubious at all. It's definite. Quite definite. He nails everything that moves."

"Is that a quote?"

"Roughly."

"I thought so. It didn't sound like you."

"It's not only that Cash is a womanizer. He's—"

"From the wrong side of the tracks. In this case, the wrong side of the bayou."

"I'm not a snob," she said defensively.

"But most people are," he reminded her gently. "And, after all, you're a Crandall from Belle Terre. What would people think?"

"It's not even as simple as that. I've never given too much thought to what other people think. Mama did. Cotton was just the opposite. He never gave a flying—I'll skip that quote." Mark laughed and it was good to hear his laughter. Shrugging, smiling, she said, "I guess I fall somewhere in between them. I don't really care what people think, but I feel a responsibility to Belle Terre to keep us respectable."

"You're getting off the subject. What about Cash Boudreaux?"

"I don't know. He's . . . It's . . ." She closed her eyes and gritted her teeth. "So damned confusing. I don't trust him and yet . . ."

"You lust for him."

She opened her eyes and gazed up at him. She'd never been able to lie to Mark. She couldn't even stretch the truth. His bald honesty with himself demanded honesty from everyone else. "Yes," she confessed softly. "I lust for him."

Mark embraced her. "Good. I'm glad. A case of raw lust is going to be very healthy for you." Chuckling, he added, "This is going to be interesting to watch, even from afar." He kissed her temple, then her lips. "Be happy, Schyler."

He released her and moved across the veranda toward the screen door. "Don't bother showing me upstairs. I know the way. Forgive me for abandoning you tonight, but I'm exhausted. The flight and all." He blew her a kiss, then stepped inside.

Schyler remained where she was, staring at the empty doorway. After several moments, she turned, still keeping contact with the pillar, and looked out across the lawn.

The red glow of a cigarette winked at her.

She was down the steps and walking through the damp, cool grass before she even realized the fluted column was no longer supporting her. It seemed to take forever for her to reach the woods, but then before she could prepare herself for it, she brushed aside a clump of crepe myrtle blooms and came face-to-face with Cash. He tossed down his cigarette and ground it to powder with the toe of his boot.

"What are you doing skulking around out here in the dark?" Schyler angrily demanded. "If you were spying on me, why—"

"Shut up."

Chapter Forty-three

He took her jaw between his hard fingers, backed her into the trunk of a pine, and forced her lips to open beneath his kiss. His tongue arrowed toward the back of her throat as his lips rubbed kiss after hot kiss upon hers. Her arms went up around his neck. She drove her fingers through his hair and held his head fast. He released her jaw and moved both hands up and down her body, touching as much of her as he could.

He tore his mouth free and locked his lustful gaze with hers. Their breaths made a thrashing sound in the dark stillness.

"Goddamn you, say you want me."

Schyler moistened her swollen, vandalized lips. "I want you. That's why I'm here."

He enclosed her wrist in the circle of his fingers and dragged her deeper into the forest. She stumbled along behind him, half laughing, half crying. She wasn't frightened. Her heart was churning with exhilaration, not fear. She didn't feel a sense of being dragged away from everything that was familiar and safe, but rather toward something that was new and exciting. And though he had her wrist imprisoned in his grasp, she felt free and unfettered.

He took her to the place on the bayou where he'd treated the dog bites a few weeks earlier. The same lantern was there, the same pirogue.

"Get in."

She stepped into the small boat and unsteadily lowered herself onto the seat. Cash pushed the boat away from the bank and stepped into it in one fluid motion. Taking up the long pole, he moved the pirogue through the shallow, murky waters by pushing along the bottom with the pole.

He stood in the prow, never taking his eyes off of Schyler. His silhouette looked large and dangerous and dark against the moonlit sky. The moon played in and among the trees that lined the bank, so that the surrounding forest was a constantly shifting pattern of light and shadow. The waters of the bayou swished pleasantly against the pirogue. Bullfrogs croaked from their natural barges and night birds called to each other.

"Why did you leave him and come to me?"

"Mark?"

"Did you break it off with him?"

"There was nothing to break off."

"You could get hurt playing me for a fool, Schyler."

She didn't doubt that for an instant. "Mark is gay. Our living arrangement was purely platonic."

He didn't laugh. He didn't accuse her of lying. He didn't express disbelief.

She would have expected any of those reactions. He said nothing, and only continued to help the slow-moving current by applying the pole to the muddy bottom of the bayou.

Sometimes the channel was so narrow that tree branches interlaced above them and formed a canopy. The bayou took twists and turns until Schyler lost all sense of direction. Even the moon seemed to change position in the sky.

She experienced sights and sounds and smells that she had never experienced before. The air felt different, still, but teeming with energy, with life unseen. It was an alien world, Cash's world. He was lord of it, so she wasn't afraid.

At last the pirogue nosed against the bank. He stepped out and dragged it to more solid ground. Dropping the pole, he reached for Schyler's hand and helped her alight. Carrying the lantern in his free hand, he led her up the incline toward his house.

They entered through the screened porch. He set the lantern on his bedside table and turned to face her. For endless moments they said nothing, just stood there, staring at each other, feeling apprehensive about what was about to happen.

Moving simultaneously, they fell on each other hungrily. His fingers sank into her hair and folded around her scalp. He angled her head back and kissed her mouth, then her throat, then her mouth again. In between those explicit kisses, he murmured even more explicit words. Some were spoken in the language of his mother's ancestors. If the words were indistinguishable, his inflection was easily understood. Schyler responded to the sexual dialect, demonstrating her willingness by arching her body against his.

The fabric of her dress was so soft, so sheer, that it seemed as insubstantial as cotton candy against the hard, demanding toughness of his body. Schyler wanted to be wrapped in his virility.

His kisses gentled. He moved his tongue in and out of

her mouth with deliberate leisure, savoring each nuance, the sleek texture, the sweet taste.

"Last time, you didn't know what hit you," he said gruffly. "This time, lady, I want you buzzing."

"I'm already buzzing." She gasped as his hands moved down the front of her dress. His palms were hot. They seemed to melt the fabric.

He looked down at her and smiled. "Good. That's good." He bent his head and kissed her mouth again. He reached for her buttons. Ending the kiss, his eyes followed the movements of his hands as he meticulously released each button from its hole. When they were all undone, he parted the bodice. Her demi-bra was pastel and floral and all for show. It seemed to disintegrate beneath his deft fingers.

And then her breasts were lying in his palms and his thumbs were sweeping back and forth over their tips. "Cash." Softly crying his name, she placed her hands at either side of his waist as her body angled back.

He made small sounds of arousal and gratification as her nipples turned as hard and rosy as pink pearls against his brushing fingertips. He bent his head toward them and laved them quickly with his tongue. He drew one into his mouth and sucked firmly.

"I can't get enough," he groaned, flinging his head up. He pressed her face between his hands and glared down at her, his intense desire bordering on fury. "I can't get enough," he repeated before assaulting her mouth again.

Locked together they fell on the bed. He worked her dress down to her hips, then he tossed it over the bed. He took only an instant to visually admire her skimpy lingerie before helping her remove it.

When she was naked, he laid his hand on her belly and rubbed his calloused palm across it. He stroked the wedge of tight, blond curls. They ensnared his fingertips. Then he curved his strong dark hand around her breast.

Holding his stare, Schyler pulled his shirt out of his waistband and slid her hands beneath it. She combed her fingers through the thick curly pelt. His eyes narrowed with increasing passion. His breath made a whistling sound through his compressed lips.

With rapid, jerky motions, he ripped his shirt buttons out of their holes and shrugged his shirt off. The buckle of his belt required a little more dexterity. He cursed it numerous times before it and his jeans became unfastened. He quickly rolled to his back and, raising his hips off the bed, pushed the jeans down his thighs. He kicked free of them, sending his boots to the floor at the same time.

Naked, warm, and hard, he rolled on top of Schyler and pinned her hands on either side of her head. His kiss would have been ravishment had she not participated with equal ardor.

"I'll kill you if you're lying to me about him."

"I'm not. I swear I'm not."

"Then this is for me? You're hot for me?"

"Yes," she cried out.

Inching his way down, he kissed her neck and chest. She laid her hands on his shoulders and gripped them hard while he stimulated her breasts with his lips and tongue until her nipples were stiff. He kissed his way down her middle, nipping her lightly with his teeth. His tongue flicked over her navel until she was gasping for breath.

Then it became impossible to breathe at all because he planted a hot, wet kiss just above her pubic hair, kissing her so strongly that he drew her delicate skin against his front teeth and made a mark. Her reaction was electric and involuntary. Raising her knees, digging her heels into the mattress, she tilted her hips up and forward.

Cash slid his hands beneath her derriere, pressed his fingers into the supple flesh, and drew her against his open mouth. He ate her with gentle avidity, letting her know he derived as much pleasure from it as he gave. Mindless as she was, and drowning in sensation, Schyler realized that Cash wanted her in the most intimate way.

His tongue pressed high into the giving folds of her body, sliding in and out in a delicious tongue-fuck. When he allowed it to slip free, he made sharp, stabbing motions with it against that kernel of flesh that had become exposed.

She clutched his hair. "Stop. Stop. Cash. No." Her belly grew taut. Her throat and breasts grew flushed. She felt as if she were poised on the edge of a cliff, looking down.

"Come," he grated hoarsely. "I want you to. Come against my mouth."

She couldn't have stopped it if she had wanted to.

When the last wave receded and she opened her eyes, his face was bending close above hers. She saw herself reflected in the swirls of gray and green and gold in his eyes. She smiled tentatively.

"What?" He playfully nudged her belly with the smooth, velvety tip of his iron penis.

"I look thoroughly debauched."

He grinned. "You certainly do." Then he sobered as his eyes wandered over her face. It was rosy and dewy with perspiration. Her lips were full and moist and slightly battered from his kiss and her own teeth. "You look beautiful."

He wasn't a man who handed out compliments frequently, if at all. Schyler had the feeling that he'd never told another woman that she was beautiful, at least not after he had succeeded in getting her in bed.

Her eyes turned smoky with the thought. Moving her fingers over his chest she said, "I think you're beautiful, too." She drew his head down and kissed his lips, licking the taste of herself off them.

Cash, hissing in sexual agony, caught her hand. He carried it down between their bodies and filled it with his erection. "Hold me. Squeeze me. Tight." He said the last word between clenched teeth, because her hand was already caressing the smooth, thick shaft. She discovered a drop of moisture on the very tip and spread it in and around the cleft.

Chanting love words, swear words, Cash reached between their bodies and separated the moist lips of her sex with his fingers. He planted himself so solidly inside of her that their body hair meshed.

He whispered, "You're tighter than a fist. Wetter than a mouth."

She massaged him with the walls of her body, contracting and releasing her muscles in an undulating motion that reduced him to a whimpering, quivering male animal, defeated by his own superb sexuality.

"Damn you," he breathed as he began to stroke her harder. "Damn you."

Again and again he delved into her body. Each time he almost withdrew, stretching and opening to give them ultimate sensation when he sank back into her. Schyler arched up to meet each deep thrust. Soon her choppy breathing matched his. When climax was imminent, they clung together and helplessly surrendered to each other, and to the rampant desire that neither wanted.

Chapter Forty-four

Lying face-to-face, Schyler lovingly examined him. "What caused this?" She touched a knick of a scar on his chest.

"Knife fight in Vietnam."

"You got that close to the enemy?"

"Not the enemy. Another GI."

"What were you fighting over?"

"Hell if I know. It didn't matter. We invented reasons for fighting."

"Why?"

"To let off steam."

"Wasn't there enough of a fight going on in the battle zones?"

"*Oui*. But that wasn't a fair fight. Most of the skirmishes in the barracks were."

"Were you a regular soldier?"

"I was *ir*regular. All of us had to be to survive."

"I meant did you specialize in something."

"Munitions and explosives." His jaw tensed. "I guess I did my share to get the body count up."

She tried to smooth the hair on his eyebrow, but it was too unruly. "If you felt that way about the war, why did you volunteer to go? I was told you kept reenlisting."

He shrugged. "It seemed like the thing to do at the time. I wasn't doing anything else."

"What about college?"

"I was enrolled, but I knew more about my major than the professors."

"What was your major?"

"Forestry."

"You didn't have to go to Vietnam to get out of college, Cash. You could have stayed here and worked."

He was shaking his head before she finished. "Cotton and I had had a falling out."

"Cotton was partly responsible for you going to war? How? What did you argue over?"

He gazed at her for a long time, then said, "Over your mother's death."

"*My* mother's death? What did that have to do with you?"

He rolled to his back and stared at the ceiling. Propping herself on one elbow, Schyler looked down at him inquisitively. He avoided looking at her. "After Macy died, I expected Cotton to marry my mother. He didn't. Wouldn't."

She rested her hand on Cash's breastbone, opening and closing her fingers like the pleats of a fan, snaring curly strands of chest hair between them. "I don't know what to say about that, Cash. I don't know much about it."

"Well I sure as hell knew what to say. I said it all to Cotton's face. We had a helluva fight. We would have come to blows if my mother hadn't intervened."

From what she knew of Monique, Schyler imagined how she must have felt when the two men she loved were at each other's throats. "What did she do?"

"Do? She defended Cotton, of course. She always defended him. She had justifications for everything he ever did. She never saw what a son of a bitch he is."

Her lover was calling her father a son of a bitch, but Schyler didn't jump to Cotton's defense. It was little wonder that Cash resented Cotton for not marrying his mother. Under similar circumstances, she would have felt the same way.

Cotton had been a good father to her and Tricia. She adored him in spite of his shortcomings. But she was no judge on how he conducted his personal life outside of Belle Terre. Until a few weeks ago, she didn't even know about his relationship with Monique Boudreaux and her volatile son. Each man was strong-willed and Schyler clearly imagined how vehemently they could disagree.

"The night we brought Gayla to Belle Terre, you mentioned that your mother had miscarried a baby."

"*Oui.*"

"My father's baby?"

His eyes flashed defensively. "*Oui.* My mother might have been unmarried, but she wasn't a whore. She didn't sleep with anybody but him."

"I didn't mean to imply—"

"I'm hungry. Are you?" He rolled off the bed and snatched up his jeans.

Troubled, Schyler took the shirt he tossed her and pushed her arms through the sleeves. "Yes, I'm hungry. What have you got?"

"Red beans and rice."

"Sounds delicious."

"Leftovers, but I'll heat it up."

Together they padded through the house, switching on lights as they went. Schyler sat in a chair at the table and watched while Cash moved about the small kitchen heating up a pan of the fragrant, hearty ethnic dish. When he passed her a plateful she saw that the beans and rice were complemented by large disks of spicy sausage.

"Just the way I like it," she said, digging in. "Hmm, wonderful. Who made it?"

"I did." She stopped chewing. He laughed at her incredulous expression. "Did you think the only recipes my mother left me were cures for warts and dyspepsia?"

Schyler ate with an unladylike appetite and finished everything on her plate. As Cash was carrying it to the sink, she studied the graceful lines of his back, the natural swagger of his narrow hips, and his long, lean legs.

He turned around and caught her looking at him with dreamy, misty eyes. "See anything you like?" he asked cockily.

"You're conceited, but, yes, I like everything I see."

"You don't sound too happy about it. What's the matter?"

"What's going to happen tomorrow?"

"Tomorrow?"

Suddenly embarrassed, Schyler glanced down at her hands, which were nervously clasping and unclasping in her lap. The hem of his shirt barely skimmed her thighs. She resisted the urge to modestly tug it down.

"I mean, what's going to happen between us? Daddy's coming home."

"I know." She looked up hastily. "I called the hospital," Cash said by way of explanation. "When you left the landing in such a hurry, I thought something might be wrong."

"On the contrary, he's doing much better. But he's still a heart patient. He can't get upset." She ran her tongue over her lips. "I don't know how he would take to something, you know, an affair, between you and me."

"He'll go apeshit."

Cash's response was not very encouraging. She continued anyway. "You know how busy we're going to be for the next few weeks. We've got to get that Endicott order filled in time. I can't let anything, particularly my personal life, stand in the way of that. There won't be much time for . . . for . . ."

Cash, leaning against the old-fashioned, corrugated cast-iron drain board, crossed his bare ankles and folded his arms over his hairy chest. His silence urged her to continue. "I'm not sure I'm ready for any kind of emotional entanglement. The relationship I had with Mark was special, even though it wasn't sexual. I'll miss him. I know you see other women."

She hoped he would enlighten her as to who and how many. Better yet, she wished he would tell her that he was through with other women now that he'd slept with her. But he remained as silent and still as a wooden Indian. It piqued her that he revealed nothing while she held nothing back.

"Dammit, say something."

"All right." He pushed himself away from the drain board. When his bare toes were only inches from hers, he reached down and grabbed a fistful of his shirt, hauling her up by it. "Get back to bed."

Minutes later, they were lying amid the sheets that smelled muskily of him, of her, of sex. She was lying on her side, facing him. His face was nestled between her breasts. He was softly caressing her nipple with his tongue.

"I've wanted to do this for a long time," he mumbled.

Schyler had conveniently dismissed her concerns for the time being. Cash had the right idea. Ignore tomorrow. Let the devil take it. Live for the moment. She might have to pay the piper a king's ransom later, but right now, with his mouth warm and urgent against her breasts, she didn't care.

"You're not going to say something corny like, 'Since the moment we met,' are you?"

"No. I wanted to do it even before we met."

"Before we met?" She looked at him with a puzzled expression. He eased her to her back and propped himself up on one elbow, leaving his other hand free to fondle.

"The first time I remember noticing that you weren't a little girl anymore, we were in the Magnolia Drug. I must have been eighteen, nineteen. You came in with a group of your friends. You were all acting silly, giggling. I guess you were still in junior high. You ordered a chocolate soda."

"I don't remember."

"No reason you should. It was just an ordinary day to you."

"Did you speak to me?"

He laughed bitterly. "Hell no. You would have run in terror if the scourge of Heaven had spoken to you."

"Is that when you rode the motorcycle?" He nodded and she laughed. "You're right. It would have been compromising to my good reputation to even say hello."

"If Cotton had gotten wind of it, he'd've had me castrated. I was banging everything in skirts that said yes. In fact, I was in the drugstore buying rubbers. I'd just paid for them when you came in. I decided to stick around. I ordered a drink at the fountain."

"Just so you could watch me?"

He nodded. "You had on a pink sweater. Fuzzy. A fuzzy pink sweater. And your breasts, or tits as I thought of them then, were making me crazy. They were small. Pointed. But they made two distinct impressions on the front of your sweater." He played with her, his motions as idle as his speech. "I made that vanilla Dr. Pepper last for more than an hour, watching you while you fed quarters into the jukebox and gossiped with your girlfriends. And the whole time, I was wishing I could reach up under your sweater, where your skin would be warm and smooth, and touch your pretty little breasts."

Schyler was mesmerized by the story. Cash stared into her wide, glassy gaze for a long time before leaning down and moistening her tight nipple with his tongue. Years of wanting went into each damp stroke.

"I knew better than to fantasize about you," he murmured. "I'd already been with more than my share of girls, but they'd all been willing partners. I never took unfair advantage of any of them. You were way too young for a man with my vast experience." He moved his face back and forth in the valley of her breasts. "Do you think I was perverted?"

"Very."

He raised his head and grinned. "But you like it?"

"Yes," she admitted with a self-conscious laugh. "I guess every woman likes to think she's been the object of a fantasy at least once."

"You were that, Miss Schyler. You were that. I was a white trash, bastard scum. You were the reigning princess of Belle Terre. I was grown. You were just a kid. You were so far out of my league, it wasn't even funny. But I had no control over myself. I wanted to touch you."

"Because you couldn't."

"Probably."

"We always want what we can't have."

"All I know is, I got so hard I hurt," he rasped, brushing a rough kiss across her lips. "After you and your friends left the drugstore, I got on my bike and drove to the edge of town. I parked and masturbated." He kissed her hard. "One phone call and I could have had a girl under me in five minutes. But I didn't want one. I wanted to get off, thinking about Schyler Crandall." Again, he kissed her. Harder.

"I've never seen Belle Terre at dawn from this side of the yard," Schyler remarked from the cab of Cash's pickup. "I've viewed sunrises from my upstairs window, but never from the outside looking in."

"I've never seen it any other way."

Her head came around quickly, but his expression didn't suggest hostility. It didn't suggest anything. She tried to lighten the mood. "I feel foolish, sneaking in at dawn."

"I wonder what your company thinks about you being out all night."

"Mark! I forgot about him. I really should be there when he wakes up." She placed her hand on the door handle, but was reluctant to officially end the night. "What are you going to do? Go back to bed?"

"No."

"Surely you're not going to work this early." The sky was still gray at the horizon.

"I've got other things to do."

"At this hour?" His eyes became even more remote. It was a visible transformation. "Excuse me," Schyler said testily, "I didn't mean to pry." She shoved open the door, which still bore Jigger Flynn's bullet hole, and got out.

"Schyler?"

"What?" She spun around, angry with Cash for not

being more affectionate and angry with herself for wanting him to be.

"I'll see you later."

His steamy look melted her thighs and her resentment. His expression and tone of voice intimated he would be seeing a lot of her later. With a slow, possessive smile, he shoved the pickup into gear and drove off.

Chapter Forty-five

Jigger woke up with a painful erection. Before he remembered that she was no longer there, he rolled over and reached for Gayla. Instead of warm, wonderful woman, he came up with a handful of grubby sheets.

Cursing her for not being available when he wanted her, he stumbled into the bathroom and relieved himself. Glancing in the mirror over the chipped, stained sink, he hooted in laughter at his reflection. "You'd make a vulture puke." He was uglier than sin. His beard stubble showed up white on his loose, flabby jaw.

Too much whiskey last night, he thought. He released a vile-tasting belch. His eyes were rivered with red streams. There was a large hole in his dingy tank T-shirt. It was a miracle that his voluminous boxer shorts kept their grip on his skinny ass.

He was hobbling back to bed, when he abruptly stopped and stood still. He had just realized what had woken him.

"What the hell?" he mumbled. He had never heard anything like that sound. He shoved aside the tacky curtains and peered through the grimy glass. A ray of sunlight pierced his red eyes, stinging him as if he had been speared through the back of his skull. He cursed viciously.

Once his eyes adjusted to the light, he blinked the yard into focus. Nothing unusual was going on. The puppies were yapping at their dam, demanding breakfast. Everything was normal.

Everything but that sound.

Jigger's gut knotted with foreboding. He had razor-sharp instincts about these things. He could smell trouble a mile away. That sound meant bad news. Menace. But where the hell was it coming from?

Compelled to find out, he didn't bother with dressing. Knobby knees aiming in opposite directions, he walked through his shabby house. It had really gone to seed since Gayla's defection. Mice scattered like a sack of spilled marbles across the linoleum floor when he entered the kitchen. Jigger cursed them, but otherwise ignored them. He pulled open the back door and pushed through the screen. The dogs in the backyard pens began barking.

"Shut up, you sons of bitches." Couldn't they tell his head was splitting? He raised a hand to his thudding temple. "Jesus." The blasphemy was still fresh on his lips when he spotted the oil drum.

It was a fifty-five gallon drum, silver and rusty in a few spots, but otherwise in good condition. It was ordinary.

Except for the sound it emitted.

Jigger recognized it now. It was a rattler. A hell of a one if the racket it was making was any indication of its size.

The drum had been left square in the middle of his yard between the back door and the toolshed. But by whom, Jigger wondered as he stood there with his hands propped on his nonexistent hips, staring at the drum in perplexity. Whoever it was had been a cagey bastard because his dogs hadn't made a racket. Either it was somebody who was used to handling dogs or it was somebody, or some*thing* spooky. Whatever it was, it was fuckin' weird. Goose bumps rose on his arms.

"Shit!"

It was just a snake. He wasn't afraid of snakes. When he was younger he'd traveled all the way to West Texas several times to go on rattlesnake roundups. That had been a helluva good time. There had been lots of smooth booze and coarse broads, lots of snake handling and one-upmanship. He'd lost count of the rattlers he'd milked of their venom.

No, it wasn't the snake that bothered him. What was giving Jigger the shivers was the manner in which the snake had been delivered. If somebody wanted to give him a present, why didn't he just come up and hand it to him outright? Why leave it as a surprise for him to discover while he still had a bitchin' hangover and before his morning coffee?

Coffee. That's what he needed, coffee dark as Egypt and strong as hell. He needed a woman here every morning to get his coffee. Yes, sir. He'd look into that today. He'd find a new woman. He had put up with that black bitch far too long. He needed one who didn't sass, one who kept her mouth shut and her thighs open. He was coming into some money soon, a goddamn fair amount, too. Nothing to sneeze at. With that, he could buy the best pussy in the parish.

This mental monologue had given Jigger time to walk all the way around the drum, inspecting it from all angles. Thoughtfully, he scratched his nose. He scratched his crotch. The lid of the drum was anchored down with a large rock. He reckoned he ought to open it and look inside to see just how monstrous this rattler was.

But damned if that sound wasn't getting to him. It was playing with his nerves something fierce. That snake was good and pissed off for being confined to that drum. He tried to remember just how far rattlers could strike.

He recalled one guy who was a fanatic about rattlers. He'd told Jigger that one could strike as far as he was long. Jigger hadn't believed him at the time. He was a born liar, and a Texan to boot. Besides, he'd been drunk as a fiddler's bitch and his tales had been nearly as tall as the blond broad who'd been straddling his lap and licking his ear.

But now, when such information was critical, Jigger

wondered if the fellow knew what he was talking about. Yet it could be that it only sounded noisy because it was in the bottom of that hollow drum.

"Hell yeah, that's it, don'tcha know. It just sounds big."

He approached the drum with garnered bravery, but as a precaution, he carried a long stick of firewood with him. His nerves were jangling as energetically as the rattler's tail when he knocked the rock to the ground, using the piece of firewood.

He moved the stick from one hand to the other, while alternately wiping his palms on the saggy seat of his boxers. Then, reaching far out in front of him, he eased the end of the stick under the rim of the drum's lid and carefully levered it up.

A bluejay squawked raucously from the tree directly overhead. Jigger nearly jumped out of his boxer shorts. He dropped the stick of firewood on his bare big toe.

"Goddammit to hell!" he bellowed. His cursing sent the pit bull bitch into a frenzy. Snarling and slavering, she repeatedly threw herself against the kennel's fence. It took several minutes for Jigger to quiet her and the litter and to scare off the territorially possessive bluejay.

Scraping together his courage again, Jigger picked up the stick and wedged it under the rim of the lid. He prized it up no more than an inch, but the volume of the sinister sound increased ten times. Jigger approached the drum on tiptoes, trying to see into it, but he could see only the opposite inside wall.

Taking a deep breath and checking to see that nothing was behind him, he flipped the lid to the ground. At the same time, he leaped backward like an uncoordinated acrobat. His heart was beating so quickly it reverberated in his eardrums, but nothing drowned out that deafening, nerve-racking, bloodcurdling sound.

No snake came striking out. He crept closer to the drum and peered over the edge, leaning forward as far as he dared.

"Jesus H. Christ."

He couldn't see all of it. He could see only a portion of a

body that was as thick as a muscle builder's bicep. Quickly he scouted the yard for something to stand on. Spotting a bucket in a pile of junk, he brought it back to the drum at a run and uprighted it. Then he stood on it, still a safe distance away, and got his first full look at his snake.

It was a monster, all right. Coiled several times around the bottom of the drum, he estimated it to be eight feet long. Six minimum. It filled up a good third of the drum. Sticking up out of the center of that deadly concentric coil was a rattling tail that looked like it would never stop. It shook so rapidly, it was impossible to count the individual rattles. But it was a great-granddaddy of a rattlesnake; it was mad as hell, and it was *his*.

Jigger clapped his hands in glee. With childlike delight, he clasped them together beneath his chin. He stared in wonder and awe at his marvelous gift. Eve's serpent couldn't have had any more sinister allure. It was entrancing to watch something so consummately evil, so gloriously wicked.

Everything about it was corruptly beautiful—the geometric pattern of its skin, the obsidian eyes, the forked tongue that flicked in and out of the flat lips, and that incessant rattle that was ominous and deadly.

Quickly, but cautiously, Jigger replaced the lid of the drum and weighted it down with the rock. He wasn't really worried that the snake could get out. If it was capable of striking over the rim of the drum, it would have by now. That snake was mean, diabolically so. Jigger instantly developed an attachment to it.

He loved his snake.

He ran for the house, full of plans on how to capitalize on the gift. It was a gift. He was sure of that now. Whoever had left it meant him no harm. He reasoned that it had been left by somebody who owed him money. That could be just about anybody in southwestern Louisiana. He wasn't going to worry about that now. His head was too full of commercial plans.

First, he'd have a flyer printed up advertising it. By nightfall his yard would be crawling with customers who wanted to see his rattler. What should he charge? A buck a peek. That was a neat, round figure he figured.

He entered his house through the back. The squeaky screen door slammed shut behind him, but he didn't hear anything over the clacking noise that his fabulous rattler made. In Jigger's opinion, it was music.

Chapter Forty-six

Cotton was a trying invalid even on his good days. Within a week of his homecoming everybody at Belle Terre was tempted to smother him in his sleep.

Tricia's affected bedside manner, never very extensive, was expended after the first day. She met Schyler in the hall. "He's always been a contrary old son of a bitch." She spoke under her breath so he wouldn't hear her through the walls of the study-bedroom. "He's even worse now."

"Tolerate his moods. Don't do or say anything to get him angry."

Schyler feared that her sister and Ken would become impatient about selling Belle Terre and broach the subject with Cotton. Dr. Collins had reiterated when she brought Cotton home that he was still a heart patient and must be treated carefully no matter how irksome he became.

Tricia didn't take Schyler's admonition kindly. "You're worried about that, aren't you? Is that what's keeping you up nights?"

"What are you talking about?"

"Come now, don't play innocent. Clever as you've been," Tricia said with a sly smile, "you haven't hidden your comings and goings in the middle of the night from us." She shook her head and laughed lightly. "Honestly, Schyler, you have the most appalling taste in men. A fairy antique dealer and a tom-catting white trash."

"And your own husband," Schyler shot back. "Insult my taste in men and you're insulting yourself. Don't forget that I picked Ken before you."

"I never forget that." Tricia smiled complacently. "And apparently neither do you."

Schyler let the argument die instantly. Insult swapping with Tricia was a tiresome exercise in futility. She could never top her sister's pettiness. As long as Tricia left Cotton alone, Schyler didn't care what she thought of her or the company she kept.

Ken avoided seeing Cotton after paying one obligatory visit to the sickroom soon after Cotton arrived. In fact, Ken kept to himself most of the time. His mood was volatile. He drank excessively and frequently carried on furtive, whispered telephone conversations.

He was particularly acerbic toward Schyler. She supposed he was still pouting because she hadn't loaned him the money he had requested. The telephone calls were probably from impatient creditors. Because of his financial difficulties she felt sorry for him. He was a grown man, though; it was time he learned to sort out his own problems.

At first Gayla was so shy around Cotton she could barely be persuaded to enter his room, but they had soon fallen into an easy rapport. He seemed to have entirely dismissed her years with Jigger and teased her often, recounting times in her childhood when she'd been a trial to Veda.

Eventually Gayla's guard relaxed. An unspoken bond developed between the two of them, which wasn't completely surprising. Each was recuperating from an assault. When no one else could convince Cotton to eat food he didn't like or to take his medication or to do his regimen of mild exercises, Gayla could.

He and Mrs. Dunne nearly came to blows the first day he was home. She had a tendency to mother him as she had her sick husband. Cotton couldn't stomach that and let her know it in no uncertain terms. Mrs. Dunne's maternal instincts gave way to a military bearing that clashed with Cotton's temper. Once the air had been cleared, however, they developed a mutual, if grudging, respect for each other.

But of everyone in the household, Schyler best handled the recalcitrant patient. She seemed to know how to mollify his temper when something set it off and how to boost his morale when he fell victim to depression. By turns she kept him calm and encouraged.

He was allowed to watch newscasts on the portable television that had been placed in his room. One of Gayla's duties was to bring him the local newspaper the moment it was delivered. But Schyler kept her answers vague whenever he asked about Crandall Logging.

"Everything's going very well," she parroted each evening when she came in to visit with him.

"Any problems on getting that order to Endicott?"

"None. How are you feeling?"

"Trains running on schedule?"

"Yes. Mrs. Dunne said you ate all your lunch today."

"Does it look like good timber their cutting?"

"Highest Crandall quality. Did you get a good rest this afternoon?"

"Are we gonna make that loan payment in time?"

"Yes. I'm sure of it. Now settle down."

"Jesus, Schyler, I hate that you're having to undo my mistakes."

"Don't worry about it, Daddy. The hard work is good for me. I'm actually enjoying it."

"It's too much for a woman to handle."

"Chauvinist! Why shouldn't I be able to handle the business?"

"Guess I'm just old-fashioned in my thinking. Behind the times." He glared at her from beneath his brows. "Like when I was your age, queers were avoided. Normal women sure as hell didn't move in with them. Is that why I never got to meet Mark Houghton? You were hiding him from me?"

"That's not the reason at all." She kept her voice even, but inside she was fighting mad. Tricia or Ken had tattled. It was probably Tricia, in retaliation for the putdown she'd received from Mark. "Mark had to leave before you got home, that's all."

She had returned home that morning from Cash's house to find a note pinned to her undisturbed pillow. In it Mark expressed his hope that she'd had an enjoyable evening. He wrote that he had been struck by a sudden case of homesickness in the middle of the night, had packed and called Heaven's one taxi, promising an enormous tip if he were driven to Lafayette where he could make flight connections the following day.

Schyler could read through the lines of the cryptic message. Mark hadn't wanted to say good-bye to her. She belonged at Belle Terre; he didn't.

Their bittersweet parting had occurred the night before, though neither had wanted to admit that's what the conversation on the veranda had been. A sad, lengthy, weepy good-bye would have put them through an unnecessary and emotional ordeal. Distressed as she had been to find his note, Schyler was glad Mark had taken the easy way out. She was sad, but relieved.

"How could you live with a guy like that?"

"'A guy like that'? You don't know what kind of guy Mark is, Daddy. You never met him."

"He's a queer!"

"A homosexual, yes. He's also intelligent, sensitive, funny, and a very dear friend."

"In my day, if one of those crossed our path, we'd beat the hell out of him."

"I hope that's not something you're proud of."

"Not particularly, no. But I'm not particularly ashamed of it either. That's just what us regular guys did. That was before all this social consciousness bullshit got started."

"High time, too. We've come a long way from rolling queers in alleys."

Cotton didn't find her attempted humor very funny. "You've got a real smart mouth, Miss Crandall."

"I learned it from you."

He studied her for a moment. "You know I was real upset about you and Ken not getting together. But now I'm glad. Damn glad. He's a pussy. Drinks too much, gambles too much. Lets Tricia run roughshod over him. She likes that arrangement just fine. But you would have hated it, and soon enough you'd have come to hate him. You're too strong for Ken Howell." He sighed in aggravation. "But once you were rid of him, what do you go and do? You shackle yourself to a man who's even weaker."

"You're wrong. Mark is a very strong individual, one of the strongest men I've ever met. It took tremendous courage for him to leave the life he led in Boston. I moved in with him because I liked him, we got along extremely well, and both of us were lonely. Believe it or not, I didn't consider your feelings about it at all. I didn't become Mark's roommate to spite you."

Cotton frowned at her skeptically. "Kinda looks like that, doesn't it? When are you going to get you a real man, one who can plant some grandbabies in you?"

"Mark could have, if he wanted to. He didn't want to."

"I reckon that's one reason you were attracted to him. He didn't pose a threat."

"I liked him for what he was, not for what he wasn't."

"Don't play word games with me, young lady," he chided her sharply. "Your problem is that you've always loved the unlovely."

"Have I?"

"Ever since you were a kid. Always taking up for the underdog. Like Gayla. Like Glee Williams."

Glad for the chance to switch subjects, Schyler said, "Speaking of Glee, he's doing very well. I called today. The doctors are going to release him from the hospital soon. He'll have to report every few days for physical therapy. I'm hoping we can find a desk job for him to do."

"Who's we?"

"We?"

"You said you hoped 'we' can find Glee a desk job."

"Oh, uh, you and I." Cotton's eyes shrewdly searched for the truth. Schyler squirmed. "Glee doesn't like taking a salary without earning it."

He grumbled, a sign that he wasn't satisfied with her glib answer. "You didn't inherit that generous nature from me. Certainly not from Macy. Her heart was about as soft as a brass andiron. Where'd you get your kindheartedness?"

"From my blood relations, I suspect. Who knows?" The conversation had taken a track that made Schyler distinctly uncomfortable. She consulted her wristwatch. "It's past your bedtime. You're intentionally dragging out this conversation to postpone it. Really, Daddy, you're worse than a little kid about going to bed on time."

She leaned over him and fluffed his pillow. Kissing his forehead, she switched off the bedside lamp. Before she could step away, he caught her hand.

"Be careful that your benevolence doesn't work against you, Schyler," he warned.

"What do you mean?"

"Vast experience has taught me that folks dearly love to bite the hand that feeds them. It gives them a perverse satisfaction that's just plain human nature. You can't change that." He wagged his finger at her. "Make sure nobody mistakes your love and charity for weakness. Folks claim they admire saints. But fact is, they despise them. They gloat in seeing them stumble and fall flat on their asses."

"I'll keep that in mind."

Cotton had a spit-and-whittle club philosophy. Schyler wanted to smile indulgently, say, "Yes, sir," and dismiss his advice as the ramblings of an old man. But it weighed on her mind as she stepped out onto the veranda through the back door. She had a strong intuition that Cotton was beating around the bush about something—specifically Cash Boudreaux. He was reluctant to bring it into the open.

She still hadn't mentioned the extent of Cash's involvement in the business or how much she depended on him.

Cotton wouldn't like it. And what Cotton wouldn't like, she wasn't telling him. Careful as she'd been to keep Cash's name out of their conversations, Cotton was too smart not to pick up signals. Piecing information together had always been his forte. He must know that Cash was running the daily operation of Crandall Logging. He no doubt resented that, but realized that Cash's experience and knowledge were necessary to Schyler's success.

What he suspected, but obviously didn't want confirmed, was Schyler's personal involvement with Cash. Because of his long-standing relationship with Monique, Cotton would certainly have misgivings about an alliance between them.

Schyler had more than misgivings. She was downright terrified of her feelings for Cash.

She had a voracious physical appetite for him. She looked forward to his stolen kisses and their hungry lovemaking. She had never felt more alive than when she was with him, nor more confused when she wasn't. He was the most intriguing man she'd ever met, but it was confounding not to know all his secrets. He was passionate and perplexing. She depended on him; yet she didn't completely trust him. His lovemaking was frightening in its intensity, but he was often aloof afterward.

When the heat of their desire had been extinguished and she languished in his postcoital embrace, the moment was invariably spoiled by her niggling doubts. She feared that Cash wanted her only because she represented something he'd always been denied. He'd been with legions of women. Certainly many of them were more fascinating, pretty, and sexy than she. What made her so attractive to him? When he entered her body, was he loving her or was he trespassing on Belle Terre?

That thought was so disturbing, it made her warm. Needing air, she stepped outside and drifted soundlessly along the veranda. As she rounded the corner, she bumped into Gayla. The young woman let out a soft scream and flattened herself against the wall of the house.

"Gayla, my God, what's the matter with you?" Schyler said, catching her breath. "You scared me."

"I'm sorry. You scared me, too."

Schyler looked at her friend closely. Gayla's eyes were round with genuine fear. "What's the matter?"

"Nothing. I was just taking the evening air. Guess it's time I went in."

Gayla eased away from the wall and turned as if to run. Schyler caught her arm. "Not so fast, Gayla. What's wrong?"

"Nothing."

"Don't tell me nothing. You look like you've seen a ghost."

Gayla's mouth began to work emotionally. Tears formed in her large, dark eyes. "I wish it was a ghost."

Schyler moved in closer, concerned for her friend's mental stability. "What's happened?"

Gayla reached into the deep pocket of her skirt and took something out. Enough light from the window fell on it so Schyler could see what it was. It was an ugly little handmade doll that bore an uncanny resemblance to Gayla. There was a vicious-looking straight pin stuck in the brightly painted red heart on its chest.

"Voodoo?" Schyler whispered. She glanced up at Gayla incomprehensively. "Is that what it is?" She didn't believe in such nonsense. "Where did you get it?"

"Somebody left it on my pillow."

"In your room? You found it in your room? Are you saying that somebody in the house did this?" The cruelty of it was inconceivable, even for Tricia. There was no love lost between the two women, but . . . black magic?

"No. I don't think it was anybody in the house," Gayla replied.

"When did you find it?"

"Last night."

"Tell me."

"I heard something out here on the veranda."

"What time?"

"I don't know. After you left." The two women shared a guilty glance, then looked away. "It was late."

"Go on."

"I thought I heard a noise out here." Gayla glanced around apprehensively. "I wasn't sure. I thought it could have been my imagination. I've been real spooked lately. I think I see Jigger behind every bush."

"That certainly isn't a figment of your imagination," Schyler said grimly, nodding down at the doll.

"I worked up my courage and came out here to investigate."

"You shouldn't have done that alone."

"I didn't want to make a fool of myself by waking up everybody."

"Don't worry about that the next time. If there is a next time. What happened when you came out here?"

"Nothing. I didn't see or hear anything. When I went back inside, this was lying on my pillow." She crammed the doll back in her skirt pocket and tucked her hands under her opposite arms.

"Do you think Jigger did it?"

"Not him personally. He's not that subtle." She thought for a moment. "But he might've hired somebody to do it, to let me know he hasn't forgotten."

"Who does that kind of thing these days?"

"Lots of the blacks."

"Christians?"

Gayla gravely nodded her head. "The early slaves believed in black magic before they ever heard of Jesus. It's been passed down."

"Does Jigger believe in it?"

"I doubt it. But he knows that other folks do, so he uses it to scare them."

"Then he's used these scare tactics before?" Schyler was remembering the two dead cats found on the veranda.

"I think so, yes."

"Do you know who he gets to do his black magic for him?" Gayla looked everywhere but at Schyler. Schyler clasped her arm and shook it. "Who, Gayla?"

"I don't know. I'm not sure."

"But you have a fair idea. Who?"

"Jigger only mentioned one hex to me in all the time I lived with him."

"And?"

"He was probably lying because it isn't a black."

"Who? Give me a name."

Gayla wet her lips. When she spoke, her voice was as soft and fitful as the Gulf breeze. "Jigger said Cash Boudreaux did it for him."

Cash heard the old board on his porch squeak under weight. He laid down his magazine and casually slipped the knife from the scabbard at the small of his back. Pressed flat against the inside wall, he inched toward the front of his house. The door was opened. Insects dived toward the screen, making small pinging sounds when they struck. He didn't hear anything else. It didn't matter. He knew with a guerrilla fighter's instincts that somebody was out there.

Moving so fast that his limbs were flesh-colored blurs, he whipped open the screen door and lunged outside. The other man was cowering against the wall. Cash's shoulder gouged his midsection. As he doubled over, Cash pressed the tip of his knife against the man's navel.

"Jesus, Cash," he cried out in fear. "It's me."

Adrenaline stopped its chase through Cash's body. His brain telegraphed his hand not to send the knife plunging in and up. He eased to his full height and slid the weapon back into the scabbard. "Goddammit, I almost gutted you. What the hell are you doing sneaking around out here?"

"I thought that's what you hired me to do. Sneak around."

Cash grinned and slapped the other man on the shoulder. "Right. But not around me. Want a drink, *mon ami*?"

"I could damn sure use one. Thanks."

They went inside. Cash poured two straight bourbons. "How'd it go?"

"Just like you said." The man tossed back his drink and, with a wide smile, added. "They never knew I was there."

Chapter Forty-seven

"What's so amusing?" Rhoda Gilbreath asked her husband from her end of the dining table. She laid her fork on her plate and reached for her wineglass. "They lock people who laugh to themselves into tiny, padded rooms, Dale."

Unperturbed, he blotted his mouth with his napkin and pushed his plate aside. Because Rhoda wanted to stay stick-figure thin, she expected him to eat as sparingly as she did. Not that he wanted huge portions of the health food she served at home. He ate sugary bakery doughnuts every morning for breakfast and a high-caloric lunch so that he wouldn't starve to death in the evenings.

"Sorry, darling. I didn't mean to exclude you from the joke." He washed down his last tasteless bite with a swallow of tepid white wine. It, too, was low cal and had no sting. "Have you heard about the latest entertainment attraction in town?"

"They've reopened the drive-in theater. Old news, Dale."

"No, something else."

"I'm holding my breath," she said drolly.

"Jigger Flynn's got a pet snake."

"Bully for him."

Dale leaned back in his chair. "This isn't any ordinary snake. It's a rattlesnake. Gruesome-looking thing."

"You actually went to see Jigger Flynn's snake?"

"I didn't want to be the only one in town who hadn't seen it," he chuckled. "That's all anybody's talking about."

"Which is a clear indication of the intelligence level in this community."

"Don't be snide. This really is a remarkable snake."

"You're dying to tell me all about it, aren't you? Well, go ahead." When he was done, Rhoda was impressed in spite of herself. "And he doesn't know who left it in his yard?"

"Claims not to. Of course Jigger is a bald-faced liar, so you can never be sure if he's telling the truth or not. Still," Dale said, recalling Jigger's giddiness as he showed off his prized possession, "I think this is more than just another of his moneymaking schemes."

"How so?"

"I'm not sure. This snake seems to have touched Jigger in some way."

"Touched? You mean mentally?"

"Psychologically." Dale leaned forward and said in a hushed voice, "I think it was supposed to."

"Isn't this where the spooky music is supposed to come up full? Doo-doo-doo-doo, doo-doo-doo-doo."

Dale ignored his wife's sarcasm. His expression was reflective, as though he were reasoning through an intricate riddle. "Whoever left that rattler for Jigger to find wanted him to be hyped up about it. Jesus, it wouldn't take long for that monster to fuck with my mind. You can hear the thing from two hundred yards. Never heard such a creepy sound in all my life."

Rhoda's slender, beringed fingers slid up and down the stem of her wineglass as she shrewdly regarded her husband. "You don't know anything about it, do you?"

Dale feigned surprise. "Who, me? No. Certainly not." At her skeptical expression, he laughed. "Honest. I don't know anything about Jigger's snake."

Rhoda took a sip of wine. "If you did, you wouldn't tell me."

"What makes you think that?"

"Because you're a provoking son of a bitch, that's why."

Dale frowned at his wife. She wasn't a cheerful drunk. Indeed, she got more surly by the glass. "I'd like to know what burr has been stuck up your ass for the last week or so. You've been impossible to live with."

"I've got a lot on my mind."

"Not the least of which is who your next extramarital lover is going to be."

He had pushed himself away from the table and left the dining room before Rhoda came to her senses. She stumbled from her chair and chased after him. She caught up with him in the den where he was calmly lighting his pipe. Before he could apply the match to the filled bowl, she caught his arm.

"What do you mean, who my next lover is going to be?"

Dale jerked his arm free, lit his pipe, and fanned out the match, meticulously dropping it in the ashtray, before giving his wife his attention. "It's all over town that your most recent stud is humping the Crandall woman. Tough luck, Rhoda."

"What does it mean?"

"Humping? It means—"

She punched him in the chest. "Stop it! You know what I meant. What does this mean to us? To your plans for the takeover of Belle Terre?"

He glowered at her for striking him, but he puffed his pipe docilely. "Their affair falls right into place with my own plans. He might be nailing her, but he has an ulterior motive. There's bad blood between him and the Crandalls, having to do with his mother and Cotton I believe."

Rhoda's spirits lifted marginally. She had cause to want the sky to fall on both Cash and Schyler. As Dale had said, it was all over town that they were sleeping together. Rhoda herself had heard it at a meeting of the Friends of the Library. Helping to spread the salacious tidings was Schyler's own sister. Tricia Howell had held court to an enthralled audience while she dragged Schyler's name through the muck.

Oh, she had put on a great act, making her avid listeners drag the information out of her, bit by juicy bit. But once she'd confirmed the gossip, she said, "Everybody at Belle Terre is thoroughly disgusted. Cash is so trashy. I mean, think what his mama was."

Rhoda wasn't fooled. Tricia was jealous of her older sister, and probably envious of her affair with Cash. The catty little bitch had then launched into a story about Schyler's life in London with a homosexual, while Rhoda sat and stewed in her own juice. Schyler Crandall was the reason behind Cash's peculiar switch in personality. He had dumped *her* for Schyler Crandall. For that, she'd pay them back in spades.

"You can play one off the other," she suggested to Dale now.

Dale stroked his wife's cheek affectionately. "You're a vicious bitch, my dear. Vicious, but so clever."

"Is there anything I can do to help further things along?"

"Thank you, but I have everything under control. I'm keeping a very close eye on the situation. I'm being kept well informed."

"By someone you can trust, I hope."

"By someone who stands to gain as much as we do."

Rhoda laid her hands on his lapels and moved close to him, nuzzling his crotch with her middle. "Be sure to let me know if there's any way I can help you, darling."

Dale set his pipe aside and reached for the fly of his trousers. "Actually there is. It also might serve to improve your disposition."

He pushed her to her knees, but she went willingly.

The blast of a car horn woke Schyler up. She threw off the covers and ran out into the hall. Looking out the landing window, she saw Cash's pickup below. He was standing in the wedge made by the open door.

"Get dressed," he shouted up to her. "We've got a problem."

"What?"

"I'll tell you on the way."

She made it downstairs within minutes. Tossing her shoes in first, she jumped into the cab of his pickup. "You certainly raised a ruckus inside this house. I hope this is important."

"A chain on one of the rigs busted. Both bolsters gave way under the pressure. We've got a helluva log spill out on Highway Nine. I called out a crew. They're working to clear the road now."

"Was anybody hurt?"

"No."

"Thank God." If the accident hadn't occurred so early in the morning, when the highway wasn't busily traveled, it very well could have cost lives. Schyler shuddered to think of the consequences. "You had a rig loaded this early in the morning?"

"I've got every man putting in extra hours. A team comes on as soon as it gets light. We've got less than a week to get the rest of that order to Endicott's, remember?"

"And if we don't get the mess on the highway cleared up, a whole crew won't be free to cut today."

"That's right. Every hour counts." Cash was driving the pickup with no regard for traffic laws or speed regulations.

"How long do you think it will take?"

"I don't know." He glanced across at her. "I should have told you to dress in jeans. You might end up lumberjacking today."

"Gladly, skirt or not. We've got to get that timber cut while the weather holds out." Gnawing the inside of her jaw in vexation, she muttered, "Why did the blasted chain have to break now?"

"It didn't." Schyler looked at him in surprise. "It was sawed through," Cash told her. "Clean as a whistle. The truck had no more than pulled onto the highway than the logs started rolling off."

"Cash, are you sure?"

"I'm sure."

"Who did it?"

"How the hell should I know?"

"Who was driving?"

He named the man and shook his head firmly. "He's been with the company for years. Thinks Cotton Crandall hung the moon."

"But what about Cotton Crandall's daughter? What does he think of her?"

He turned to her with a leering smile. "Sure you want to hear it word for word?"

The way he asked made her certain she didn't want to know. "He's loyal?"

"Loyal as they come."

"What about the others on that crew?"

She gave him time to run through the list of names mentally. "I'd trust any of them with my life. What would be a logger's motivation to deliberately screw things up? He would lose his job permanently if Crandall Logging goes out of business."

"Not if he were bribed with a large amount of money."

"Sudden riches would be a dead giveaway. The traitor would never survive the others' revenge. None of them would be stupid enough to try it. Besides, they're as loyal to each other as they are to your daddy."

"An independent?"

"Again, what's his motivation? You've created an active, local market. He's making more profit because his hauling expenses are reduced."

"But you still think it was sabotage?"

"Don't you?"

"Jigger?" she asked. They stared at each other, knowing the answer.

That was the last quiet moment they had for the next several hours. A state trooper was already on the scene when Cash and Schyler arrived. He was engaged in a heated argument with the logging crew.

Cash shouldered his way through. "What's going on?"

The trooper turned around. "You in charge?"

"I am."

"I'm gonna ticket you, mister. This rig was overloaded."

"Find me one that isn't."

"Well you got caught," the trooper said in a syrupy voice.

"A chain busted."

"Because you were overloaded. And just because everybody else overloads doesn't make it right. I'll make an example out of you." He took a citation pad out of his pocket. "While I'm doing it, tell your driver to get his rig off the road."

As it was, the trailer rig and the logs were blocking both

lanes of the two-lane state highway. "Look," Cash said, with diminishing patience, "we can't just scoot that timber aside. It's got to be reloaded onto another trailer."

"Yeah?"

"Yeah. We'll have to scare up a loader that's not in use and get another rig out here. It'll take awhile. They're not built for speed."

"We can't shut down this highway. You'll have to do that at night."

"I'm afraid that's out of the question. I wouldn't risk the lives of my men by having them work after dark."

At the sound of the feminine voice, the trooper spun around. He gave her a once-over that was calculated to intimidate. "Who are you?"

"Schyler Crandall."

The name worked like a splash of water on a growing fire. "Oh, Ms. Crandall, ma'am," he stammered, tipping his hat, "well I was just telling your man here—"

"I heard what you told him. It's unacceptable." The startled trooper opened his mouth to protest, but before he could say a word Schyler went on. "I suggest a compromise. Could you keep open the east-bound lane and close only the west-bound? That might slow traffic down, but it will slow down because of gawking drivers anyway. Having only one lane closed wouldn't stop traffic and it would be a tremendous help to us. I think we can move all our equipment in and work from one side of the road. We could get this cleared much sooner and that would be to everyone's advantage. Am I right?"

"Am I right?" Cash mimicked her moments later, fluttering his eyelashes.

"You weren't getting anywhere with him," she said. "It was a macho, Mexican standoff. What was I supposed to do?"

"Well, a blow job might have done the trick quicker. As it is, what you did worked okay."

She gave him a fulminating look, but he missed it. He was already stalking away from her, issuing orders. Though it seemed like little was being done at any given time and confusion reigned, one by one the immense pine logs were lifted by crane and swung from the highway to the trailer rig. Cash himself sat in the knuckle boom and operated the loader. He carefully chose each log before loading it and stacked them all to achieve the perfect balance.

The accident did stop traffic, but it was the fault of rubbernecked drivers and not Crandall Logging. By midmorning the state trooper was literally eating out of Schyler's hand since she brought him a doughnut when she catered a snack to the crew assisting Cash.

"Thanks," Cash said curtly as he opened the soda Schyler handed him. Unlike the others, who were taking a ten-minute break, lounging on the shoulder of the highway in the shade of trees, Cash was checking the bolsters and chains on the rig that had arrived to replace the damaged one. He drank the cold drink in one long swallow. "Wish it was a beer," he said, handing Schyler the empty can.

"I'll buy you a case of it if you make up this morning's quota before dark."

Staring her down, he grimly pulled on his beaten leather gloves and put the hard hat back on his head. Turning away from her, he shouted, "All right, up off your asses. This isn't a goddamn picnic. Back to work." The loggers grumbled, but they complied with his orders. Schyler had seen only one other man who commanded both obedience and respect from his crews—Cotton.

As the morning progressed, the heat became unbearable. Waves of it shimmered up off the pavement. The humidity was high; there wasn't a breath of air. The men removed their shirts when they became sodden and plastered to their backs. Handkerchiefs were used as sweatbands beneath hard hats. The state trooper kept his uniform intact, but large rings of perspiration stained his shirt beneath his arms. Frequently he removed his hat to mop his forehead and face. Schyler stayed busy at the bed of Cash's pickup dispensing ice water.

He never took a break, so she carried a cup of water out to him. He put a chunk of ice in his mouth and poured the water over his head. It dribbled off his head and shoulders and through his chest hair. His discarded shirt had been tucked into his waistband. It hug over his hips like a breechcloth.

"You shouldn't be out here," he said after giving her a critical look. "You'll cook. The tip of your nose is already sunburned."

"I'm staying," she replied staunchly. She wouldn't desert her men.

But as she walked back to the pickup, she pulled the tail of her blouse from the damp waistband of her skirt. Sweat trickled between her breasts and behind her knees. Her hair felt hot and heavy on her neck. Luckily she found a rubber band in her purse and used it to hold together a wide single braid. She'd never felt grittier or more uneasy. Even after gathering her hair off her neck, it continued to prickle with sensations that were so unpleasant as to be uncomfortable, almost as though someone had her in the cross hairs. Slowly, warily, she turned her head and looked toward the woods behind her.

Jigger Flynn was standing partially hidden behind the trunk of a pecan tree. He was staring at her, clearly laughing to himself.

Schyler sucked in a quick breath of stark fear, though she retained enough control over her reaction not to let Jigger see it. His malice toward her was palpable, but Schyler held his stare. His eyes were so small and so deeply embedded that she couldn't really distinguish them. It was his overall expression that conveyed his silent message of vengeance. He was mocking her, gloating over the havoc she was sure he had caused. He was daring her to confront him and warning her that if she did, he would retaliate. This was only a mild example of the cruelty of which he was capable.

She briefly considered running to the trooper and pointing out Jigger as the one responsible for the log spill, but she vetoed it as a futile idea. Jigger was an adroit liar; he would only deny the charge and produce an alibi. She needed proof.

As for alerting Cash, he already knew that Jigger was the most likely culprit and had made no effort to go after him. She doubted he would.

Jigger seemed to discern her dilemma because he smiled. The devil's face couldn't look any more sinister than that smile. Schyler actually shuddered, as though the evil he embodied were passing through her body. She felt it as an assault and physically reacted to it.

Panicked, she spun around. She opened her mouth to summon Cash, but she realized he was involved in loading the last log onto the rig. The trooper was speaking into the microphone of his patrol car radio. She was alone. She had to deal with her fear of Jigger Flynn by herself. She had to face him.

Drawing a deep breath, she turned around to confront him, but there was nothing beneath the pecan tree except its branches and their leaves, dropping in the heat. All Schyler saw were shadows and dappled sunlight. Jigger Flynn had disappeared without a sound through the tall, dry grass. It was as if hell had opened up and taken him home.

Schyler was brought around by the cheer that went up from the men as the last log was placed on the rig and the load was secured.

"Get that rig unloaded at the landing and then bring it back to the site," Cash shouted to the driver as he ran toward his pickup. To the other men he said, "Hitch a ride on the loader. I'll meet you at the site after I drop Schyler off. When I get there I want to see trees dropping like whores' panties."

He jumped into the cab of his truck. "Get in," he barked at Schyler, who was still standing and trembling with fear. She got in. Cash slipped the truck into first gear and pulled out onto the highway. As they drove past the trooper, Schyler waved her thanks at him.

"Did you two make a date?" Following so closely on the heels of seeing Jigger, his acerbity was too much for her nerves.

"Do you care?"

"Damn right." His arm shot across the seat and his hand plunged between her thighs. He squeezed her possessively. "This is mine until I get through with it, understand?"

Enraged, Schyler removed his hand, throwing it away

from her. "Keep your hands off me. And while you're at it, go to hell."

"What would you do without me if I did?"

She averted her head and didn't look at him again. As soon as the pickup came to a stop on the other side of the Laurent Bayou bridge, she bolted out the passenger door. Cash was hot on her trail and caught up with her at the door of the office. He spun her around and, pressing her shoulders between his hands, drew her against his bare, damp chest. He kissed her hard enough to take away her breath.

His tongue ground its way between her unwilling lips. Schyler's resistance slipped a notch, then snapped. He tasted like salty, sweaty, unrefined, fearless man. Feeling a desperate need for a mighty warrior's protection, she greedily kissed him back.

As suddenly as he had grabbed her, he pushed her away and released her. "I warned you that I was never kind to women. Don't expect me to be any different with you."

He drove off, leaving a cloud of white powdery dust swirling around her.

Chapter Forty-eight

Schyler watched until the lights of the caboose disappeared in the tunnel of trees. Wearily pushing back a wispy strand of hair that had escaped her clumsy braid, she turned around, but instantly stopped short.

Cash was leaning against the exterior wall of the office. She hadn't known he was there, though she should have smelled the smoke from his cigarette. It was dangling precariously from the corner of his lips. His shirt was unbuttoned. He had his thumbs hooked into the waistband of his jeans.

"Well, we did it," Schyler said. "We recovered the production time we lost this morning."

"Oui."

"Several times today I doubted that we would."

He took one last drag on the cigarette before flicking the butt into the gravel bed between the train tracks. "I never doubted it."

"Thank the men for me."

"One of the drivers brought back word to the site that you mentioned a bonus."

"I did."

"They'll hold you to it."

"They'll get it. As soon as I get a check from Endicott and the bank note is paid in full."

"You owe me a case of beer."

"Is tomorrow soon enough?"

"Fine."

She entered the landing office by the back door. She didn't sit down behind the desk, fearing that if she did, she would lay her head on top of it and fall asleep right there. Instead she switched off the lamp, picked up her purse, and made her way toward the front entrance.

"You still mad at me?" Cash followed her out, making certain the door was locked behind them.

"Why should I be mad?"

"Because I don't court you with flowers and presents."

She turned to face him. "Do you think I'm that shallow? That silly? If you gave me flowers I'd know you were mocking me, not courting me. All that aside, I don't want to be courted by you. By anybody."

"Then why are you mad?"

"I'm not."

Schyler headed toward her car, only to realize that her car was at Belle Terre. She reversed her direction. Cash caught her arm. "Where're you going?"

"To call Ken to come pick me up."

"Get in the truck. I'm taking you home."

"I—"

"Get in the truck, dammit."

Schyler knew that it would be lunacy to stand there and fight with him when she felt this tired and this grimy. It was grossly unfair of a man to engage a woman in an argument when a hard day's work had left him looking ruggedly appealing and left her looking like hell. If she'd had access to a lipstick and a hairbrush, then maybe she would have stayed to fight. As it was, the deck was stacked against her. She was too exhausted to think, much less argue with him. She got in his pickup.

"Want to go by Jigger's and see his rattlesnake?"

Jigger was the last topic she wanted to talk about. She still shuddered every time she recalled his leering grin. But what Cash had suggested was so out of context and so preposterous, she couldn't help asking an astonished, "What?"

"His rattlesnake. Jigger's got a new pet rattler. I hear it's a helluva snake. He's even charging admission to look at it. Want to stop by on the way home?"

"I hope you're joking. If you are, it's in very poor taste. I don't want to have anything to do with him, except maybe to bring charges against him for assaulting Gayla . . . and that only tops a very long list of offenses. I can't believe you'd go near him either. He might have been responsible for sabotaging that rig this morning."

"I thought of that."

"And you still pander to him?" She spread her arms wide. "Oh, but I forgot. He's a customer of yours, isn't he?"

"You mean the medicine?"

"Yes, the medicine."

"I was doing Gayla a favor, not Jigger."

"But you took Jigger's money."

"It's green. Same as anybody else's."

"Money is money, is that it?"

"*Oui*. To somebody who's never had it, that's it, Miss Schyler. You wouldn't know what poverty is like."

"You grab at money no matter where it comes from?"

"It matters. I didn't kill those pit bulls for you, remember?"

"So there are a few things you wouldn't do for money."

"Very few, but some."

What about making a hideous little doll and placing it on someone's pillow, Schyler wondered. Cash had at least a smattering knowledge of voodoo. Gayla had heard his name in connection with it, but surely he didn't know anything about that doll. He couldn't have treated Gayla so kindly the day they found her in the woods, only to later put a curse on her. On the other hand, could anyone count on Cash's loyalty? It seemed to extend only to himself.

Schyler turned her head away and stared through the open window, letting the wind cool her down for the first time that day. Cash was practically inviting her to tell him about the doll. She didn't because she didn't trust him enough. That disturbed her deeply. There were no boundaries to their physical intimacy, but she couldn't trust him with her secrets. She didn't even want to mention Jigger's appearance at the site of the accident that morning.

He pulled the truck to a stop while they were still a distance away from the mansion. "I don't want to give Cotton another heart attack by coming any closer," he said bitterly.

"You drove right up to the front door this morning."

"This morning there was an emergency. Even Cotton could understand and forgive that."

"Better than he could understand and forgive you for delivering his inebriated teenaged daughter?"

He laughed shortly. "I could deny it till kingdom come and he'll always believe that I was the one who got you drunk that night at the lake. He probably thinks I took sexual liberties, too."

"But that's not what you argued about."

His grin evaporated. His eyes homed in on her face as though it were the target and they were a laser weapon. "What did you say?"

Obviously that night was a sore spot with him. She considered dropping the subject then and there, but she was compelled to solve this riddle, to find the clue that had always been missing. "I said that's not what you and Daddy argued about that night."

"How do you know what we argued about?"

"I overheard you yelling at each other."

He stared at her for a long moment. "Oh, really? Then you tell me. What did we argue about?"

"I can't remember." A crease formed between her eyebrows as she strained her memory. "I was so woozy. But I remember you shouting at each other. It must have been an argument over something important. Was it Monique?"

"That's been over ten years ago." He slumped down in the seat behind the steering wheel and cupped his hand over his mouth, staring out into the darkness. "I've forgotten what it was about."

"You're lying," Schyler said softly. His head snapped around. "You remember. Whatever you argued with Daddy about still isn't resolved, is it?" Cash didn't answer her. He looked away again.

"Ah, to hell with it," Schyler muttered. It was between the two of them. Let it fester. She was too tired to try to lance that ancient wound tonight. "Thanks for everything you did today. Bye."

Schyler put her shoulder to the door. It was necessary for without that boost, she doubted she would have had the strength to open it. As soon as her feet hit the ground, she bent down and slipped off her shoes. The grass felt wonderfully cool and clean and soothing beneath her feet.

Keeping within the shadows beneath the trees, she made her way toward the house. The purple twilight made the painted white bricks of Belle Terre look pink and ethereal, like the castle in Camelot. The windows shone with mellow, golden light. The bougainvillea vine that garnished one corner column of the veranda was heavy with vivid blossoms.

A pang of homesickness and love seized Schyler until it was painful to breathe. Physical and mental fatigue had brought her emotions to the surface. She braced herself against a chest-high live oak branch and stared through the balmy dusk at the home she loved, but which always seemed just beyond her grasp.

She had lived there most of her life. The walls had heard her weeping and her laughter. The floorboards had borne her weight when she learned to crawl and when she learned to waltz. She'd watched the birth of a foal and received her first kiss in the stable. Her life was wrapped around the house as surely as the bougainvillea was wrapped around the column.

But the spirit, the heart, of the house eluded her. She could never touch it. It was inexplicable, this feeling of being an interloper in her own home, yet it was undeniably there, a part of her she couldn't let rest. It was like being born without one of the senses. She couldn't miss it because it had never belonged to her, but she knew she was supposed to have it and felt the loss keenly. A sense of loss that made her sad was perpetually in the back of her mind.

She knew Cash was there before he actually touched her. He moved up behind her and folded his hands around her neck. "What's bothering you tonight, Miss Schyler?"

"You're a bastard."

"I always have been."

"I'm not referring to the circumstance of your birth. I'm referring to *you*. How you behave. How you treat other people."

"Namely you?"

"What you did and said to me this morning was crude, unnecessary, and unconscionable."

"I thought we settled this at the landing."

She made an impatient gesture with her shoulders. "I don't want hearts and flowers from you, Cash, but I do expect a little kindness."

"Don't."

Her head dropped forward in defeat. "You don't give an inch, do you? Never. You never give anything."

"No. Never."

She should have walked away from him, but she couldn't coax her feet to move, not when he was a solid pillar to lean against. She needed a shoulder to cry on. He was available, and he, more than anyone except her father, would understand how she felt.

"I'm afraid, Cash."

"Of what?"

"Of losing Belle Terre."

His thumbs centered themselves at the back of her neck and began massaging the tension out of the vertebrae. "You're doing everything you possibly can to make sure you don't."

"But I might. In spite of everything I do." She tilted her head to one side. He massaged the kinks out of her shoulder. "I take one step forward and get knocked back two."

"You're about to cash in on the deal that'll put Crandall Logging in the black and free up Belle Terre. What are you afraid of?"

"Of failing. If we don't get it all there, then the timber we've already shipped doesn't count. This last week is the most crucial. My saboteur knows that as well as I do." She breathed deeply and clenched her fist. "Who is it? And what does he have against me?"

"Probably nothing. His quarrel might be with Cotton."

"That's the same thing."

"Hurt Cotton, hurt you?"

"Yes. I love him. I couldn't love him any more if he were my natural father. Maybe because I understand why he loves this place so much. He came here an outsider, too. He had to prove himself worthy of Belle Terre."

Cash said nothing, but his strong fingers continued to knead away her tension and distress. The massage loosened her tongue as well.

"Macy was never a mother to me. She was just a lovely, but terribly unhappy, woman who inhabited the same house and laid down the rules of conduct. Cotton was my parent. My anchor." She sighed deeply. "But our roles have switched, haven't they? I feel like a mama bear fighting to protect her cub. I'm desperately inadequate to protect him."

"Cotton doesn't need your protection. He'll have to pay for his mistakes. And there won't be a damn thing you can do about it when the time of reckoning comes."

"Don't say that," she whispered fiercely. "That frightens me. I can't let him down." Cash had moved up close behind her. His lips found a vulnerable spot on the back of her neck beneath her braid. He lifted her hands to the branch of the tree and placed them there. "Cash, what are you doing?"

"Giving you something to think about besides all your troubles." Now that her arms were out of the way and he had an open field, he slid his hands up and down her narrow rib cage, grazing the sides of her breasts.

"I don't want to think about anything else. Anyway, I'm still angry with you."

"Anger's made for some of the best sex I've ever had."

"Well I don't think of it as an aphrodisiac." She sucked in her breath sharply when he reached around her and cupped her breasts. "Don't." Responding to the feebleness in her voice and not to the protest itself, he pulled her blouse apart, unfastened her bra, and laid his hands over her bared breasts. "This is . . . no. Not here. Not now. Cash."

Her objections fell on deaf ears. His open mouth was moving up and down her neck, taking love bites, while his fingers lightly twisted her nipples. He tilted his hips forward. Reflexively she pressed her bottom against his erection.

"You want me," he growled. "You know you do. I know you do."

He slipped one hand beneath her skirt. He pushed down her panties and palmed the downy delta at the top of her thighs. She sighed his name, in remonstration, in desire. "No," she groaned, ashamed of the melting sensation that made her thighs weak and pliant.

He hissed a yes into the darkness as his fingers sought and found the slipperiness that made her a liar. He raised her skirt and pulled her against him. The cloth of his jeans against her derriere was rough, soft, wonderful.

Then his thumbs, stroking her cleft, down, down until they parted the swollen lips. She pressed her forehead into the hard wood of the branch and gripped it with her hands. "Cash." His name was a low, serrated moan of longing.

He deftly unzipped his jeans. His entry was slow, deliberate. He was ruthlessly stingy with himself until his own passions governed him and he sheathed himself within the moist, satiny fist of her sex. He ground against her. The hair on his belly tickled her smooth skin.

Schyler flung her head back, seeking his lips with hers. Their open mouths clung together; tongues searched out each other. He fanned one tight, raised nipple with his fingers. His other hand covered her mound. His stroking middle finger quickly escalated her to an explosive climax.

His coming was long and fierce and scalding. When it was over, he slumped forward and let her support him. Both might have collapsed to the carpet of grass had not Schyler been braced against the limb of the tree.

Eventually he restored her clothing and his. Schyler let him. She was too physically drained to move. And too emotionally unstrung to speak.

My God, what she had just done was unthinkable. Yet it had happened. She wasn't sorry, only deeply disturbed, because while he'd been holding her she'd been inundated with him. She had forgotten her problems. She had forgotten everything, including Belle Terre.

She spun around when she heard the engine of his pickup being gunned to life, not realizing that he'd slipped away. It was just as well, she thought, as she watched the truck disappear down the lane. She wouldn't have known what to say to him anyway.

Parked on the edge of the ditch, Cash waited until the last of Jigger's gawking customers left before he pulled up in front of the derelict house. Even over the noise of the pickup's motor, he could hear the rattlesnake in the drum.

He cut the motor and got out. Through the screened back door, he could see Jigger hunched over the kitchen table counting the day's take. Cash knocked loudly. The old man whirled around. He was holding a pistol aimed directly at the door.

"Calm down, Jigger. It's me."

"I nearly blew your fool head off, don'tcha know." He dropped his money on the table and shuffled toward the door.

"What do you do with all your money, Jigger? Stuff it in

mayonnaise jars and bury it in your yard? Or maybe under your kennel?"

The old man's eyes glittered. "You want to know, Boudreaux," he taunted, slowly waving the pistol back and forth just beneath Cash's nose, "you try to find out."

Cash laughed. "Do I look stupid to you?" Then his smile disappeared altogether. "I assure you, I'm not."

Jigger lowered his head and peered up at Cash from hooded eye sockets. "I should shoot you anyway. You helped my black bitch get away. You took her to Belle Terre."

"You nearly killed her."

"That's none of your business."

"Oh, but it is. You didn't leave her alone after the miscarriage like I told you to. I take that personally, Jigger."

"It wasn't me. It was a customer."

"It's still your fault."

Jigger executed a Gallic shrug. "She's just a woman. I'll get me another one."

"Fine with me," Cash said with deceptive nonchalance. "But if you ever work over another woman the way you did Gayla Frances, I'll come here, cut off your cock, and stuff it down your throat until you choke. Understand, *mon ami*?" Cash leaned against the door frame where the paint was chipped and peeling. His eyes didn't blink, but there was a trace of a smile on his lips.

"You threaten me?"

"*Oui*. And you know I don't threaten lightly."

Jigger's face split into a parody of a grin. "You got the hots for the bitch, hey Boudreaux?" Then he shook his head. "No. You're fuckin' Schyler Cran-*dall*."

"That's right, I'm fucking Schyler Crandall," Cash said tightly. "But I'm still looking out for Gayla."

The two men eyed each other antagonistically. Finally Jigger threw back his head and cackled. Cash Boudreaux was perhaps the only man in the parish who intimidated him. Jigger was smart enough to know when retreat was prudent. He didn't want to test the other man's reputed temper and skill with the knife that always rode in the small of his back. If one were measuring meanness, they were equal, but Cash was twenty years younger, thirty pounds lighter, and much swifter. Physically, Jigger was no match for him.

Cash relaxed his tense stance and eased himself away from the doorjamb. "Are you going to show me your rattler or did I drive out here for nothing?" He angled his head in the direction of the oil drum.

Jigger shoved the pistol in the waistband of his trousers. He strutted across the yard toward the drum. A light cord had been strung from the house. A bare bulb dangled over the drum. Jigger switched it on. With a proud flourish he knocked the rock off the lid and prised it open with a tire tool.

"Look at that son of a bitch, Boudreaux. Ever see such?"

Unlike most spectators, Cash approached the oil drum with a casual, intrepid stride. He walked right up to it and peered over the rim. The rattler's tail was flicking, filling the still night air with its insidious racket. Even the nocturnal birds and insects in the trees had fallen silent out of respect and fear. The pit bull bitch barked, then whined apprehensively.

Jigger waited excitedly to hear Cash's reaction. He was sorely disappointed when Cash shrugged, unimpressed. "Fact is, I have seen such, lots of times, in the bayous."

"Bloody hell."

"I'm not lying. Once a flood washed up a whole colony of cottonmouths. *Maman* wouldn't let me play outdoors for days. The yard was working alive with those snakes. All sizes. Some as big or bigger than this. Could have swallowed a dog whole."

He leaned over the barrel for a closer look and stayed a long time. Jigger peered over his shoulder. When Cash spun around abruptly, Jigger dropped his short crowbar and leaped backward.

Cash smiled with sheer devilment. "Why, Jigger, I do believe this snake makes you nervous."

"Bull*shit*." Angrily Jigger picked up the lid, tossed it back onto the drum and maneuvered it into place with the crowbar he'd retrieved from the ground. When he was done, he stuck out his hand. "One dollar."

"Sure." Never breaking his stare, Cash fished in his tight jean pocket and came up with a crumpled one-dollar bill. "It was well worth a dollar just to see you jump like that." He strolled toward his parked truck.

"Boudreaux!" Cash turned around and faced the man standing in front of the drum. "You know who sent me this snake?"

Cash only grinned through the darkness before disappearing into it.

Chapter Forty-nine

Schyler slept late. When her alarm went off at the regular time, she rolled over, shut if off, and promptly went back to sleep. Hours later she woke up. She glanced at the clock and discovered that it was closer to lunch than breakfast. She should feel ashamed; but after the hellish day she had had yesterday, she decided that she deserved to take a morning off. She showered and dressed quickly and was soon in the kitchen doing damage to a honeydew melon.

"You can have chicken salad for lunch, if you'll wait an hour for it to chill," Mrs. Dunne told her.

"Thanks, but I need to get to the office." Sometime during the night, in her subconscious, a thought concerning their last shipment to Endicott's had struck her. Luckily she remembered it this morning and was eager to discuss it with Cash.

"Well if you ask me, you're working too hard."

"I didn't ask," she retorted, but kindly, as she winked at the housekeeper on her way out. As she went past the parlor doors, she saw Gayla in there dusting the books on the shelves. "Gayla, I asked you to catalog those books, not dust them. That's what I pay Mrs. Dunne to do."

"I don't mind. I ran out of chores. I feel guilty just sitting around mooching off you."

"You're not mooching." Schyler smiled up at Gayla, who was perched on a ladder. She got only a faint smile from Gayla in return. "Is something wrong? No more voodoo dolls, I hope."

"No." Distractedly Gayla gazed through the wide windows. The expansive lawn, full of sunlight and serenity, hardly looked threatening. "It's just that I...I..." She sighed and shook her head in self-derision. "Nothing."

"What?"

Gayla made a helpless gesture with her dust cloth. "The yard looks so peaceful and harmless now. But when it gets dark outside, I have the eerie feeling that something or someone is out there watching us."

"Gayla," Schyler chided gently.

"I know it's stupid. I jump at my own shadow."

"That's understandable after all you've been through. The doll was a very real threat. I was reluctant to call the sheriff's office to come out and investigate, but if you want me to I will."

"No," Gayla exclaimed. "Don't do that. Besides, it wouldn't do any good. The sheriff is a friend of Jigger's."

"Then you're certain he was responsible?"

"He probably paid somebody to put it in my room."

"I'm sure he just wanted to scare you. I doubt it'll go any further than that. For all his chicanery, Jigger Flynn wouldn't dare set foot on Belle Terre."

"I hope not." There wasn't much conviction behind Gayla's voice.

Schyler lowered herself to the padded arm of an easy chair. "That's not all, is it?"

"No."

"Tell me."

Gayla climbed down the ladder and dropped her cloth into a basket of cleaning supplies. Her narrow shoulders lifted and fell on a deep sigh. "I don't know if I can pinpoint what's wrong, Schyler."

"Try."

"You're too busy to listen to my whining."

"I've got time. What's on your mind?"

Taking a moment to collect her thoughts, Gayla said, "I've just been wondering what I'm going to do with the rest of my life. I don't have enough college to get a good job. I'm too old to go back to school. Even if I wasn't, I couldn't afford it." She raised troubled eyes. "What is there for me to do? Where should I go? How will I live?"

Schyler rose and embraced her fondly. "Don't rush yourself to make a decision. Things will get sorted out in time. Something will turn up. In the meantime you have a home here."

"I can't go on living off you, Schyler."

"It makes me angry when you say that."

She tilted Gayla's head up. Looking into Gayla's eyes was like looking into twin cups of chicory coffee. They were that large, that dark, that fluid. They should be laughing; instead they were full of despair.

It was disappointing to Schyler that Jimmy Don Davison hadn't responded to that letter she had mailed him in prison. She had hoped that once he knew Gayla had left Jigger in fear of her life, he would contact her. She had gambled on him being curious about his lost love at the very least. Obviously he wasn't.

A forgiving letter from Jimmy Don would be like a tonic to Gayla. It would imbue her with optimism for the future. Schyler had no way of knowing how Jimmy Don felt about his former sweetheart, but surely once he was acquainted with the circumstances, he wouldn't hold Gayla's recent past against her.

"It's too pretty a day to worry about the future," Schyler said softly. "I don't want to think about you leaving Belle Terre. It makes me sad. I don't know what I would have done without your friendship these past few weeks."

Gayla's eyes cleared of misery, but they flashed with anger. "Tricia's been so hateful to you. How do you stand it?"

"I try to ignore the swipes she takes at me."

"I don't see how you can. And her husband just stands

there and lets her get by with it." Gayla shook her head. With a wisdom beyond her years that was probably inherited from Veda, she added, "There's something wrong there."

"Wrong where?"

"With them."

"Like what?"

"I'm not sure. They're sneaky. Both of them. They carry on whispered telephone conversations. Are you aware of that? When I walk past, they hang up, or start talking real loud, like I'm too stupid to tell that they're faking it." She looked at Schyler worriedly. "I wouldn't trust them if I were you."

Those furtive telephone conversations were probably being placed to realtors. Gayla didn't know about the Howells' plan to put Belle Terre up for sale. Schyler laughed off her warning. "I doubt they're plotting to smother me in my bed."

"Mr. Howell hasn't got the balls. But she does. She hates you, Schyler. I don't know how two girls can be raised as sisters and turn out so differently."

"We come from different stock."

"Well I think Tricia is a bad seed. Mark my words."

"She's just insecure about her self-worth." Gayla's intuition made Schyler more uneasy than she wanted to acknowledge. Still, and to Gayla's annoyance, she defended Tricia. "Mother ignored both of us, but Daddy made no secret of favoring me. Years of living with that turned Tricia sour."

"I respect you for taking up for her. But don't give her your back."

With that warning echoing in her ears, Schyler left Gayla in the parlor and headed toward the back of the house. She checked Cotton's room, but he wasn't there. She found him outside, sitting in a lawn chair and feeding shelled pecans to squirrels that ate the treats right out of his hand. When Schyler appeared, they scattered across the lawn and into the nearest trees.

"Spoilsport," Cotton said, frowning at her.

"Good morning to you, too." She leaned down and gave

him a quick kiss before dropping into the chair beside his. "How are you this morning? I feel glorious." Pointing her toes far in front of her and reaching high over her head with both arms, she stretched luxuriously.

"You should. You've slept away half the day."

"Well after yesterday, I thought I deserved it."

"Reckon you do. Quite a mess, wasn't it?"

"How did you know?" He'd already been asleep when she came in last night.

She followed his gaze down to the morning newspaper lying on the small table between their chairs. Even reading upside down, Schyler could see that the front page was dominated by an account of the Crandall Logging rig accident. The accompanying picture featured Cash, standing astride one of the massive logs, overseeing the chore of clearing the highway.

"Cash was right there in the thick of it, I see."

Schyler knew better than to take her father's comment at face value, but she pretended to. "He's a born organizer. The other loggers would walk through a wall of fire for him."

"Hmm." One of the squirrels had decided that Schyler posed no danger and had crept back for more nuts. Cotton leaned out of his chair and tossed it a pecan half.

"Does Mrs. Dunne know you've got those? Pecans that pretty should be going into a pie."

"Don't change the subject," Cotton said crossly.

"I didn't know there was one," Schyler fired right back.

"Why didn't you tell me about this accident?"

"I haven't seen you since the accident."

"Why didn't you ask for my advice when Boudreaux came roaring up here yesterday morning?"

"I'm sorry. Did he disturb you?"

"He's always disturbed me."

She ignored that and answered his original question with forced calm. "I didn't tell you about it or ask your advice because frankly I didn't think about it."

"I'll have you know, young lady, that I'm still the head of this goddamn company," he bellowed.

"But you're temporarily out of commission."

"So you've turned the whole operation over to that Cajun bastard."

"Now wait a minute, Daddy. I depend on Cash, yes, but I still make the decisions. On most of the major ones, I've consulted you. Yesterday was an exception. I had to act spontaneously. I didn't have time to weigh my options. There were no options."

"You could have phoned. You could have kept me posted."

"I could have, I suppose, but since your surgery I've tried to insulate you from the day-to-day hardships of running the business."

"Well don't do me anymore goddamn favors. I don't want to be insulated. I'll be insulated for a long time when they seal me in a friggin' casket. Don't rush it."

It took an enormous amount of self-control for Schyler to remain silent and let that go by without comment. Like a catechism, she mentally recited all the reasons why she should overlook his unfair allegations. He wasn't to be excited or upset. Stress of any kind could be dangerous, if not deadly. He was prone to depression and contrariness when his pride was in jeopardy.

In a carefully regulated voice she said, "Now that you're obviously feeling so much stronger, I'll consult you on business matters. It was only out of consideration for your health that I hadn't before now."

"That's bullshit." He jabbed a finger in her direction. "You didn't consult me because you've got Cash to talk to." A vein in his temple began to throb, but neither of them noticed. "Do the two of you talk shop in bed?"

Schyler flinched guiltily. She stopped breathing for a moment. When her involuntary responses eventually took over again, she raised her chin a notch and bravely challenged her father's censorious stare.

"I'm a grown woman. I won't discuss my personal life with you."

He banged his fist on the arm of his chair. "We're not talking about your personal life. You got passed over for your sister. She duped us all into believing Howell had knocked her up. You lived with a goddamn fairy for six years. After all that, why would I start caring about who you're screwing? I don't."

"Then what are you shouting at me for?"

He moved his face closer to hers. "Because this time your bedmate is Cash Boudreaux."

"And that makes a difference?"

"You're damn right it does. He's too close to my business, my home. Your affair with him affects everything I've worked my ass off for."

"How?"

"Because that Cajun bastard—"

Schyler shot out of her chair and bore down on him. "Stop calling him that! He can't help being born illegitimate."

Cotton flopped back in his chair and looked up at his daughter with disbelief. "God almighty. You're in love with him."

Her face went blank. She continued staring at her father a few thudding heartbeats longer, then turned away. She braced her arms on the back of the chair she'd been sitting in, leaning against it for additional support.

Cotton wasn't finished with her yet. He sat up straight and scooted to the edge of his seat. "You dare to defend that man to me. To *me*." He thumped his chest. Inside it, shooting pains were leaving fissions in the walls of his heart. He was too irate to notice. "Have you made the pitiful blunder of falling in love with that skirt chaser, with Cash Boudreaux?"

She flung herself away from the chair and angrily confronted Cotton again. "Why not? You were in love with his mother."

They glared at each other so hard that neither could stand the open animosity for long. They lowered their eyes simultaneously. "So you know," Cotton said after awhile.

"I know."

"Since when?"

"Recently."

"He told you?"

"No, Tricia did."

He sighed. "What the hell? I'm surprised you didn't

know all along. Everybody else in the parish did." Cotton cracked another pecan, dug out the meat and passed it to an inquisitive and intrepid squirrel. "I committed adultery with Monique for years. I made her an adulteress."

"Yes."

"And I would do it again." Father and daughter looked at each other. "Even if it meant burning in hell for eternity, I would love Monique Boudreaux again." He leaned back in his chair again and rested his head against the wicker. "Macy wasn't a... a warm woman, Schyler. She equated passion with a loss of self-control. She was incapable of feeling it."

"Monique Boudreaux was?"

A ghost of a smile lifted his pale lips. "Ah, yes," he breathed. "She was. She did everything passionately, laugh, scold, make love." Schyler watched his eyes become transfixed, as though he were looking into a mirror of memory, seeing a happier time. "She was a very beautiful woman."

Schyler was amazed by the expression on his face. She'd never seen Cotton's features look that soft. His vulnerability affected her deeply. "I think Cash is a beautiful man."

Instantaneously Cotton's expression changed again. It grew hard and ugly. His smiling lips turned downward with contempt. "He's done a real number on you, hasn't he? You actually trust him."

"He's been invaluable to me. I depend on him. He's the most intelligent, instinctive forester around. Everybody says so."

"Dammit, I know that," Cotton snarled. "I depend on his professional judgment, too, but I don't crawl into bed with him. I don't even turn my back on him for fear I'll get a knife in it."

"Cash isn't like that," she said, wishing she believed it herself.

"Isn't he? When he was telling you about Monique and me, did he mention all his threats?"

"Threats?"

"I see he didn't."

"I know the two of you have had several vicious arguments. One being the night he brought me home from Thibodaux Pond. Remember that? It was right after Mama died."

"I remember," he answered guardedly.

"Cash helped me that night. He wasn't the one who plied me with beer. You unfairly blamed him for my condition."

"Cash never does anything out of the goodness of his heart. He might not have been the one that got you drunk, but don't be misled into thinking he was concerned with your welfare."

"What did the two of you argue about that night?"

"I don't remember."

He was lying, too, just as Cash had. "Monique?"

"I don't remember. Probably. When Macy died, Cash demanded that I marry his mother."

Schyler searched his face, looking for the soft expression of love that had been there only moments ago. "Why didn't you, Daddy? If you were so in love with her, why didn't you marry her when Mama died?" Feeling guilty she asked, "Because of Tricia and me?"

"No. Because of a pledge I had made Macy."

"But she was dead."

"That didn't matter. I'd given her my word. I couldn't marry Monique. She understood and was resigned to it. Cash wasn't."

"Can you blame him? You made his mother's life hell. Did you know she had miscarried your child?"

Cotton's eyes clouded with tears. "Damn him for telling you that."

"Is it true?"

"Yes. But I didn't know she was pregnant until afterwards. I swear to God I didn't."

She believed him. He might have lied by omission, but he'd never told her a lie that was an outright contradiction to truth. "Monique lived in a very gray area, an outcast of society. She couldn't even observe her religion because of her life with you."

"It was her choice as much as mine to live as she did."

"But when Mama died, when you had a chance to rectify that, you didn't."

"I couldn't," he repeated on a shout. "I told Cash that. Now I'm telling you. I *couldn't*." Cotton paused to draw a deep breath. "That's when Cash swore on his mother's rosary that he would get vengeance. He accused me of making her a whore. He promised not to stop until he's brought ruination to me and to Belle Terre." He gasped for sufficient oxygen. "Why do you think a man with his expertise has hung 'round here all these years, living like white trash down there in that shanty on the bayou?"

"I asked him that."

"And what did he say?"

"He said he had promised his mother on her deathbed that he would never leave Belle Terre as long as you were alive. She asked him to watch over you."

That gave Cotton pause. For a moment, he stared sightlessly at Schyler, then into near space. Finally, he shook his head stubbornly. "I don't believe that for a minute. He's been biding his time. Waiting like a panther about to pounce. You came back from England with sex-deprived gonads and *bam!*, he saw his opportunity to finally get his revenge. Because I was laid up, he had access to you that he'd never had before. He took full advantage, didn't he?"

"No."

"Didn't he?"

"No!"

Cotton's eyes narrowed to slits. "Didn't he seize a golden opportunity to pay me back for screwing his mother? Everybody around here knows how I feel about you, Schyler. The boy's not dense. If he wanted to fuck me real good, the best way he could do it was fuck the daughter I love best."

Schyler crammed her fist against her lips and shook her head vehemently while tears of doubt filled her eyes.

"He's as cunning as a swamp fox, Schyler," Cotton rasped. "Monique was proud. She never would take any money from me. They barely scraped by. Growing up as he did messed with Cash's mind. He's warped. He hates us.

He has all Monique's charm, but none of her compassion or sweetness."

Cotton wagged his finger at her in warning. "You cannot trust him. Do, and we're doomed. He'll do anything, say anything, to bring us down. Don't doubt that for a single instant."

Schyler, unable to tolerate another word, turned and fled.

Chapter Fifty

It wasn't true, she told herself.

By the time Schyler reached the landing office, however, the doubts that Cotton had raised obscured her certainty like a thundercloud blotting out the sun.

She braked and shoved open the car door. Cash's pickup was parked beside one of the scales. He was here, not in the forest. She was glad she wouldn't have to chase him down. This confrontation couldn't wait. She wanted to know, and know immediately, that Cotton was wrong. She needed to know that she was right.

She bolted into the office and swung the door closed behind her with a loud crash. Cash was sitting at the desk, entering data into an adding machine. He glanced up. His brow was beetled, his lips a hard, narrow line. "You're not going to believe this, Schyler. Ken Howell's been screwing you."

"So have you."

Her voice was soft, but chilly and taut. It was obviously not what he had expected. His brow gradually smoothed itself out. He regarded her carefully. She was standing rigidly against the door, blinking rapidly with indignation, like a temperance marcher who'd just detected demon rum in the punch. His eyes leisurely swept down her highly strung posture, then back up. He casually tossed the pencil he'd been using onto the littered desk and stacked his hands behind his head.

"That's right, I have. And so far I haven't heard you complaining about it."

Her breasts shuddered with her uneven breath. "Why do you? Why did you want to in the first place?"

"Why?" he repeated on an incredulous laugh. When he saw that she wasn't being facetious, he answered flippantly. "It feels good."

"That's the only reason, because it feels good?" Her voice was hoarse. "Then any woman would do, right? So why me?"

He lowered his hands and stood up. Coming around the corner of the desk, he propped himself against the edge of it, studying her all the while. "What brought this on all of a sudden? A bad case of cramps?"

"Just answer me, Cash," she said in a shrill, impatient voice. "Just about any woman could give you an erection and make it feel good, so why me?"

He gnawed on the corner of his lip. "You want it straight?"

"I want it straight."

"Okay," he said insolently. "I guess you just make it feel better than anybody has in a long time. I wanted you that day I saw you sleeping under the tree. Every time I saw you after that, I wanted you a little bit more. Until I had you."

"That must have been thrilling for you. My capitulation."

"It was," he said with brutal honesty. "It was thrilling for you, too."

She bit her lip hard to keep from crying. "Why didn't you say anything?"

"When?"

"After the first time."

"Because you looked down at me like you expected an

apology. I never apologize to a woman. For anything. But especially not for screwing her."

"You had what you wanted. I had surrendered. I'd even come to you. Why didn't you just leave it at that?"

He looked at her strangely. "Because I wasn't satisfied. I'm still not. I like your tits, your legs, your ass, your mouth, those breathy little sounds you make when you come, and the way you give head. Now should I go on or stop with that?"

Schyler's emotions waged war. The lady that Macy had groomed wanted to slap his face and storm out. The woman in her wanted to fling herself against him, kiss him, love him. Cotton's daughter wanted to scratch and claw at him. She wanted to inflict pain that would hurt him as much as the cold detachment in his voice was hurting her.

"Why . . . why did you take me last night at Belle Terre?"

"I got the urge."

"Why in that particular way?"

"Don't pretend you didn't like it. You were dripping."

"I didn't say I didn't like it," she yelled. "I asked you why you did it then and there."

"Because it felt—"

"Good?"

"*Oui*!" he shouted. "And right. It felt right. I went with the flow, okay? I didn't stop to reason it out. My cock was doing my thinking."

"From what I hear, it usually does."

He made a hissing sound through his teeth. "Look, you wanted it. I wanted it. I was hard. You were creamy. We did it and it was fine with both of us at the time." He stood up and advanced on her. The lock of hair hanging over his brow was trembling with anger. "So what's the big fuckin' deal, huh? Why the cross-examination? Can we drop this and talk about something important, like how your brother-in-law has been cleverly skimming off the books for years?" His eyes turned dark. "Or better yet, why don't you climb on my lap and do something about this monstrous hard-on I've grown as a result of our conversation?"

"That's not funny."

"You're damn right it's not."

Seething, Schyler said tightly, "Tell me about Ken."

"Simple. He's a crook. He's the reason the company's been losing money in spite of steady business. I don't know if Cotton knew and overlooked it because Howell is family, or if he's gone dotty in his old age. It was Howell who robbed Endicott. Apparently he endorsed Cotton's signature on their check, cashed it and pocketed the money, but failed to mention that order and advance payment to anybody." He waved his hand toward the ledgers on the desk. "Those records are shot full of holes that he made."

"How do you know all this?"

"Glee uncovered the number-juggling Howell had done to make the sums come out right."

"Glee?"

"You said he needed something to do. I took duplicate records over to him. He's been going over them. He said they weren't—"

"Who gave you the authority to do that?" Schyler was furious.

"What?"

"You heard me."

He tossed back his hair with a jerk of his head. "Let me get this straight." His left knee unhitched, throwing him slightly off center and into an arrogant stance. "You're upset because Glee turned up the goods to send your ex-lover to jail?"

"No," she ground out. "I'm upset because you assumed authority that I didn't give you."

"Oh, I see," he said coldly, "I overstepped my bounds."

"That's right."

"Does this have anything to do with our previous discussion? Am I overstepping my bounds every time I take Miss Schyler Crandall to bed?"

"Isn't that part of the kick for you? Overstepping bounds? Flaunting authority? Trespassing? Isn't that why you make love to me?"

"I don't make love."

Schyler tried not to flinch. "I see. You don't make love. You rut."

He made a dismissive motion with his shoulder. "I guess that's as good a word as any." He saw the pale, bleak expression settle over her face. It brought a soft curse to his lips. "I call a spade a spade. I don't believe in the word love, so I don't use it. It doesn't mean anything. All I've ever seen people do in the name of love is hurt each other. Your father claimed to love my mother."

"He did. He told me so this morning."

"Then why did he stay with a woman he didn't love, didn't even like? Because this grand love he claimed to have for my mother wasn't as strong as his own goddamn ambition and greed. My mother claimed to love me." He swiped the air in front of him to cancel out the protestation he saw rising from Schyler's lips.

"But when she died, you know who she was crying for? Cotton. Cotton! Who'd treated her like shit. She cried because she didn't want to leave Cotton." He shook his head in bewilderment and disgust. He laughed bitterly. "There's just no percentage in this love bullshit. The inventor of it got nailed to a cross. So explain its attraction. Sure, you can toss the word around if it makes things look prettier than they are. If it justifies the reasons people do things, go ahead. Use the word. But it doesn't mean a damn thing."

Schyler said gruffly, "I'm sorry for you."

"Save it. I don't want anything to do with love. Not if it means letting people mop up the floor with me and then begging them to do it again. Fuck passive resistance. Cash Boudreaux fights back."

"An eye for an eye."

"Precisely. And then some."

"So since Cotton used your mother, you felt justified to use me the same way." Her eyes moved up to meet his. There was no life in them, no compassion or human warmth. They reflected only her own disillusioned features. "Didn't you?"

"Is that what you think?"

She nodded slowly. "Yes. That's what I think." Her heart begged him to deny it. He didn't.

"I take it Cotton opened your eyes to me," he said calmly.

"He said you threatened to ruin him. Did you?" Cash said nothing. "You swore on your mother's rosary to destroy him and Belle Terre. Does that include frightening me? Tampering with the equipment? Causing delays? Making certain that a contract that would put the company on solid footing again doesn't get filled?"

His eyes glittered. "You're a smart lady. You figure it out."

"And it would be a big joke on all of us if you were sleeping with me at the same time, wouldn't it?"

"It brings a smile to my face just thinking about it."

But his face wasn't smiling. It was remote and cold. Wanting to crumple, Schyler forced herself to stand tall. "I want you out of here immediately. Don't come back. Don't go around the loggers either."

"You think you can stop me?"

"I won't have to. You wield tremendous influence over them. You could probably get them to walk off their jobs this afternoon." She tipped her head to one side. "But I wonder if they would go on strike if it meant giving up those promised bonuses. I wonder what they'd do to you if they suspected you of sabotaging the shipments and preventing them from getting those bonuses."

"I see you've got it all thought out."

"I want you off Belle Terre within a week. Vacate that house. Burn it to the ground for all I care. Just don't come back. If I ever see you on my property again, I'll shoot you."

He tried to stare her down, but she didn't succumb. He shrugged, went to the door, and pulled it open. "You'll never make the deadline without me, you know."

"I'll die trying."

He gave her a slow, assessing glance. "Maybe so."

Even the click of the latch when he closed the door behind him sounded as ominous as a gunshot.

Chapter Fifty-one

Schyler walked into the dining room at Belle Terre. Without a word, she slapped a manila folder on the table in front of Ken. "What's that?" he asked.

"Enough incriminating evidence to send you to jail."

Across the table, Tricia's fork halted midway between her plate and her mouth. Ken played innocent and smiled sickly. "What the hell are you talking about, Schyler?"

"I don't want to talk about anything in here where we might be overheard by Mrs. Dunne and Gayla. I'll meet you in the parlor."

Minutes later she was seated in a wing chair. Her bearing was indomitable, but she felt more like the feathery ball of a dandelion blossom on the verge of disintegration. She was ready to fly apart.

As Ken and Tricia entered the room, she said, "Please slide the doors closed."

"My, we're being so dramatic tonight." Tricia snuggled into a chair across from Schyler and draped her legs over the arm of it. She plucked several white grapes off the stalk she had brought in with her and popped them into her mouth. "I adore all this intrigue, but why is it necessary?"

"I'll let Ken tell you." Schyler, ignoring Tricia's irritating insolence, looked at her former fiancé. Comparisons were unfair, but she couldn't help measuring his failure against Cash's success. Ken had had all the advantages. He'd come from a good family, had a private school education, had money. He had squandered all those advantages. Cash had begun with nothing, not even legitimacy, and had built a successful life for himself. He still didn't have many material possessions, therefore his success couldn't be measured in dollars and cents. But he had earned more respect than ridicule.

She had loved both men. Both were liars and cheats. That was a worse reflection on her than on them. Obviously she had a tendency toward choosing the wrong men to love.

Ken tapped the edge of the folder against his palm. "Look, Schyler, I don't know what you think this file proves, but—"

"It proves that you've been embezzling money from Crandall Logging almost since my father put you on the payroll."

Tricia sat up straight and swung her feet to the floor. *"What?"*

"I don't know what the hell you're talking about," Ken sputtered.

"The figures are there in black and white, Ken," Schyler said evenly. "I've seen Father's forged signature on canceled checks."

Ken nervously wet his lips. "I don't know who put this . . . this outlandish idea into your head, but . . . It was Boudreaux, wasn't it? That son of a bitch," he spat. "He'll stop at nothing to cause disruption. Don't you see what he's doing? He's trying to turn you against me."

Schyler bowed her head and massaged her drumming temples. "Ken, stop it. Please. I've known for weeks, ever since I went to Endicott's, that there were discrepancies in the bookkeeping. I couldn't figure out why Daddy had ignored them until the company was on the brink of bankruptcy."

"I'll tell you."

All heads turned toward the sound of Cotton's voice. He hadn't parted the wide sliding doors that separated the parlors, but stood in the doorway that led into the hall. He was thinner than before his illness, but when he stood at his full height, as now, he could still be intimidating and seemingly invincible.

He came into the room. "I ignored it because I didn't

want to admit that there was a thief living under my own roof."

"Now just a—"

"Shut up," Cotton commanded his son-in-law. "You're a goddamn thief. And a liar. You're a gambler, which I could forgive if you were any good at it. But you don't gamble any better than you do anything else. I know all about the heavies you owe money to."

Ken had started to sweat. At his sides his fists opened and closed reflexively.

"What's he talking about, Ken?" Tricia asked.

It was Cotton, however, who answered her. "He's in debt up to his ass with a loan shark."

"Is that why you asked me for money?" Schyler wanted to know.

Ken foundered for an answer. Cotton frowned at him disparagingly. "I was kinda hoping they'd get rough and scare some sense into you. But you're too stupid to take their warnings seriously. Then I started hoping they would go ahead and kill you. This family would have been shed of you and we could pass it off as robbery and murder."

"You better stop right there, old man," Ken warned.

Cotton paid no attention to him. "I never could stomach you, Howell. You might have hoodwinked both my daughters, but I had your number the day you let that little bitch," he said, pointing at Tricia, "get by with that lie about carrying your kid. You're a weakling, a sorry excuse for a man, and I can't stand the sight or the smell of you. You stink of failure."

Schyler left her chair. "Daddy, sit down." Cotton's face was florid. He was gasping for breath. She took his arm and led him to the nearest chair, easing him into it.

Her ministrations annoyed him. "You all seem to think that when my heart went on the blink, my brain did, too. You've been pussyfooting around this house, not wanting the old man to get drift of what was going on. But I know, all right. I know everything. And I can't say I like much of it."

"All the trouble started when Schyler came home," Tricia said peevishly. "Things were rocking along fine until then. She just moved in and took over."

"What did she take from you?" Cotton asked.

"My husband," Tricia replied venomously.

"That's a lie!" Schyler cried.

Cotton gave Schyler a baleful look. "Do you still want him?"

"No."

He looked back at Tricia. "She doesn't want him. I'd think she was crazy if she did. What else have you got to bellyache about?"

"She took over the management of this house. She fired the housekeeper."

"Thank Jesus, Mary and Joseph," Cotton said. "That Graves woman was a shriveled-up, dried-up old shrew who couldn't cook worth a damn. I say good riddance."

"What about that black person who's living with us?"

"Veda's girl? What about her?"

"Thanks to Schyler she's got the run of the place. God only knows what kind of diseases she brought with her."

"That's a dreadful thing to say," Schyler exclaimed furiously.

Tricia glared up at her. "You'd turn this house into a refuge for every color of riffraff if we'd let you. Mama would roll over in her grave."

"Your mother never had a kind thought for anybody," Cotton said to Tricia. "And neither have you. At least Schyler doesn't have your prejudices."

Tricia's breasts heaved with indignation. "Of course. Sure. Certainly. Take up for Schyler. No matter what she does, it's okay with you, isn't it?" Her blue eyes flashed. "Well, did you know she's sleeping with Cash Boudreaux? *Cash Boudreaux*! I mean, my God, that's scraping the bottom of the barrel, isn't it? What do you think about your precious Schyler now, Daddy?"

"I didn't come in here to discuss Schyler's love life."

"No," Tricia shouted. "Of course not. Schyler's perfect even if she's bedding down with lowlife."

"That's enough!"

"Daddy, calm down."

"Tricia, just shut up," Ken yelled.

"I won't," Tricia screamed at her husband. "Daddy's right. You are a weakling to just stand there and not even defend yourself. Why don't you defend me?" She jabbed her index finger into her breast. She was bristling with rage. Spittle had collected in the corners of her lips. "I stayed here in this tacky, rundown old house for years while Schyler was living the high life in London. I stayed and took care of you," she said, turning to Cotton, "when Schyler deserted you. And this is the thanks I get. You still throw her up to me as an example to live by."

Cotton's gaze penetrated Tricia to the core of her being. "You stayed here with me so Schyler couldn't come home. That's the only reason. It wasn't out of affection."

She collected herself and drew in several deep breaths. In a small voice she said, "Why that's simply not true, Daddy."

Cotton's white head nodded. "Oh, yes it is. You didn't want Ken. You just knew that Schyler did. And you didn't want to live at Belle Terre. You knew that it killed Schyler's soul to leave it." Staring at her, he shook his head sadly. "You've never had a single unselfish thought, Tricia. If you ever had a drop of charitable blood in your veins, Macy polluted it with her autocratic philosophy. You're a self-indulgent, spiteful, lying bitch, Tricia. Much as it grieves me to say so."

Tricia shuddered under his verbal attack. "Whatever I am, it's your fault. You knew Mama didn't love us. You made up for it with Schyler. But not with me. You ignored me. You couldn't see me through Schyler's golden aura."

"I tried to love you. You won't let anybody love you. You're too busy being defensive about not coming out of Macy's womb. It never mattered to me that I didn't spawn you, but it sure as hell mattered to you."

Tricia came out of her chair slowly. Her eyes glowed with evil fire. "I'm glad I'm not your real daughter," she hissed. "You're coarse and crude, just like Mama always said you were. No wonder she wouldn't let you darken the door of her bedroom. You strut around like God almighty, but you're little better than white trash. That's exactly what you'd be if you hadn't married a Laurent."

She turned to Schyler. "And I'm glad I'm not your blood sister. You weren't content to come back and upset the household that I'd kept together even though I despise this place. You made my husband look like a fool for not seizing control of the business. Now you're accusing him of being a thief."

"He is a thief," Cotton barked.

It was easy for Schyler to disregard Tricia's vindictiveness. She was concerned for Cotton. This stress was what he needed least. "Daddy, we can talk about all this later."

"We'll talk about it now," he shouted, banging the arm of his chair. At the risk of upsetting him more, Schyler held her peace. Cotton focused his attention on Ken again. "You've bled my business for years. I should have put a stop to it when I first figured it out. I guess I hoped you'd grow some balls and stop before someone caught you at it."

"I wouldn't have had to dip into the company till if you'd paid me a decent salary."

"A decent salary?" Cotton repeated in a raised voice. "Goddamn you. What I pay you is more than three times what an average logger gets. And he sweats and strains and ruins his back and risks his life for every friggin' dollar." Cotton leaned forward in his chair. "What did you ever do to earn your handsome salary? I'll tell you. Play golf three afternoons a week and keep your butt folded over a padded pink leather stool at the country club bar."

"I've given six good years to Crandall Logging."

"With nothing to show for it," Cotton yelled back. "Nothing, that is, except a criminal record."

"If you had treated me like a man—"

"You never acted like a man."

"If you had given me more responsibility like you did Boudreaux, I'd've—"

"You'd've fucked up even worse," Cotton finished curtly.

That was like the final blast of steam out of a factory whistle. It was followed by a profound silence. Schyler spoke first. "We're all tired and short-tempered tonight. Maybe airing our differences has been good for us." She glanced down at her father. It hadn't been good for Cotton. He was leaning against the back of his chair, looking utterly exhausted. "Let's not talk anymore tonight. I think once this Endicott order is filled, we'll all feel a lot better."

"Is that all you ever think about?" Tricia asked.

"Right now that's all there is," Schyler replied shortly. "If we don't get the last shipment there in time, we don't get paid. If we don't get paid—"

"Belle Terre will be foreclosed upon. Well that would suit me just fine." Tricia's statement roused Cotton from his brief respite. He raised his head and looked at her as though he hadn't heard correctly. "In fact I hope that's exactly what happens."

"Tricia, shut up."

"Daddy may just as well know now how Ken and I feel, Schyler."

"Not now."

"Why not? We might not get another chance at a family discussion like this." She looked at Cotton. "Ken and I want to sell Belle Terre. We want our portion of the money and then we want to leave here and never come back."

Schyler knelt down in front of her father's chair. She grasped his hands. "Don't worry about it, Daddy. It'll never happen. I swear that to you."

"Careful, Schyler," Tricia taunted. "With all the things that have been going wrong, I'm not so sure you can get that order filled in time."

Schyler surged to her feet and confronted Tricia. "I can and I will. We've got several more days before the note at the bank comes due."

"Not much time."

"But enough."

"Not if something else causes a delay."

"I'll make sure nothing does. In fact, I'm not going to wait until the last minute. Today I ran a quick inventory of the timber we've got at the landing. I think I can ship enough to fill the order by Wednesday. No need to wait until next week."

That was the plan she had wanted to discuss with Cash. Now, even without his advice, she had decided to act on it. She would get the jump on anyone who had notions of seeing her fail.

"Tomorrow morning, I intend to step up operations. Start an hour earlier, work an hour later. With the bonuses I'm offering as incentive, I think everyone will be more than willing to put in the overtime."

"Leave organizing the loggers to Cash." Cotton was absently rubbing his chest.

Schyler noticed. She mentally flipped a coin on whether or not to tell him she had fired Cash. She decided that it would relieve Cotton to know that she was no longer involved with him. "Cash won't be acting as foreman any longer. I fired him today."

The three were stunned by her announcement, Cotton most of all. "You fired Cash?"

"That's right. I ordered him off Belle Terre. He'll be gone within a week."

"Cash is leaving Belle Terre?" Cotton parroted in a thready voice.

"Isn't that what you wanted?"

"Of course, of course," he said. "It's just that I'm shocked to hear that he agreed."

Her announcement hadn't been met with the reaction she had expected. She wanted to pursue it with Cotton, but Tricia distracted her.

"You're going to bring this about all by yourself?"

"That's right."

Tricia snickered. "If nothing else, it's been hightly entertaining to watch the rise and fall of Schyler Crandall. And about that sale of Belle Terre, Daddy, I don't think the choice will be left up to us. Not even to you. Coming, Ken?" She glided out of the room.

Schyler rushed to the doorway and called for Mrs. Dunne. "Help Daddy get to his room and into bed," she said the moment the housekeeper appeared. "He's upset, so give him his medication even if it is an hour early. He needs to go to sleep."

"Don't fuss, Schyler," he said cantankerously as he labored to get out of his chair. "I'm still standing. It'll take more that Tricia, Ken, and their hush-hush plans for Belle Terre to kill me."

"You knew they'd been talking about it?"

He smiled at her, tapping his temple, and winked. "I'm a mean son of a bitch. I learned to take care of myself on the docks of New Orleans. Not much gets past me."

"You own Belle Terre. Nobody is going to take it away from you."

He shook his head, his expression reflective. "No one can own Belle Terre, Schyler. It owns us."

He let himself be led away by Mrs. Dunne. Schyler watched him go. He looked frail as he shuffled down the hall. She wasn't ready for him to be aged and feeble. Her daddy was strong. Nothing could bring him down.

More than ever she regretted the years they'd been separated by the misunderstanding based on Tricia's lie. She echoed the sentiment Tricia had voiced earlier. She was very glad the same blood didn't flow through their veins.

Her shoulders stooped with fatigue, she turned into the room again. She had almost forgotten that Ken was still there. "I thought you went upstairs with your wife."

He was pulling his lower lip through his teeth. "No, uh, we left a matter up in the air."

"What matter?"

"That." He nodded down at the file. Schyler had forgotten about it.

"I'll cover for you, just as Cotton has."

"Don't do me any favors," he said sarcastically.

"Then you'd rather go to jail?" Schyler's nerves were shot. Ken should have known better than to press her when he was ahead.

Apparently her tone of voice brought him to that same conclusion. "No, of course not. But I want you to know, Schyler, that I'm not a thief."

"You stole something that didn't belong to you. That's the generally accepted definition of a thief."

"I only took what I felt I had coming."

"You only took what you needed to keep the loan sharks from breaking your legs."

"And to keep Tricia off my back about money. That woman thinks she's a Vanderbilt and has to live like one. Cotton's a stingy bastard. He never paid me according to my ability."

Schyler looked away, not wanting to point up the obvious, but Ken saw her expression and took issue with it. "I guess you're going to say that my contribution wasn't worth even what I got."

"I'm not going to say anything except good night. I'm exhausted."

He barred her way to the door. "I know what you're thinking."

"What?"

"That I've been putting moves on you just for the money."

"Haven't you?"

"No."

"You're right. That's what I was thinking. Not very flattering to either of us, is it?" She looked him in the eye. "Not that it matters. I would have rejected you anyway."

She tried to go around him. Again he blocked her way. "Are you going to fire me? Is that your next duty as CEO of Crandall Logging?"

"I haven't really thought about it, Ken. I can't think about anything until I get a check from Endicott and endorse it over to Gilbreath."

"But firing me would be just your style, wouldn't it? You like throwing your weight around. You must have what the shrinks call penis envy. You want to be the son your daddy never had, don't you? That's probably what went wrong between you and Boudreaux. There can't be two studs in one bed."

"Good night, Ken." When she tried pushing him aside, he caught her arm roughly.

"Tricia was right. Everything turned to shit when you came back. Why didn't you stay with your gay friend? That relationship was more suited to you. You could be the man. Why'd you have to come back here and screw everything up?"

Schyler wrenched her arm free. "I came back to find everything already screwed up, thanks to you and Tricia. I'm going to put things back the way they should have been all along. And nothing is going to stop me."

Chapter Fifty-two

From where she stood out on the veranda, Gayla heard Schyler's exit line. Through the windows, she watched her enter the hall and head toward her father's bedroom. Gayla saw Ken Howell in the parlor, working free the knot of his necktie with one hand and pouring himself a stiff bourbon with the other. He muttered deprecations to Schyler, to Cotton, to his wife.

Gayla considered Ken a dangerous man. He was like a wounded beast. He would lash out at anything or anyone, even someone who tried to help him. Weak men were often the most dangerous. They felt threatened from every direction. They had something to prove.

Gayla hadn't been eavesdropping intentionally. She and Mrs. Dunne had been drinking coffee together in the kitchen when the hue and cry went up in the back parlor. They'd glanced at each other, then took up their conversation, trying to ignore the raised voices and what they might signify. After Mrs. Dunne had been summoned to take Mr. Crandall to bed, Gayla had slipped out the back door.

It had become her nightly ritual to walk the entire veranda several times before going to bed. It was a masochistic exercise. Nothing scary had happened since the appearance of the doll on her pillow. She never saw anything unduly alarming on these nightly excursions.

But she knew that someone, something, some *presence* that bore malice toward the people of Belle Terre was out there in the darkness, lurking, watching, biding his time.

Schyler, she knew, passed off her skittishness to ethnic superstition at best and to her remnant fear of Jigger at worst. Gayla was sure that in the latter respect, Schyler was right. She was terrified that one day he would seek retribution for her desertion.

She had ridden into town with Mrs. Dunne for the first time only the day before. When they arrived at the supermarket, however, she had refused to go inside with her. Instead she had sat in the car, sweltering in the noon heat, with all the windows rolled up, anxiously glancing around.

Her fears were childish. But one glance at her scarred naked body was sufficient to remind her that they were justified. The worst of her scars didn't show. They were on her mind and in her heart. Jigger had marred her soul. She prayed for his death each night. She would burn in hell for that, and for being his whore, and for betraying Jimmy Don's sweet, pure love.

The only comfort she could derive was that Jigger would burn in hell, too. Hopefully there were stratas of hell, where those who sinned because they had no choice were dealt with more kindly than those who sinned out of meanness.

She only hoped that before she was consigned to hell, she would know that Jimmy Don was out of that awful place. Gayla felt guiltily responsible for Jimmy Don's imprisonment.

She had just about come full circle. She rounded the corner of the veranda, but immediately she ducked back, clamping her hand over her mouth to keep from uttering a squeal of fright. A tall shadow had made a dent in the rhododendrons the instant she'd stepped around the corner.

Her instinct was to run as fast as she could for the nearest door, but she forced herself to stay where she was. After several seconds, she peered around the corner again. Every leaf on the shrub had fallen back into place. The blossoms were motionless. There was no shadow, no evidence that anybody had been on the veranda.

Maybe she had imagined it. She crept forward, inching along the wall. At the parlor window, she glanced inside. Ken was pacing the floor, drinking and bad-mouthing his misfortunes beneath his breath.

Gayla slipped past the window unseen. She figured that anyone on the inside couldn't see out onto the veranda because the lights in the parlor were so bright. But anyone on the outside could see inside clearly, as well as hear everything that was said. It would be like watching a picture show.

But there hadn't been anybody there. A bird had probably disturbed those rhododendron bushes. She had imagined the shadow. Her overactive nerves were making her see things that didn't exist.

Gayla had almost convinced herself of that when she turned and caught, on the still evening air, the unmistakable fragrance of tobacco smoke.

At two minutes past nine the following morning, Dale Gilbreath took a telephone call at his desk.

"What do you mean she's going to ship ahead of time!" He sat bolt upright in his reclining chair.

"She's sending the timber out on Wednesday."

"Why?"

"Why do you think?" his caller asked impatiently. "She's a damn clever bitch. She's trying to avoid exactly what we had planned for that last shipment."

Dale quickly assimilated the information. "I don't think this will cause any problems. Flynn's agreed to our price. He's willing to do it. More than willing since that Frances girl is at Belle Terre."

"Are you sure he knows how to use the materials?"

"Yes. You just see to it that he gets them. I'll notify him about the change in the date. What time Wednesday?"

"If the train is on schedule, it arrives Wednesday afternoon at five-fifteen. I rechecked this morning."

"You know," Dale said thoughtfully, "that if anyone on that freight train gets killed, it'll be murder."

"Yes. Too bad Schyler won't be on it."

* * *

Wednesday dawned hot and still. The hazy sky was the color of saffron. Area bayous seemed to lack the energy to flow at all. Their viscous surfaces were unbroken except for an occasional insect skimming them. Thunderheads built up on the horizon in the direction of the Gulf, but at five-ten in the afternoon, the sun was still beating down.

The explosion occurred a mere quarter of a mile from the Crandall Logging landing. It blew the glass out of the office windows and showered the desk with flying shards that ripped the leather upholstery of Cotton's chair.

A large column of black smoke rose out of the pile of twisted metal. It could be seen for miles. The boom was loud enough to have heralded the end of the world. The impact of it rattled the beer bottles behind the bar at Red Broussard's café.

One of Red's frequent customers, sitting alone at a table, smiled with supreme satisfaction. He'd done a damn fine job.

Chapter Fifty-three

"Stop looking at me like that, Daddy. I'm fine."

Cotton's cheeks were flushed. He was propped up against the pillows on his bed. Schyler was glad he wasn't up and moving about.

"You don't look fine. What happened to your knees?"

She glanced down, noticing for the first time that her

knees were raw and bleeding, as were the heels of her hands. There were particles of gravel embedded in the flesh. She brushed them off, trying not to wince at the stinging pain.

"I was standing out on the platform, watching the train approach. The blast knocked me off my feet. I landed on my hands and knees beside the tracks."

"You could have been killed."

She thought it best not to tell him that she probably would have been if she'd been sitting behind the desk in the office. "Thank God no one was."

"No one on the train?"

She shook her head. "It was pushing two empty locomotives. They sustained the worst damage. The engineers in the third diesel weren't even bruised. Scared, naturally. It was a costly, uh, accident, but thankfully not in lives or injuries."

"Accident, my ass. What happened, Schyler?" He frowned at her. "And don't sugarcoat it for the heart patient. What the hell really happened?"

"It was deliberately set," she admitted with a deep sigh. "They used—"

"They?"

"Whoever . . . used some kind of plastic explosive. Once the smoke had cleared and we had made sure nobody was hurt, the sheriff conducted a preliminary investigation."

"Investigation," Cotton scoffed. "Patout doesn't know shit from shinola. He wouldn't recognize a clue if it bit him in the butt."

"I'm afraid you're right, so I stayed right there with him. That's one reason I'm so grubby." She swept her hand down the front of her dress. "There are a thousand and one unanswered questions. Since the train is interstate, several government agencies will be going over the scene with a fine-tooth comb. It'll take weeks, if not months, to sort through all the debris."

"And in the meantime, the tracks are unusable."

"The tracks look like iron hair ribbons all knotted together." Dejectedly, she sat down on the foot of his bed. "What I can't figure out is why the explosives were set to go off before the train reached the landing. If someone wanted to stop that shipment, why didn't the explosion occur after the train was loaded with Crandall timber and not before?"

"Somebody wanted to put us out of commission, and they did."

"Like hell," Schyler said, with a burst of enthusiasm. "I swore to you, I swore to myself, that I was going to meet that deadline and I'm going to."

"Maybe you should let it go, Schyler." Cotton's face looked heavy and old with defeat. The familiar zest was absent from his blue eyes. There was a hopeless lassitude in his posture that had nothing to do with his repose. He didn't look at rest; he looked resigned.

"I can't let it go, Daddy," she said huskily. "To let it go is tantamount to letting Belle Terre go. I can't. I won't."

"But you can't do this alone."

He struck at the heart of her most basic fears. She was utterly alone. Cotton could coach from the sidelines but, through no fault of his own, he was a weak and unreliable ally. She wished she had someone to act as a backboard for her ideas, her apprehensions.

She wished she had Cash.

She desperately needed his counsel on what action to take next. But he might be the very one who had blown up the tracks. She tried to forget his telling her that he'd been an explosives expert in Vietnam. He was clever enough to have disabled Crandall Logging without hurting anybody. But was he capable of such wanton destruction? And why would he destroy all he had built?

She recalled his face the last time she'd seen it, hard and cold, reeking contempt. There hadn't been a spark of human feeling in the eyes that bore into her. Yes, he was capable of doing anything. Mere pride wouldn't prevent her from going to him on her knees and begging his advice, but consulting him now was out of the question. He was a suspect.

She thought of calling Gilbreath and humbly appealing to his emotions, but she seriously doubted he had any. If he wouldn't extend the deadline of the loan in light of Cotton's heart illness, what would compel him to do it in light of this catastrophe? Besides, for all his unctuous mannerism, she suspected him of celebrating each mishap that had befallen her and Crandall Logging.

Most unsettling of all was that only a handful of people knew that she had changed the day of the shipment. They were the people closest to her, people she should have been able to trust.

Ken. There was hostility there to be sure. Her discovery of his embezzlement had only stoked his resentment. He had hurled vicious insults at her, but Schyler doubted there was a violent bone in Ken's body. He was all talk and no action. An explosion just didn't seem in keeping with his personality. Besides, he would lack the ambition and knowledge to pull it off successfully.

Tricia. She was certainly vindictive enough. She would rejoice in the company's failure because it would expedite the sale of Belle Terre. But again, she wouldn't have the expertise to do something of that caliber.

Jigger Flynn. Motive, yes. But no opportunity. He couldn't have known about her secret change in plans.

Cash wasn't among those who knew either, but Cash could have found out. The loggers must have known something was in the wind by the way she'd been pushing them the last few days. They drank together in the local watering holes in the evenings. Cash could have overheard tongues lubricated by too much liquor.

Whoever the culprit, he was still around and very close to her.

"I'm afraid for you," Cotton's raspy voice jostled her out of her brooding.

She forced a confident smile. Through his socks, she massaged his feet. "I'm more afraid for Belle Terre. If we were forced out, we'd have to change our personal stationery. Imagine what a hassle that would be."

He didn't crack a smile at her attempted humor. "Did Cash do this to us?" The disillusionment in his expression made his whole face appear ravaged.

"I don't know, Daddy."

"Does he hate me that much?" Cotton turned his head

and stared out the window. "I probably haven't been fair to the boy."

"He's not a boy. He's a man."

"He could be a better one. Monique was so proud, she wouldn't let me buy him clothes, wouldn't let me pay for anything. When he started school, he was laughed at. Made fun of." He squeezed his eyes shut. "That works on a kid, you know. It either makes him a pansy or a mean son of a bitch. Cash started fighting back. That was good. I knew he'd have to be tough to make it in this world. But Jesus, that boy has turned into a pain in the ass."

"Whatever tiffs you've had with him, nothing warrants what happened today," Schyler remarked. "If it's ever proved that he was involved, I'll see to it that he's punished to the full extent of the law."

Cotton's chest rose and fell heavily. "Monique would hate to see him locked in some goddamn jail. Cash belongs in the forest, on the bayous. That dark water flows in his veins instead of blood, she used to say." He gnashed his teeth. "Christ."

Schyler stroked his thick white hair out of compassion for his suffering. "Don't worry about Cash. Tell me what I should do. I need your guidance."

"What can you do?"

She thought a moment. "Well, the timber is still intact at the landing. They were hauling the last—"

Suddenly she broke off. Her mind halted and then backtracked as she recalled the last half hour before the explosion when the landing had been a beehive of activity. "Daddy, when you first took over the company, how did you transport the timber?"

"That was before I built the landing and weasled the railroad into laying the spur."

"Exactly. How did you haul the timber to the various markets?"

His blue eyes flickered. "Like most of the independents do now. Rigs."

"That's it!" Schyler bent down and planted a smacking kiss on his lips. "We'll drive that shipment to Endicott's. Right up to Joe Jr.'s front door."

* * *

"Why wasn't it done right?" the caller hissed into the telephone receiver.

Gilbreath had been sitting hunched over his desk, asking himself the same question. "Jigger must have been drunk. He misunderstood our instructions. Something. I don't know. For some reason he didn't realize that he was supposed to blow the tracks after the shipment was loaded, not before."

"We were fools to depend on him."

"We had to."

"I think I'm a fool to depend on you, too. I can do this by myself and cut you out entirely."

"Don't threaten me," Dale said coldly. "We haven't lost anything yet. It didn't go as we expected, but there's no way in hell she can get that shipment off in time."

"Want to bet? Tomorrow night."

"*What?*"

"Yes. Tomorrow night. By truck."

"Crandall's doesn't have that many rigs."

"Schyler's been mustering them all day. Everybody in the parish who owns or has access to a rig, she's enlisting. Paying top dollar. She'll make it, I tell you, unless she's stopped."

Gilbreath's palms began to sweat. "We'll have to use Jigger again."

"I guess so. I'll let you handle that, but you make damn certain he knows what he's doing this time."

"I'll see to it. Don't worry."

"Funny. I do."

Gilbreath, choosing to disregard the dig, asked, "What time tomorrow?"

"I don't know yet. I'll have to call you when I find out."

"That means Jigger will have to use a timer."

"Probably."

"The stakes are higher this time. There will be men driving those rigs."

"I can live with a guilty conscience if you can."

"Oh, I can," Gilbreath said with a chuckle. "I just wanted to be sure you could."

"Don't doubt it."

"After your call tomorrow, I don't think we should speak to each other again. And for a long time after this is over."

"I agree. Too bad we won't be able to have a celebration drink."

"When Rhoda and I are ensconced in Belle Terre, we'll invite you out for cocktails."

There was a laugh. "You do that."

Chapter Fifty-four

"I'll get back some time tomorrow." Schyler squeezed Cotton's hand affectionately. "I can tell you're worried. Don't be. Endicott is expecting us. I explained why the convoy would be arriving in the wee hours. He thinks I'm crazy, but I think he's a jerk, so we're even," she said with a laugh.

Cotton didn't laugh. His expression was grave. "I'll feel much better when you're back safe and sound."

"So will I. I've got a lot of hard work ahead of me before then."

"Why do you have to go yourself?"

"I don't have to. I want to. This will be the culmination of everything I've worked for. I want to accept that nice, fat check in person. I promise to ride with the best driver. Whom do you recommend?"

"Cash."

"Cash?" she asked in surprise. "He won't be going."

"I know. But he's who I would recommend you ride with if I had first choice."

Cash would be her first choice as well. He should be

there beside her when Joe Jr. handed over that check. Tonight would be the culmination of all Cash's hard work, too. Or had his hard work been a screen just like his love-making?

Correction. Cash didn't make love. He'd said so with brutal explicitness: *I don't make love.*

Schyler cleared her throat of a tight constriction and put on a phony, bright smile. "Who would be your second choice?" Cotton named an independent logger. "I'll ride with him then. Now," she said, placing her hands on Cotton's shoulders and easing him back against the pillows of his bed, "you get a good night's sleep. Not long after you wake up in the morning, I'll be home." She kissed him good-bye. "Good night, Daddy. I love you."

At the door she turned to give him a thumbs-up sign, but his eyes were closed.

"What a marvelous idea," Rhoda cooed as she languished in the bubble bath her husband had drawn for her. She reached for her stem of chilled champagne and sipped, then rolled her tongue over her lips, intentionally making the movement seductive. "There's room for two in here, if we get real chummy."

"No. I'd rather watch."

"And take pictures?"

"Yes. Later."

"Are we celebrating?"

Dale knelt beside the tub and parted the mountain of bubbles so that Rhoda's surgically edified breasts were visible. The nipples bobbed upon the surface of the water. He stuck his finger in her glass of champagne and dribbled the cold wine over them until they tightened.

"We are."

"What are we celebrating?"

Dale removed the champagne from her hand and replaced it with a bar of scented soap. "Wash yourself."

Eyes lowered to half-mast, Rhoda took the soap between her wet hands and began rubbing them back and forth until they were dripping foamy lather. She laid them on her breasts and squeezed the stiff, red nipples between her slippery, soapy fingers.

Dale's eyes glazed over. His breathing accelerated. "We're celebrating our success."

"Hmm. Does our success have anything to do with the explosion at the Crandall landing the other day?"

"No, that didn't go quite as planned."

"Oh?"

"Wash down there, too," he instructed raspily as he unfastened his trousers to accommodate his erection.

Rhoda smiled indulgently as she parted her thighs and rested her feet on opposite rims of the tub. She slid the bar of soap between her thighs. Dale groaned.

"What went wrong at the landing?"

In panting bursts of dialogue, he explained the snafu. "It slowed her down, but it didn't stop her. We're stopping her tonight. Nothing's going to go wrong this time. We've got the timing right, everything."

"Good." She blew aside a clump of bubbles so Dale would have an unrestricted view. She would have enjoyed his bedazzled expression more if she hadn't been puzzling through her own thoughts. "That doesn't sound like Cash. To make a drastic error like that."

"Move your hand faster, darling. Yes, that's it," he panted. "Boudreaux? What has he got to do with it?"

"Everything, I thought. Wasn't he the one who set the explosives?"

"Hell no. Jigger Flynn did."

Water sloshed over the rim of the tub as Rhoda suddenly sat up. "But Cash planned it, showed him how, right?"

"No."

"I thought you were using Cash. You said you had plans for him."

"Initially I did. But I changed my mind. He's too closely tied to Belle Terre. I couldn't be sure how loyal he is to Schyler."

"He's sleeping with her."

"He sleeps with everybody," Dale yelled defensively, not liking Rhoda's tone. It suggested he was stupid. He added silkily, "So far Cash Boudreaux hasn't shown much discrimination."

"You bastard." Rhoda stepped out of the tub, splattering Dale with water and reaching for a towel. "So you hired that Flynn character."

"He can be trusted because he wants to see Schyler Crandall ruined."

"But does Cash?" Rhoda demanded of her husband. "Where is he tonight?"

"Out of the picture. She fired him."

"You fool!" Rhoda cried. "He might be pissed off at her, but he's not going to stand by and idly watch as Belle Terre falls into our hands. He wants the place himself. He told me so. Who's keeping an eye on him tonight?"

Dale, realizing what a serious blunder he'd made, left the bathroom at a run. He knocked the bedroom telephone to the floor in his haste to dial.

"What's all this?"

Ken entered his bedroom to find it in a state of utter chaos. Two suitcases were lying opened on the bed. The clothes from Tricia's closet were draped across chairs and every other conceivable surface. Bureau drawers had been disemboweled, their lacy entrails spilling over their sides. Tricia was busily picking and sorting.

"What does it look like I'm doing? I'm packing."

"For where?"

"New Orleans. Dallas. Atlanta." Tricia shrugged and smiled prettily. "I haven't really decided. I think I'll drive to Lafayette, then head out on the interstate and see what strikes my fancy."

"What the hell are you talking about?" As she sailed past him, Ken caught her arm. She jerked it free.

"Freedom. I'm talking about getting out of Heaven and never looking back."

"You can't just leave."

"Watch me." For emphasis, she tossed a pair of shoes into one of the suitcases. They landed with a plop that sounded final.

"You haven't got any money."

"I'll use plastic money until I get some cash."

"And where will that come from?"

"Don't worry about it, honey. I'm not asking you for any." She ran her palm down his clammy cheek.

When she stepped away, however, he caught her against him again. "I'm your husband. Where do I fit into all your plans?"

"You don't. Our marriage is over."

"What do you mean over?"

Tricia sighed with vexation. She didn't want to waste time explaining to him what should be obvious. "Look, Ken, we started out this marriage on a lie. Let's at least end it on a truth. We don't love each other. We never have. I tricked you into marrying me. The only reason I wanted you was because you and Schyler wanted each other. Well she doesn't want you anymore, so neither do I."

"You bitch!"

"Oh, please. Spare me a theatrical scene and don't look so wounded. You've lived the life of Riley these last six years. Personally I don't like it, but Belle Terre is considered to be a fine mansion by most people's standards. You've had the privilege of residing here without paying a dime in rent. You haven't had to pursue a career. You've bled the family coffers of God knows how much money and got off scot-free.

"We each knew what we were getting when we got married. You know I am manipulative and selfish. I know you are weak and unambitious. Our sex life has been adequate. To my recollection I never said no and when you visited the bawdy houses, I looked the other way.

"The arrangement worked well for us while it lasted, but it's time to call it quits." She went up on tiptoe and kissed his lips softly. "You'll do just fine without me. Lay off the bourbon for a month or two and firm up your belly. You're still good looking. You'll find a wealthy woman just dying to take care of you."

"I don't want a woman to take care of me."

"Why of course you do, sugar. That's what you've always wanted, somebody to make all your tough decisions for you."

The telephone on the nightstand rang. Smiling her rehearsed Mardi Gras Queen smile, Tricia dismissively patted Ken's cheek and went to answer it. But her smile collapsed; she barely got out a hello before she fell silent and listened intently.

Jigger woke up with a roaring headache and a hairy tongue. He rolled over and buried his face in the pillow. It smelled sourly of him and hair oil and sweat. The ringing in his head wouldn't stop. When, after several minutes it became apparent that he couldn't go back to sleep, he sat up on the edge of the bed, gripping the mattress for balance.

His head was muzzy. He tried to shake off the grogginess. He tried to yawn away the ringing in his ears. It persisted. He shouldn't have drunk that pint of whiskey so fast. He chastised himself for it as he stumbled through the dark house.

He had returned home from his nefarious errand at dusk. It was full-fledged nighttime now, but he didn't turn on any lights in deference to his headache. He bumped into several pieces of furniture before he made it to the kitchen sink and turned on the faucet. He had to get that foul, furry taste out of his mouth.

He didn't begrudge guzzling a whole pint. He'd been due a drink. He had risked getting caught by placing those explosives when all that activity was going on at the landing. Several times he'd spied that Crandall bitch herself sashaying in and out and about, issuing orders like a goddamn drill sergeant. It wouldn't be long before she'd get hers.

Smiling evilly, he filled a glass with tap water and raised it to his mouth. It was only halfway there when he realized what had awakened him. It wasn't the noise in his head. It was the lack of it.

His rattlesnake had stopped rattling.

The glass shattered when Jigger dropped it. Water splashed over his muddy shoes, but he didn't notice as he lunged through the back door. In his haste, he almost fell down the concrete steps. At the bottom of them he drew up short, chest heaving.

It was still there. The oil drum was glowing silver in the pale moonlight. The lid was on top of it and anchored down by the large rock. He glanced around the yard. Just as on the morning the snake had been mysteriously delivered, everything appeared normal. He glanced toward his kennel. The pit bull bitch looked at him curiously. Her ears had perked up when he came barreling through the door, but she lay quietly letting her litter suck.

She hadn't barked all evening. His nap had been a deep sleep, but not so deep that a yelping dog wouldn't have roused him. He could swear his snake had been in that drum, making that bloodcurdling sound when he got home at dusk.

So why not now? What was it doing in there that prevented it from making its characteristic sound? Was it digesting that field mouse he'd tossed in there? No, that had been days ago. Why had that son of a bitch stopped rattling?

Was it dead? Shit! It seemed like everything he touched here lately turned to shit. He had planned to use the snake to take up the slack while he was training his pit bull pups to fight. He had thought about taking it on a tour, putting it in a carnival sideshow, or working up an act with it and one of his whores. Now if his snake was dead, all his fancy planning wouldn't be worth a damn.

Or maybe it wasn't in there at all. Maybe some low-down, sneaky bastard had heard of his plans and had come along and swiped his snake while he'd been in there sleeping off a pint of cheap whiskey! He would find him, he would . . .

Cursing, he ran toward the drum and pushed the rock off. It landed with a hard thud on the ground, sending up a little cloud of dust. Jigger grabbed the lid, ready to swing it off. He caught himself just in time. As much as he admired his snake, it was still a helluva rattler. He respected its deadliness. He let go of the lid quickly and snatched his hands back. They had begun to sweat. He wiped them on his pants legs.

Why wasn't it rattling?

Was it even in there?

Muttering, he went to the woodpile and picked up a stick of firewood. For the sake of his paying customers, he'd courageously dispensed with that precaution, but he felt better about having it in his hands now. Again he approached the drum. It looked the same, but damned if it didn't seem spookier now that the sound had stopped.

He had to relieve himself badly. His breath was choppy. He stood staring at the lid of the drum for a long time before he poked it once, quickly, with the stick of firewood. There was not even one little rattle.

The snake wasn't in there. Was it? Jesus, he was going fuckin' nuts. He had to know.

Using the stick, he pushed against the rim of the lid. It didn't budge. It was stuck. Swearing, Jigger applied more force. The lid didn't move a fraction. He dug his heels in and put his weight behind it.

Suddenly the lid slid off and clattered to the ground.

Inertia propelled Jigger forward. He fell against the silver drum belly first. His head went over the rim. He yelled in startled fright.

Regaining his balance, he laughed nervously at himself. Goda'mighty, he was edgy tonight! He was relieved to see that his snake was still there, all right, coiled up in the bottom of the drum. But why wasn't it rattling? Was it dead?

He leaned against the drum and peered over the rim.

When he did, an iron hand clamped down hard on the back of his neck.

Jigger squealed like an impaled pig.

"He's still in there, you cock-sucking son of a bitch." The voice was whispery, laced with hate and rife with malevolence. "He's asleep now on gasoline fumes. But when he wakes up, he's gonna be mad as hell and he's gonna take it out on you."

Jigger screamed. Panicked, he kicked his feet out backward and flailed his arms. His struggles did him no good. His head and shoulders were being held over the open drum by a strong arm with a body sufficient to back it up.

"Before he wakes up, you'll have a while to think about all the mean things you've done. This is Judgment Day for you, Jigger Flynn, and your road to hell is going to be long and scary."

The chain landed heavily on Jigger's back. He grunted with pain. Terror made him weak. His efforts to escape were ill-timed and ineffectual. An ordinary pair of handcuffs had been linked to the end of the chain. Jigger watched in horror as they were clamped to his wrists. His arms were stretched across the drum and down the other side until his head and shoulders were bridging it. He was staring facedown at his splendidly wicked snake. The chain was wound around the drum, securing his feet and legs to it.

Jigger tried to keep his eyes closed, but he couldn't. He gaped at the oily coil of muscle beneath him. Those muscles were beginning to ripple. He screamed and peed in his pants.

"That's right, scream. Scream real loud. Scream so every devil in hell hears you." Jigger was swacked across his buttocks with the stick of firewood. "I ought to cram this up your ass, but I don't want you to die that way. I want you to die looking eyeball to eyeball with a snake just like yourself. Wonder how many times he'll get you before you die?"

"Let me up. God, Jesus, please. Let me up. Sweet Jesus. Hail Mary, Mother of God, blessed art thou . . ."

"That's it, Jigger, pray."

"Oh, Jesus God. What'd I ever do to you? Who are you, you son of a bitch?"

"I'm an angel of the Lord. I'm a demon from hell. It doesn't matter to you who I am." He opened his hand wide over Jigger's head and pushed his face down farther into the drum. He whispered with insidious delight, "You're gonna die. You're gonna die in excruciating pain."

"Oh, Jesus, Jesus," Jigger whispered. "I'll do anything. Please. Please. I'm begging. I'll give you anything. Money. All my money. Every friggin' cent. Oh, Jesus, help me."

The vindicator got tired of Jigger's screams and his pleas

for mercy. He unwound the bandanna around his throat and stuffed it into Jigger's mouth. Jigger tried to spit it out, but all he succeeded in doing was gagging himself on scalding whiskey that his stomach tried to reject. Jigger squirmed frantically, bucking against his restraints.

"You won't be alone for long, Jigger. You'll have company real soon. You know how swelled up your head is gonna be by morning? Your face'll look like a meat platter, with those twin holes all over it. Bye-bye Jigger. Next time we see each other, we'll be in hell."

The vindicator stopped at the kennel to hand-feed the pit bull bitch a snack. She'd come to expect that from him. He spoke to the puppies; they licked his hands with affection and trust. Then he slipped into the darkness of the forest, becoming one with all the tall dark shadows.

Jigger wiggled against the barrel as much as the chain would allow. He screamed, but it only echoed inside his terrified brain. His heart knocked painfully against his ribs. The acrid sweat of stark fear ran into his eyes. He blinked it away only to see the slitted black eyes of his beautiful snake.

The rattling tail began to twitch.

Gayla would be glad when this night ended.

Lordy, what a night. First Schyler had left for the landing. Gayla thought she was crazy for going back there after the explosion. It would be a tremendous load off her mind when Schyler got through with her business in East Texas and came home.

Schyler would have been enough to worry about, but then Tricia had pulled her stunt. She had run out of the house like the devil was after her, only to come storming back inside seconds later. "Where the hell is my car?"

Gayla had had the misfortune of being the only one available to answer her. "Mrs. Dunne took it to town."

"What!" Tricia shrieked.

"Her car broke down. This is her night off. Schyler said she could take your car since you weren't going out."

"Well I *am* going out."

"Then I guess you'll have to drive Mr. Howell's car."

"I can't," Tricia said through her teeth. "It's a stick shift. I never learned to—" Exasperated, she raked her hand through her hair. "Why in God's name am I standing here explaining it to *you*?"

She whirled on her heels and stalked out the front door, letting the screen door bang shut behind her. Gayla watched her run across the yard and disappear into the barn. A few minutes later, she rode out barebacked on one of the horses. Wherever she was going, it was in a hell of a hurry.

Then Ken had come downstairs and gone into the parlor. Gayla heard him scraping open drawers and banging them closed, apparently searching for something. She didn't dare cross paths with him. He seemed as upset as Tricia. Gayla watched him leave the house and, looking like a man with a purpose, drive off in his sports car.

She would have been relieved to see them go, if their stormy departures hadn't left her alone in the house, except for Mr. Crandall, who had been sleeping peacefully the last time she checked on him. Schyler had asked her to keep a close eye on him and to call Dr. Collins if he showed any signs of pain or distress.

She didn't mind the duty. In fact, she enjoyed taking care of him. She seemed to have an instinct for knowing when he needed something but was too proud to ask for it. He rarely thanked her out loud for her unasked for attention, but he looked at her kindly.

When darkness fell, Gayla's nervousness increased. She patrolled the house, checking to see that all the doors and windows were locked. She didn't take her nightly stroll around the veranda. She couldn't bring herself to step outside.

She tried to watch television, but the programming didn't hold her interest. She tried to read, but couldn't sit still for any length of time. She was glad when the clock in the hall chimed the hour, indicating that it had been an hour since she'd last checked on Mr. Crandall.

She went to his bedroom and opened the door. Craning her neck around it, she peered through the darkness. His form was clearly delineated beneath the covers. His medication had worked well; he was sleeping soundly. She listened closely until she was certain she heard his breathing, then backed out of the room, pulling the door closed.

The attack was so sudden, she didn't have time to scream before a hand was clamped over her mouth. The arm that curled around her waist was as supple as a tentacle and as strong as a vise.

She was dragged backward down the hallway. When she scraped her heels along the floor trying to get traction, she was lifted up and carried. She clawed at the hand over her mouth and kicked her feet, doing some damage to her attacker's shins, but not enough to be released.

She was pulled into the parlor, spun around, and slammed back against the wall.

Reeling and dizzy with fear, gulping for breath, she raised her head. Her eyes went round with disbelief and apprehension. Her mouth formed the name, but no sound came out.

"Jimmy Don!" she finally whispered.

Chapter Fifty-five

He was probably drunk. Some drunks imagined seeing pink elephants. He was imagining he saw a woman on horseback, a blond woman on horseback. She reminded him of Schyler. His gut curled with desire and his loins got thick and tight and he wished to hell he would stop having these physical reactions every time he thought about her.

He took a deep swallow of his drink. It was the third or fourth bourbon he'd had since he'd returned to his house only a short while ago. It was a hot, humid night and he had had a lot of ground to cover. He had slogged through swamps and tramped through dense forests for hours, but he had a niggling suspicion that he had left one stone unturned. It was the important stone, the one that counted. It pestered him like a gnat. He couldn't brush it away.

What had he overlooked?

Pacing restlessly, drinking steadily, he had tried to push his worries aside. Hell, it wasn't even his problem anymore. Why was he letting it bother him? Yet he couldn't relax. The steady intake of booze wasn't helping. It was only making him see things. A blond woman riding barebacked. Jesus!

Once again, he paused at the window. This time, he slowly lowered the glass from his lips. Damned if there wasn't a woman sliding off the back of a horse and running up to his door. He set his glass down and went to answer her knock.

"Hi, Cash," she said breathlessly, splaying her hand over her bosoms.

"Are you lost?" He would have had to be blind not to notice that she was braless beneath her snug T-shirt.

She appeared to be out of breath, as though she'd been jogging instead of riding horseback. Spreading her hands wide, she shrugged, a movement that did great things for the nice set of tits. "In fact I am," she said around a giggle. "Can you tell me how to get back to Belle Terre?"

Cash stepped through the screen door. "I don't know," he drawled. "Can I?"

Tricia simpered as Cash backed her up against the cypress post. "From what I hear about you, Cash Boudreaux, you can lead a woman just about anywhere. Even some places she doesn't want to go."

"Is that a fact?"

Her glance lowered to his impressive chest, seen through his unbuttoned shirt. "Um-huh. That's what I hear." She looked up at him through her eyelashes. "'Course I don't know that for sure."

"You could ask your sister."

Tricia's smile faltered. "Schyler? Are you referring to her? She's not my real sister, you know."

Cash propped his shoulder against the post and leaned in close. He ran the knuckle of his index finger across her collarbone. "You could still ask her."

Tricia invitingly leaned into his caress and gazed up at his provocatively. "There are some things I'd rather find out for myself."

Cash, giving her a cool, steady stare and a sly grin, eased himself away. "Want a drink?"

"Thank you, I'd love one. I'm fairly parched."

He held open the screen door. "After you."

She went past him, dragging her body against the front of his and giving him a knowing, sidelong glance. "Why, this is just charmin'. Absolutely charmin'. Look at that cute little chair. Handmade?"

"*Oui*. Bourbon okay?"

"And just a splash of water. Ice, too, please." She pivoted slowly, taking in the quaintness of his house, with its pronounced Cajun flavor. "So this is where my daddy spent so many passionate hours with your mama."

"Now the way I see it," Cash said, deliberately thunking two ice cubes into a glass and covering them with liquor and water, "is that if Schyler isn't your sister, then Cotton isn't your daddy." He turned in time to catch Tricia's hostile glare, which hastily righted itself into a smile.

She took the glass from him, deliberately brushing his fingers with hers. "I guess you're right." She immediately took a sip of her drink, as though she desperately needed it. Her eyes darted around furtively. She kept trying to steal glances through the windows. "Fact is, I don't feel like I have any attachments here anymore."

"Oh?"

"I'm leaving Heaven."

"Alone?"

"Yes. Ken and I are finished."

"Too bad."

"I don't think so."

"When are you going?"

"Tomorrow probably."

"Where?"

"I'm not sure."

"You picked a funny time to go horseback riding."

"Well, I . . ." she stammered, "I got tired of packing. Besides, I guess I wanted to say a formal good-bye to Belle Terre."

"Hmm, and you got lost."

She took another drink, looking at him over the rim of her glass while she drained it. Her voice was husky when she said, "You know why I came here, Cash."

"You want to get laid."

His ability to see through her was disconcerting. His candor was unkind and offensive. She pretended it was flattering. Pressing a hand over her heart again, she said, "My goodness, you're so blunt. Shame on you, Cash Boudreaux. You know I'm nervous. You plumb take my breath."

Cash started unbuckling his belt as he moved toward her. "I've known you since Cotton and Macy adopted you. You never gave me the time of day, Miss Tricia. Each time we passed on the street, you made it a point to turn up your nose and look the other way. If you've got such a powerful crotch throb for me, what took you so long?"

Tricia followed the slow, deliberate movements of his hands as he unsnapped his jeans. She moistened her lips. "I've heard other women talk about you."

"And just what do they say?"

"That you're the best. I wanted to find out."

"You could have found out sooner. Why'd you wait?"

"I guess I was working up my courage."

Cash was standing directly in front of her now. His eyes were half-closed as he looked down at her. He reached for the hem of her T-shirt and began working it up. "What I can't figure out is why you came here tonight, since you were so busy getting packed and all." He peeled the shirt over her head and dropped it to the floor.

Tricia draped her arms over his shoulders and arched her lush body against his. "We're wasting time with all these silly questions."

Cash sank the fingers of one hand into her hair and pulled her head back. His breath was hot and flavored with fine bourbon as he lowered his mouth close to hers. "One thing you ought to know about me, Miss Tricia. I never waste my time."

She should have known things were going too smoothly. Something disastrous was bound to happen. Schyler had wondered what form the first sign of trouble would take. A half hour before they were scheduled to leave, she found out. It didn't come from outside the ranks of the trusted, but from within.

The loggers stubbornly refused to drive the timber to East Texas unless Cash was in the lead rig.

"Mr. Boudreaux no longer works for us," she told the disgruntled group. That didn't faze them. There were nearly a dozen of them facing her, unresponsive to her reasoning. "He doesn't want to work for us."

"Boudreaux don't quit on a job 'ntil it's did," one said from the back of the crowd. Others murmured in agreement.

Before she had a bona fide strike on her hands, Schyler reminded them of the bonuses. "You won't get them. None of the loggers, the saw hands, the loaders, the drivers, nobody will get a cent if this deal with Endicott falls through. You all know the terms of the contract."

"Everybody's behind us. We're authorized to speak for everybody. We ain't budgin' if Cash don't go." The ultimatum was punctuated by a stream of tobacco juice. They all chorused their agreement.

Schyler's shoulders slumped with defeat. She couldn't drive the whole convoy to East Texas. She didn't have time to recruit other drivers from outside the parish, and it seemed that all the locals had pledged fealty to Cash. It was the eleventh hour.

She had no choice.

"All right, wait for me. I'll be back. By the time I get here, I want every rig ready to roll. Got that? Check your chains and bolsters every few minutes while I'm gone. Keep an eye out for anybody lurking around who doesn't belong here."

She had carefully timed their departure and arranged with Sheriff Patout to provide them with a police escort to the state line. At ten o'clock two units from his office were to meet them on the other side of the Laurent Bayou bridge. As she ran to her car, she consulted her wristwatch. It was twelve minutes till ten.

She floorboarded the accelerator of her car and sent it skimming over the rough dirt road that led to Cash's house. There were endless negative possibilities of what she would find when she arrived. He could laugh at her. He could slam the door in her face. He could have already left town. He could be sick, drunk, asleep, or all of the above.

Her headlights made a sweeping arc over the front of his house when she pulled up. There were no lights on inside. God, please let him be here.

She left the car's motor running and the door open as she raced for the front porch, calling his name. She banged on the frame of the screen door.

"Cash?" she called out. Seconds later, he materialized behind the screen. "Cash, thank God you're here. Listen to me, please. I know I don't have any right to ask. I don't want to ask. But you've got to help me. You've got to—"

The rushing fountain of words dried up the instant Tricia appeared beyond Cash's shoulder. She pulled her T-shirt over her head. Schyler watched as she smoothed it over her breasts and cleared her hair from the neck of it. Seeing Tricia in this place was so astonishing that Schyler stared at her with bewilderment.

Then her eyes moved back to Cash. She noticed his unbuttoned shirt, his unfastened jeans, his rumpled hair, the insolent expression on his face. And the smug one on Tricia's.

She actually fell back a step. "My God." She couldn't catch her breath. Unconsciously she gripped a handful of her shirt directly over her heart as if to hold it together. It seemed to be collapsing inside her chest. She closed her eyes and prayed to God she wouldn't disgrace herself by fainting. She didn't want to give either of them that satisfaction.

She was reliving that nightmarish moment at her engagement party when Tricia had announced her pregnancy by Ken. She felt herself being sucked into that chasm of despair again. The woman she had called her sister was wearing the same gloating smile now as then. And as before, the other guilty party was saying nothing, neither confessing nor denying. Cash would never feel the need to justify himself. It would never occur to him to make apologies or amends. He would watch her sink into that black pit and do nothing to help lift her out.

Schyler's impulse was to turn and run until she fell down dead. Instead she drew upon resources she didn't know she possessed. Taking a deep breath she said, "Forgive the intrusion. I didn't know you had . . . a guest."

"What's the problem?"

She gripped her hands together, swallowed, and said the hardest words she'd ever had to say. "I need you." Once those three words were out, the rest seemed relatively easy. "The drivers refuse to drive the rigs unless you're with them. I can't change their minds. They won't be swayed by threats or promises. I'm running out of time to negotiate. The sheriff will give us an escort to the state line, but we've got to go now. So tell me yes or no. There's no time to think about it. I've got to know now. Will you help me one last time?"

He didn't say anything. He gave the screen door the heel of his hand and stalked across the porch past her, refastening his clothes along the way. Schyler fell into step behind him.

"What about me?" Tricia trotted after them. "Cash, come back here. You can't just leave me here by myself."

"Get home the same way you got here," he told her as he slid behind the wheel of Schyler's car.

"Cash, why are you going with her?" Tricia wailed. "What do you care what happens to that wretched timber? Schyler fired you. Don't you have any pride? Cash, don't you dare leave me here."

"If you don't want to get left behind then get in the goddamn car." Fuming, Tricia scrambled in. Cash executed a hairpin turn before she had even closed the back door.

Schyler kept her knuckles pressed against her lips for the

duration of the trip. She wanted to rail at both of them. She wanted to physically punish them. Except for her secret love for this man, she had no right to. The pain of this second betrayal might very well kill her, but later. Not tonight. Once she had Belle Terre's future secured, she might die of her twice-broken heart. She wouldn't succumb tonight; she wouldn't let herself.

The loggers were sitting around glumly, smoking, talking desultorily among themselves when the car pulled into the clearing. They rose from their sullen postures and looked toward the car expectantly. A cheer went up when Cash stepped out.

"What the hell is going on around here?" he bellowed. "Get off your fat asses and climb behind the wheels of these rigs. You want that timber to take root before we get it to Endicott's?"

His harsh words galvanized them like a sprinkling of fairy dust. Their lassitude vanished and they sprang into action. Laughing and slapping each other on the back, they ran toward the cabs of their rigs.

"Which one do you want me in?" Cash asked Schyler.

"The lead one." She fell into step beside him.

"Where are you going?"

"Where do you think?"

"Endicott's?"

"Yes, and I'm riding with you. Cotton recommended that I should."

He stopped. She did likewise. They turned to face each other and exchanged a puissant stare. Schyler didn't look away until the two sheriff's cars pulled to a stop on the far end of the bridge. "It's time to go." Without waiting for his assistance, she climbed up into the cab of the lead truck.

Cash went around and got behind the steering wheel. He started the motor. He checked the rearview mirrors on both sides, stepped on the clutch, and pushed it into first gear. They moved forward only a few feet.

"Wait!" Schyler cried. Cash braked. "That looks like Ken's car."

"What the hell is he doing?"

They watched through the wide windshield of the rig as Ken sped between the two sheriff's cars and braked in the center of the bridge. The rear end of his car swerved to one side before shuddering to a halt. Cash tooted the horn of the truck. Schyler leaned out the window and waved her arms.

"Ken, what are you doing? We're on our way out. Don't block the bridge."

Ken got out of his car. Schyler shaded her eyes against his headlights. She could barely make out his silhouette against the glare that filtered through the cloud of dust he'd raised.

"What on earth is he doing?" she asked rhetorically.

"Beats the hell outta— Oh, *shit*!"

In the same instant, Schyler saw what Cash had. She gasped, "Oh, my God, no."

Ken had raised a revolver to his temple. He took a few steps forward. "You all thought I was stupid." His speech was slurred. He'd been drinking. But his gait was steady and so was the hand holding the pistol to his head. "You thought I didn't have any balls. No brains. I'll show you. I'll show you all. You'll know I've got brains when I splatter them all over this motherlovin' bridge."

"We've got to do something." Schyler opened her door.

Cash grabbed her arm and held her inside. "Not yet."

"But he could pull the trigger any second."

"He will if you go barging across the bridge and freak him out."

"Cash, please," she said, trying to wrest her arm free.

"Give me a sec," he said. "Let me think."

"*Get off the bridge, you idiot!*"

They turned in the direction of the scream. Up until then, they had forgotten Tricia. They spotted her cowering against the exterior wall of the office building.

"What's the matter with her?" Schyler wondered out loud. "Why isn't she—"

"Get off the bridge!" Cupping her hands, her voice frantic, Tricia shouted to her suicidal husband. "Ken! Do you hear me? Get off the bridge."

Schyler whipped her head around to look at Ken again. "I don't understand her. What—"

"Jesus!" Cash shoved open his door. Dragging Schyler across the cab, he jumped to the ground. "Get out of the truck!" He pulled her to the ground with him. She hit it at a dead run.

A split second later the explosives Jigger had meticulously set blew the Laurent Bayou bridge to smithereens.

Chapter Fifty-six

Gayla ran her hands over Jimmy Don's chest, his face, down his arms. "I can't believe you're here. That I'm actually touching you. And . . . and that you don't despise me." Tears filled her eyes. By now she should have cried herself dry. Since Jimmy Don had appeared out of nowhere, she'd been crying. First in fear, then in shame, now out of love.

"I don't despise you, Gayla. At first I did. All the time I was in prison I hated you. But I got a letter from Cash the very same day I got one from Schyler. He told me to come see him when I got paroled." His hand lovingly grazed her cheek. "He told me how it had been with you, why things had turned out the way they had."

"Then why have you been spying on me?"

He grinned in the darkness and gave the porch swing a push. "Cash hired me to."

"He hired you to spy on Belle Terre?"

"To keep an eye on it. He was scared Jigger was gonna do something to get revenge."

She digested that. "Cash was worried about Schyler?"

"About everybody. Schyler, you, the old man."

"You made me afraid. I knew somebody was out there, watching, waiting till the time was right to do something terrible to us."

"There was." His nostrils flared. "It wasn't just me sneaking around. Jigger was, too. One night I saw him go inside."

"So he did leave the doll on my bed."

"A doll?"

"Voodoo."

"I didn't know what he was doing in there. There wasn't anything I could do to stop him without letting him know I was watching him. I just made sure he came out without hurting you and then I followed him home."

"A few nights ago someone was eavesdropping outside the parlor."

"That was Jigger, too. I saw you come out onto the veranda. I held my breath, wanting to warn you not to step around that corner, but Cash had told me to lay low until Jigger tipped his hand."

"But he hasn't."

Jimmy Don shrugged. "It's too late for him to. That timber goes out tonight. Cash has been as jumpy as a cat these last few days. I don't know how many times he's scouted the area around the landing."

"Looking for what?"

"That's just it. He didn't know. He was just convinced that somebody had it in for Schyler. Whoever blew up the railroad tracks wasn't going to stop there. Cash was sure they would do something to stop that convoy."

"They?"

"Cash didn't think Jigger was working alone."

Out of habit, Gayla shivered at the mention of his name. "You've got to stay away from Jigger, Jimmy Don. If you're seen with me, he'll want to kill you, too."

Her hand was protectively sandwiched between the ones that had carried a football across the goal line more times than anyone in Heaven High School history. "Jigger isn't gonna hurt you, or anybody else, ever again."

He spoke with such surety that Gayla's heart froze. She gazed up at him apprehensively. "Jimmy Don, you didn't ...?"

He laid his finger vertically along her lips. "Don't ever ask me."

For a moment they stared at each other, then she made a small sound of gratitude and pressed her face into the hollow of his throat. He held her.

Eventually she eased herself out of his embrace. She went to stand against one of the columns. "I've been to bed with too many men to count, Jimmy Don."

He came to his feet and moved to stand beside her. "It doesn't matter."

"It does to me." She looked down at her hands through eyes blurred with tears. "Before I went to work in that beer joint, I'd never had anybody else but you. Swear to God."

He laid his hands on her shoulders. "I know that. We both suffered 'cause of that evil man, Gayla." He turned her to face him. "Things were done to me in prison that ..." His voice tapered off. The memories were too painful for him to vocalize.

Intuitively she knew that. "You don't have to tell me anything," she whispered.

"Yeah, I do. I love you, Gayla. And I want to be with you. I want to marry you like we always talked about. But I can't ask you to marry me." She tilted her head to one side, gazing up at him inquiringly. He cleared his throat, but he couldn't blink away the tears in his own eyes. "There were men in prison who forced themselves on me." He turned his head aside and squeezed his eyes shut. "That killed something inside me. I, uh, I don't know if I can ...if I can be with a woman anymore. I think I might be, uh, impotent."

Gayla laid her hands on his cheeks and turned his face toward her again. He opened his tearful, troubled eyes. "I don't care about that, Jimmy Don," she said with soft earnesty. "Believe me, baby, I've been worked over so many times I don't even remember what it's like to want a man in that way. Just be gentle and tender and sweet with me. Love me. That's all I want from you."

Tears streamed down his smooth, dark cheeks. He clasped her to him and held her tightly. At that moment nothing could have parted them except the explosion that rattled the windows at Belle Terre and lit up the night sky like the Fourth of July.

"Good God!" Jimmy Don cried. "Looks like Cash was right."

"Schyler!"

"You stay here." Jimmy Don set her away from him.

She reached out. "I want to go with you."

"You've got to stay with the old man." He vaulted over the railing of the veranda.

"All the cars are gone."

"I'll run." His powerful, record-breaking legs started churning.

"Be careful, baby. Call when you know something." He waved to her to let her know he'd heard. She watched until he disappeared around the bend in the lane. At the squeaking sound of the screen door, she spun around. "Mr. Crandall, get back to bed!" She rushed forward and braced him up on one side. He seemed on the verge of collapse. The red glow of the fire was reflected in his eyes.

"That's the landing."

"I'm sure everything's all right. Jimmy Don's gone to check. He said he would call."

Cotton didn't ask about Jimmy Don. It didn't seem to register with him that an ex-convict had spent the last few hours in his house. Either that or he didn't care. He was staring at the hellish red light rising above the treetops.

"I've got to get to the landing," he wheezed.

"You'll do no such thing. You're going back to bed."

"I can't." He wrestled with her, though he was so weak it was no contest.

"Mr. Crandall, even if I'd let you go, we don't have a car. You've got no way of getting there."

"Goddammit!" He slumped against the doorjamb. His breathing was rough. His hand was making squeezing motions over his heart.

Gayla was frightened. "Come on back to bed now."

"Leave me alone," he rasped, shaking off her assisting hands. "I'm not a baby. Stop treating me like one."

Any further badgering would only cause him stress. Gayla relented. "Okay. We'll sit out here on the veranda. We can hear the phone ringing from here."

Cotton let himself be led to one of the wicker chairs. Once he was settled, Gayla sat down on the top step and wrapped her skirt around her shins. Together and in silence they watched the night sky turn the color of blood.

The pickup rumbled up to the front walk. Gayla was still sitting on the top step, leaning against the column, asleep. She didn't come awake until the door of the pickup was closed. She raised her head and shielded her gritty eyes against the morning sunlight.

Cash and Schyler were coming up the front walk. Both looked like they'd been in a combat zone. Jimmy Don climbed out of the bed of the pickup and jumped to the ground. She smiled at him shyly. He smiled back.

"Daddy!" Schyler exclaimed. She ran the rest of the way up the steps and onto the veranda. "What on earth are you doing out here? Why aren't you in bed?"

"He refused to go back inside, Schyler," Gayla told her. "Even after Jimmy Don called and told us that you were all right, he flat refused to go back to his room."

"You've been out here all night?" Gayla nodded in answer to Schyler's question. The women exchanged a worried glance. Cotton didn't look well. "Well, I won't hear of such shenanigans from you," Schyler said bossily. "You might have intimidated Gayla, but you don't intimidate me. You're going back to bed immediately."

Cotton pushed his daughter aside. "I want to know one thing." Though his voice was as fragile as tissue paper, it stunned them all with its impact. Using the arms of the chair for support, he struggled to stand at his full height. "Did you do this to me?"

He looked directly at Cash. His blue eyes were deeply hooded by scowling brows. Cash returned his stare. One was as steady and antagonistic as the other.

"No."

"It was Jigger Flynn, Daddy," Schyler said quickly.

She was trying to outrun a storm about to break. The air was sulfurous. The instant Cotton and Cash came face-to-face, the scene had become as still and electric as the atmosphere before a tornado. She had known there was antipathy between them, but she'd never expected it to be so palpable that it could be tasted.

In short, concise sentences, she related to Cotton what had happened during the night. She didn't go into details. They could be doled out to him like medication when he was well enough to hear them. She didn't tell him that Ken had been killed in the explosion seconds before he planned to take his own life. She didn't tell him that Tricia, months earlier, had formed an unholy alliance with Dale Gilbreath. At that very moment Tricia was giving her deposition to the sheriff in the presence of her attorney. He was already planning to plea bargain. Tricia hoped she would get a lesser sentence if she turned state's evidence. If not, she would stand trial with Gilbreath and Jigger Flynn for the murder of her husband among a variety of other charges.

No, all that could wait until later, when Cotton wasn't swaying on his feet.

"The fire looked much worse than it was, Daddy," Schyler concluded anxiously. "Most of the timber was saved. We'll deliver it to Endicott in good time, but we don't have to worry about the deadline at the bank."

Cotton seemed not to have heard a single word. He raised his hand and pointed a finger at Cash. "You're trespassing."

"Daddy, what's the matter with you? Cash has done the work of ten men for you tonight."

His pointing hand began to shake. "You . . . you . . ." Gasping, Cotton clutched his pajama jacket and fell back a step."

"Daddy!" Schyler screamed.

Cotton went down on one knee, then fell backward onto the veranda. Schyler dropped to her knees beside him.

"I'll call the doctor," Gayla said and ran inside. Jimmy Don bolted after her.

"Daddy, Daddy." Schyler moved her hands over her father frantically. His pasty face was beaded with sweat. His lips and earlobes had an unhealthy bluish cast. His breath whistled through his waxy lips.

Schyler raised her head and looked up at Cash in desperate appeal. His taut expression startled her. His face was suffused with color, as though he had an overabundance of blood while Cotton didn't have enough.

Kneeling, he reached down and secured a handful of Cotton's pajama top in his fist and yanked him up. "Goddamn you to eternal hell if you die now. Don't you die, old man. Don't you die!"

"Cash, what are you doing?!"

Cash shook Cotton. His white head wobbled feebly. His eyes were fixed on Cash's tortured face. The younger man's sun-tipped hair had fallen over his brows. Tears were making his hazel eyes shimmer.

"Don't you die until you've said it. Look at me. Say it!" He clenched the pajama top tighter and pulled Cotton up closer to him. He lowered his head and ground his forehead against Cotton's. His voice cracked with yearning when he pleaded through clenched teeth. "Say it! Just once in my whole godforsaken life, say it. *Call me son.*"

With an effort, Cotton lifted his hand. He touched Cash's stubbled cheek. The bloodless fingertips caressed it, but the name he rasped wasn't his son's. Drawing a rattling breath, he sighed, "Monique."

And then he died.

His hand fell away from Cash's face and landed with a thud on the boards of the veranda. Gradually the muscles of Cash's arms relaxed and he lowered the sagging form. He kept his head bending over it for a long time, staring into the sightless blue eyes that had always refused to see him.

Then he pushed himself to his feet and staggered down the steps of the veranda. He drove away, but not before Schyler, speechlessly kneeling at Cotton's side, had had a glimpse of his shattered expression.

Chapter Fifty-seven

Every sunset at Belle Terre was beautiful.

Today's was more gorgeous than most. It had rained earlier in the day, but the sky overhead was clear now. On the western horizon enormous violet thunderheads looked like a cluster of hydrangea blooms. The sun was shining through them to create a sunset that was celestial.

It reaffirmed one's belief in God.

Schyler gazed at the spectacular sunset through her bedroom window. Long shadows were cast along the walls and floor. Dust motes spun in the glow of the warm, fading sun. The house was quiet. It usually was. She and Mrs. Dunne didn't create much noise.

Gayla had moved out. She and Jimmy Don were living as newlyweds in a duplex nearer town. Gayla was planning to enroll in a nursing school in the fall. Jimmy Don was working for Crandall Logging. He had taken over the bookkeeping responsibilities that Ken Howell had once had. His parole officer was pleased. Schyler had high hopes for the couple. They would make it, especially since they had been extricated from the blight of Jigger Flynn.

Schyler had been shocked to hear the horrible and mysterious circumstances surrounding his death. Though it was one of the grisliest murders to ever occur in Laurent Parish, not a single clue had turned up. Most everybody had formed an opinion and had made their list of possible suspects, but none were coming forward. Jigger had cultivated enemies like most folks cultivated summer gardens. Few lamented his ghastly demise. His murder would be entered in the record books as an unsolved crime.

Cotton Crandall's funeral was one of the largest the parish had experienced in decades. The First Baptist Church had been filled to capacity. Extra chairs had been set up in the aisles. When they were filled, the crowd stood on the grounds outside. The service had been abundant in pomp and circumstance. The preacher had never been so eloquent. The whole choir had sung. When they reached the last verse of "Amazing Grace," even those who had called Cotton an opportunist who had married well had tears in their eyes.

But his funeral wasn't what had people all abuzz; it was his private interment. He hadn't been buried beside his wife in the Laurent family cemetery as everybody had expected him to be. He'd been laid to rest in an undisclosed and undisturbed spot on Belle Terre. Only Schyler knew where. Only she knew that another grave lay beside his.

She also knew Cotton approved her decision.

The day before his funeral, she had gone to New Orleans to entomb the body of Ken Howell with his family. Pitifully few attended. Tricia remained tearless. She had refused to look at or speak to her sister. She was led away by policemen as soon as the brief service was concluded. Schyler was paying for Tricia's defense attorney. Beyond that, her sister wouldn't accept her help. She had refused to see her when Schyler tried to visit her in jail.

During the darkest days of her bereavement, Schyler had telephoned Mark in London. He'd been sympathetic and consoling, but there was a difference in their friendship now. Each knew it and each was saddened by it, but each accepted that they couldn't return to the way they'd been before.

So Schyler was very much alone in the large house and never more alone than this evening. She'd taken a lingering bath in the old tub. Her clothes were carefully folded into neat piles on the bed. All that was left to do was place those neat piles in her suitcase and go to bed. But she would put that off as long as she could because tonight was the last night she would ever spend under Belle Terre's roof.

When the sun finally gave up its valiant struggle to survive one more second and sank beyond the edge of the earth, she shook off her despair-induced lethargy and turned away from the window.

He was standing in the doorway of her bedroom, one shoulder propped against the frame, silently staring at her. He was dressed as always in jeans and boots and a casual work shirt, which made her feel even more uncomfortable being caught in nothing more than her slip.

"I see your manners haven't improved since the last time I saw you," she remarked. "Couldn't you have at least knocked?"

"I've never needed to knock to get into a lady's bedroom."

He levered himself away from the door and swaggered into the room. He withdrew an envelope from the breast pocket of his shirt and tossed it onto her dressing table. "I got your letter."

"Then there's nothing left for us to say to each other, is there?"

He picked up a crystal perfume bottle and sniffed its contents. "I think so. That kind of news is usually delivered in person."

Schyler felt naked, not just her body, but her spirit. His presence in the feminine room was unsettling. He prowled it, touching things, making her feel violated. "I thought it would be best for us not to see each other. My attorney advised me to notify you by mail."

"Did he vote in favor of your decision to sign over Belle Terre to me?"

"No."

"Because I'm Cotton's bastard."

"That wasn't his objection. He . . . he thought I should let Daddy's will stand as it was written."

"Dividing the property equally between you, me, and Tricia?"

"Yes."

"But you didn't think so?"

"No."

"How come?" He sprawled on a linen-covered chaise and propped one booted foot on the end of it. The other he left on the floor. His bent knee swung from side to side.

"It's difficult to explain, Cash."

"Try."

"My father . . . *our* father . . . treated you abominably."

"You're trying to right his wrongs?"

"In a manner of speaking."

"A kid born on the wrong side of the blanket has no rights, Schyler."

"You were more than that to him."

He laughed bitterly. "A living guilty conscience."

"Perhaps. When he left New Orleans, he didn't mean to desert you and your mother. He loved her. Fiercely. His will proved that he loved you, too."

"He never even had a kind word for me," he said angrily.

"He couldn't afford to." That got his attention. The insolent knee stopped wagging. His eyes held hers, begging to be convinced. "He loved you, Cash. He just couldn't let himself get too close. He knew if he allowed himself to show his love just a little, it would be obvious to everybody." Schyler's brow wrinkled in puzzlement. "I don't understand why that would have been so bad. Why didn't he acknowledge you when he was alive?"

"He had sworn to Macy that he wouldn't. That was their bargain. Cotton could have my mother as his mistress, but he couldn't have his son."

"But after Mama died, why didn't he recognize you then?"

"Macy's deal was for life. Cotton's life. At least that's what he told Mother and me when I wanted him to marry her. Macy had no choice but to leave him Belle Terre. She just made damn certain he wouldn't be too happy in it."

"He placed Belle Terre above his own happiness. Above his own son," Schyler said sadly. "He loved you, Monique, me. But he loved Belle Terre more than anything."

Looking down at him she said quietly, "And so do you, Cash. That's why you've stayed here all this time. In the back of your mind, you knew Belle Terre was rightfully yours. You've been waiting all your life to claim it, haven't you?" He said nothing, just stared at her. "Well, you don't have to wait any longer. I gave up my share of it to you. It says so in that letter.

"Everything's in the clear," she went on after a short pause. "The deed to the house is no longer tied up as collateral. It's written out in your name now. Endicott's check covered the bank note. You've got plenty of operating capital. With an honest bookkeeper taking care of the budget, I'm sure that you'll make Crandall Logging what it was in Cotton's heyday. Probably even better. Daddy taught you well. And what he didn't teach you, you learned on your own. He always said you were an instinctive forester. The best. He was proud of you."

She smiled at him faintly. "You'll probably want to change the name of the business, won't you, now that you've inherited Belle Terre?"

"I'd rather have a woman than a house."

Schyler took a quick little breath. "What?"

He rolled his spine off the chaise and stood up. He moved so close she had to tilt her head back to look up at him. "I didn't sleep with Tricia," he said. "I never wanted to. In any event, that bitch wouldn't have let my shadow fall on her before that night. I knew she had probably been sent as a decoy. I was just going through the motions until she cracked under pressure and I could get information out of her."

He reached around Schyler with both hands and took hold of her hair, pulling her head back. "You love this place, Schyler. Why'd you give it to me?"

"Because I've always felt like it was on loan to me. I sensed, always, *always*, that it didn't really belong to me. I didn't know why. Now I do. You're Cotton's flesh and blood. His son." She shook her head at her own stupidity. "You're so like him. Why didn't I see it?"

She gazed into his face, loving it so much it was painful and she had to look away. "After he died, I finally remembered what had been said the night you brought me home from Thibodaux Pond. It had never made sense before.

Daddy told you to stay away from the house. You shouted back, 'I've got more right to be here than they do.' You were referring to Tricia and me, weren't you?"

"Oui. I lost my temper."

"But you were right. You belonged here. Not us."

"I've been obsessed with Belle Terre since the first time my mother said the words to me." He brushed a kiss across her lips. "But I'm not going to be like my daddy. I'm not going to place Belle Terre above everything else. It's not what I want most. I knew what I wanted most when I saw you asleep under that tree."

"Cash?"

"Why'd you give me Belle Terre?"

"You know why," she groaned against his lips. "I love you, Cash Boudreaux."

He kissed her. His lips were warm and sweet as they parted above hers. His tongue gently explored the inside of her mouth. He combed his fingers through her hair, then let them drift over her shoulders and down her chest to her breasts. He caressed them, touched their centers with his fingertips, then slid his hands down her ribs to her waist. Holding their kiss, he pulled her forward as he backed up. When the backs of his knees made contact with the mattress, he sat down on the edge of the bed and positioned her between his spread thighs.

He kissed her breasts through her slip, flicking the ivory silk charmeuse with his tongue. "You aren't going anywhere," he growled as he planted a kiss between her breasts. "You're staying here with me. And when we die, our children will bury us here together. On Belle Terre."

Tears stung Schyler's eyes. Joy and love pumped through her. She tunneled her fingers in his hair and held his head against her.

Cash nuzzled the giving softness of her belly. "Schyler?"

"Yes?"

Several ponderous heartbeats later, he whispered, "I love you."